The Tides That Lie

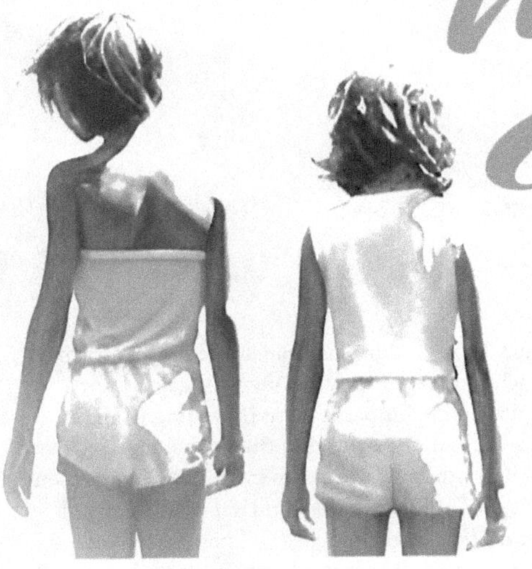

Jenn J McLeod

The Tides That Lie. First edition. January, 2024 (07/2024)

Published by Wild Myrtle Press.

Copyright ©Jenn J. McLeod

National Library of Australia Cataloguing-in-Publication entry

Creator: McLeod, Jenn J., author

Title: The Tides That Lie/Jenn J. McLeod

ISBN: Paperback 978-0-6485708-7-5 and ISBN: eBook 978-0-6485708-8-2 (epub)

Subjects: Modern & Contemporary Fiction, Family Relationships, Australia

Dewey Number: A823.

Cover design by Annie Seaton

Photo credit: © Sigal / Adobe Stock

Font: Alpine by Charles Borges de Oliveira / Adobe Fonts

Printed and bound in Australia.

To my fabulous mum and amazing dad who took three kids camping every holiday.
Thanks for the memories.

To my tribe (my hunters and gatherers who love to fish while I write): thanks for making me finish this story.

To my sister, Kris, with whom I share an unbreakable bond.

And, as always, to Jeannette (The J) McAnderson—my seahorse for life. Thanks for never letting go in turbulent waters.

thalassophobia (noun)
a clinical phobia characterised by extreme and irrational fear of the sea

Word origin:
Greek thalassa (sea) + phobos (fear)

EPIGRAPH

My father loved life—and us—but he died, and I let it happen.

Over thirty years ago, the high tide swept him and my recollections away. But some memories, I'm learning, are not so easily taken. No matter how high the tide or fierce the ocean, they remain on the edge of the sand—the edge of our minds. And, like the tidal detritus we pick through, some we discard, some we treasure.

I guess that's why, despite the years, I'm back at Sandbar, still missing Dad, still commemorating him, still wishing I'd chosen differently that day. But being here doesn't explain why I've left behind the family home I love—my fortress—to camp alone in a tent and with the sound of waves pounding the beach. The ocean is not my friend; it will never be. Not even the type of friend that requires a certain cautiousness and restraint when in their company.

I want to trust the tides again, and myself, because the more I fight life's ebb and flow, and the more I thrash about, indiscriminately clinging to everything I treasure, the more I risk drowning—and pulling my family down with me.

If Dad were here today, he'd offer profound advice, like, 'Have faith in the rhythm of life, Chelsea-girl. Ride the waves and reach for the horizon'. Then he'd say, 'But remember, just as you can't see where the earth ends and the ocean starts, you must convince yourself it's okay to not know some things'.

But is it?

All I know as I sit in a storm-battered tent, alone and hearing waves pounding the sand, is I'm both a lousy decision maker and a woman who holds too tight to all the wrong things. So tight that I failed to notice the most precious treasures of all slipping away.

My husband and my family.

Social media now keeps tabs on the people I love, telling me where in the world my travel-agent sister is, and in which country Mum is spending husband-number-three's money. Meanwhile, with my boys deployed to the other side of the world, and the emotional battle with my daughter ongoing on the other side of the country, I'm a mother lacking purpose, a wife short of a husband, and a daughter struggling with guilt and regret. And yet I'm here, preparing to face the thalassophobia monster.

My fear of the sea is an irrational one. There are no evil ocean-dwellers; nothing lurks beneath the surface, and nothing can hurt me. Nothing. I'm already three decades beyond the worst hurt in the world. The angriest of oceans will not stop me reclaiming my life. My need right now is for my big sister—the one who used to love and protect—to recognise the day and commemorate Dad with me.

But that's unlikely after all these years, even though there's supposed to be an unbreakable bond between sisters. While I'm proof such bonds do break, I'm unsure what estranged us. That's Layla's story to tell.

My story starts thirty-four years ago.

ROCK FISHING WITH DAD, 1981

'Can we go, Dad? It's *freeeezing!*'

For the first time *ever*, I hate fishing. Hate, hate, hate it. The sky is no longer blue, my toes—rubbed raw by my thongs—sting in the salt water, and without rubber soles under my feet, the rocks are slippery and unsafe.

While I picture Mum and Layla back at camp with their beauty masks, both trying not to laugh in case their faces crack, Dad's face is set in a strange scowl as he stares out to sea. He's not talking much—not even when he lands *another* fish. Today, the tailor are running, so while we won't 'bring home the bacon' like Dad promised Mum, we sure won't go hungry. Dad's bucket is chock-a-block.

'Don't we have enough?' I ask, getting more tired and cross by the minute.

Worst still, the promised secret spot isn't so special. We're fishing the same rocky point as always, but the northern end, which you can't get to from Sandbar Beach. There's so much to explore and lots of new rock pools. I ask Dad if I can go beachcombing and explore the caves. He says no, which is why I'm sitting on a rock, bored out of my brain, and craving our caravan's cosy interior that will be smelling of Mum's pan-fried cheese and Vegemite sandwiches.

Even when Dad mutters something about the time and the tides turning as wishy-washy as the weather, and then announces a different bait should do the trick, I don't budge from the rock. Maybe, like Layla,

I've outgrown the tidal pools and make-believe mermaids in magical underwater worlds. Once already I've almost broken my neck on the slimy green moss, and while looking for shells—I'm only allowed to collect broken ones—I reckon I saw a blue-ringed octopus hiding under a rock. Mum would go ape if she knew how close my hand had come to touching the deadly creature.

I call to Dad, 'Mum will have a timer on us, and she'll be cross if I get a cold.'

A dreadful thing to catch, for sure. I can almost smell the steaming bowl of eye-stinging eucalyptus she'll force my face over after covering my head and shoulders with a towel. An accusation will follow—*This is your fault, William*—and ordinarily I would silently disagree. I mostly side with Dad. Not this time, though. If a cold results from us staying out late in this weather, it *will* be his fault because we'd walked so very far through sunless scrub after leaving camp too late in the day.

Why did we wait?

When it comes to fishing, he's usually up with the sun and raring to go —Dad says 'raring to go' a lot—but for most of the day he'd lollygagged. Mum uses the word 'lollygag' to describe how Layla wastes time when she should be studying. But before setting off today, Dad had insisted on a big family lunch with a fire and an old-fashioned fry-up of fresh fish rissoles.

After wrapping vegetables in foil and burying them in hot coals alongside the damper in a camp oven, Dad suggests we play cricket. Soon after eating, he takes Mum to the caravan 'to talk'—like he does sometimes— telling us girls to 'go for a walk and make it a long one'.

We do what we're told, even though I didn't want to waste more of the day. I want the secret spot with the promised rock pools.

My parents finally emerge—all lovey-dovey and giggly—and Dad tells Mum he loves her almost as much as he loves fishing. When Mum smacks his bottom and they kiss again, I know at that moment I will meet a man just like him and we'll live happily ever after.

When finally on our way, Dad and I walk single file on the skinniest path. Dad talks mostly to himself, until I ask how much further. His reply is more of a hurry-up, followed by more walking and more climbing—up, up, up.

I'm about to ask if we're walking all the way to the horizon when we come upon a big flat space with fallen-down buildings made from rocks and wrinkly tin sheeting. At the centre of the clearing is a round, concrete *thingamabob*. The colour of rust, to match the chunky length of chain at its centre, it reminds me of a giant bath plug, like the old brown one in the laundry tub out back. Branching off the big plug are tunnel-type structures, like drains but draped in vines boasting pretty blue flowers. When Dad ducks inside one opening, calling me to follow, my tummy wobbles.

I'm scared because I'm reminded of the open storm water drain that runs under the road outside the school. Local kids gather there to smoke cigarettes and stuff. Dad says they're dumb, and Layla and me are too smart to do anything so dangerous. So why is he calling me to follow him into a drain?

'Come on, you're safe with me. These tunnels are the secret bit in the secret spot. They'll lead us safely to the rocky platform. It's the only way down from the headland.'

'I don't want to go in there.' *What if it rains?* Dad says the storm water drains are extra dangerous in the rain.

'Okay, well, the best rock pools in the whole world are within your reach, but if you want to go back to your mother and sister while they paint nails and braid hair—or whatever you girly girls do to occupy yourselves while the hunters gather food—we can do that. We can go.'

I bite my lip so hard it hurts. 'Um, what if we came back again tomorrow—in the morning?' I suggest. 'It's late now.'

'And getting later by the minute,' Dad mutters, checking his watch. 'Besides, the tide will be all wrong tomorrow. Then we head home. I guess I'll be keeping the secret to myself.'

'Are you sure there's no other way?' I ask. 'The beach maybe?'

'You know crossing Sandbar's estuary isn't safe, and the high tide will stop us from getting back to camp. It's this tunnel to the northern side of the headland, or nothing. So, what's it to be? And don't dillydally when deciding. The day is getting away from us. You won't want the incoming tide to swallow all those rock pool riches, and you don't want to make me regret bringing you.'

I don't understand 'regret' and can't think of anything except how tired my arms are from lugging my fishing gear.

'Would it help if I carry your load?' Dad asks. 'I'm going to leave my backpack here. We won't be needing it after all.'

I think about asking what it is he's carried all this way for nothing, but Dad seems sort of angry and anxious all at once.

Then he says, 'Very well. Back to camp and then home. Just give me a minute.' Suddenly, Dad slumps to the ground, his body hunched, head in hands.

'What, Dad? What's wrong?'

Though he doesn't lift his face, not even when he speaks, it's not hard to tell; the man who loves to laugh is crying.

'This … I thought this was the best way. Maybe I'm wrong. Maybe I should be content to go home, too. It's just … I'm tired.'

'Tired of what, Dad?' I plonk onto my bottom to sit crossed legged, ready for the rant that is bound to follow, like when Mum goes on and on about being 'tired of this and tired of that'.

'Tired of treading water,' he says in an almost whisper. 'I'm drowning in that house, Miss Fix. Out here I can breathe.'

Chelsea almost chuckles. 'You're being silly, Dad. You can't drown. You're almost as good a swimmer as me. Besides, people don't drown in houses.'

'They do,' he tells her, head still bowed. 'We can drown anywhere, anytime.'

Like in the bath. I recall the day—a few years ago—when my dolls had needed a good wash behind the ears. While yanking out the bath plug, Mum said I could've drowned. Then she declared the bathroom out of bounds.

'You know what?' I pat Dad's knee the way he does when telling me and Layla to buck up and be brave. 'If you were drowning for real, I'd save you.'

Looking up, his smile small, he asks, 'And how, Miss Fix, would you manage that?'

'Easy.' I puff up like an abandoned blowfish on the beach. 'Even if the plug was as big as that one,' I point behind me, 'I'd yank it out and let the water run down the drain.'

'That is a big plug!' A bigger smile wrinkles his face and squeezes a fat tear from one eye. 'I love you to the horizon, Miss Fix. Remember that.'

'Love you, too, Dad. And if it makes you feel better, we can stay for fishing. We're here now; we might as well go all the way.'

'You're right, and you are my brave girl,' he says with a hug. 'Come on. I'll carry this lot for you.' He reaches for my gear.

As one tunnel turns into two, then splits again and slopes away, I imagine I'm a tiny silver ball in a palm puzzle tilting this way and that. On and on I roll through the maze, wondering if we'll ever find the way out. Then … Daylight.

'Stay on the track and watch your steps,' Dad says.

I do, but I'm mesmerised by the cave-like construction of rocks and concrete we pass. 'Is that like a cubby?'

'A bunker,' he explains. 'During the war, soldiers would hide here to keep watch. This headland has two: one looks north, and one overlooks Sandbar Beach to the south. The entire coastline is littered with wartime bunkers.'

'Can I go look inside?'

'Not now,' he says, tugging me in the opposite direction. 'Time's ticking and we have the tides to think about. The best fishing is on an incoming one. Watch your feet. It's steep.'

At last! We reach the rock platform and it's pockmarked with a million magical tidal pools. I'm so happy I almost wet my pants with excitement. The very first pool has my favourite Neptune's Pearls, so I snap two small strands and drape the bauble-like seaweed over my ears as earrings. The next rock pool has sea anemone, a family of five warning me off with their spiky venom-filled tentacles.

'Careful,' Dad warns. 'And remember, Chelsea, when you get home, this place must remain our secret. Understand?'

I nod, knowing Mum would have a fit and yell the house down if she learned how far we'd come. She yells at Dad a lot and says mean things, like telling him she'll call the police and have him taken away for being a bad husband and father. And that they'll believe her. The police always believe the wife, she reckons.

Dad never yells back. He just slinks away to the garage or the back-yard. For that reason, I won't ever tell Mum this secret—or Layla. I can't get Dad in more trouble. Not ever. Dad's the best, and I'm safe with him. He's always looking out for Layla and me and teaching us stuff like, "Observant fishermen don't die" and "Follow the rules, read the rocks, monitor the tides, never turn your back on the sea".

'Chelsea, that pout of yours will scare the fish.'

'But it's been ages. It's almost dinner,' I say, my mouth watering from the imaginary hot Milo milk and toastie oozing with hot cheese.

Dad looks around at his watch, out to sea, at the sky, and back at his watch. 'Another hour and it'll be time.'

'Time to go?' I can only hope.

'Yes, but first go grab fresh bait. We'll give the old cunjevoi a try. The fish have gone off pilchards.'

'Cunjevoi?' I scan the rocky platform, looking for the clumps of leathery brown tubes normally abundant at low tide. 'There is none, Dad. The tide's come in fast.'

'There's a bunch of the stuff back towards the track.' He points. 'Behind those boulders. Where we turned right, remember?'

I nod, even though I'm not good with my left and right.

'Take a bucket, go all the way past the big round boulders and you'll see where the rock ledge falls away to the sand. Go left—or right, depending on which way you're facing, of course. I saw loads of cunjevoi when we arrived.'

'But …' I'm curious. We have more than enough for dinner, and Dad usually grumbles about blokes who catch more than they need, just to show off back at camp. 'Your bucket's full of fish already.'

'Then empty *your* bucket. Here, take *it*,' he says, scattering my collection before I could scream …

'But my shells!' I snatch up the unbroken conch that I planned on sneaking into my jacket pocket.

'Chelsea Scott!' he snaps while passing me the now-empty green bucket covered with mermaid stickers. 'We don't take away. We appreciate Mother Nature, we learn, and we leave.'

When my bottom lip buckles into a sob, Dad squats, grasps both my arms, and says, 'I'm sorry; only snapper are allowed to snap, right?' He waits for my nod. 'Remember I love you, Miss Fix.'

My head bobs like the bobbing dog on Dad's dashboard.

'And you love all the creatures in the sea,' he adds, 'which is why these treasures stay behind. Now …' He stands and checks his watch. 'Time is ticking. Do you need your dad's help, or are you a Cunjevoi Collector extraordinaire?'

Feeling silly for crying, I puff up. 'I can go by myself.'

'Yes, you can,' he says, ruffling my already windblown hair, dank with sea salt. 'Remember, Chelsea-girl, you can go anywhere and do anything. Follow your heart and let your dreams guide you.'

'Guide me how?' I ask. 'To where?'

'To the place that makes you happiest. That's where you should be, my darling girl. That's where we *all* deserve to be.'

'Dad?' I whisper, forced to squint into the brilliant orange sun slowly sinking behind the headland. 'The place I'd be happiest right now is back at camp with Mum and Layla.'

Dad's laugh sounds sort of sad as he lifts me onto my tippy toes for a hug. 'You'll be home with your mum and sister soon and they'll spoil you and fuss over you and paint your nails. Whatever you want. But first, go get that magic bait. There's one more big fish in the water with your name on it. And take your time so you don't slip.'

Waterlogged cunjevoi is much heavier than the clumps I usually find dried up on the beach. It's a lot to carry, especially given only the creature's bright orange innards get used for bait. Tiptoeing over the slimy rocks, I call out to Dad up ahead, but he doesn't turn around. He just sits there all hunched. At first, I giggle. Such a big man sitting in a small rock pool looks so silly. Then I see his pained expression, a rip in his pants, and a blood-soaked fishing rag wrapped around one leg. I'm frightened.

'I'm hurt bad, Chelsea. Tide's coming in quicker than I realised, and a rogue wave hit, washing your shells under my feet.'

My bottom lip quivers. 'My shells made you slip?'

'Don't blame yourself. Accidents happen. Your thongs washed away as well. Should've kept them on your feet, kiddo.'

I stare down at my toes, blue with cold—now the same colour as my lost thongs—then at the blood-stained water swirling around Dad's knees. 'Does your leg hurt a lot?'

He nods. 'Seems we've got ourselves in a bit of a pickle. The cold water dulls the pain, but it's a nasty injury. I won't be walking out of here without help.'

'What do I do, Dad?'

'You can't fix this alone,' he says. 'You'll need to get back to camp as quick as you can.'

I turn in the direction of Sandbar Beach. If I run very fast, I'll reach the dune track before dark.

'No! Not that way. Even if you can climb over those boulders, crossing the estuary alone is dangerous, especially at high tide. The only way out is up and through the tunnels. You'll need to retrace our steps.'

'Oh, okay.' I wish I could sound more certain. We've come such a long way. 'But, Daddy, what will you do? You can't stay here.'

I'm only twelve, but Dad has taught me everything about the ocean and the tides. I know its magic, its dangers, its fury, and its fickleness. And he knows I know.

'I'll be fine,' Dad says. 'Last night's high tide mark is all the way down there.' He points to the line of pumice and seaweed. 'Tonight's will be much the same.'

'Are you sure?'

'The tides don't lie, Chelsea-girl.'

'I could stay, Dad. Whenever we're out late, Mum sends Layla. She'll find us.'

He reaches for my hand, squeezing it. 'What am I going to do with you, my contrary girl? One minute you're pestering me to go, and the next you're wanting to stay in the cold and dark. Remember, this spot is our secret. Layla won't look for us here. So, think hard about what you want because once properly dark, we'll be here until morning. Or,' he adds, 'you can hurry back up to the headland and run back to camp.'

'Mum's gonna be really mad, isn't she?'

'Yes, my girl. She's probably already rung the police.'

'The police?' I panic. 'Will they take you away for being a bad father? I don't want you to go.'

He tilts his head to one side and grins curiously. 'No one and nothing can take me from my girls. I'll always be in here.' He touches me where my heart thumps wildly at the thought of the journey ahead. 'Go quickly, Chelsea-girl. Soon it will be dark.'

'Okay,' I whimper, wishing I had a torch.

I don't like the dark.

1

CHELSEA - DAY 1 OF 7, 2015

'You're doing what?'

Chelsea didn't understand why her friend was yelling. Was dodgy phone reception the problem, or was Vicki also in a dark and scary place with a howling wind and lashing rain?

'I'm camping,' Chelsea shouted back, expecting her pop-up camping cocoon to lift off any second. 'C-A-M-P-I-N-G.'

'As in T-E-N-T?' came Vicki's reply. 'And what's the noise I can hear?'

'Probably wind,' Chelsea says.

'Then I'd avoid the tinned beans, sweetie. They're only camping essentials for cowboys in old American westerns. Speaking of beans, Timmy is shoving one up his sister's nose. Hang on.'

Chelsea could always rely on Vicki for a laugh or a good shake up, and both were in order tonight. As well as being a regular running mate, her friend filled the sisterly void left behind after Layla, in her early twenties, distanced herself from the family. Vicki was also the one person Chelsea could text and, unlike her mother and sister, get a reply. Communicating with her mother, Wendy, was always a mistake—a prelude to disappointment—while Layla was deliberately incommunicado around this time of year. She sure wouldn't care to know Chelsea was at Sandbar Campground today to remember their father.

Vicki had been a constant in Chelsea's life—rock-solid and reliable— while daughter, Gabby, kept in touch by tagging Chelsea in Facebook posts showing her beautiful grandbabies. Twins, Travis and Tyler, recently shifted to the next big thing—something called Instagram—because the app focused on pictures rather than words. Like their mild-mannered granddad, Chelsea's sons were creative and gentle souls. Not Gabby. The Holt's firstborn had inherited her Aunty Layla's aloofness.

Immensely proud of her three children, the family had benefitted from Chelsea being a stay-at-home mum. Growing up in the old Scott family home, and with the financial security of her dad's insurance policy payout, the Holts had wanted for little. Perhaps her husband needed reminding of William Scott's contribution to their comfortable lives next time he complained about the daily train commute or missing his beloved beach. Both were a small price for Dale to pay. Besides, her dad had sacrificed in much the same way when his wife insisted a new house in the fast-developing Penrith plains district would be a smarter move than renting 'a rat-infested flat in Bondi's back blocks'. Sure, growing up out west in the eighties and nineties meant 'a day at the beach' translated to 'a half day on the sand and three hours on the road'. But the Holt family was better off than their peers, and the kids would always have a familiar place to land—if ever needing somewhere to call home.

Because security and stability were important to Chelsea, and not the fact they were sitting, as Dale said, 'on a fortune and in the worst house on the best street', she constantly pushed back when it came to selling. More than a home, The Beach Shack—her dad had named the place by nailing a sign under the letterbox—remained Chelsea's fortress, protecting her family and preserving her memories.

Memories like those weekends during summer when Dale and the kids would barrel through the front door late on a Sunday, their saltwater hair dried stiff on the long, hot trip home. Or on a Saturday, with victorious faces muddied from football, and only the occasional broken limb.

Chelsea sighed. As much as she might have preferred to keep her three children safe by locking them in their rooms forever, or making them afraid to do what they loved, the Holt children made their own choices. In doing so, they'd left behind parents who had forgotten how to be alone—with or without each other.

'Still there, hon?' Vicki's voice snapped Chelsea back. 'Bean crisis averted. Where were we?'

'I was about to say I'm hungry enough to eat tinned beans. I went walking earlier when I should've finished setting up. I tried making the beach, but it was too much too soon. Then, suddenly, it was dusk and raining, so I grabbed one bag from my car. Now I'm starving and stuck in a tent in a storm with a supply of snacks but no wine, which proves the only thing worse than my timing is my decision making.'

'Wait! Spell the place you're staying,' Vicki demanded. 'I'm checking *weatherradar.com*.'

Chelsea suggested she try Whale Rocks. 'It's bigger than Wandarri, and a few beaches north. Vik? Hello? You there?'

'Good grief!' her friend screeched. 'This is why I avoid places with no cocktails, cabana boys, or cyclone shelters. Chelsea, sweetie, get in the car and come here where it's dry and you have solid walls, a real bed, a hot shower, *and* wine waiting.'

Though hardly cabana boy status, Chelsea toyed with telling Vicki about Mr. Tight Fly sitting outside his old caravan, and how his hat and sunnies, along with a sun-creamed nose and delta-shaped torso, had reminded Chelsea of her father; especially the way Dad lounged in his camp chair like lord of the manor at the end of a day's travel. Beer in hand, he'd crow, 'Wouldn't be dead for squids'.

Without fail, Mum would shout a reply, 'The saying is *quids*, not squids, idiot,' and Dad would wink at Chelsea.

'Oh my!' Vicki trilled. 'I Googled *Wandarri* and *camping* and found Wandarri Eco-Community. Seriously? Doesn't a hippy nudist cult in the jungle have a cabin or a yurt for hire?'

With every adorable exclamation to escape her friend's lips, Chelsea's angst subsided. She even laughed.

'What on earth did you search, Vik? Besides, hippies do not live in yurts; it's a forest not a jungle; and Wandarri, as far as I can make out, is an off-the-grid community—not a cult. There are none on the north coast.'

'That you're aware of,' Vicki persisted.

'True,' Chelsea chortled while stripping down to her bra and undies, shoving the wet clothes in a plastic bag. 'But I've not spotted one nudist. I've actually seen very little of the area because the weather changed not long after I popped my cocoon.'

Vicki hooted. 'Don't let anyone else hear you talking that way, sweetie. They'll think you're crazy.'

'What I am is delirious from no dinner, melting from the humidity, and I'm about to run out of phone battery. As soon as the rain stops, I can charge in the camp kitchen and call you back.'

'Does Dale know where you are?'

Chelsea was about to answer when something sounded outside her tent. 'Uh-oh!'

'Uh-oh what, sweetie? What's wrong?'

Chelsea cupped her hand around the phone and forced a whisper. 'I think I see legs outside my tent door.'

'What do you mean "you think"? What sort of legs? Hairy ones?' Vicki didn't wait for a reply. 'Stay where you are, turn off the lights, and pretend you're not home. Whatever you do, Chelsea, do not answer the hairy legs.'

Despite her increasingly soggy situation, and the possibility her airbed might float away, Chelsea found another chuckle. 'I'll call you back, Vik. Hairy Legs is saying something.' And Chelsea thought she recognised the voice.

It was the same one on the other end of the telephone earlier today.

'Pick any camping site anywhere you like. Plenty of choice,' the man had said during the requested phone check-in process.

'Anywhere?' she'd queried. 'That's great!'

It was a lie, and her 'great' a reflex response. Decision-making had never been Chelsea Holt's strong suit; not since the age of twelve when a wrong decision—the kind that made a mother not love a daughter very much—broke the Scott family forever. Layla, four years Chelsea's senior, had made up for their mother's emotional absences, until also drifting out of Chelsea's life.

Enter Aunty Rita. Not a real aunt, but their mum's friend from school who had comforted the family, intervening as needed to guide both girls through their grief. While Chelsea never fully recovered from the trauma of losing her dad, as people said she would, her mother, Wendy, moved on too quickly—in Chelsea's opinion—while Layla's multiple coping mechanisms morphed over the years from mournful crying to medicines, booze, and self-inflicted body piercings. One day, she'd talked Chelsea into a home-made tattoo. The design—a starfish—was supposed to represent regeneration and renewal.

Nowadays, her sister's drunken depiction of a starfish remained an odd blue freckle at the base of Chelsea's left thumb. If only it could help with letting go of the past, because renewing and restarting by moving forward was something her husband seemed committed to, with or without his wife.

2

———

TADPOLE

Adrenched Thaddeus Poulle—Tadpole to Sandbar campground regulars and Wandarri locals—waited in the dark for a reply from inside the odd-looking tent. When no answer came, he headed towards the camp kitchen. Surely, she' was there and taking advantage of the sturdy, dry and well-lit structure. Tad hoped so. For reasons unknown, the woman had occupied his thoughts all afternoon.

He'd earlier spotted the solo traveller struggling to peg her tent in the windy conditions; unsurprising given she'd left herself exposed to the elements. Experienced tent dwellers usually tucked in behind the thicket of coastal vegetation to avoid the unpredictable south-easterlies; especially during December, which was pretty much mid storm season. Even when a wind gust had sent her loose tent fly into a flap, and the woman looked certain to become a human kite, he'd resisted the urge to offer advice; mostly because only one thing was worse than sandflies sneaking under your board shorts and that was an independent female who saw a gentleman's offer of help as an affront.

As Tad had been bitten too many times, he'd observed from a distance, intrigued that a tent could look so much like a blue igloo. He also took comfort from knowing, should everything take off in a stiff wind, he'd be sure to witness the woman and her tent sail by Mary Poppins style. After which he'd help pick up the pieces and mend whatever was broken. In such matters, Thaddeus Poulle had ample experience.

Around dusk, Tad had been resting under his shade awning, and

13

surrounded by his *wheel estate*—the only real estate he bothered with these days—when the woman stopped short of the beach track entrance, worry evident in her expression. She'd hesitated a little, fiddled with her phone a lot, and then retraced her steps back.

'G'day!' he'd called out. She'd looked up from her phone briefly to wave but turned away. 'Could get a storm,' he'd added. At the same time, Tad had grabbed his groin and grunted in response to sudden nerve pain gripping the stump that was his leg these days—and a sure sign of rain. 'I find keeping a tight fly helps,' he'd called again, thinking a hint wouldn't hurt.

Faux pas realised when her pace quickened, Tad laughed. He no longer apologised for being the person he was, and Lucky sure didn't care about the occasional faux pas or politically incorrect perspective. A happy observer of nature, life, and good-looking women, Thaddeus Poulle remained unapologetic. Not only totally, madly, and deliriously in love with life at Sandbar Community Campground, he was a man on the other side of sixty who enjoyed spearing the nose of his board headfirst into a shimmering crest of a wave—at one with the sea. But these days he needed to nudge Lucky into action. The dog would stand, allowing Tad to fit the assistance harness and the two-wheeled gig specially designed to tote a surfboard. After years together, his working-dog knew the score. Second to surfing was watching newcomers, like Miss Lily-white legs with the discernible digital dependency.

Some Wandarri old-timers objected to folk visiting Sandbar. Not Tad. He enjoyed watching their bodies unwind after a day of driving, when the slump of harangued shoulders straightened out, and faces squinted at sunshine rather than at phones. As a rule, Sandbar holidaymakers started out with the same cautiousness of bare feet on nature's carpet, before easing into a lazy amble by holiday's end. Having returned home to Wandarri Eco-Community ten years ago, Tad easily recognised certain traits, and a person's gait said heaps about them. But this potential Mary Poppins had accelerated away from the beach track like something nipped at her heels.

With Sandbar Beach usually the first thing people aim for after establishing camp—the weary traveller drawn to the golden sands and lively breezes—whatever this jittery woman's problem was, the one-kilometre stretch of pristine coastline waiting on the other side of the dunes would surely loosen those slender shoulders. So, why turn back before the bush track, especially when dusk was the perfect time for beachcombing? Bounded by ocean, estuary, and a pristine forest—and bookended by two bluffs—Sandbar Beach could be a million miles from anywhere, while Wandarri rarely rated a mention on road maps. Rather, the state's first intentional community was everything the parcel holders wanted it to stay: a commune-style habitat hidden away on the north coast of New South Wales; its shacks lost amongst the sprawling stretch of protected forest.

As a child of Wandarri, Tad had spent his youth shoeless and not wearing very much at all. In his twenties, when fishing the estuary and surfing waves no longer fulfilled him, he'd left for Sydney. After his mum passed away quietly—even though Prudence Poulle rarely did anything quietly—Tad found himself the reluctant owner of a single-room shanty; one of sixty in the long-established Wandarri Eco-Community. But with self-imposed seclusion not his thing, Tad sold the Poulle land parcel for a nice profit, started renovating disused caravans, and set himself up at Sandbar as campground caretaker—and sort-of landlord. More recently, he'd established *Surf-Able*—a website and program encouraging amputee kids to embrace their passion for surfing, and to not be afraid.

These days, Thaddeus Poulle survives on sunshine, sand, and peak-season tariffs, because when Sandbar campgrounds swell to bursting, and colourful tents sprinkle the grass like confetti, his *wheel estate* pays him triple the low-season rate. His pride and joy, *Sea-Esta*—all sixteen fabulous feet of her—had been abandoned on-site three decades ago. Left to rust away, the lovingly refurbished Viscount caravan now sat proudly on the concrete slab opposite Tad's geriatric and aptly named caravan: *Thisldo.*

'This'll do us, eh, Lucky? Sandbar is perfect—rain, hail, or shine,' Tad said while checking the camp kitchen and thankful he was able to fix a plastic roller blind that had come loose and was flapping wildly in the wind. His caretaker role could be hard work—life with only one leg came with challenges—but Thaddeus Poulle was a survivor. Having endured more than one tragedy, he needed very little, wanted for less, and with a past he couldn't change and a future he couldn't predict, Tad remained hopeful of finding someone to share what was left of his very simple way of life.

'Left of me,' he muttered while massaging the stump below his knee. 'There must be a woman out there somewhere, Lucky. One who sees Sandbar as the ideal place in the world to live.' And no better place to die, he mused, aware when his time came, locals need only drag him to the shoreline. The tide will do the rest.

Even if *Thisldo* could come out of retirement and off the bricks, Tad's roaming days were over, and while nothing was going to budge him from his piece of paradise, the same could not be said about the little blue tent now bearing the brunt of an east coast low, and likely with a petrified Mary Poppins still inside.

'Come on, Lucky, we'd better check again.'

Glad to find the tent holding firm, he moved closer and called louder. 'Are. You. Okay. In. There?'

3

CHELSEA

Despite the echo of her friend's warning, Chelsea had no choice but to answer the hairy legs this time. He was very persistent, and if the wind didn't blow her away, she'd soon float away.

So much for the waterproofing and the fifty-dollar fly! The lightweight cover was supposed to keep rain out if pulled taut enough. *Tight fly! That's what the guy had meant this afternoon. It's him.*

'Hold on,' she called, reaching for the door zipper. 'Oh no!' The abrupt movement caused the undulant, half-inflated mattress to heave, catapulting the phone off the bed and onto the flooded floor.

Now down on all-fours, Chelsea poked her head through the tent opening, only to have headlights blind her, and sideways rain slap her face.

'Figured you might be damp in there,' Hairy Legs said.

'Not as wet as you out there,' Chelsea retorted, pulling the blue nylon flaps bonnet-like around her chin before looking up. With a hooded high-vis raincoat concealing his facial features, she saw only floral board shorts and two legs—one a prosthetic. Beside him, a German Shepherd dog eyeballed Chelsea. 'Do you need my help with something?'

'We wanted to ask if *you* needed *our* help. I have a caravan at the far end of the park. She's clean and dry and safer than a tent in this weather.'

'That's kind of you, but I'm fine.' Chelsea even contemplated adding the line about her husband being home any minute. *If only!*

'I'm offering my *spare* caravan. *Sea-Esta* is a rental,' he clarified. 'You walked right by her—and me—earlier. I waved.'

'Ahh, you're Tight Fly Guy!'

Either oblivious to or ignoring her faux pas, he explained a last-minute cancellation meant the van was hers for the night.

'If you want it. I'm the campground caretaker, not some weirdo pervert. This rain isn't expected to ease for hours, and without a tight fly, you're exposed to the elements.' As if to prove his point, a wind gust slapped wet leaves over her face.

'What about the tent?' Chelsea spluttered, grateful most of her gear remained dry in the car.

'A few solid pegs will help,' he said over a crack of thunder. 'I'll come back and batten down the hatches, as they say. First things first. Let's get you settled and safe.' At that, he raised an arm, and an umbrella mushroomed. 'Take this, get in your car, then follow us.'

Snatching the few belongings close at hand—her soggy mobile phone, handbag, and a shopping bag of snacks—Chelsea crawled out, stopping to zip the tent before standing and making a dash for her car. After slamming the driver's door shut behind her, the hooded man collapsed the umbrella into a walking aid and trod the soggy ground that earlier had presented as the perfect camping spot. With powerful strides—despite the one sneakered prosthetic and one thong-wearing foot—he and his torch guided Chelsea through the pitch-black campground and across a gravel road turned sludge.

As the car's wipers juddered and pushed mushy leaves back and forth over the windscreen, her headlights caught his high-vis raincoat, one arm urging her to veer left, then right. By the time Chelsea had steered her little car under the cover of a corrugated tin carport, and grabbed her travel bag from the backseat, the caravan door was open, lights ablaze. Welcoming.

Relieving Chelsea of her load, the hooded man slid the soft bag across the caravan floor, shouting over the million raindrops hitting the metal roof. 'Up you go. Dryer inside than out.'

'I need to pay you.'

'Tomorrow is fine. If you need anything, call. Number's above the door. I'm staying close, tucked into my old van across the road. The one with the Tibetan prayer flags. *Thisldo* is my shelter from the storm, and my office. I won't sleep much. Never do on nights like this. I need to stay alert and on hand, in case.'

'Okay, well, thanks. This will definitely do,' she said.

He grinned. 'Towels are on the bed. Oh, and the stove is LPG. I'll turn the bottle on as I go but give the gas time to come through.'

'I understand how it works,' she shouted. 'Thanks, again. See you tomorrow.'

Locking the door, checking it twice, Chelsea towelled her arms and legs until she'd stopped dripping.

'A bit of water hurts no one,' she could hear her dad say, unperturbed that his straw hat and board shorts would get a soaking while fixing a leak in the caravan. Board shorts were William Scott's go-to, while on top he mostly wore a tiny pot belly, which he rubbed each time he burped, much to their mother's displeasure. Also earning Wendy's wrath was the collection of leather neck chokers, usually adorned with a feather or some kind of totem.

The family's caravan, Vinnie the Viscount, had braved Mother Nature's fury on numerous occasions, requiring many buckets and all hands on deck to batten down the caravan hatches and hammer more annex pegs into the ground.

'Storms pass,' her dad would espouse. 'We get through each one only to wonder what the fuss was about.'

While surveying *Sea-Esta's* cosy interior, she noted its coordinated cushions and window coverings in shades of red. The compact kitchenette featured beige cupboards and red retro food canisters lined up on gold-speckle laminate. Grateful the restoration included vinyl and not fabric dinette seats, Chelsea lowered her still-soggy self, sighing long and deliberately loud as she realised the van was similar in size and shape to the one the Scott family had holidayed in decades ago.

So strong was the memory of Vinnie, and of William Scott standing outside and urging her to help—hammer and spare tent pegs in hand—the years rolled back to when Chelsea was eleven years old and working alongside her dad.

CAMPING WITH DAD, 1980

Being the Scott family's fifth annual holiday in Vinnie the Viscount, I'm an expert at just about everything when it comes to setting up camp. First, I chock the wheels with lumps of wood. Then I place the slops container to catch the kitchen sink water. Only when my chores for Dad are done do I help Layla erect the two-man tent Mum lets us sleep in. Once the caravan is unhitched and levelled, and the gas turned on to get the refrigerator cold real quick, coz Mum likes cold wine, Dad double-checks the tent pegs while me and Layla take turns blowing air into our Lilo mattresses.

'Tea might be nice, love. No rush,' Dad calls into the open window. 'Chelsea-girl, go in and grab my hat off the bed.' He flops into a camp chair. 'This is the life, eh? Wouldn't be dead for squids.'

'It's quids!' Mum grumbles from inside, where she dribbles water on the drainboard. 'Water's running to the back of the sink,' she tells the entire park. 'No one goes anywhere until we're level.'

Hoisting himself up, Dad dons his hat, winks, then walks to the drawbar at the front of the caravan where he winds the jockey wheel handle, winking again. 'Happy wife, happy life, Chelsea-girl.'

I'm keen to skip the tea-drinking part of setting up. Unlike Layla, who at almost fifteen fakes liking the watery brown goop to look grown up, I reckon tea tastes disgusting when black and totally puke-worthy with milk. Besides, it's plain dumb to waste perfectly good beach weather. We can drink tea at home.

'Can't we go to the beach, Dad? Please?'

'If I find the Thermos, we'll take tea with us,' he replies, ducking as he enters the caravan door before turning back to me. 'As usual, your mother has brought everything from home except the kitchen sink. You girls, take your buckets, head into the trees at the back of the park. We need kindling for tonight's fire. I'll be in here helping Mum look for the Thermos and the toasting marshmallows. I may need to tickle their location out of her, so take a walk and take your time, girls,' he adds, closing the door to muffle their mother's cackle.

With so many trees surrounding the campground, finding firewood isn't difficult, but I don't hurry. I've half-filled my bucket—green and covered with the Little Mermaid stickers I snaffled from the breakfast cereal box—when my sister downs Dad's red bait bucket to tug her pony-tail tighter and to huff. Layla has taken to huffing a lot lately.

'Hey, Layla? How can Mum hate almost everything about camping? Do you reckon she and Dad have *anything* in common?'

'Their initials?' Layla chuckles and wraps an arm around my shoulder. 'And us.'

'And we'll always have them, right?'

Layla shrugs. 'Old people grow older and get sick, like Gran and

Gramps. No one lives forever, Chels, but I'm not going anywhere. You'll have your big sis until we turn old and grey. Come on, let's go check out this year's Christmas decorations.'

Leaving our half-filled buckets on the ground, Layla and me wander the small streets where permanent park dwellers live in mostly dilapidated caravans they've chocked with bits of wood and bricks. Each December, residents drape their homes and tiny pot plant gardens in tinsel, and stake Santa cut-outs into the sandy soil. Some residents get real creative, with most happy to offer a treat when polite visitors pass by and admire their efforts. White Christmas fudge is my favourite.

'Oi! You two!' Dad finally calls from the open van door as we're wandering back to camp. 'You haven't been bothering the permanents, I hope. We can't go until the firewood is stacked, so make it snappy. Fish are waiting to bite my hook.'

'You go with Dad,' Layla tells me. 'I'll finish.'

'Okay. See ya!' I dash across to Mum for a goodbye hug, but dart away before the woman can reposition the dorky canvas hat.

'Be good and be careful, and for goodness' sake,' Mum calls, 'look after your idiot father.'

'Are you sure you don't wanna come, Layla?' I ask, hopeful. But I know the answer, even if I don't understand why growing up means missing out on the fun stuff, like body surfing, building sandcastles, and standing side by side on the beach casting a fishing line with Dad.

'What on earth have you got in that thing?' Mum calls as Dad settles the straps of a bulging backpack on both shoulders.

'Wouldn't you like to know!'

With Dad already walking away from camp, I run to catch up. I love him so much; I love the rowdy holiday version even more. Gone is the quiet man who takes the morning train Monday to Friday before I'm even out of bed, and who comes home too late and too tired to bother with bedtime stories. With Mum mostly lost in what Dad calls 'her brooding billionaire books', Layla has become the family's storyteller—and she's good at it. When tucked up in bed, my sister invents nonsense tales, and we laugh and laugh until Mum, in the next room, reminds us Dad has an early start.

I'll have no trouble falling asleep tonight. I'm struggling to keep up with Dad's big strides across the campground. We're headed for the skinny bush path that traces the back of the dunes and goes forever. Dad loves hiking. Some mornings, he gets up before anyone, grabs his back-pack, and doesn't return until after Mum has washed up after breakfast.

With today windy, the rustling leaves make Dad's chatter hard to hear. But he claims to have found a secret fishing spot on the far side of the biggest headland.

'Can we *please* go to the secret spot now?' I beg.

He shakes his head. 'Tide's all wrong for rock fishing. Maybe next year, when the tide's right, I'll take you. But never tell Mum there's a special spot. Okay? Now, sit tight for a bit while I go bush.' He disappears into the thick undergrowth, returning a few minutes later, looking relieved.

'All set,' he announces, adjusting his grip on the fishing rod, tackle box and net. 'Up and over, Chelsea-girl.'

Tea thermos in one hand and my green bucket in the other, I charge uphill until both feet sink ankle-deep in the soft sand.

Finally, I'm atop the mountainous dune and surveying my sea king-dom. Sandbar Beach is so pretty, and while I love fishing, it's the treasures waiting to be discovered that make my tummy tingle.

'Look at me! I made it! I'm Queen of the castle. Hey, Dad?' I ask when he stops on the crest beside me. 'How long would it take me to swim to the end of the ocean?'

'There's no end to the ocean, Chelsea-girl. The sea goes on well beyond the horizon. In fact, it just goes and goes and goes.'

'Goes where, Dad?'

'Everywhere, but nowhere.'

I'm confused. 'How can something go everywhere but nowhere?'

'Easy. Your imagination does all the time.' He chuckles when I scrunch my face. 'You probably think your imagination is stuck in here, right?' He taps my skull. 'But it goes places if you let it. Lots of fabulous places.'

'Like where, Dad?'

'Wherever you want. When*ever* you want. You'll understand when you're older. Come on.'

When he nudges me into action, I plant my heels firmly to slow the dune descent in sand so fine and soft it threatens to swallow me whole. Racing ahead, I jump over dried and greying pumice stones set in lines by the morning's high tide, while Dad stops to pick up a piece of twisted driftwood about the size of his forearm.

'One small bit won't hurt,' he says, answering the surprise in my wide eyes and open mouth. 'I promised your mum. She wants me to make a Christmas centrepiece for the table at home. Don't you worry. We'll return this one to nature on our Sandbar trip next year.' He examines the many twists and knots from different angles. 'Perfect specimen for your mum: dried-up, gnarly, and weathered. But don't tell her I said so.' He laughs and lets the wood drop with a thud into the bucket.

If that's a Dad joke, I don't understand. Just like, at eleven, I don't get the importance of table centrepieces. Christmas is about Santa stockings, presents, roast vegies, and fruit pudding with its hidden coins.

'Hey Dad,' I say as we near the shoreline, 'if not the secret spot today, where *are* we fishing?'

He drops his gear. 'Reckon this spot in front of us has your name on it.'

I giggle, eyeing the long stretch of beach with our two footprints side by side. 'No, it doesn't.'

Taking up the stick of driftwood, he scratches the words MISS and FIX in the sand.

'Does now.' He grins. 'Let's get fishing.'

'What made you call me Miss Fix?' I ask.

Dad stops digging in the tackle box to tussle my hair before positioning the sunhat hanging down my back. 'That's for me to know and for you to figure out.' A tap to my head settles the hat almost over my eyes. 'Let's get these lines out. The best fish are caught on an incoming tide. Once the waterline washes those letters in the sand away, the tide will have peaked and the fish we didn't catch will head home—as will we.'

Yes, I think, but not before I make him chase me down. He'll catch me —he does without fail—hug me tight while calling me 'a giggling sack of beach worms', then charge into the water, throwing us both into the tumbling waves. Eventually, Dad will make for the shore and suggest Mum will have the timer on us. Then, hoisting the bucket containing our catch, he'll say, 'Enough for dinner and no more. Come on, Miss Fix. Last one back to camp is a rotten egg.'

4

LAYLA

Childless by circumstance rather than by choice, the siren-like scream of a toddler in full tantrum mode while in the confines of economy-class would ordinarily poke Layla's fifty-year-old buttons in all the wrong ways. Fortunately, she could snuggle into the spacious business-class seat, mutter her appreciation to the travel gods for providing an upgrade for the return flight to Sydney, and feel smug about other inflight perks bestowed by the airlines on travel agents. Enduring a long-haul flight any other way would push her to the point of madness. And not for the first time.

Layla had worn *Looney Layla Scott* as a label in her late teens following several attention-seeking self-harm incidences. Looney probably *wasn't* the word do-gooders used while literally picking her out of the gutter on her twenty-first birthday. That inglorious incident had put her on Doc Dashing's very comfy couch for the first of many sessions. For years, Layla drifted aimlessly back and forth between gutter and do-gooder, drawn to abrasive people and sharp objects, aware anything or anyone damaging had the potential to end her misery. The day Doctor Trent Dashwood—the out of bounds bachelor with the honeyed voice and smoldering eyes—marked her file *NO LONGER A DANGER TO HERSELF*, she'd believed the impossible.

He'd saved Layla from Layla. What he couldn't fix, however, was the relationship with her sister. *Or your intolerance for badly behaved kids,* she mused while tuning out of the squeals in economy by tuning into the familiar and soothing hum of the aircraft's engines. Was it Layla's good fortune—or any potential child's—that she'd never ventured down the parenting path? The closest thing to a motherly urge was during those rare, long-ago visits to the old house in what used to be called "the Penrith boonies". Gabby, her amusing niece with the mischievous spark, had made the morbid family get-togethers tolerable. The occasional pill and alcohol overindulgence also helped Layla cope with Chelsea's insufferable reminiscences about their father. But when the determined Doc Dashing had denied Layla such vices, she'd resorted to nicotine hits, slipping into the backyard to smoke.

That was until her teenage niece started pestering her for a puff. Although delighted young Gabby had considered her worth emulating, Aunty Layla with the addictive personality—not to mention one monstrous family secret—had not been appropriate mentor material for a growing girl. Add to that the skeleton in the Scott-family closet—certainly no little white lie—Layla's survival and sanity had remained best served by distancing herself from family gatherings. Invitations still came, but her travel job provided an endless array of excuses, making it ages since she'd seen her sister in the flesh. Texting was best; the pair agreed.

As news captions on the inflight screens updated passengers on the day's global happenings, Layla wondered how Chelsea was acknowledging the dreaded anniversary. Was she at home this minute, setting his place at the dinner table and announcing the centrepiece display was courtesy of a backyard shrub or tree their father had nurtured and loved? *Lucky trees!* After the meal, would her sister insist they watch home movies or play stupid board games? The go-to in the Scott household on wet or windy days had been *Mouse Trap*. An ironic choice for their family, given the game starts with players working together to build a ridiculously complex and totally over-the-top Rube Goldberg-like mouse trap, only then to turn against each other once they'd finished the project. How did Chelsea's husband and kids tolerate such ritualistic crap? Or had time curtailed Chelsea's obsession to commemorate the man Layla never wanted to remember?

Adjusting the airline-provided eye mask and pillow, Layla knew one thing. Flying from one side of the world to the other would help her sleep through the anniversary. If only there was a way of avoiding the bustling baggage claim area overflowing with tear-filled greetings and happy family hugs. The only thing waiting for Layla each time she landed in Sydney was a painful truth and a one-bedder flat.

Her luck ran out in Singapore where a change-over and an over-booked flight saw an end to the perks, putting Layla back in the economy section, but with a window. Seat 41A might not be so bad had a rambunctious mob of five not spread themselves across row 40.

The Scott family had squabbled over all kinds of things, but never over seats on a long-haul flight. Their holidays never amounted to more than a trip to Sandbar Campground where Layla would work on her tan lines while staring up at contrails in the sky and imagining exotic locations—anywhere other than the New South Wales north coast. If Layla never saw that campground again, it would be too soon.

With the squabbling siblings in Row 40 impossible to ignore, Layla leaned back and let their excited squeals trigger the movie reel of childhood recollections. Playing on the insides of her eyelids were images of her five-year-old self happily cramming Cabbage Patch Caroline into a cupboard, ready to play protective big sister to a real-life baby. For years, she and Chelsea had giggled over silly secrets, held hands on the way to school, played Hide and Seek, and pretended to be famous. As the lanky one in the family, Layla had dreamed of being a model or an air hostess—or both. She had their mum's light-blue eyes and dyed-brown hair so thick and rebellious it repelled every rubber band and any attempt to hold it in place.

A chorus of 'shhh' made Layla lift one corner of the eye mask. Three girls of varying ages but with matching brown eyes stared back from Row 40, smiling through identical mouths.

'We're going on an adventure,' one said. 'You'll never guess where.'

Layla and Chelsea used to enjoy family holidays—the muddier, sandier, or wetter the better—until keeping up appearances mattered more to Layla than beach and bush expeditions with little sisters and dorky dads.

'Do you want to know?' another whispered. 'It's a secret, but I can tell you.'

'No, thanks. No more secrets for me,' she managed as the mother cast Layla an apologetic look before wrangling her trio back into their seats,

Layla needed no more secrets. On her sixteenth birthday, she'd discovered a family skeleton and a lie devastating enough to turn her tears to stone. Not having asked for the secret, nor knowing what to do with one, she'd held it tight to protect her sister, until the weight of truth became too painful, and Layla tried too hard, too many times, and too many ways to stop the hurt.

Besides, she was far too preoccupied with the text message that had dropped onto her phone while in Singapore. It was from her mother and the news was not good.

5

CHELSEA

With the same finger she'd scribbled the words MISS and FIX in the condensation on the caravan's foggy front window, Chelsea flicked a tear from one cheek.

What are you doing here? She couldn't even claim the decision to come camping as hers alone.

Two so-called trauma and phobia experts on talk-back radio had been debating the pros and cons of self-imposed exposure therapy. One expert claimed emotional wounds were healed by recalling and then modifying the bad memory into something else. Apparently, if done in a place that feels safe, the brain disconnects the discomfort and sense of panic that might otherwise turn a traumatic incident into a lifelong phobia. The other expert espoused the benefits of facing fears head on through repeated exposure to whatever triggered the bad memory or phobia.

If she achieved nothing else, Chelsea hoped to return home renewed and ready to cauterise the emotional wounds she was bound to incur while preparing her beloved Beach Shack for the market. While not yet ready to tell Dale she was letting go, in case the plan went pear-shaped, and Chelsea changed her mind—again—she owed her mother a heads-up.

Having dried her phone as much as possible, Chelsea began a text message. No salutation needed—the Scott family hadn't bothered about such civilities for years.

Not sure where in the world you are, Mum. We need to talk about the house.

'You remember the house, don't you?' she paused to mutter. 'The family home you abandoned for husband number two—and way too fast, in my opinion.'

> There's so much stuff in boxes under the house.
> And don't forget the emotional stuff you and Layla
> left behind when basically walking out of my life.

Deleting the last sentence, feeling all the better for having written the words, Chelsea instead typed:

> It's been a long time and you've moved on.

'To husband number three.'

> I hoped you might, at the very least, want to revisit
> the boxes in storage under the house. I don't want
> the responsibility of choosing what stays and what
> goes. To me, it's all precious. But taking everything
> kind of defeats the purpose of downsizing.

' … which my husband is insisting we do now the kids are grown. My very absent husband who left to give me space and time to think about what I wanted.'

Chelsea's tapping on the keyboard began to sound somewhat hopeful.

> Maybe, Mum, you'll visit the house. Any day that
> suits—or night is fine. When are you next in town?

'In the actual country?' she grumbled.

> I'm away for the next week—camping. You'll never
> guess where. Sandbar!!!

Three exclamation points seemed appropriate, and when the angry rumble of distant thunder confirmed as much, Chelsea chuckled, saying, 'Yes, that's right, Mum, I'm camping.'

> I had to come back. I need to forgive myself, and
> to do that I need to remember and …

'What rubbish!' With a growl, and the same expletive repeated over and over, she deleted the draft message in its entirety, only to begin again using the more familiar mother-daughter morse code.

> Selling house. Will email when home. Camping at Sandbar!!! Talk later.

After pressing SEND, the phone screen went black.

'Oh no! No! No! No!' Could the day get any worse? Did Chelsea need more signs to confirm this trip was a dumb idea? It sure wasn't the alone time she'd imagined.

All afternoon, her blue nylon dome had garnered interest from fellow holidaymakers. People in nearby caravans had peered, understandably curious about the middle-aged woman struggling with her fresh-out-of-the-packet pod-like shelter, its manifest fold lines and pristine pegs glinting under the summer sun. The purchase had seemed like a good idea, with impromptu trips away doable since Fred's passing. The pop-up contraption was also reminiscent of when the Scott sisters would share an old-fashioned A-frame tent, whispering in the dark before sleeping, then giggling awake each morning.

While much of Sandbar Campground appeared unchanged, the same could not be said about Chelsea. As a girl, she had loved the outdoors, especially the beach. Ten minutes after setting up camp, she would be in her togs and headed for the water. With no fear, she would race her dad into the ocean, dolphin-diving through the waves over and over until her nose ran, her eyes stung, and her bikini bottoms turned heavy with beach sand.

Now grown, the only diving Chelsea had wanted to do earlier today was back into the igloo-like structure to hide from nosey people, like the grey-haired woman under the awning of a caravan who'd raised a full-to-the-brim wine glass. With the big, upward curve of her lips that said 'come join us', Chelsea had retreated like a threatened turtle pulling its head inside a blue nylon shell.

No way! Having happy hour—or *yappy* hour—from three in the afternoon with a bunch of grey nomads was not why she'd returned to Sandbar. There was no *happy* anything about her spur-of-the-moment getaway, and nothing to raise a toast to unless she counted having successfully erected the Cosy Camping Pod without losing an eye. Thankfully, the hunky adventure-store salesman had alerted her to the potential hazard. Unfortunately, he'd neglected to mention the pod's cosy interior would have little spare floor space once she'd fully inflated the *'super-plush mattress'*. But where she slept for the next week hardly mattered if she achieved what she hoped: to change the sad narrative of her empty-nester existence by facing her demons and learning to smile in the place she'd cried as a child.

Those radio theorists had agreed on one thing. It was not possible to overcome trauma or feel genuine regret for something that could not be fully recalled, and Chelsea's memories seemed selective, as if she wasn't supposed to remember the detail. For that, she blamed her mother and sister who'd insisted the way to recover from grief was to forget. Chelsea's nightmares eventually stopped, morphing into weird recollections, but she never forgot the nature-loving man, or his lessons about living an honest life and never settling for less.

Ha! Chelsea huffed at the irony. *Settling for less?* Wasn't Dale expected to do just that all these years? To settle and give up on his dream of owning a place with a water view and sea salt in the air? No amount of ocean-breeze room deodoriser in a three-bedder weatherboard house in Penrith could ever satisfy his longing to live by the beach. But Chelsea struggled to let go. She had suffered a complicated grief, with her loss bringing out the best and the worst in the people around her. Her mourning had not come in prescribed stages. For a guilt-ridden twelve-year-old, grieving had been messy and confusing, and to this day still whispered its painful reminders.

While there was no changing the past, she *could* mend her marriage, but only once Miss Fix fixed herself. And so she was back in *Nowhere* to remember the good times, like helping Dad load the old Viscount caravan, Vinnie, and always with the same conversation starter:

'Where we goin' for holidays, Dad?'

'Nowhere,' William Scott replied.

'*Daaaad!*' Chelsea would giggle. 'We can't be going *nowhere.*'

'Yes, we can. We can go anywhere and do anything *if* we want it desperately enough. Remember my words, head for the horizon, and never settle for less, Chelsea-girl.'

Though too few, those family camping holidays had taught Chelsea what it meant to want *desperately*. Like when she and Layla would beg their dad to drive faster so they might snaffle the top camping spot before anyone else. Until they'd staked their claim closest to the beach track, Chelsea's insides never stopped churning with anticipation.

Truth was, it took years to truly grasp the meaning of *desperate*. Like *desperately* wanting her children to need her and her husband to come home. More than anything right now, Chelsea *desperately* wanted to find better and happier memories to assign to this time of the year, and to the father who had loved life and looked for the magic in it everywhere.

The phone trilling—melody intermittent, screen blank—ended her one-person pity party.

'Hello?'

'Thank goodness,' said the familiar voice. 'Vicki's been on the phone to me. Something about rescuing you from a storm. Where are you, Chels?'

'Nowhere,' she told her husband.

'Why can't I see you?' he asked. 'Or hear you properly. Press the Face-Time feature.'

'I can't see it. My phone got a dunking. Hold on. Plugging into power might help.' The charging *beep* sounded, but the screen stayed blank. 'You there?' she asked, settling awkwardly onto the bed, wishing for a longer electrical cord.

'More to the point, why are you *there*?' Dale asked. 'What's going on?'

'I bought a tent.' If *tent* was the right word for the pop-up pod she'd abandoned in the dead of night. 'I'm where I need to be, Dale.' She pictured his piercing blue eyes blinking in disbelief.

'Hon, *I've* always taken the kids camping because you hate it. I'm worried. What can I do?'

Tempted to suggest he either let her go or come back home, she instead bit down on her quivering bottom lip and lied; maudlin was not what she wanted to be.

'Nothing, I'm fine. The camping idea was a quick decision.'

I at least deserve points for making one, she mused while covering her head with the throw rug to dull the deafening ricochet of hard rain on a metal roof.

'Hon, you're completely *koozy*, and I love you.'

Chelsea let those three little words—I love you—play in a loop like a happy GIF. She wanted to believe his declaration was not simply habit; the call and the worried voice were surely proof of his sincerity. The reason she hadn't told Dale about the Sandbar trip was because her husband was a worrier. He'd looked out for her since the first day she'd walked into his Year Ten classroom as 'the new girl'.

The change of school had been Aunty Rita's idea, with the fresh start in a different suburb ideal. Ideal for Aunty Rita, maybe, who for four long years had travelled from her Narrabeen Beach house to western Sydney to check on both Scott girls, fill the refrigerator, and lecture Wendy on her responsibilities. Wendy's growing number of acquaintances, however, took precedence over parenting, while Layla's disconnect from family, and from society in general, worsened. Dark became her sister's signature —clothes, hair, nails, makeup. When Chelsea's schoolwork started to suffer, Rita relocated her to Narrabeen Beach 'for both their sakes'.

From day one, her uniform cleaned and pressed crisp, right through the last two years of study, Chelsea Scott was Dale Holt's *koozy girl*. The *kooky* and *crazy* girl who would stare across the room in detention, silently introducing him to her secret blink code. Dale had taught her to smile again, and they'd laughed throughout their marriage, until recently when he said those other three words and made her cry: 'I am leaving'.

'Have you heard from your sister today?' Dale was asking.

'No. I-I thought you might be Layla calling.'

Her husband replied with a hum of understanding, his mind no doubt turning over with ways to help. Dale liked to help. He spent his days coaching kids to cope with change, which allowed him to understand Chelsea's grief and her lifelong habit of retreating to her bedcover cubby. As a teenager, while on a date at the local McDonalds, Chelsea had divulged everything about her home life to Dale, listing every flaw and confessing to every sin—from stealing coins from her Mum's purse, to unintentionally flushing her sister's favourite earrings down the loo, *and* setting Layla's journal on fire. A Big Mac, fries, and a soft serve later, Dale was holding Chelsea while she cried over not being able to fix the family she'd broken. Years later, Dale had confessed to falling in love with her that night.

The man still loved her, but—yes, there were often buts—he was ready to *move forward*. More specifically, he moved to the other side of the country for work, leaving Chelsea with her empty-nester emotions as company, and a crippling guilt rendering her unable to move or to make a decision in case it was the wrong one.

Or plain stupid, like this solo return-to-Sandbar-psychotherapy-caper!

Hearing the beep of an incoming call, and with her screen remaining blank, Chelsea asked Dale, 'Is that for you or me?'

'Me,' her husband replied. 'Hang on.'

Naturally, the call was for him. No one needed Chelsea. No kids demanded dinner; nor was there an animal to feed. *Poor old Fred!* Tears for the little Terrier tipped over onto Chelsea's cheeks. Not only had she taken the vet's advice and said goodbye, but she'd also lost her last excuse for *not* selling the house. No longer could she claim unnecessary cruelty for forcing an old, blind dog to adapt to new surroundings.

'Let's hold off on moving,' she'd tell Dale. 'He won't be with us forever.'

If it wasn't hard enough farewelling the dog alone, returning home had made Chelsea realise the void old Fred had filled. No family member needed her like Fred had—not today, not yesterday, and not in the months since Dale packed his bags for the Perth posting.

The same pressure his giant hands had placed on the over-stuffed suit-case to close it tight that day, Chelsea had felt on her chest as she'd struggled to find the right words. Strangely, all she'd told her soon-to-depart husband at the time was how windy it could get in the west, so ... 'Best throw in a second coat. And a hat,' she'd added. Dale did look fantastic in the fedora Gabby had sent last Christmas.

'Sorry, hon.' Dale's voice jerked Chelsea from her wretched ruminations. 'Work call. I'm back. Where were we?'

She might have replied, *miles apart on opposite sides of the country*, or enquired about the west coast weather, but surely more important topics needed discussing. Subjects such as the state of their marriage, her daughter's increasing aloofness, or how Dale's departure had left Chelsea to mourn alone when the vet said: 'A quick end is kind.' For Fred, she'd wished the man had clarified.

When Vicki had suggested Chelsea adopt a new dog, she'd agreed company and a beating heart to love her back might be nice. She could rescue another Fred from the pound: an old dog, abandoned, one needing love and comfort in its final years. But each time Chelsea came close, common sense stopped her adopting. Owners rarely surrendered their pets unless sick, nippy, recalcitrant, or recidivist runaways. With Chelsea already feeling abandoned by a family moving forward without her, the final straw would be a rescued dog running away. Besides, a pound visit required decisions: Puppy or mature? Big or small? One or two? Black, white, or brindle? How would she ignore the hundreds of hopeful faces and wagging tails to choose a single dog?

'You there, Chels?'

'Yes, but I'm not sure about the phone. With no screen, I've no way of knowing if it's charging or even ... Damn! Hello?'

Ordinarily, Chelsea might have thrown her head back on the pillow in frustration and cursed the lost connection, but truth be told, she was too miserable to talk to Dale tonight. After seven hours driving, two detours around road works, followed by ten uncooperative tent pegs and a floppy fly—all on top of her thwarted effort to make the beach—Chelsea was not only drained and disillusioned, but she was disappointed her dad's anniversary was passing by without the reflection and commemoration it deserved. This special date was partly why she'd come to Sandbar so impulsively.

She could try calling Dale back, or she could get off the bed and unpack the other essentials from her car, like the bottles of red on the back seat. A drink would lift her mood. Instead, stripped of wet clothes and prone on the mattress, staring up at the overhanging cupboard covered in stickers, she recalled the time Layla had got cranky with Mum and gouged a rude word into the underside of Vinnie's overhead cupboards. Covering the underside of *these* overhead cupboards were sheep stickers. Dozens of cartoonish creatures ready for the counting by exhausted holidaymakers. But Chelsea couldn't sleep.

The only thing not a blur from that last camping holiday thirty-four years ago was her twelve-year-old self screaming at the wicked and wild sea responsible for snatching her daddy away, and the tearful trip home curled up with Layla in the back of a police car, while in the front, their mum had howled.

For weeks afterwards, a constant flow of friends and strangers visited The Beach Shack. All offered the same warped solace: 'At least your father died doing what he loved. It happens'. The notion had terrified Chelsea back then; she loved all the same things: the adventures, the bush, the sea.

Tempted to hide in a bedcover cubby like she'd done as a child, the phone's crackly ringtone sounded, and the screen flickered twice before turning black.

Chelsea shook the phone; frustration shook her voice. 'You stupid bloody—'

'It's me again,' Dale announced. 'I'm worried you're alone in that place.'

'Well, don't be. The truth is, I should've come back a long time ago.'

I should have done a lot of things years ago, she told herself.

'But you're not cut out for camping, Chels.'

'I was once,' she retorted. 'Once upon a time I was lots of things and I intend finding that person—for me more than anyone else.'

'But the beach, Chels? Really? I witnessed your meltdown at Bondi when we went for the twins' tenth birthday. You haven't put a single toe in the ocean in all the years I've known you—and for good reason. I get that. What I don't get is why you waited until I was on the other side of the country to do something this crazy.'

Another silent question screamed through her. *Why be on the other side of the country?* But Chelsea knew the answer; her stubbornness had pushed him there. And as much as she might've wanted Dale to drop everything and race home, she wouldn't force him to choose her over the job he loved. Because he would come—if she asked. *Wouldn't he?*

'Look, hon, I might tease you about never making a decision, but are you sure about this one? What will being in that place achieve? Especially at this time of year.'

Doubt swamped Chelsea. What *was* she doing? Saying goodbye to her dad? Did she believe a person's spirit only crossed over once whoever had wronged them acknowledged their mistake? Would being here wipe away all guilt, or tell Chelsea more about that day? Might she finally stop obsessing? That had been her daughter's criticism before moving out of home. At least *obsessive* was an improvement on *indifferent*, Chelsea remembered pondering. *It is better, isn't it?*

'Dale, I'm sure a few days in the sun will do me *and* my phone good. Even if it rains the entire time, being here feels right. In fact,' she added while poking a corner of one sheep sticker refusing to adhere to a gouged section of wood, 'this *caravan feels* inexplicably right.'

'Well, if you need me … And, Chels, honey …?' Dale spoke those three words like she might break. Was it a good or a bad sign Chelsea recognised the tone?

'I'm okay,' she reassured. 'And thank you for recognising his anniversary—and for caring. My mother doesn't, and my sister is incapable of recognising the importance.' Her prerogative, Chelsea had conceded years ago. 'It's taken me a while, Dale, but I'm finally waking up to the fact that everyone else has moved on. It's my turn.'

'Sorry, hon, gotta go,' her husband announced in a whisper. 'A team member is hovering. I'll try you later.'

Team member? Working at this hour? Perth was three hours behind the east coast, but it was late to be at work. *Don't go there, Chelsea.*

6

CHELSEA

Chelsea sat up on the bed, avoiding the hazardous overhanging cupboard. From the tunnel bag at the foot of the bed, she plucked out the toiletry bag, unzipped it, and stared into the mirror glued onto the inside flap. For a split second, she saw her father looking back. Then she noticed the crow's-feet and dark shadows around her eyes. Did she look like him? Even if she recalled the details of his face, Chelsea, at forty-six, had grown older and lived years longer than her life-loving dad. The man who'd wrapped his family in sunshine and magic, taking them on fun, faraway adventures—real and imagined—died too young; lost at thirty-seven to the dark world of wicked sea witches. Every night in bed, young Chelsea had bargained with the evildoers, prepared to sacrifice anything to bring her daddy home, or to rewind the day and make different decisions.

Not until years later, while helping Dale study guardianship law, had Chelsea learned the part of the brain responsible for decision making and sound judgements did not fully develop until a person reached their mid-twenties. Still, she blamed herself, with her mother's words from all those years ago painfully clear.

'You left your father alone,' she'd wailed. 'They would have rescued you both. If only you'd stayed put.'

The irony of those words was not lost on Chelsea. Here she was three decades later, determined to stay put in the family home and losing Dale because of it. Had her stubbornness not shushed him every time he'd hinted about moving to a better, more modern place, might their relationship be different and her marriage happier? Had she not batted away every suggestion, or had her indecisiveness not crippled her all these years, Dale might not be on the other side of the country? The man couldn't have made his thoughts any plainer over the years, any time the subject came up, and always starting the same way.

'Chels? About the house …'

Those three words, and the home she treasured, caused most of their marital spats. Their first fight was twelve years ago, as the boys prepared for high school.

'About the house,' Dale began. 'I get what you're saying about the twins' schooling, but the commute is killing me.'

Commutes don't kill, Chelsea wanted to respond. Oceans do. Giant sea-going monsters with white foam fingers snatch people from rocky shelves and pin them to the sea floor where the sea witches live. Of course, she didn't say any such thing, rehashing instead the lines her husband knew verbatim.

'You understand what this house means to me, Dale; what it means to us. I grew up here and our children are growing up here. It's their home.' She pointed towards the myriad cherished features: the laundry door with two generations of growth charts marking the frame, the backyard with its forty-year-old fig trees, and the eighty-four handmade pavers fashioned by her father and laid in the chequerboard pattern to match her mother's kitchen linoleum. And who could forget the living room with the corner bar made from old surfboards and hula skirts? 'I want to stay put, Dale. That's that!'

'And what anyone else wants doesn't matter?' he asked.

'The twins matter,' she replied. 'Moving house now will mean a new school, and at the worst time. I remember feeling new and awkward when starting high school, but I was lucky. I found you.'

'And they'll have each other, Chels. That's the benefit of twins.'

'But what about Gabby?'

'Our Miss Independent?' He let out the laugh Chelsea adored. Dale laughed love. 'Playground prima donna by day's end—guaranteed! A new school can be life changing. Remember?'

'I do,' Chelsea conceded.

'Then get on board and let's find *our* place. With renovations and the current real estate market, the timing is perfect. *And* we're mortgage-free, thanks to your family.' He spoke the last part with the usual disdain. 'We can find a beach suburb north of Gosford. The choice is ours.'

'That's my argument,' Chelsea said. 'Dad never got to choose. Moving west was a huge sacrifice, but he agreed renting was a waste of good money. Buying a house meant keeping a roof over our heads and—'

'... and full bellies. Yeah, yeah, all hail William bloody Scott,' Dale cawed. 'What about my sacrifices? Living so far from the beach was not my first choice, and to be honest, I'm sick of feeling like a visitor in this place.'

The same argument played out the same frustrating way every few years, ending with Chelsea accusing Dale of being unfair. The most recent episode had concluded with her husband taking the fedora hat from her hands, throwing it on top of his Perth-bound suitcase, and pulling her into a farewell hug while the taxi driver waited.

'I'll miss you, hon, and I understand the connection to your dad, but I'm drowning under the weight of your father's memory. I'm drowning in his house.'

So violent was Chelsea's reaction to the statement that she gasped and gagged, and her eyes teared up. 'Don't ever say that!'

'Sorry, but it's how I feel.' He stroked her shoulders, his face angled to meet with her downcast eyes. 'I thought we'd finally whittled our selection down from six potential suburbs to two. I'll happily agree to any house, anywhere you choose. If not the coast, what about The Blue Mountains? I left a Leura house brochure under a magnet on the fridge. We could fit two houses on the block. Maybe even a granny flat for visiting kids.'

'The property is five train stops west,' she said, incredulous. 'The commute you complain about would be longer. How is that moving forward?'

'It'll be ours,' he said quicker than a blink. 'Yours and mine—together.'

'So, you're saying my family home is—'

'*Our* home, Chelsea,' he corrected. 'It's *our* home and supposedly a steppingstone to a bigger house more suited to *our* family. Something we can choose together and get excited about. A place to make memories in —yours and mine and with *our* kids. All I'm asking while I'm committed to six months in Perth is to pick a suburb. Decide what you want.'

'Why me?' she said, sounding like a ten-year-old. 'If you want to move so badly, you choose and let's be done with it.'

'No! I'm over being the sole decision-maker. At least ask your mother or call your sister—or whoever you need to consult about getting the place sorted and ready for sale. Or don't,' he said. 'I'm not forcing this to make you sad, Chels. I'm asking you to choose *us*. To treasure our lives more than your father's beloved Beach Shack. Please, commit to *our* future. It's coast or country. Leura is west, Woy Woy is north, and both regions have commuter services. Because they are chalk and cheese, choosing should not be difficult. Just decide what is it you want for us. Okay?'

No! It's not okay, she silently shouted through sobs as Dale's taxi sped away and Fred's front paws inched their way up her left leg. Cradling the little dog, she kissed the soft fur between his ears. 'At least I have you, buddy. Don't you leave me.'

During the months following Dale's departure, she'd rattled around the house no one in the family but Chelsea loved. At work, keen to convince colleagues and acquaintances she was fine, she'd boldly talked up the benefits of being home alone. Then Fred died and Chelsea's tearful teachers' lunchroom meltdown had ended with a recommendation she didn't wait until the end of the school term to take a break.

'A couple of weeks away before the Christmas crazies might help,' said the principal.

The so-called Christmas crazies had been behind her parents' decision to pull Layla and Chelsea out of school early each December—destination: Sandbar Beach. Now here Chelsea was in a caravan, and fully cognisant she could no longer keep both The Beach Shack *and* her husband; nor could she continue resisting change.

Incredibly, Fred's passing had let Chelsea see that beating hearts, and not material memories, made a house a home. But with Chelsea the sole custodian of the family footprint—until Gabby or the twins took over as the curators of their grandfather's legacy—she would hold tight to William Scott's memory through special mementoes. As for the numerous boxes under the house? Even though Wendy had walked away at the first chance she got, and Layla might lack any skerrick of sentimentality, sorting the contents without their input was both morally wrong and emotionally unfair.

Hopefully, a lovely couple would inspect the place and buy with their heart, unconcerned about the foundations drying out and twisting the frame so much the internal doors no longer closed properly. A 'heart buyer' would fall in love with the quaint and quirky, like the garden sculpture made from rusty anchors, and the collection of mooring floats eternally entwined in two giant gum trees out front. Though not the neighbourhood's most treasured feature, the multi-coloured marine detritus that draped like festive baubles made every day feel like Christmas.

'How do I say goodbye?' she asked, staring up at the rain-spotted caravan hatch with the increasing condensation on the inside.

As a drip fell—*splat*—on Chelsea's forearm, a tear escaped from the corner of one eye and trickled into her ear. Was Perth getting rain tonight? What about Sydney's west with the acre of trees and garden William had planted, that Wendy had later neglected, and Dale had restored? As Chelsea dabbed the wet spot from her cheeks, the Beach Shack's ocean-blue exterior with sandy-yellow trim on the doors and window frames materialised. The place had gained quirky status when developers began snapping up neighbouring acreages and selling modern monochrome homes designed to blend into the landscape.

'What landscape?' Chelsea and Dale would scoff. 'Concrete and bitumen?'

Apart from her dad's handmade pavers, the only concrete on the Scott property was the path to the clothesline Wendy had insisted on. The day Chelsea and Layla had helped mix concrete in the wheelbarrow, father and daughters had dropped to their knees to press their handprints into the curing mix. Not their mother. Wendy was a wife inclined to oppose her husband in every way. Like Leura and Woy Woy, Wendy and William had been chalk and cheese.

Good grief! Was Chelsea turning into her mother? *No!* She was too like her dad—family-centric and not fussed with fancy stuff, which was why she'd baulked the day Dale had suggested engaging a business to help ease Chelsea's burden. *Clear-a-house.com* claimed it could help sellers prepare their house for the market.

Chelsea had almost spat the mouthful of breakfast tea over Dale's iPad while reading the sales blurb.

Clear-a-house can vamoose what's not valuable, redo any duds, and renovate or remove the worthless. We'll restyle stale homes to add the street appeal that attracts serious buyers, leaving you with a squeaky-clean, neat, and decluttered shell ready to sell.

'Seriously, Dale? A shell ready to sell?' But before he could utter a word, Chelsea was yelling. 'No way will strangers strip all the things that make this place special. It's not a bloody showroom. This is a beloved family home made of quality hardwood, and with features you won't find in those McMansions down the street. Pinewood frames with trusses stapled together and made to look like brick castles are popping up all around us. Somewhere out there is a family who will appreciate The Beach Shack's characteristics and want to live in it, *not* pull it down. I couldn't stand seeing my beautiful home in a demolished heap.'

'*Our* home, Chelsea,' Dale said pointedly. Then, after sighing long and deliberately loud, he planted both palms firmly on the countertop. 'While you keep digging those heels in, I'm moving on—to Perth, if that six-month secondment in WA is still available.'

'What? Why?'

'Because I'm tired of this merry-go-round we're on. Let's get off, Chels. Come with me. We'll have an adventure together.' When Chelsea hesitated, he added, 'Or, while I spend quality time with Gabby and our very special grandies, you can stay put and enjoy your quality-built house with its *special* characteristics.'

With another tentative trill from the still-blank phone, Chelsea hissed several expletives while slamming the unresponsive device into the mattress.

'Mum? Mum, are you okay?'

As Chelsea flipped the phone over, there was her daughter's pixilated face.

'Oh my, Gabby!' *She's remembered the anniversary after all, bless her.*

'I can't talk for long,' her daughter replied. 'The moronic paper shufflers at my ex-superannuation company have sent forms for me to sign, but to my old address. Has anything arrived for me?'

'No, nothing,' Chelsea replied, tempted to add: *It's been three years!* 'I'll keep an eye out, though, and forward mail to your Fremantle address. Are you still there?' she queried, concerned the crackly connection had disconnected them.

'Yes, Mum, all *four* of us are still here, still together and happy.' A suitable amount of surprise and cynicism accompanied the retort; Gabby had misunderstood Chelsea's query. 'We'll stay put here until the twins are older. If I learned anything from you, it's how kids benefit from stability.'

'Just not too much, Gabby, if I've remembered correctly.' Regret slapped Chelsea silent. 'I'm sor—'

'Hang on, Mum. Come on, babe, I said take this one from me. That is a Dadda squeal, not a Mummy cry.'

With her daughter too distracted to realise the phone camera was doing an accidental sweep of the living room littered with baby bouncers, toys, and piles of unfolded laundry, Chelsea was unexpectedly privy to a slice of her daughter's life.

'Hey, quit that, bozo! Can't you see I'm on the phone to Mum?'

As a slap, a giggle, and a deep voice sounded, Chelsea pictured the playful interaction between the bearded biker and her willowy, big-eyed daughter—a.k.a. the spitfire who spoke first, only to write vague apologies a few weeks later. Gabby's last bout of silence had left Chelsea stewing for six weeks until a birthday card had arrived with a note inside. Her daughter was sorry: sorry for yelling, sorry for calling Chelsea 'obsessive and overbearing and unwilling to let go of the past', and sorry for hanging up on her.

There'd been similarly hurtful outbursts as Gabby had slammed eighteen years of belongings into suitcases and shoved bulging plastic bags into the Honda Civic hatchback, destination Western Australia—a.k.a as far away from this place as possible. Her daughter's parting words from three years ago still landed like lemon juice on an open wound, the sharpness stirring Chelsea's insides as she recalled the discussion.

'Shit happens, Mum!' Gabby said while breaking her embrace to deliver one of those annoying twenty-something shrugs. 'And unlike you, I'm not afraid of cutting the bow lines and losing sight of the shore.'

'I am *not* afraid,' Chelsea protested as Gabby upturned another drawer of knickers over the already bulging packing box.

'Yes, you are,' she said with irksome millennial impudence. 'And you've tried to make my brothers and me afraid. You're scared of everything, Mum, but mostly you're afraid to want.'

Not true! Chelsea silently disputed. She did *want*. She wanted to know right there and then what the hell her daughter meant about making them all afraid.

'I'm sure about what I want, Mum, and this is *my* life. You can't stop me.'

'My purpose in life, Gabby, is to love and protect. It's not to block you. I've known since you were a child you are like your Aunt Layla. There's no holding either of you down. And while I'll always support you, I … Well, I mean … The man *is* almost twice your age; having things in common with your partner is important.'

'The *man's* name is Mick, and you simply don't get it,' Gabby declared. 'Love is love. Gender or age shouldn't matter. But you seem happiest living as if it's nineteen-freaking-eighty, and *we're* all stuck in the past with you and Grandad's ghost. I hate so much about this place.' Gabby swung her arm to point out the room she'd occupied since old enough to demand privacy. 'Throughout school, I was the weird girl from the weird house who got picked on and teased. But Mick loves me, warts and all, and if me loving him *is* a mistake, I'll manage the fallout. But it's not,' she was quick to add. 'You're just like Gran. You used to tell us kids about how Wendy got embarrassed when Granddad walked around the neigh-bourhood in his swimmers and thongs, wearing leather chokers and bracelets, and with his hair tied into a ponytail. Well, you're no different to her. Mick's not your idea of a son-in-law and you're freaking out about what people will think.' Gabby's palm flash gagged Chelsea, which was just as well. 'The thing is, Mum, you only care about my decisions when you don't agree with them. I know, I know—' Another palm flash. 'That's your prerogative, but before criticising my choices, try making a few decisions of your own. Why can't you be more like Aunty Layla? She and Gran aren't dwelling on the past. Losing anyone is a shit, but they moved on to live full lives.'

Chelsea hadn't known whether to laugh or cry at her daughter's observation, so she did neither, saying instead, 'Gabby, darling, distance makes everything harder. I'll miss you. Tell me it's not forever.'

As always, regret showed itself in the reddening of Gabby's cheeks. 'It's ideal for the time being, Mum,' she said, her voice softening. 'Mick's fly-in fly-out contract makes Perth practical.'

'If only you'd given me a chance to like Mick,' Chelsea said. 'Our one meeting was too brief.'

Gabby's exaggerated shoulder slump and sigh conveyed more than words ever could. 'Because, Mum, that was *the* most excruciating and embarrassing meal. I couldn't wait to get Mick out of the house and explain the whole shrine-place-setting-at-the-head-of-the-table thing—*and* the DAD Christmas stocking ritual. As for that stupid *Mouse Trap* game you insisted we play … I should've warned Mick.'

'And you might have warned me about Mick's—'

'What? Tattoos? Bike? Man bun? Earrings?'

'No!' Chelsea retorted. 'That he was previously married to one of the soccer mums. Next time, when I see him, I won't act so surprised.'

'And I'm sure you'll suffocate us with your insincerity. I can hear it now. "What a lovely couple you make".'

'Gabby, darling, did I make you this bitter?'

'Best if we leave it there, Mum. I must get on the road. I'll call.'

A hug and a quick kiss on a tear-streaked cheek and, like that, the baby girl she'd given birth to twenty-four years earlier stomped her stilettos over her granddad's hardwood floors for the last time, squeezed the final box into the car, and drove to the other side of the country.

Gabby's laugh now echoed down the telephone; her joy palpable.

'Oh, Mum! You should see Mick with the twins. He's all thumbs and totally no idea.' Another giggle reminded Chelsea her daughter was not *all* Layla. Like Dale, when their daughter laughed over her babies, she laughed love. 'Don't drop them, idiot! Give Lucy to me. Gotta go, Mum.'

'Wait, Gabby, I want to tell you I'm at Sandbar Beach, and in a tent. At least I was until—'

'Sorry, Mum, Mick's juggling babies here. Just forward the mail, okay?'

'Sure. Hug the twins for me, and Dad when you next see him,' Chelsea added, but she was talking into a void.

Either the phone reception had cut them off or Gabby had hung up, keen to get back to her full and purposeful life with her babies, and with her husband with the zillion tattoos.

Had Chelsea judged a book by its cover when first meeting Mick?

Pressing the iPhone's power button, hoping a reboot might reconnect her—to the mobile network at least—she sighed as messages from Travis and Tyler popped onto the screen. The twins were thinking of her, their texts both ending with the words: *Love you to the horizon, Mum. xx*

Chelsea brushed the tears from wet cheeks and smiled at the memory of her father saying the same.

TO THE HORIZON WITH DAD, 1979

'I'll love you to the horizon and back, Miss Fix.' Dad says, pointing out to sea.

'Is that like forever, Dad?'

He smiles, but his eyes stay sad. 'Nothing is forever, Chelsea-girl. Not the good things and luckily not the bad. And the horizon isn't forever either,' he adds.

'But it is a long way away, right?'

Dad squats so his eyes are level with mine. 'Like in life, it depends how you look at things. The furthest point you can see from all the way down here where you are, and while on the beach, is the first part of the horizon. You'd see much more if you stood as tall as me or went higher still— say to the top of Bunker Headland. You should do that, Miss Fix.'

'Climb to the top of the headland, Dad?'

'No. I mean, stand tall, want for more, go further, and climb as high as you can in life, even if it means bravely stepping beyond the horizon to find *the more*.'

'The more of what? I'm confused.'

This time when he laughs, he tousles my hair, sending a spray of sand over my shoulders. 'You'll understand one day, Miss Fix.'

'But when?'

'When you're ready to want *the more*. That's when the horizon and your life will make sense.'

7

CHELSEA

As comfortable as the mattress felt when Chelsea stretched out in her track pants and T-shirt, she craved her abandoned blue pod—a reminder of the bedcover cubby a sad, frightened teenage Chelsea had found comfort in.

A tent had not been on her shopping list that day. Her trip to the adventure store was to buy a replacement silk mantle for the old kerosene lantern she'd rescued from under the house when dumping Fred's smelly old bed in the kerbside collection pile. Initially thinking the lamp would add a rustic touch to a patio, she'd cleaned the glass of Daddy long-leg spiders, cobwebs, and dust, and added a new mantle for the lamp to the shopping list. Dale would be less keen on the retro restoration, even suggesting her clinging to bygone days was no way to move forward.

'Face the past,' he'd likely say when she showed him. 'Please don't live in it.'

A wave of sadness washed over Chelsea. She'd left the original Scott-family camping light, complete with new mantle, taking pride of place on the plastic hook at the center of the Cosy Camping Pod's domed roof. The urge to race back and rescue the lamp came at the same time as a crackling sound from her phone.

She sat up too quickly and her head clipped the overhead cupboard. 'Ouch!'

'Are you off that bed yet?'

As promised, her husband was calling back. When Dale said he was

47

going to do something, he did—from telling Chelsea Scott in detention class that he'd marry her, to warning his wife of nearly twenty-eight years he was serious about a fresh start in a new house.

'Get up, go for a run,' Dale suggested. 'You say it clears your head.'

'My head's not my problem,' she said, rubbing the sore spot. 'Besides, you're three hours behind. It's later over here and pouring rain, remember?'

'Bet you're doing your bedcover cave thing.'

'I am not.' She sighed, immediately regretting the soppy tone. She wasn't weak or needy, or an insecure stay-at-home mum like the ones her tennis group gossiped about. 'How did we get here, Dale? I miss us.'

'Me too.' His reply sounded sincere and a little sad.

'I get that I'm obsessive and difficult to live with, but—'

'You're not obsessive,' he interrupted. 'And living with you is not the issue. It's not even about me hating the house. I love the old place for the start it gave us, and that our children padded down its hallways as toddlers, and as teenagers they hid in its small spaces to smoke durries in secret. Remember how, as adults, they'd staggered drunk down the same hallways and fallen into their beds? But, hon, are you aware when Gabby talks to her twins about growing up in Sydney, she refers to the place as Granddad's house?'

No, she was not. Chelsea knew only that she treasured a house nobody wanted to live in.

'Hon, things might make more sense if we were splitting up over a person.'

Splitting up? Had Dale used that phrase before? The Perth secondment position was temporary, or so she'd thought. How could their marriage—an enduring one—be ending?

'What I mean is,' he continued, 'if this discontent *was* over another guy, I'd have hope. I could change my ways, or I'd try harder to win you back. Maybe I've neglected that part of us and let other stuff, like work, take priority. But Chels, this is all over a stupid house.'

'A stupid house that's been good to us and continues to grow in value,' she railed. 'Keeping it in the family makes sense.'

'Yeah, well, I guess I should be grateful we were teenage sweethearts, and I was your first and only.'

'Meaning what exactly, Dale?'

'Face it, hon. Back then, had there been another guy on the scene, and you'd had to pick one of us, he and I would still be waiting for you to make a decision.'

'That is not the least bit funny.'

'I'm not trying to be funny,' he said. 'Decision-making is not your strong point. You're the only person I've met who failed a multiple-choice test because you refused to choose. I'm surprised you got your *I do* out when the minister asked.'

Chelsea bristled. 'More exaggeration, but point made.'

'Sorry, bad joke,' he said, adding, 'I didn't ring to make points. I rang to tell you I'm worried and I want us back.'

'You do?' There was that needy whimper again.

'Of course, yes, but—'

Ah, the but! She braced.

'Not if you're going to make me stand still when I need to be moving forward with my life.'

'Seriously, Dale?' Chelsea despised the term *moving forward* as much as the word *journey*. 'You sound like my mother. Getting on with *her* life had meant abandoning her daughters.'

'I'm not your mother or your father,' Dale insisted, his words metered, considered. 'And taking a break is not walking away. I'm simply asking you to let go of the past to walk *with* me. The two of us can do anything. Go anywhere.'

Tempted to tell Dale her dad had once spoken those same words, she refrained. Nothing good came from such comparisons.

'For the first time since our wedding, hon, we no longer need to consider what's best for the children.'

'Yes,' she said, 'and from *that day forward*, you were fine deciding for us both. You loved being the man of the house, you found my faults endearing, and my needing you wasn't a source of frustration then. What happened?'

'We grew up, Chels.'

'I guess we did, Dale.'

After more silence and a mutual 'miss you', the phone's soggy circuitry —or poor reception—ended the call, sparking distress inside Chelsea as she realised the real reason for not selling.

Chelsea wasn't merely afraid. She was terrified of discovering a change of house won't fix her relationship with Dale and she will have lost her husband *and* her beloved family home.

8

DALE

Dale checked his watch. Time to head home.

He huffed. *Home?* At forty-six years of age, Dale Holt—successful in business, devoted husband, and loving father of three—was, in his heart, as homeless as the day he was born, and the lifeless Scarborough Beach apartment was no more 'home' than William Scott's so-called Beach Shack, west of Penrith.

Dale eyed the desk piled high with folders. A fifteen-minute meeting had resulted in fifteen hours-worth of paperwork and five new clients—all vulnerable children needing his one hundred percent focus. If only he could stop thinking about his wife.

'How did we get here?' Chelsea had asked on the phone.

They'd been crazy in love on their wedding day. The memory of his wife shedding swathes of white chiffon from shapely curves could still make Dale's breath catch. The pair hadn't rushed into a relationship, mostly because his career aspirations had meant high school studies took priority over pretty girls, and the shy new girl had been a stubborn nut to crack. So he'd waited, hoping Chelsea would realise she liked him as much as he liked her.

After school came life lessons, like learning how to be careful in the backseat of a car. Although not careful enough, as evidenced by the baby bump hidden under Chelsea's puffy wedding dress that magical day.

'So glad I married you, Mr Holt.' His wife of three hours peeled away white pantyhose. 'And ten times gladder the night is over. Sorry about my family. They can be so painful.'

'I saw no one but you.' He moved behind to breathe in her bare shoulder skin, locking the smell into his memory and knowing, from this day forward, if he ever got lost, the scent of her would lead him home—to *their* home; one he couldn't wait to create.

Dale only had to work and save hard, and together they'd hunt out the perfect place. Not that *perfect* was a prerequisite. Anywhere was better than Aunty Rita's second bedroom/sewing room, where the newlyweds were about to make love at low volume. While grateful for Rita's generosity, and the Sydney property's prime position putting the beach at the backdoor, Dale would easily give his beloved surfing away to carry his bride over the threshold of their first home. What fun they'd have testing in-store mattress displays and lugging their new bed home on the roof racks. Laughing over flat-pack instructions and too many leftover parts, they'd cross their fingers and christen the bed, then cuddle while planning the photo gallery for the wall opposite. Dale wanted lots and lots of family pictures randomly hung on lots and lots of hooks. Sticky tape and thumb tacks could also do the trick because, for the first time in his life, he could use them liberally without getting a kick in the butt from a fed-up foster parent.

One day you'll have it all, Dale told himself while staring at his brand new and adorable wife in the frilly white knickers and bra he'd not seen before.

As weddings go, the night had been a simple affair. Chelsea invited people from the hairdressing salon where she worked, and Dale asked a few blokes—mates he hung with at the beach. Rather than buy gifts, guests split the Chinese banquet bill between them, while Aunty Rita insisted on paying for the separate function room.

'Can you believe how excited Aunty Rita was giving me away?' Chelsea chortled. 'Tonight was perfect, Mr Holt.'

'And the night is far from over, *Mrs* Holt.' Pressing his body into her back, he reached for the barely there baby bump. 'We are all just beginning. You've never looked more beautiful.'

'And while you looked quite the spunk in your tuxedo, I'm loving the understated underpants look you've got going on.' She twisted an arm behind her, hooked a finger in the waistband of his Bonds undies and let the elastic snap back on bony hips. 'Are you aware your nickname on campus is Dale The Holt Hunk?'

He stopped nibbling her earlobe. 'And you know this how?'

'I have ears,' she giggled, 'and they're ticklish, so quit it.'

'And I have eyes, Mrs Holt.'

As his groin ground against her buttocks, Chelsea moaned and angled her face back to accommodate his lips.

'What made you fall in love with me?' she asked.

The question stopped Dale mid-kiss. Not the words themselves, but the way she spoke them, as though she didn't quite believe he *was* in love. Resting his chin on her shoulder, arms cradling his soon-to-be first born, Dale observed their reflection in Rita's antique dresser mirror. Her need for affection and willingness to love had endeared Chelsea to him, mostly because Dale craved someone to love back. They fit together perfectly.

'On our first date at McDonalds, I discovered we wanted the same things. I recall you were determined to be "the best homemaker in the world".'

'Oh, don't tell me I used the word homemaker.'

Dale held in his laugh, mindful of Rita's proximity. 'Music to my ears. I couldn't wait to have a home of my own—finally—and you couldn't wait to be a mother.'

'Hmm, sorry about my rush on that score.' She entwined her fingers with his where they pressed on her belly. 'Do you suppose people noticed?'

'Who cares? Come to bed.' He tugged her arm. 'I want to show you I am not at all sorry about the rush, or about getting into detention all those times. Do you remember your first day? I do.'

Twisting back and forth in his office chair, Dale Holt—advocate for children and young people—recalled the moment the classroom door opened, and all eyes shifted to the prettiest girl. Although tall, her hair bleached almost white and her limbs suntanned and kind of glistening, Chelsea Scott's shoulders seemed weighed down by sadness, her eyes downcast, too.

'The bag, Mr Holt!' Miss Pidgeon, his teacher, had decried while directing Chelsea to the spare seat next to Dale.

Cheeks burning from the snorting and snickering of his classmates, who knew Cupid's arrow had hit his heart dead-centre, Dale looked everywhere but at the girl slipping silently behind the adjacent desk. Later, the school grapevine alerted him to the unhappy circumstances behind Chelsea's relocation from 'the boonies'. Painfully familiar with being shunted from place to place, Dale knew about starting over and fitting in, but he knew little about Sydney's outer suburbs. Only one placement saw him moved away from the coast. For five frustrating months, he'd hitched or bused-it back to Narrabeen where the regular surfers knew him and let him borrow their boards when taking a break. Young Dale might have been passive, indifferent, and numb, but repeated unsuccessful foster home placements soon fuelled his aspirations and determination. The only thing Dale Holt was more passionate about than surfing was getting a job to improve the lives of kids in care. His more immediate challenge, though, was making the new girl laugh, because for sure, it would sound as beautiful as she looked.

The pair had kept each other laughing until the last day of school when Dale got a place at university, while Chelsea, who'd struggled to concentrate, settled for a hairdressing indentureship. When fatherhood demanded Dale reshuffle his goals—taking travel off the agenda—Chelsea suggested they could save money by living in the vacant Scott family home. He agreed. As it was owned by family members, the house offer came with a sound financial arrangement requiring a nominal rent if they improved the property. Not a hard task given the place had sat neglected for several years.

While the temporary move out west meant no more beach, Dale's days of sponging off mates and sofa-surfing in living rooms smelling of stale beer and God knows what else were over. Dale Holt, the kid no one had wanted, would be the best dad, even if it meant changing universities, finding another part-time job, and learning to be a handyman around the quirky old joint that was a long way from the home of his dreams.

9

CHELSEA

Dale's comment about her Sandbar return being pointless strengthened Chelsea's resolve to rid herself of the relationship-sabotaging self-reproach. Admittedly, the D-I-Y exposure therapy concept was far-fetched, but being here and focusing on her phobia couldn't hurt. And she was delaying the packing task waiting for her at home; not to mention *un*packing boxes and deciding what to do with the myriad memories. Some cartons had been under the house for decades, put there by a tantrum-throwing Wendy who, in the months following her father's memorial service, changed—a lot.

Offers of emotional and hands-on support from concerned neighbours and friends had been plentiful, but with her mother adamant nothing was to be tidied, vacuumed, mopped, cleaned, or chucked out, most of Dad's everyday effects had stayed where he'd left them, as if he was expected home any minute. But all that changed seemingly overnight when Wendy's mood shifted from sad acceptance to raging resentment. Aunty Rita tried explaining the seven stages of grief to Chelsea and Layla, but nothing could explain or justify the tantrum Wendy tossed, discarding both the precious and everyday reminders of her husband. Some things went into boxes, others into garbage bags destined for the kerbside rubbish collection.

That same night, having squeezed into an old dress, set her hair and applied way too much makeup, their mother left Layla in charge of Chelsea. But with that one night out turning into a forty-eight-hour absence, the sisters had time to coerce Layla's latest boyfriend to fight cobwebs and drag the chock-a-block garbage bags and boxes to the furthest reaches under the house where their mother would never venture.

The bags and boxes were still under there, all of them, untouched for decades, prompting Chelsea to sit up on the bed, fossick for a pen, and start a To-do list on the back of a shopping docket. Some tasks she could cross off while at Sandbar, like texting Layla to ask for help with the sorting. With luck, her sister would be in the country soonish, and in an affable frame of mind. Although one never knew with Layla. According to their dad, controlling his capricious and impassioned eldest daughter was a lot like tying down a beach umbrella on a windy day.

'You never know how tight to hold on, or if she'll take off without warning,' he'd told Chelsea.

How right he'd been.

1 0

LAYLA

Layla whispered a string of expletives when forced to side-step two snickering women whose abandoned baggage blocked all three hand basins. Was she too old for long-haul flights, or too grumpy? In the good ol' days, she would've shrugged off inconveniences, like being bumped off the Sydney leg to accommodate a full fare passenger, and hit the club lounge to wait out delays with a drink. They were the days she would use pills to pep her up and the oblivion of opioids.

Nowadays, thanks to the dashing Doctor Trent Dashwood—shrink, stickler, and stick-in-the-mud—Layla relied on no such panaceas.

As the warm water washed away her irritability, Layla studied her quinquagenarian face in the soap-spotted mirror. Where was the rebellious young woman who would've burst into public toilets, giggling and being a nuisance? The face staring back at her was so altered: no pimples, no piercings, no heavily made-up lashes, nor eyeliner to end up as dark circles under dull eyes following a drug-filled bender. How wretched she must have looked when delivered to the rehab facility—for the first time. Though no one had cared to know or enquire, that day twenty-nine years ago had been Layla's twenty-first.

'Hip hip hooray!' She muttered into the mirror, letting the years roll back until she was that tough, young girl being herded into a sparsely furnished room by Nurse Ratched's wicked sister.

56

SESSIONS WITH TRENT, 1986

Seated at the opposite end of the oblong table, his back to a wall of dark glass, is a shrink trying to hide his nerves. Layla might suggest the bow tie and blazer is a neon sign to his newness in the job, but speaking is not Layla's strategy today. Silence has been her safety net since her eighteenth birthday. Silence works.

They are alone now, with only the clunk of a noisy wall clock ticking over.

'Why blue, Layla?' he says, pointing to his own eyelashes. Dark and luxuriously long, they require no enhancing.

'Well, Doc, maybe because *I'm* blue.' She folds her arms, pushing up the push-up bra, then slumps further into the moulded plastic chair—the stackable type found in hotel beer gardens. If only she was in one and downing a few drinks at a bar, rather than self-consciously picking at her caked mascara, and answering inane questions.

'You feel sad, Layla?'

She scoffs. 'What I feel, Doc, is pissed off. Make that *bloody* pissed off to find myself in your modern-day Cuckoo's Nest.'

'What makes you describe the facility in such terms?'

'Because, while checking me in, creepy Nurse Ratched's twin sister raided my handbag and stole everything *except* my blue freaking mascara. I get that scissors and nail files are a potential problem—for some—but who the frig self-harms with a kohl stick and lip gloss?' Layla kicks out a foot, connecting with a table leg bolted to the floor. She doesn't stop at one kick, or at the one little toe silently screaming in pain.

'Do you mean to hurt yourself?'

The care and concern in his question seems so genuine it catches Layla off-guard. But rather than answer, she asks, 'I suppose my mother insisted on rehab? Silly Wendy!'

'Why is your mother silly?'

'How long have you got, Doc? For one, if she's serious about me keeping my mouth shut, she should butt out and let me kill myself. Not too many souls to tell my secret to where I'm going.' With no reaction from Doc Dashing—not even an admonitory brow arch—Layla wonders if she's misjudged his rookie status. She might have to re-strategize, try harder.

For several years, she'd let Doc Dashing try to save her, while she'd tried to die every way she knew how. Then came the big day; time to say goodbye to Doctor Trent Dashwood and to rehab. As the man's lips had curved into a self-congratulatory grin, Layla guessed he was feeling pretty good about bringing Blue Girl back from the brink.

Job done, Doc! Pop that cork and make a toast. Only don't give any booze to the patient.

Despite Doc Dashing's persistence and months of praiseworthy psychobabble, Layla returned to rehab numerous times, always keen to reassure Trent her relapse was not his failure. The blame was all Layla's because of who she was, what she was, and the secret she could never tell —the cruel family skeleton that had made her wish do-gooders had let her die each time she'd tried.

Like any recovering addict, Layla remained a work-in-progress today, which meant until she passed by the various airport eateries with their 24/7 alcohol service, she kept her head bowed, eyes focused on the mobile phone in her hands, and drew strength from one of Doc Dashing's copious diktats. Yes, he was still in her life—still caring, still dashing—but she'd friend-zoned him years ago to avoid falling into the man. Trent Dashwood could do far better than Layla, who, according to Wendy Scott, was 'best in short doses'. For that reason, and with the Arrivals Board lighting up with flight cancellations and delays due to the east coast deluge, Layla's text to her niece, Gabby, stated:

> A quick catch-up only, sweetie.

Whether the overnight delay was fate or good fortune hardly mattered; Layla Scott didn't believe in either. She did, though, enjoy seeing her niece; the occasional catch-up yet another secret Layla kept from her sister. The phone pinged with a reply from Gabby.

> Hey, Aunty Layla, did you know Dad's living in Scarborough? If you like, I can see if he's free. Oh, and Mum's gone totally gaga and gone camping. You'll never guess where. Can't wait to see you.

A text message in Singapore, from Wendy, let Layla know about Chelsea being at Sandbar. *But Dale living in Perth? What the ...?* Her stroll through the airport quickened. She had to see Gabby and find out what her adorable brother-in-law was doing here when Chelsea was going to need him after Layla detonated her bombshell. Chelsea sure won't look to her secret-keeping sister for love and support.

A rush of doubt and dread stopped Layla part way along the concourse. Playing overhead on the television screen was silent news footage showing cyclone-ravaged Queensland communities. At the bottom of the screen, the moving news ticker displayed: *Former Tropical Cyclone Minnie hits southern Queensland ... Severe east coast low expected to bring damaging winds and heavy rain overnight to parts of northern New South Wales ... Holiday-makers warned to seek shelter.*

Why a drenched and wind-whipped reporter in the street—microphone clenched in one hand—risked flying debris to deliver the latest news to camera, Layla didn't understand. Did he also have a death wish? What she did know was tomorrow's flight back east would likely be an eventful one. Nothing new for a seasoned globetrotter, she mused. Layla knew what to expect; she could see it unfolding.

On approach to Sydney, when the captain's customary announcement cut in overhead, alerting passengers to a rougher-than-usual landing, a willy-willy of anxious exclamations will whip around the cabin. At that point, Layla would consider an announcement of her own to calm and reassure her fellow travellers.

'No need to panic,' she'd tell them. 'You'll be fine. Nothing will happen to the plane while I'm on board. No one will die. Layla Scott has never been that lucky.'

11

LAYLA

Right now, with her sister in the last place on earth Layla wanted to think about—let alone be—she needed a dose of Trent Dashwood's tranquillising voice. Despite the man's continued habit of asking more questions than he answered, he could disarm Layla of dangerous thoughts and deeds—usually. Although, no reply text or email from her mother added to Layla's angst. With hindsight, the rushed message alerting Wendy to her plans may have been unwise. Her sister's return-to-Sandbar camping caper could end up uneventful; a sympathy stunt of some kind and a part of her ritual to remember the man Layla tried hard to forget.

But what if it wasn't? *What if . . . ?* The thought of Chelsea being in that place drove Layla's determination and fuelled her anger; what struck the match was how the man had used his youngest daughter all those years ago, doing the most unthinkable and evil thing a father could do to a child —to his own daughter. How had Layla thought keeping quiet was best for everyone? It clearly wasn't for her sister, whose marriage was falling apart because of what he did to her all those years ago.

Early in Layla's rehab, Trent had suggested Chelsea's obsessive behaviour was a coping mechanism. He'd explained how details from the past—especially distressing ones—don't grow as people grow. Some fade, while others become reimagined moments, with the victim fabricating facts to fill the memory blanks, or to paint rosier pictures of something ugly.

'These people aren't deceiving themselves,' he'd said. 'They're surviving.'

Layla had understood. She'd coped by walking away from her family. Turning her back on Wendy had been easy enough but leaving Chelsea behind had broken Layla's heart. Cutting ties had become necessary and safer than being truthful and crying it out together. According to Wendy, the only way to not ruin all their lives was for her and Layla to forget and never again discuss the letter or its contents.

On the rare occasions Wendy would request a catchup, Layla's calendar entry read *Ceasefire Coffee*, with the notation denoting adversaries meeting in No-man's-land. No longer acting like mother and daughter, the pair became co-conspirators fighting different battles, but stopping briefly to exchange trivialities over untouched coffees, and following the golden rule of keeping your enemies close. Such strategies were an imperative when sharing a destructive family secret.

Little did Wendy know, however, her eldest daughter had amassed innumerable secrets over the years. One had involved a bath with razor blades and booze. Another was a pity party with pills followed by a late-night dip in the ocean. Layla hadn't counted on more do-gooders dragging her out of the sea, or on Doc Dashing attending her hospital room. Then again, she hadn't counted on seeing through her twenty-fifth birthday.

SESSIONS WITH TRENT, 1990

Layla is late for her appointment. How late, she's not sure, because a week ago, desperate for a fix, she gave her watch to a dealer.

'A new tattoo, Layla?' Doc queries the minute both she and her shoulder bag land on the sofa opposite his wingback chair.

'Hey, hey, Doc! Eyes up. Your job is examining my brain, not my boobs. But thanks. The bra's also new. I can thank the lazy assistant in the lingerie store who basically ignored me. Big mistake. Huge! Seen the movie, Doc?'

'What movie?'

'Pretty Woman. Classic happy-ever-after. Splurged on a ticket for my birthday. Oh, and this.' Layla adjusts her black singlet to reveal more of the tattooed snake biting into an apple. '*Happy birthday to me! I'm alive and twenty-five*,' she sings. 'Like it?'

'Interesting design,' Doc replies. 'You chose the biblical symbolism for a reason?'

'Temptation, of course,' her voice purrs. 'Has something tempted you recently, Doc?'

'What tempts you, Layla?'

'You do.' Her answer is the type she's trained him to expect, and Layla doesn't like to disappoint. 'I'm tempted now,' she adds, knowing he'll scold her. Any time he does, Layla is pleased. Doc Dashing's gentle berating and you-crossed-the-line expression can satisfy her craving for a fatherly reprimand. But with Trent now extra cross, it's up to her to get their doctor-patient relationship back on track. Sharing something personal usually does the trick. 'Don't get your knickers in a knot, Doc. Saying *I'm tempted* refers to my urge to reveal the truth—to finally confess all.' She has his attention. 'You can't tell anyone what I say in our meetings, right? That's a rule, isn't it?'

Doc nods. 'No cameras or recorded sessions if that's worrying you. Remember, we agreed on the level and the limits of confidentiality—and our professional relationship. But if you feel the need to review the contract, or the boundaries we set, or if you would prefer another counsellor—a female maybe—'

Layla bolts upright. 'Hell, no!' She feels bad now, and that's not good. Feeling bad often ends in a self-harm episode. 'Look, Doc, it's not that I *can't* tell you. I just haven't—yet. I've told no one.'

'You've told no one what?' He sounds unusually impatient and skeptical, as if she's toyed with him too many times.

'The truth,' Layla announces. 'I've never told you the whole truth, or Chelsea. Not even when I had the chance after finding out. I couldn't. My sister was young, and Wendy said they'd take her away.' Layla stops to suck the blood spot from the thumb cuticle she's picked raw.

'But you're ready to tell me now?' Doc asks.

'Maybe.'

It's only fair, Layla muses, especially given she's opened the can a smidge, and the worms are restless. Using a trickle technique—telling him a little at a time to gauge his reaction and test that confidentiality clause—is unnecessary. She trusts Trent. It's herself she can't trust.

'Sorry, Doc,' she says, shaking her head. 'Maybe in another five, ten, fifty years from now I'll be ready to bare my soul; the one I sold to my mother.'

'Won't you at least think about your sister? If you can't tell me, then tell her.'

'No! If I was going to tell, it should've been years ago. There's no point upsetting Chelsea's life. She's happy and with a wonderful husband and a young family to love and grow. That's all I've ever wanted for her, and the truth will simply shatter her world for a second time. I've broken my sister's heart once already. Never again.'

12

CHELSEA – DAY 2 OF 7

Something about the beach is not right. Where are the usual sounds—the cawing gulls, the thunderous ocean pounding the shore, the excited squeals as children frolick? Instead, there are no waves, no foam, no rivulets carving wet trails in the sand. Someone has pulled the ocean's plug and drained the beach bone dry. Even the fish left to flounder on the exposed seabed seem surprised, their mouths agape, eyes clueless and fixed with confusion.

Moments before, Chelsea was running across the rocky platform, barnacles and shells ripping her shoeless feet raw. Now she's prone on blood-stained sand, her gills expanding—desperate for water—and her thrashing mermaid tail tangled in seaweed.

'Daddy!' she cries out. 'Where are you?'

'Over here, Miss Fix. Save me. I'm drowning in this place.'

'But I don't have legs, Daddy. I can't go anywhere. I'm stuck.'

'You don't have to stay stuck,' he tells her. 'You can do anything and go anywhere, Chelsea-girl. Remember that and head for the horizon.'

They are her father's last words, waking Chelsea each time to her own screams.

'The plug! The plug! Help me find the plug. Help me … Ouch!' Rubbing the spot where her head hit the overhanging cupboard, she cussed some more and knuckle-scrubbed sleep from her eyes, only to find tears welling. 'This stupid, stupid trip idea! How many bloody signs do you need?'

After a shower and something to eat, she would pack her bags, rescue her tent and Tilley lantern, and head home, stopping at the local shelter to rescue a dog—or two. But, she thought while staring out the window, not before doing the one thing she'd come here to do. After all, the track to the beach she'd walked hundreds of times over six annual trips to Sandbar *was* less than fifty paces away.

While the last family holiday remains a blur, recalling the first camping trip was easy because it was special. That was the year they'd gotten early Christmas presents. Chelsea had unwrapped a mermaid beach towel, and the entire family got new swimming togs because, according to their mum, who often spoke about their family in third person, 'The Scotts might holiday like trashy trailer folk, but they will not look like a pack of misfits'.

As Wendy would regularly refer to her husband as a misfit, young Chelsea had considered the term an endearing one; like when Dad called Mum a fishwife, and Chelsea his 'Miss Fix'. Chelsea never did discover the origin of her nickname.

But maybe, Miss Fix, it means you can fix your fears. There is nothing out there that can hurt you.

Having slipped into gym pants and a sweat top, she left her feet bare, keen to rediscover the comforting sand-between-her-toes sensation she'd loved as a girl. But as Chelsea neared the start of the beach track with its archway of gnarly bushes, she faulted. Observing from a safe distance, an echo of an earlier time prompted the happy memory of a bikini-clad Layla racing ahead and calling over her shoulder.

'Come on, Chelsea. Last one in is a rotten egg.'

Sadly, Layla wasn't in Sandbar. Chelsea was facing the *thalassophobia* monster alone. But when three deep breaths failed to move Chelsea towards the beach, she turned away from the path. She needed more time and to slow her hammering heart.

To distract herself, she examined the curious array of camping configurations, including the happy hippy van dwarfed by an adjacent motorhome. What if luxuriously appointed rigs—complete with coffee machines, wine fridges, hot showers, and flushing toilets—had been an option for the Scott family, rather than the musty, mildewy hot box with the double bunks at one end and a dinette that converted into a double bed each night? Might Mum have shown more enthusiasm at holiday time? Might her parents have lived a long and happy life together, living the dream like the two caravaners currently looking up from the paper map stretched across their laps? The pair waved at Chelsea.

Returning the smile was not difficult. Chelsea saw her dad in them, his own map of Australia permanently glued to the garage wall, and with as many cobwebs covering the continent as his dotted lines denoting the dream trip he never made.

'One day,' he'd said, 'when you kids are doing your own thing, I'll talk Mum into doing the big lap of Oz real slow.'

'Not in this life,' Mum had replied.

A sudden wind gust sent both Chelsea's hat and the sad recollection flying. As the hat blew with abandon towards the bush track, almost mocking Chelsea by forcing her to follow, two medium-sized black dogs, with two sets of teeth competing for the same stick, burst into the clearing. Close behind were two blowzy boys with fishing rods and buckets. As the pair blustered across the sandy patchwork of coastal grass and weeds, jostling each other, one picked up the hat and raced towards Chelsea.

'Thank you!' she told the boy whose willowy frame and suntanned face was the excuse she needed to return to the caravan and try a reply text to her own boys.

Closing the door on *Sea Esta*, she was contemplating breakfast options—cereal without milk, followed by coffee without milk, or leftover crackers and red wine—when a female voice sounded over a rat-a-tat-tat.

'Yoo-hoo! Anybody in there?'

Fashioning her hair into a haphazard bun at the back of her head, Chelsea opened the door to a woman wearing a multi-coloured outfit and turban, her wispy, white hair wafting like an abandoned cobweb left to blow in the breeze.

'Good morning?' There was no keeping the question out of Chelsea's salutation. The visitor looked like a cross between a geriatric unicorn and a walking rainbow.

'Every morning I wake up to is a good one.' As the woman raised the foiled-covered plate, her kaftan—an intricate chorus of earthy colours in perfect harmony—billowed against the sea breeze. 'Taddy mentioned he had a lady in *Sea-Esta* who needed a proper feed.'

Chelsea's eyes widened. 'Is that so?'

'And I have fresh pikelets.'

'Pikelets for breakfast?'

'As Australian as meat pies and lamingtons! If it helps, think of them as pint-size pancakes.' The visitor hoisted herself into the caravan with surprising agility, forcing Chelsea to get out of the way—and quickly.

'Okay, well, I'd offer you a hot drink, but with no milk I—'

'We take our English Breakfast black,' the woman said with a nod towards the colourful kitchen canisters.

We? Pausing briefly to scan the area outside, Chelsea shut the door before any flies found their way inside. When she turned around, her visitor had peeled the tinfoil lid away to expose the doughy stack.

'I'm Elmie. What's your name, dear? You do remind me of someone.' The woman cocked her head to one side, eyes narrowing. 'It'll come to me. Or Connie will recall. She'll be along with jam. Pikelets aren't pikelets without her homemade jam—and tea.' The woman's painted-on eyebrows arched towards the canisters.

'Oh, tea, yes.' After a shake of the kettle to check the water level before igniting the gas jet, Chelsea dived a hand into the canister with the big T on the front. *Teabags! English Breakfast! Well, well!* 'Lovely to meet you, Elmie. I'm Chelsea.'

'Messy night,' her visitor said. 'Bet you were snug as a bug in here. *Sea Esta* is a lovely restoration, don't you think? A good ol' Viscount, circa 1960. Built to last, like me. My sister, Connie, would agree, further suggesting we can all do with a patch up and a re-coating.' Elmie's two thin lines of garish orange lipstick curled into a crooked grin.

'Should we wait for Connie?' Chelsea asked, taking three hanging mugs from the hooks above the sink.

'Oh, no, dear. She's the difficult, unpredictable one in the family. Do you have a sister?'

Chelsea paused. A 'yes' would have very little truth to it—except for the difficult and unpredictable bit. But before Chelsea could utter her answer, Elmie yelped.

'Ooh! Almost forgot.' She loosened the drawstring on the hessian tote slung over one shoulder. 'Not having jam is my excuse for lots of butter. *Ta dah!*' The tub of spreadable margarine hit the table with a thud. 'All one needs is a knife.' The way she reached a hand into the nearby cutlery drawer suggested Chelsea wasn't the first holidaymaker to, in Tad's words, 'need a proper feed'. Next, a heart attack-sized dollop of yellow margarine hit the doughy delight with a plop, the knife barely flattening the greasy lump before Elmie shoved her pikelet-laden palm in Chelsea's direction. 'Eat, dear, before they go cold.'

'Thanks.' Chelsea took the proffered pikelet, carefully nibbling the unbuttered edges.

'What brings you to Sandbar, dear?'

'My dad.' The words were out before she could stop them. 'He loved camping. We had a Viscount caravan called Vinnie, only the dinette folded down into a double mattress and there were two single beds at the back.'

'This one too, until Taddy got his hands on her. A lovely restoration.' Elmie looked up from her half-buttered second helping. 'Dad is no longer with you, dear? Sad business, losing those we love.'

The sparkle in her eyes dulled. Perhaps the woman spoke of her own sorrow. A sad widow filling lonely days by welcoming strangers with pikelets. *At least she has a sister.*

'None of us stay forever, dear, but those of us left behind keep their stories alive. My mother told her story on walls. Today, I wear those stories on my kaftans.'

As Elmie ran a hand over the material's intricate Indigenous design incorporating undulating lines, dots, and silhouetted shapes, Chelsea slipped into the dinette for a closer look.

'How lovely!' While the striking swathe of fabric was beautiful in both sentiment and in design, more intriguing was why Chelsea found this older woman's presence unsettling.

Elmie fixed her gaze. 'I see you carry your memories in a different way, dear. Grief weighs you down. Your father?'

'Um, yes, but we *lost* Dad a long time ago.'

Chelsea never used the words dead or dying when speaking about her father. She'd never stood over his coffin or set flowers at his gravestone. Instead, a framed photograph and a floral wreath on a table in a surf club hall one Sunday had allowed hope to settle in her young heart. Hope that William Scott was not gone forever, the ocean had not swallowed him up, and one day, from her seat on the front porch, she would see her dad get off the bus and stride down the street, arms wide and ready to receive. For that reason, whenever her mother had called Chelsea inside to set for dinner, she had put his placemat and beer glass at the head of the table. Then, each Christmas, she'd bought a Nestlé Golden Rough chocolate and sneaked it into his stocking. She'd encouraged her own children to keep the family's festive traditions alive, and for a time they had, until Chelsea's promise to never forget drove her family away: First Wendy and Layla, then Gabby. *Now Dale!*

Elmie reached across the table, covering Chelsea's clasped fingers like cupping a crystal ball. The woman tilted her head back, closed her eyes and hummed yogini-like.

'I see black. I sense your sorrow. I do. And I know you, my dear. I believe we've met before. A long, long time ago.' Her eyelids slammed wide open, a little spookily in Chelsea's opinion. 'Possibly in another life.'

Unsettled by the psychic undertones, Chelsea slid out from the table and stood. 'I am sad, Elmie. Sad about abandoning my new tent mid-storm last night. The gentleman was lovely for allowing me to stay in here, but I should get organised.'

'Taddy is a doll, isn't he?' As she eased her ageing body out of the seat, Chelsea tried ignoring the lump of yellow accumulating at one corner of Elmie's lips. Then, like a frog catching a fly, the woman snared the buttery blob with one flick of her tongue. 'I hope the storm hasn't frightened you away and you'll stay on and enjoy Sandbar.'

'The weather will decide for me. I'll check the forecast and hope for sunshine.'

'We make our own sunshine, dear,' Elmie chirruped.

'That sounds like something my dad would say. He used to capture the sun's rays in his magic jars. He even wore a tiny glass vial version on a leather choker. Claimed it was like keeping the beach with him all day.'

Elmie hooted with delight. 'Imagining a beach when you don't have one? Marvellous! I must tell Connie. As for the weather, I'm sure Taddy won't mind you keeping on in *Sea-Esta*. I can ask for you.'

'No need, thanks.' Chelsea was curious about a man who would call himself Taddy, and even more curious about the mysterious missing sister, Connie, as the greasy coating in her mouth had Chelsea wishing there'd been jam. 'Actually, Elmie, when you arrived, I was about to check my campsite.'

'And I've kept you.' The woman fussed with the kaftan that had slipped off one cadaverous shoulder turned crisp from decades of too much outdoors. 'You do what you need to, dear. I only popped in to say hello; I knew you'd be lovely. All the ladies who stay in Taddy's van generally are.'

Ah, so, it's like that, is it? Taddy Tight Fly is a ladies' man!

'Thanks for the pikelets, Elmie.'

And for the heads-up!

A part of Chelsea panicked when she saw the crushed blue cocoon covered in tree branches. The rest of her pondered if the tent had made a popping noise, like when washed-up bluebottles on the beach burst underfoot. Thank goodness she'd left nothing behind of any value: an inflatable air mattress that refused to stay inflated, sodden shoes, and the torch—a gift-with-purchase promotion attached to the silk mantles for her ...

Oh, no! My poor lamp! Asking someone to find the buried treasure crossed her mind. Maybe the two burly blokes in safety vests attacking limbs with handsaws and tree loppers. Or the man stacking the chopped wood into a box trailer hitched to the tow ball of a dirty ute. Nearby, but keeping a safe distance from the activity as if he knew to stay away, a young boy mimicked the chainsaw action, while to his left, a couple of backpackers outside their hand-painted hire van huddled behind a single mobile phone screen. Chelsea's squished tent would no doubt feature in their Facebook feed. Behind her, a cacophony of cocky caravaners shared their storm survivor stories from locations far more exotic than Sandbar Beach. Even locals ventured out of their shanty village for a look, with their busy back and forth, and the way they bumped into each other briefly, reminding Chelsea of an ant trail.

Wondering what to do next, she automatically reached for the phone in her jeans pocket, but hesitated. Not only was she disinclined to fall back on Dale for comfort, but Chelsea also imagined his response when she told him her only hurt was realising she'd lost a precious William Scott keepsake. Calling Vicki was an option. While a terrible listener, giving advice was her forte. Chelsea would not have survived months alone in the house if not for her friend suggesting the occasional boozy night in front of the television—and always Vik's favourite McLeod's Daughters DVD collection. Watching her friend sob uncontrollably was entertainment in itself. But Chelsea's real fascination with the show was more about episode-after-episode of gutsy, good-looking young females amid a man drought, each woman completely capable and infuriatingly independent. *Damn them!*

'And damn this phone,' she grumbled, slapping the discommodious device against her palm.

With the chainsaw entertainment over, the backpackers bored, and the grey nomads already shanghaiing hanger-oners for three-o'clock *yappy* hour this afternoon, Chelsea's thoughts turned to her car crammed with more clothes than food. Tinned stores, dehydrated noodle and pasta packets, tea, coffee, wine, and Pringles would not go far. She'd only packed enough for a couple of days because, according to the campground's website, the Wandarri Eco-Community Co-op stocked stone-fired sourdough, general produce, homegrown foodstuffs, locally made crafts, and fishing and camping essentials. Listed as *within walking distance*, Chelsea pictured the tiny shop from her youth; the one that had the audacity to sell paddle pops and bait from the same refrigerator—apparently just to annoy fish-loathing Layla.

'Lucky I came along last night when I did, eh?' A worker, wearing a Billabong-branded peak hat pulled low to shade everything but his mouth, had sidled up to Chelsea. With his unshaven face and greying rat's tail of hair a heart-wrenching reminder of the holiday-version of her dad, Chelsea said nothing for a moment. 'Last night is why I'm constantly onsite and on hand,' the man continued. 'Better that I stay alert until the danger has passed. You never know who'll need rescuing.'

Though bearing little resemblance to last night's water-logged rescuer, Chelsea assumed he was Taddy. About to ask, his earsplitting whistle startled her two steps back.

'Oi! Kai! Home time, kiddo.'

The young sound-effects master stared through thick spectacles held in place by a band of white elastic that carved a deep crevasse through his afro fuzz. Then ... '*Swish! Swish! Swish!*' His imaginary sword sliced through the carefully raked debris, showering the geriatric German Shepherd dog standing unsteadily on sagging hips, tail wagging, his eagerness for the leaf pile clear.

'Leave,' Taddy growled while dusting his hands on the backside of the heavy-duty work trousers. 'I see you're dying to dive in, buddy, but I'm dying to get into my boardies and get some serious surf time.'

'Surf! Surf! Surf!' the boy mimicked.

'Tomorrow, kiddo. If Mum says so.' The boy looked as crushed as Chelsea's tent until his pretend enemy put him *en garde* again.

'*Swish! Swish! Swish!*'

'Kids!' Taddy said. 'It's Chelsea, right? Nice name. Don't hear it much.'

Had she said her name last night? He may have found her details on the park register. Understandable, given he'd handed his rental van over to a stranger in a storm.

'Yes, Taddy, my dad chose my name,' she told him. 'As well as being an Old English expression meaning *safe landing place or harbour*, Chelsea means *seaport*. So ...' She shrugged, grinned. 'After last night, I can lay claim to being my own *port* in a storm.'

The man's gaze stopped on her dying smile. 'Did you call me Taddy?'

Oh, no! She groaned inwardly. 'I, um, so you're not Taddy?'

'To Elmie I am.' His lips slipped into a smirk. 'She's the only one to get away with calling me that.'

'I see. And the rest of the world calls you …?'

'The unabbreviated version is Tadpole. Has been since I was ten. Same age as young Kai, here …'

'I see.' Chelsea wondered how being referred to as frog larvae could be preferable to Taddy. 'So, that's Tadpole as in …?'

'Wrigglers, yeah, on account of I grew up in the water. The day I wriggled into my first wetsuit, my scuba mates reckoned I looked like a tadpole. The name stuck.'

The man wasn't young but he had a typically manly physique; the top end all muscle with broad shoulders that tapered to a narrow waistline and hips.

'If you prefer,' he said, breaking her train of thought. 'Mum named me Thaddeus. Not that she christened me; Wandarri-ites never bothered with formalities. We all got born and married with little fanfare until the world, and the authorities, got nosey. About twenty years back, they forced *The National Census* on us. They tried.' Tad winked. 'Some Wandarri-ites will never trust the government, and for good reason. Anyway, enough political talk. All good in *Sea-Esta*?'

'Yes, Tadpole,' Chelsea replied. 'Thank you so much for last night *and* for rescuing my tent this morning.'

He grimaced and glanced over his shoulder. 'Not sure about the rescue bit. Recovery only. The tent and contents are basically … Well, buggered.'

'Making this the shortest camping trip ever.' Chelsea sighed.

'Stay on in *Sea-Esta*. Elmie mentioned you were deciding what to do next.'

Hmm, for a woman of her vintage, Elmie sure was swift of foot and of tongue.

'So, you live here full-time?' she asked, noticing the slight facial tick that occasionally turned one corner of Tadpole's mouth up.

'I was born here, so it'll always be home. Not quite how I saw myself living out my days, but close enough—and rewarding in a weird way. Selling all I owned to downsize was *the* most liberating experience of my life.'

'You sold *everything*?'

He nodded. 'Gave away most of it. There was a time when life got pretty crazy, so I disconnected from all the material things and tried the whole *Eat Pray Love* pilgrimage *thingo*. Needed to find "my happy". Any possessions that didn't fit or have a purpose went to charity stores. Won a few hearts in the Op Shop, I can tell you.'

'And did you find your … *happy?*'

Tadpole's grin suggested he'd noticed the eagerness in her enquiry. 'They say clarity comes when you least expect it, but there was one point when I knew.'

'Knew what?' Chelsea asked, genuinely curious.

The man raised two fists, fashioning his fingers and down-turned thumbs into a heart shape before holding his hands against his chest, and with a solemn expression, he said, 'I. Complete. Me.'

Chelsea barked a laugh, only to have her cheeks warm when Tadpole remained straight-faced.

'I'm serious,' he said. '"Knowing others is wisdom. Knowing yourself is enlightenment"—a direct quote from Lao Tzu. I bought the fridge magnet in a Hong Kong duty-free shop,' he added with a wink.

'Oh, ah, I'm not sure I've heard of him,' Chelsea admitted.

'Fascinating guy. I researched him; figured I might enjoy the teachings of a bloke whose mysteriousness is only matched by his philosophies. All was good until I read his mother supposedly carried him in her womb for eight years—some claim it was as much as eighty—after which she gave birth to him through her left flank. Why are you laughing?' Tad asked through his cheeky 'gotchya' grin. 'Look it up for yourself on that mobile phone you have a fascination for. Hate the things myself. Then again, I've heard they have apps that are useful for checking weather and storm warnings.'

'I'll keep that in mind.' Chelsea giggled—yes, giggled—her moment of *happy* not only unexpected but courtesy of an amusing and intriguing stranger.

While no Tom Cruise, and considerably older than Chelsea, the man seemed, well, interesting—*if* she looked beyond the work trousers slung low on bony hips, and the torn T-shirt exposing neck tattoos.

Enough about his looks, she silently chastised. Taddy—aka Tadpole— seemed perfectly nice, and his equally charming old Viscount caravan for rent was a gentle reminder of happier days.

'So, do you want to grab *Sea-Esta* before anyone else does?' He spoke as if people lined up for the opportunity. 'A last-minute cancellation makes this your lucky day.' He returned his attention to the wheelbarrow overflowing with leaves. 'A quick decision is a good decision, so they say. Fifty a night is fine, as is online bank transfer.' When she didn't say no, he hoisted the handles of the wheelbarrow. 'I'll drop over with the account details and, if you need to, you can access my hotspot whenever you're ready.'

'Your, ah, hotspot, Tadpole?'

'Mobile reception can be erratic, and I have a business to run,' he said, missing—or ignoring—her unstoppable smirk. 'Down that end of the park, I use a booster to strengthen my dongle.'

Every double entendre uttered by this utterly amusing man poked another hole in the pressure-pack Chelsea had carried around since Dale left for Perth. Dale, who needs to move forward—with or without his wife.

Dale, your husband.

'My phone isn't faring well after last night's big wet,' Chelsea said, flipping the blackened screen to show Tadpole.

'Reception can be stronger on the hill. Might help, and the co-op has all kinds of stuff if you need to stock up. Turn right outside our gates and you're on your way. About two kilometres and almost a straight line. Hilly, which makes it feel further.'

'Thanks for the tip.' She patted the pocket in her shorts for her asthma inhaler, the little blue puffer a constant companion.

'If you want to go now, my little warrior man can lead the way,' Tad said. 'Time he got going. Oi!' A slap to Tadpole's thigh moved both boy and dog. 'School's in soon and Mum hates a lollygagger. Meanwhile, me and Lucky will fit in a well-earned surf.'

'Surf! Surf! Surf!' Kai chanted, spraying spittle over Tadpole's T-shirt.

'Thanks, buddy. On second thoughts, Chelsea, I'm dressed for kid stains. Leave this little guy to me. I don't need a swim after that shower.'

'Oh, please, don't worry. I raised three children of my own, plus I work with special kids part-time at the local school back home. I'm surprised Wandarri has a school.'

'Home-schooling,' Tad clarified. 'Mum's a top teacher, eh Kai? Or is Dad top of the pops this week?'

'Dad! Dad! Dad!' Kai chanted.

Tad laughed and high-fived his son. 'Boy-power!'

'Boy pow-*wahhhhhh!*' Kai mimicked.

'That's right, kiddo, but we'd better keep our little secret and not tell Mum she's runner up in the home-schooling stakes. Off you go, little mate. Chelsea, you'll find Talia at the co-op.'

'You have a lovely name, Kai,' Chelsea said, hoping to engage with the boy and stop him from wandering too far ahead.

He stopped swishing the stick to look back at her. 'Kai means sea.'

'How wonderful! My name means sea*port*,' she said, catching up. 'That must make us instant friends.'

Kai appeared to contemplate the information before continuing to the exit gate and onto the gravel road. Content with his own company, Chelsea wondered what the world looked like through his special lens. This area sure was a picturesque part of the world—to those without painful memories to shroud the prettiness.

Chelsea's recollections of the old campground were of a bushy space bounded by thick forest, and popular among fishermen and itinerants whose tents, comprising metal poles and guy ropes pegged to the ground, sat within painted demarcation lines denoting their temporary piece of paradise. While the buzz of conversations about big catches, the click of ring-pull beer cans, and the fizzle of fish frying in pans had been the soundtrack of a Scott summer holiday, Wendy's big proviso, and the only thing her parents ever agreed on, had been pulling both girls from school before the end of term to avoid the craziness of the Christmas crush.

What fun times they'd shared before grief unglued them. Wendy found comfort in the Coolabah Wine Cask, Layla changed from a protective big sister to a gnashing, not-to-be-trusted eighteen-year-old, and Chelsea carried her guilt in silence.

Still!

13

CHELSEA

Balanced on a stepladder, adding a pottery bird feeder to the shop's array of dangling arts and crafts, was a slim, tanned woman dressed in a flowing peasant-style skirt, and with a tie-dyed top knotted at her blinged belly button.

'Hey there, kiddo!' she called while climbing down the ladder, her voice as melodic as the bamboo wind chime collection. 'What have we found today?' she asked as Kai thrust the bunch of worse-for-wear wildflowers and weeds towards his mother. 'Gosh! They are almost as beautiful as you, my darling boy.' She kissed his head before glancing at Chelsea, curiosity and concern etched into her expression. 'And you've collected a new friend along the way.'

'Hi! Talia? I'm Chelsea.' She thumbed awkwardly in the direction they'd come from. 'I'm staying in the park. Thaddeus wanted a quick surf, so Kai and I walked here together.'

Another smile lit Talia's face. 'Thaddeus?'

'I, ah, mean Tadpole.'

'Yes, I realise that. It's just ... Hearing his real name surprises me. After all these years, Tadpole surprises me. If you've met him, you'll understand he's a one-of-a-kind kinda guy.' The brown-skinned woman, her wild black curls partially strangled into submission, peeled her son's arms from around her waist, inspecting his palms. 'Kai, kiddo, save some hugs for when Dad gets back. Go clean your hands. Workbooks are on the table.'

A tap on his back propelled Kai off the porch and along a well-trodden path passing a rusting petrol bowser that had seen better days, and a paintless public phone box without a phone. As he turned towards the adjacent cottage, the boy hurdled the low fence made from nautical rope slung between wooden posts. One post was home to a not-so-subtle notice: *Private Residence.* He disappeared, swallowed up by a thicket of green ferns, Bird of Paradise plants, and sprawling Frangipani trees devoid of colour. Instead, its fragrant flowers formed a striking carpet of white, pink, and yellow.

'Such a shame,' Talia said, mirroring Chelsea's thoughts. 'Last night's winds played havoc with the plants—and my dreamcatcher display. Won't be a sec.' She was back on the ladder and passing a feathery creation to Chelsea. 'Would you mind holding this one?'

Rather than the usual macrame hoop and lacework centre, Talia's dreamcatchers featured intricate, egg-shaped designs carved out of a chalky white material. Cuttlefish bone, perhaps. Chelsea was about to ask when Talia announced ...

'All done. Thanks. Your timing was perfect.'

'The dreamcatchers are lovely. Unique.' Like the woman herself, Chelsea concluded.

Up close, Talia was even more beautiful, her features as finely chiseled as the dreamcatcher carvings. That said, she was possibly older than Tadpole. How much older, Chelsea couldn't be sure; islander women seemed blessed with ageless complexions and timeless beauty. Not that such differences mattered these days, she reminded herself. Love is love, despite age disparity, gender sameness—or the number of tattoos and earrings a son-in-law can fit on his body.

'Way up here you'd cop the wind from every direction,' Chelsea said, taking in the bird's-eye view of the dreaded Sandbar Beach. Bounded by extensive forestry to the north, from a distance, the compact crescent-shape of sand bookended by headlands seemed hardly menacing. Walking its length should be easy enough.

'I never tire of the view,' Talia said. 'The sea goes on and on and on.'

'There's no end to the ocean,' Chelsea parroted her dad before peeling her gaze away. 'You're isolated up here, though. Don't you miss having people around?'

Talia laughed. 'There'll be no shortage come the holidays. I suggest you enjoy the lull in the lead up to school break. I do,' she said. 'Don't get me wrong. We welcome the tourists—we need them—but when it *is* just us again, the way it was when I met the man of my dreams, right here on this very veranda many moons ago … Well, what can I say?' She sighed. 'Those were the days. Two peas in a pod we were until baby pea made three.'

What were the odds? Chelsea wondered. What forces allowed two perfectly matched people to find each other in a tiny place like Sandbar Beach? Were Talia and Tadpole another case of shared consonants, like Wendy used to say about her and William? Were initials the problem with Chelsea's marriage, and not her sentimentality and stubbornness over the house? How different might life be for Chelsea had she married a Chuck, a Chad, or a Chandler? Instead, a D popped into her life. D for Dale: dependable, doting, diplomatic, dedicated, and Darcyish.

'You're looking flushed after your walk uphill. Come inside,' Talia beckoned. 'We have fresh lemonade.'

Chelsea had noticed the same four words on a timber-framed chalkboard by the door. 'You make your own?'

'My mum used to say "when life gives you lemons …" And with a bait and hardware store not every woman's go-to when holidaying, Mum made complementary lemonade to lure the ladies inside for some lively conversation. I've kept the tradition going and added local produce, groceries, and crafts to the offering. Come on, take a seat. I'll get us that lemonade.'

The shop's interior was surprisingly big, with three rows of shelving to the right extending deep into the store. At the far end sat refrigerated display cases with posters advertising paddle pops and other frozen treats. The nautical decor included a wall of old fishing rods, with nets draped to disguise peeling paint on the ceiling. Coloured mooring floats hung like giant baubles, and there were jars of sea glass, driftwood ornaments, and carved signs. There was even a vintage cork hand-line collection in a giant-sized glass ball. Gosh, how many fishing lines had Chelsea untangled in her youth? But the trip down memory lane darkened when taking in the series of framed photos—a pictorial of Sandbar Beach through the ages. Although faded, the images brought a familiar tightness to Chelsea's chest.

'The walk uphill takes it out of me, too,' Talia announced as Chelsea pocketed the asthma inhaler. 'Something cool to drink while you sit will set you right. Here!'

'Thanks.' Chelsea gladly took the proffered plastic tumbler before lowering herself into a canvas deck chair; one of three seats circling a small table holding a flower-filled vase and an open magazine.

'Excuse the Kai crystal,' Talia said. 'Non-breakable plastic is necessary with my son. Speaking of which …' The woman stood, head tilted to listen. 'Can you hear anything?' But before Chelsea could utter a syllable, Talia was flinging the Nemo-patterned curtain fabric aside to reveal a dark hallway. 'Won't be a sec.'

The lemonade, Chelsea decided after a second sip, would taste good in a tin cup, like the recognisable rainbow-coloured tumblers neatly stacked in a brown-vinyl carry case and on display in the cabinet featuring other retro reminders of an earlier time. Whatever happened to the Scott family's set? Chelsea's cup of choice had been red, Layla's orange, Dad's blue, while Mum refused to drink anything from metal, much less wine. Then again, her mother disliked anything that didn't match or impress the neighbours. The Beach House might have been Dad's castle, but the colour-coordinated contents were all about Wendy keeping up with the Joneses.

And, oh, how the woman would arc up every time Dad dragged 'the crappiest caravan in the street' out of the shed. When it was time to head off, he'd drag Wendy into the car—figuratively, of course; William Scott was the gentlest and kindest man who surrendered to his wife's many demands all year in return for two measly weeks of camping at Sandbar.

'You don't get quality these days, Wendy,' he'd say each time she'd demanded a modern caravan. 'And I'm happy to prove my point any time. I can fold down the dinette, and we'll test ride the suspension.' Mum would bark her disapproval before laughing and smacking his wayward hands. But with William a fit man, and tall, he won every mock battle, easily maneuvering his wriggling, giggling, and griping wife into the van. Layla and Chelsea would watch, squealing with delight at their parents' antics, and soon all four Scotts would be in a tangle of tickles and chuckles on the van's double bed.

'Happy thoughts?' Talia asked, settling into the chair opposite.

'Nostalgic,' Chelsea qualified. 'Find your noise source?'

'I did.' Crossing her legs, Talia bundled the excess fabric of her peasant skirt over her knees. 'Do you have children?'

'Gabby, the eldest, and twin boys.' Chelsea's cheeks warmed. 'Twin boys! Makes them sound like babies when, in fact, both are serving overseas. I'm proud, but I miss them.'

Talia's perennial smile faulted. 'My Kai will never leave me; he'll need his dad even more. They're so alike—water babies both. I've always said I willed the two of them straight from the ocean.' She laughed at Chelsea's obvious bewilderment. 'It's a bedtime story. I tell Kai how I asked the ocean spirits and the stars for a family, and how he and Dad crawled out of the sea and sacrificed their fins for feet to find me. The Little Mermaid story, but with a gender twist,' Talia explained needlessly. 'It's good for growing boys to imagine women as decisive and strong. With Wandarri not booming with role models, I tell Kai he can be whatever he wants, wear whatever he wants, and be whatever comes naturally. I wouldn't have it any other way. Sadly, however, what he'll never do is see much of the world. And so we travel in books.'

'Have you travelled?' Chelsea asked.

'Enough to know where I wanted to end up,' Talia replied. 'After boarding school, I went to London and toured Europe, but this is my place.' The woman topped up both glasses with lemonade. 'Mum and Dad lobbed here when there was no official town status, no Wandarri, and the shop, rundown as it was, serviced a mostly itinerant population, providing petrol, an unofficial post box, and basic items. They'd left Dad's home in Victoria's high-country, planning a slow trip along the east coast to Queensland. He was taking Mum back to see her people until a detour brought them here. They stopped for petrol and saw the business and house were for sale. Mum happily stayed. To her, home was wherever Dad put down roots.

'I arrived on the scene, and the Wandarri community was officially established a few years later. The place boomed, business grew, and life was good until Mum fell ill while I was in London. They found an itinerant jack-of-all-trades in need of work who looked after the place until I could get home. Dad continued to care for Mum while I worked the business, and that jack-of-all-trades ended up the man of my dreams, with Kai surprising us late in life. So, here I am with a bait shop, a child, and a husband. Add to that a father I am desperate to hold on to for as long as I can. And that's my life in a seashell. But enough about me. What's your story?'

Chelsea sipped her drink, uneasy about sharing her past with a stranger. Then, like a fish in her hand that refused to stay caught, the words kind of wriggled free.

'I lost my dad when I was twelve. Mum's basically been AWOL ever since, and my sister—four years older—*was* close. I miss her. As for Dad … I've never stopped missing him, probably because I've never truly grieved his loss.'

'May I ask why not?'

Chelsea looked into Talia's gentle and inquiring eyes. 'Because I've never let him go.'

The woman nodded. 'Losing any loved one is hard. Sons and fathers bond, but there's no connection quite like that between a father and daughter.' She reached for Chelsea's hand. 'It is said a father is a son's first hero but a daughter's first love. Oh gosh, now I've upset you.'

Chelsea shook her head. 'No, no, it's not you. This solo trip is harder than I'd imagined. But Dad loved Sandbar and I … Argh! I should let you work. Not sure my conversation style is the lively type your mum enjoyed, nor worthy of lemonade.'

'Stay.' Talia tugged two paper napkins free from under the heavy, hand-painted sinker, passing them to Chelsea. 'Even though my father is still with us, I understand your loss. Dad loves life, his fishing, his grandson, and this shop, but we're losing him slowly to dementia; a disease at its most cruel when you witness a smart man struggling through his confusion. But what can a girl do?' Talia brightened. 'The men in my life keep me on my toes—and young.'

Chelsea sniffed and pinched the napkin to her nose, feeling calmer. 'And here I am blubbering over losing my father when I was twelve. I didn't stop to think—not about what I was saying and not about this pointless pilgrimage of mine. I do like that Tadpole found his "happy", as he calls it. Not sure I will.'

'No journey is trivial, Chelsea. Mum raised me to not think about the past or the future because we can't control either. "Inhabit the now and let your heart guide you", she'd say. She followed her heart.'

'But she never got to go home,' Chelsea said.

'She did, in her own time and way. But she's also still here with me in one form or another: a plant, a bird, a butterfly. Our loved one's embrace exists in those elements surrounding us.' Talia's voice softened. 'I wondered if last night's windstorm was Mum's reminder that our spirit form continues to flow around us, through us and out of us even after our physical form has passed through death.' Talia squeezed Chelsea's hands in hers. 'If this is the place you feel your strongest connection to a loved one you miss, coming back makes perfect sense. Whether you're here to hold on or let go—if you're looking for a sign to guide you—live in the now, because the past can't hurt you and your future is already determined. Free your heart of the negative, Chelsea. Open yourself up to the universe and you'll draw good things to you.'

Chelsea sniffed into the napkin. 'Like you drew your husband and child over the sand?'

'Exactly! And if you understand that, you're halfway there.'

'Thank you, Talia. I needed a pep talk as much as I needed the lemonade.'

'I'm delighted you stopped by. Anything you need in the way of supplies? You *are* staying?'

'Yes, I'll grab a few things and let you get back to Kai.' As she stood, Chelsea spied the five-dollar cotton carryall on a hook by the cash register. Taking one, she toured each aisle and chatted. 'Tadpole says you home-school?'

'My days happen around my family, and around my customers who mostly lob for bait early, or last minute. But a woman can only chat about bait and the weather so many times without a little girl talk in between. I wonder, though,' Talia sung out to Chelsea, who'd stopped to examine the bulk canisters of dry goods requiring customers to supply their own reusable glass jars: honey, psyllium husk powder, oats and other beans, seeds, and grains. 'Would we have met during your holidays at Sandbar, Chelsea?'

'My sister, maybe,' she replied. 'She had the sweet tooth. I was rarely out of the water. Besides, before leaving the house, Mum would pack the caravan with every conceivable kitchen appliance and foodstuff. She didn't think much of camping, or trust food stores beyond the city limits. As for bait …' Chelsea paused by the small chest freezer displaying the *Tweed Bait* decal. 'Dad preferred finding pippy shells at low tide, or he'd nip beach worms as they poked their heads out. Other times we used green weed.'

'The cunjevoi is a favourite in Wandarri. Kai and his dad *love* a good cunjevoi fight.'

Pinching back the sudden urge to cry, Chelsea headed to the counter, telling Talia, 'Your son would be a formidable opponent when armed with a sea squirt. I've witnessed his imaginary swordsmanship.'

'Oh, but the smell!' Talia quipped. 'Give me a prawn any day.'

'I agree.' Chelsea's chuckle pushed the sad memories away. Selecting a keyring-sized torch from the point-of-sale display, she placed it alongside the tube of sunblock, a packet of powdered milk sachets, a loaf of locally made bread, a tub of butter, and more snacks. With her lantern lost to last night's storm, and her mobile phone light unreliable, the torch was a necessity. The packet of snacks, too. 'My preference was prawning at night, with all four of us working the net as Dad dangled the Tilley lantern. You enjoy fishing, Talia?'

The woman followed Chelsea's gaze to the floor by the door curtain where a lime-green box sat. 'That old thing? Dad's tackle, bless him. You'll find every conceivable hook, lure, and knot in there. We use this box during the holiday season. Tad and I hold beginner fishing classes with the kids because, of course, our world needs more men with fishing addictions, right?' The woman grinned. 'Seriously, not only is the program good for business, throwing out a line at sunrise or sunset is great for mental health at any age. You're welcome to borrow our equipment. We sell bait.' Talia handed Chelsea her change.

'If my dad was here, he'd say: "There's a fine line between fishing and standing on the shore like an idiot, Chelsea-girl".'

'Well, my dad,' Talia added, 'would tell you I talk too much to be any good. He's the dedicated fisherperson in our family. He was.' She added the afterthought. 'This place spoilt us with seafood daily. But that was before. Lucky for the fish in these parts, my nature-loving husband is more the kiss-and-release type. With him, it's less about the catch and more about standing on the beach and being at one with the elements. Fortuitously, I find the untangling of line therapeutic. As is our chat, Chelsea,' Talia added. 'I've so enjoyed meeting you.'

'Thank *you*, Talia. I'm feeling more settled about being here but suffering from too little sleep overnight and too much tree this morning.'

Talia's face wrinkled. 'You'll have to explain "too much tree".'

'A limb came down in the storm. Crushed my tent. I wasn't inside, thank goodness. Your lovely husband stopped on his way to the beach earlier to help clear the mess.'

'He did?' Talia sounded surprised, or a little suspicious. *Awk-waaaard!* 'And will you be staying long, Chelsea?'

'I had no plans other than the week in a tent.'

The woman sighed. 'Oh, no plans! Sounds heavenly.'

'I thought you didn't believe in plans.'

'No, I shared my *mother's* beliefs with you,' Talia said cheekily. 'Between the family and the shop, I can only dream of nothing to do. Wait! Can you hear that?'

Chelsea listened. 'No, nothing.'

'Me either.' Talia craned her neck to spy through the gap in the curtaining, 'And that is a problem when you have an old dad with selective hearing; one I can't trust to pick up on the cues of a silent child. Two secs. Let me check on the pair. Hey, you two, what's going on out here?'

As the door curtain dropped back into place and Talia's voice and footsteps faded, Chelsea imagined a life with both father and husband living together. Dale would suggest that's exactly what he contends with daily because, according to him, William Scott is everywhere in their house, and the reason for every argument in recent years. Chelsea conceded she had overloaded shelves and walls with Scott-family memorabilia, but it wasn't, as Dale inferred, because William Scott was more important. Memories of her dad littered her mind, and the house, because he *wasn't* around; Dale was there every day. Or he was before Perth. How had they let their relationship deteriorate to this point?

Slinging the strap of her carryall over a shoulder, Chelsea thought back to Talia's comment about sacrifices. Had Chelsea expected Dale to bend to her needs? To crawl over sand and forego fins for feet to live in *Chelsea's* world—and not as the hero but playing a bit part in *her* version of happily ever after, and in *her* family's house.

'Duty calls, Chelsea,' said a flustered-looking Talia. 'I'm sorry. We'll catch up again.'

14

DALE, PERTH

'Morning, Dale!' Sheila Matthews leaned on the partition separating their two workstations, slender legs squeezed into fluro active wear, a white towel draped around a neck slick with sweat. She beamed, nodding at the photo of Gabby and the twins he'd unconsciously picked up while musing over the past. Sheila was bubbly and bright, but the type of workmate whose smile flashed a warning. Even her voice held effervescent qualities.

'I think those super-adorable twins are going to take after their adorable granddad.'

'Lovely of you to say,' Dale said, keeping the requisite reply suitably robotic. On day one of his secondment, when introduced to his team, he'd identified Sheila as the most capable, but the one requiring the most caution. 'One good thing about Perth is seeing my daughter playing mother. Makes me feel old, though.'

'Only one? Surely you can think of more good things about being here. And by the way, you *look* fabulous! But you work too hard. I didn't think anyone else was mad enough to start their day this early. Did you sleep here last night? Bed at home not comfortable?' she asked, her singsong voice ending on a suggestive high note.

'Bed's fine, Sheila.' The only thing wrong with the one in his apartment was too much space, but he didn't share such detail.

Equal in ambition, the pair had hit it off professionally straightaway. Intellectually, Sheila Matthews was Dale's perfect match, and he appreciated and benefitted from the female perspective she brought to his case discussions. If Dale impressed the boss, Sheila was the reason.

'Do you often run to work?' he asked her.

'Best part of the day. And no one else uses the staff showers. I'm headed there now to wash off this sweat, but only after I've shed this impossible-to-peel-away active wear. Oh, and don't forget Jack's farewell at the pub tonight. You *will* be there, Dale. You know what they say about all work and no play?'

'I'll be there. I like Jack. Thanks for the reminder, Sheila.'

15

CHELSEA

When a gust of hot Wandarri wind whipped gravel dust up the hill, Chelsea turned away to shield her face. With one hand, she secured her hat. In the other were her purchases, with the hemp and organic cotton tote growing heavy—along with her mood.

Talking with Talia had come easily, but she'd walked away envious of the woman: a loving family, a simple existence, happy peas in a pod dealing with life's ups and downs together. While not venturing beyond the shop's curtain and into the residence, Chelsea couldn't imagine the many mod-cons Wendy had regularly demanded, only to walk away from it all and leave deep cupboards crammed with stuff; some still in the original boxes: the idolised 70s fondue set and distinctive Corningware casserole dish collection, the must-have mixer and umpteen Tupperware containers designed to outlive Armageddon. With no shortage of space, unused items found their way to the back of the cupboards, which was fine. Chelsea had no problem hanging onto things. *Except your daughter and your husband!*

There everything stayed, surviving two kitchen spruce-ups. Dale had enjoyed turning the Scott's circa 1950s shack into a home for their family. Fastidious in his preparation of the high ceilings, ornate cornices, and picture rails, he'd almost finished one coat of Watermelon Pink in the baby's room when Gabby decided to not wait for permission to be born. With a colicky baby, sleepless nights and a long daily commute, Chelsea had suggested he put his tertiary studies before the renovations. Time flew, and after two years of living in a partially painted house, Dale arrived home from work with a surprise. A Peter Rabbit wallpaper border he'd found in a bargain bin.

'Cute, huh? I even like the name Peter for a boy.'

'Great minds!' she'd said while downing her cutlery to reach under the table for the matching stuffed rabbit toys. 'I bought these two in town after my ultrasound today. Oh, and we'll need a second name to go with Peter.'

Fork midway to his mouth, his eyes already welling, Dale asked, 'We're having twins, Mrs Holt?'

'Two boys as wonderful as you, Mr Holt.'

But amid the mayhem of motherhood, and following the twins' first day at school, she and Dale experienced their first serious fight. The first of many to come, and all about the house. Chelsea had mistakenly announced some news in the same fun way she'd announced the twins. Only this time, when Chelsea reached under the dining table—quick to reassure a panic-stricken Dale this was not another baby—she produced a small gift box.

'Ta-dah!' She flipped the lid to display an ordinary brass key stamped with the word *Lockwood*.

'You've changed the locks?' he asked, his cautious chuckle edged with worry.

'No, silly, the key is symbolic of how one door closes and another opens.'

'Out with it, Chels,' he insisted. 'What is this?'

'Good news. I got Mum and Layla to agree. Oh, and Sharon Hawthorn, the conveyancer down the road—the one with the sign out the front—said it was a sound investment. She believes bringing a property as old as ours up to market standard would require costly renovations. Her advice, given the high-growth area we find ourselves in, is to keep the property. And she should know. She and her husband have done well over the years.' Chelsea's excitement faded. 'Why are you staring, Dale?'

'Chels, I thought you were a lousy decision-maker.'

'I am lousy, but Sharon made me see sense. It's a win-win. The most practical way forward is to stay put and let our investment grow. This house is the key to our future security and, as of today, it's all ours. *Ta-dah!*'

'This house isn't *our* investment,' he snapped back. 'It's meant to be a steppingstone while we save up.'

'Yes, Dale, and we also agreed the nominal rent Mum and Layla set was financially beneficial. With you putting so much of your wages into our investment portfolio, and with it doing so well—'

Dale's thump on the table rattled the cutlery they'd abandoned on their plates. 'You sold shares to buy your family out?'

'Of course not!' The stiffness in her husband's shoulders fell away until . . . 'I used my trust money, Dale. We no longer pay rent at all. The house is ours.' The ticking grandfather clock in the next room grew supersonic as her husband sat mute and unblinking. 'What's the matter? I-I don't understand, Dale. You've wanted to own a house. It makes sense to reap the rewards from the one you've put so much love into. Mum talked to Layla who agreed—and to be honest, the price was ridiculous, as it should be after all our work. Mum hardly needs money, and Layla's never wanted the place. As landowners in the fast-developing west, the only way for us is up, especially with the completed town bypass and ... Say something, Dale.'

The only sound was his chair's legs clawing the kitchen linoleum as he stood before storming from the room.

'Dale?' Chelsea followed him.

First stop: the photo gallery where Holt and Scott family pictures hung on the wall in a happy shamble. Next, he paused at the sideboard— home to a decorative assortment of William's magic jars, sea glass in bowls, and carved cuttlebone figurines. Further along were more photos of Chelsea with her father: on the beach, around the campfire, standing on the front porch in his usual it's-all-mine and I'm-king-of-the-castle' stance.

Finally, Dale turned to face her, his expression a blend of disbelief and defeat. 'You could've used our joint savings, Chelsea. At least the place might be partly mine.'

'Don't be silly, Dale. What's mine *is* yours. *We* have a house—finally.'

He muttered something about 'a freaking shrine' and snatched his car keys from the hallstand.

'Where are you going?' Chelsea called.

A sonic boom would not have drowned out the angry retort. 'Anywhere but here.'

A week later, after dismantling the so-called *freaking shrine* on the sideboard, and de-cluttering the bookcase of William Scott knick-knacks, life in the Holt household returned to a kind-of normality. Little did Chelsea know the subject of selling would raise its hurtful head every few years. There was never a way to know how or when, but every discussion ended with Dale going for a long drive before coming back—calm, but quiet.

Returning from one such cooling off episode, Dale had found Chelsea at the dining table, cursing the ceiling fan that had waited until summer to stop working.

'I've been thinking,' he said as they tucked into their evening meal. 'We can afford something nice now. Our forever home—with air con, or a sea breeze. Not close enough to see the waves—I'm understanding of your phobia, Chels—but the kids could bike-it to the beach. And an ensuite bathroom would be practical. It's been a long time since we showered together without a gatecrashing kid. Imagine a new house with an entire bathroom to ourselves.'

'You seriously want to talk about moving again, Dale? You want to go there tonight? Seriously?' Chelsea stiffened, prepared for the same argument, but Dale was unexpectedly coy.

'Ah, actually, I *was* suggesting a shower together might be fun, but we can argue instead while discussing our growing family.' He let his cutlery drop on the plate. 'With the amount of land under us, and in a seller's market, we can use this house as equity and get something to tick all our boxes. Where did you put the business card from the last bloke? You said the guy had shifty eyes, and you'd check out other real estate agents and make a list so I could make a decision.'

'Oh, so *you* get to choose?'

Dale looked dumbstruck. 'Yeah, like I've regularly chosen ice cream flavours and what DVD to hire—and everything else, for as long as I can recall. Remember when we were on a date and you—'

'Dale, I'm not ready to move. Not yet.' She reached for the stemmed glass and threw back the last of the wine. 'I've got a mothers' network here; the twins have made friends; *I* have friends and a volunteer job I enjoy, and Gabby is at an age when, well, you know better than anyone a teenager needs stability. She's always been a handful.'

'She's hardly a child,' Dale mumbled, taking up arms and attacking his steak with renewed vigour.

From that point on, The Beach Shack became the elephant *in the room* —and *on their dinner table* and *in their bed*—while the phrase 'let's discuss the house' became code for 'let's raise our voices, dig in our heels, and make each other miserable'. Before she knew it, her children had grown up. Gabby was arguing back and accusing Chelsea of being obstructive and obsessive, while the twins were being deployed overseas.

Now, with Dale on the other side of the country and Fred gone, Chelsea was alone at Sandbar and at breaking point.

Well done! She sulked. *You have an empty house and a bathroom to yourself. Yay!*

Bending to grab a long stick in the middle of the road, she batted a pebble, sending the stone high and long before it hit a tree truck with a dull thud.

'Howzat!' she heard her dad shout.

CRICKET WITH DAD, 1981

'But *daa-a-ad!*' I complain, eager to lodge a leg before wicket appeal.

'No disputing the umpire, Chelsea-girl. Change of batsman,' Dad declares before calling across to Layla. 'You're up!' But when my sister doesn't budge from her prostrate position on the beach towel, Dad looks at his watch, then at me. 'Never mind. We have an extra-special lunch to eat. Then it'll be close to fish-biting time, Miss Fix.'

We head towards the caravan, Dad tossing the ball in one hand, his other arm draping heavy around my neck. 'Do you reckon they'll miss us when we're not here?'

'Huh?' I'm confused, so he nods at Layla, then at Mum, the pair already baked brown on their striped sun lounges.

'Check the forecast, William,' comes Mum's muffled diktat.

'Nah, she'll be right, Wendy. We've been bringing home the bacon for years in all kinds of weather. Me and Miss Fix are all-weather anglers.'

I'm about to dispute the notion of catching bacon when Mum lifts the sunhat from her face and tells Dad, 'I don't care about you, William. I don't want Chelsea getting wet and catching a cold if you stay out late. And you'll stay until the fish stop biting.'

I don't say so, but getting wet and cold is not the fun bit. At twelve, I'm acquiring a taste for grownup things, like suntans and tea—with milk and one sugar—and taking to girly hair braids, lip gloss, and the frosty-blue nail polish Layla painted on our nails last night.

'You're not piking out, are you Chelsea-girl?' Dad says. 'You can't today. I'll need my Chief Bait Collector on hand. And don't forget all those rock pools.'

I'm torn. *Go with Dad or stay with Mum?* Once the clouds roll in proper, and the weather is not good for sun baking, Layla will set up the caravan as a pretend beauty salon and do facials. But it's Dad's promise of a sheltered spot and the perfect rock-hopping tide that wins out. Besides, Chief Bait Collector sounds cool. I've never been one of those before.

After lunch, ready to head off, Dad walks over and kisses Mum goodbye, hugging her long and tight.

'Quit that! You're blocking my sun,' she snaps, adding a shoulder slap and a shove. 'What on earth has got into you this trip?'

'I'm thanking you, my love. I appreciate you worrying about our girls,' he says. 'I don't say it enough. They're in good hands. You're a good mum.'

'Better than you are a fisherman,' she retorts.

Dad winks, steps away, grabs his gear. 'It's time to say goodbye. Give Mum a hug and let's go, Miss Fix.'

'We won't be holding our breath for a fish dinner, will we, Layla? I'm not even sure why you're going today, William. This is an easterly wind blowing. Don't you say if the wind is in the east, they bite the least?'

As usual, Layla pipes up. 'Hetty Vaughn's mum says a fisherman is a jerk on one end of the line, waiting for a jerk on the other.'

'Hetty Vaughn's mum married a jerk,' Dad says. 'And you know, Wendy, it's also said a woman who never sees her husband fishing will never know what a patient man she married.'

'Don't need to see it. You tell me often enough.' Mum rolls onto her tummy and opens her latest billionaire boyfriend book with the pink cover. 'All I want to know is you'll catch dinner, so we don't go hungry. I've got nothing out of the freezer for tonight.'

Dad's mood falls serious. 'I made a promise when we married, Wendy, and I've never shirked my responsibilities as a father, a husband, or as a provider. No matter what happens, my family will never go hungry.'

Mum grunts and says, 'I hope you have jackets in that backpack of yours. You'll be needing them.'

'I have all I need.' Dad hoists the bulging backpack onto his shoulders. 'And I have the best bait collector coming with me. Miss Fix and I are the hunters and gatherers, and we're survivors. Come on, Chelsea-girl, it's time to find out what big and exciting things await us on the other side of those dunes.'

Later that December day, 1981, a wave washed William Scott out to sea.

16

LAYLA

It's not fair, Layla thought as a fresh-faced Trent Dashwood appeared in the Skype window on her laptop. Men weren't supposed to glow. Maybe the man's sunflower-covered shave coat contributed to his bright-eyed look so early in the morning.

'Sunflowers, Doc?'

'Samantha's going away gift. *Her* going away!' he added.

'Yeah, well, what can I say? It was inevitable.' Layla lifted her shoulders and let them drop. 'No idea why you two married.'

He ignored her triteness. He always had. Forever the professional, Trent's expertise was in keeping a conversation on track, despite the ardent distractions Layla had attempted in the early days.

'I needed someone to want me,' he said. 'Samantha did, for a few years at least. She asked after you when I dropped off Toby the other day.'

'That's nice.' Layla downed the last of the fizzy drink she'd helped herself to from the hotel's minibar, plonking the empty bottle on the bedside table. '*She's* nice, I guess, but Blind Freddy and I could see you weren't right for each other.'

'Speaking of blind, Layla,' he said, 'I need my glasses and the big monitor to see you properly. Hold on while I shift into the office.' Trent was en route before Layla could object or suggest blurred was a better look after a long-haul flight. 'Then we're going to stop talking about Samantha and start talking about why you're calling me at such an early hour. Okay,' he said, reclining into a black executive chair, hands cupped behind his head. 'Start by telling me from which faraway land you're calling. The background décor has me stumped. I see the bedhead is the timeless, button-tufted type, and above it is an elaborate frame holding a painting of vineyards, hills, and rows of cypress trees. The colours alone suggest luxury villa, Tuscany, Italy.'

In dramatic contrast to the doc's colourful description, Layla replied somewhat monochromatically. 'Budget motel, Perth, layover.'

'And the reason for your call? You look pensive.'

Layla leaned back against the studded velveteen headboard, raised her knees, and leaned the laptop against her thighs. 'I'm wondering about the ramifications of telling you something I've kept to myself for three decades.'

'I see,' Trent said, his demeanour equal in both perceptiveness and compassion. 'And the ramifications of *not* telling me are what?'

The question almost drove Layla off the bed. If only she could be in the Doc's office, snuggled into the latest in a lineage of swallow-me sofas. Layla had felt safe and protected there. Alone in a hotel room, she remained exposed, scared, and distrusting—of herself.

'Is this the same long-held secret?' Trent asked.

'Sure is,' Layla mumbled while chewing on a fingernail. 'Confessing is hard.'

'I always say secrets are easy to tell if the reason is strong enough. Start with one word,' he suggested. 'The rest may flow.'

'That's what I'm afraid of.' Squinting at the framed certificate behind Trent's left shoulder, she asked, 'Did I ever tell you about *my* accreditation? I was young when The University of Liars and Con Men awarded me an honorary master's degree in Secret Keeping. Sure pips your Counselling 101 qualification, or whatever the hell you shrinks need to screw with people's brains.' She flashed a smug look.

'Is that what you think I did all those years? Screw with your brain?'

'All your questions did. I would've preferred to screw you, but I well and truly screwed that up. Sensing a theme, Doc?' Layla slid down the headboard, adjusting the laptop screen to suit. 'Go ahead. Hit me with the next question.'

'Why, after all this time, does telling the truth bother you?'

'Did I say it bothered *me*? It's my sister I worry about.'

'And you're afraid the truth will hurt Chelsea?'

Layla repositioned, rolling over into a kind of fetal curl, taking the laptop with her so she was staring at Trent's face as if he was right there, curled beside her, his head sharing her pillow.

'That's just it, Doc. I don't know what this will do to Chelsea—to what's left of our relationship. She was young when it all went down. Mum and I protected her. Well, I did. I'm unsure how much detail she remembers, or if she would want the whole truth.'

'Speaking as a friend, Layla, and one who understands childhood trauma in a professional capacity. Memory is malleable and easily contaminated by life experiences. The older we get, the more beliefs we bring to a memory, the more muddied our remembrances. As adults don't store memories in pristine form from childhood, we don't get the option—come old age—to play everything back on a kind of personal recording device in our heads. What a child with limited life experiences recalls of a single moment in time, traumatic or not, will likely distort as they grow. So, yes, you may find your sister's recollections different from yours. Likewise, your current emotional and physical state, especially after a long-haul flight, may influence the replaying of an event and, in turn, influence your actions. So, I'm asking. Why now, Layla? What's the rush?'

'I wouldn't call thirty years rushing it, Doc. I was a teenager.' She dragged the spare bed pillow into her body, cuddling it tight. 'What I discovered about him when I was eighteen haunts me.'

Trent leaned forward until Layla could make out the amber specks in his eyes. 'I am listening,' he said. 'Trust me.'

Over an hour later, Layla's stranglehold on the pillow eased, and she sat up on the bed.

'And there you have it, Doc. The truth, and the reason I was wild with rage for so long. Do I wish I'd never found Dad's letter? Hell yes! Some bloody birthday that was. Fully prepared to call him out, Mum's threat stopped me. "By all means, tell the world, Layla", she'd said, "and watch your mother go to jail, and your sister go into the foster system". When I screamed I didn't care, and that I'd protect Chelsea always, she'd laughed. "What makes you think you'll be together? Tattletales and troublesome teenagers aren't foster family favourites. No one will want you. No one". So, Doc, I kept the secret, and guess what? I still ended up alone.'

'And you never said a word to anyone about what he did?'

Turning her face towards the ceiling, she blinked hot tears back to where they'd been dormant all these years. Seconds later, cynical Layla re-emerged, her heart as cold as her mother's words that day.

'Mum told me he wasn't worth remembering. Then she grabbed my shoulders, looked me in the eyes, and said, "We weren't enough for your father. The sooner you get that through your thick skull and forget him, the better".'

Neither surprise nor shock revealed themselves on Trent's face as Layla rounded off her story with a good dose of sarcasm and swear words.

'How's that for a family skeleton?'

'So, you never asked your mother more about it? Did she know the full extent of his actions?'

'Sure, I asked heaps over the years. Mum was super talkative after a few wines. Then she got sad, then angry. I discovered my parents' marriage was not typical, their relationship hard to figure out. One day, they'd be cuddling and kissing. The next Mum would lash out at Dad—verbally *and* physically. I was too ignorant to recognise domestic abuse. William was a softy, and he'd make out her anger was a pretense. He'd say stuff like, "Water off a wetsuit". But I know better now. Life was all about Mum and what she wanted. She was the violent one, controlling him, forcing his compliance. Dad conformed to keep the peace. He never raised a hand or a fist to anyone. A real shame, too.'

'Why a shame?' Trent asked.

'Because an occasional smack when I mucked up might have let me see he cared—about me.' She gave a little snort. 'Turns out, William Scott hurt us without lifting a hand, and all because marriage to Mum made him miserable. One way or another, he was getting out.'

'Thank you for trusting me, Layla. Understanding all you've endured makes you more impressive. You're a survivor.'

'Courtesy of two deadbeat parents,' she mocked. 'Wendy survived by adopting an "every woman for herself" strategy, while I dropped out of school to work at KFC, hoping I'd make manager. I aspired to greatness back then. Regrettably, my sister aspired to keep Dad's bloody memory alive by fixating on ways to remember him at Christmas and birthdays and every other bloody time. When I visited, the house was like a museum, and she pulled out photo albums, and then insisted we all play dumb board games.'

'And you dislike board games?' he queried.

'I disliked how my sister's obsession cemented Wendy and me as co-conspirators and drinking buddies and relegated to the backyard. Removing ourselves was all we could do to cope during those occasions. One day, I decided to stop being curious about any Scott-family member —living or dead. I walked away; I drank, I did drugs, and when the self-harm started, I got myself a VIP pass to your very first, and very comfortable shrink's couch. Not sure why you got rid of the sunny yellow one. I liked it. It would go well with your sunflower shave coat.'

'You know I've always cared for you, Layla, and more than was appropriate. As my first *client*, I've known you longer than any other woman, including my mother, bless her. You matter to me and I'm here for you. I'll always be here for you in whatever capacity you need.'

'Thanks.' Layla didn't mention William Scott had sprouted similar sentiments before leading Chelsea away that day to commit a father's cruelest betrayal. 'You're the best thing about my shitty life, Doc.'

'You get what I mean by "here for you"?'

'Yeah, I do.'

With Lay a troubled teen, and Trent the other a nerdy new shrink, the pair had danced around their developing but inappropriate attraction for years. He was her perfect match: easy to talk to, totally professional and, as her psychologist, ethically out of bounds. Until he wasn't. Now his "here for you" meant "when you're ready to accept love" *and* accept the ring he'd bought well before Samantha came along with her matching university degree and designer high heels.

'You get what I can't let myself do, Doc,' Layla said. 'Besides, no one in their right mind wants someone with my baggage hanging around 24/7. "Good in short doses only" will be my epitaph. I mean, look at you! You're Richard Gere in *Pretty Woman* and I'm Kit de Luca, the druggy who'll never amount to anything because only the pretty woman who gets her act together gets the guy. So, here we are—mates—talking, as usual. We do it well, don't you think?'

'Did you get any sleep on the plane?' Trent asked.

'Oh, you know me. I'll sleep anywhere.' She shot a wink his way, but Trent stayed stony-faced.

'Why say things like that? You don't think I see the real you?'

How can you? She wanted to ask him. *I don't know the real me or trust myself to have a real relationship. Sleeping with strangers in exotic destinations is far safer; much easier to walk away from and no one gets hurt.*

Keen to change the subject, she put on her brave face. 'I can share one thing the unscrupulous William Scott taught me, which might explain a lot. I've never forgotten his words: "Having nowhere to go doesn't mean it's right to stay".'

Trent leaned closer, as if trying to see through the computer screen and into her soul. 'One day, Layla, you'll find your *somewhere* and a reason to stay. Let's talk tomorrow.'

'Sorry, Doc, I won't be here tomorrow.'

When Trent's body visibly stiffened, forcing a squeak out of the office chair, and putting his professional mask back into place, Layla understood. She'd said those words years before, as Doctor Trent Dashwood had attempted to schedule another appointment. Two days later, after the emergency department doctors had pumped Layla's stomach of pills and booze, Trent had sat by her hospital bed.

She could still picture his pained expression—the one saying he'd failed her as a psychologist, as if he'd held her down, opened her mouth, and poured the bottle of benzodiazepines and codeine down her throat.

SESSIONS WITH TRENT, 1991

She knows he's close by, and has been for a while, because the pungent scent of sandalwood aftershave and hair product is a change from hospital disinfectant.

'You didn't show up for your appointment, Layla. Want to talk about what you did?'

'Maybe.'

'Were you aware of the baby before you took the pills?'

'Maybe.'

'And how did you feel when the doctors told you what happened?'

'Maybe.'

The art of avoiding and shutting down questions, especially those with painful answers, is part of her DNA. From whom she inherited such skill, Layla will probably never discover. All she knows at this moment is bringing a life into the world—a mistake and a bastard—only to hand the baby over and expect strangers to shower it with love is not happening to another child.

'Is this to do with your mother?' the hot doc asks.

Smiling, she replies, 'My mother is not my problem. She and I have loads in common—mostly secrets—which means we get on like a house on fire. Only in our case, it's more paper on fire. Eight years ago. I was eighteen.'

The shrink cocks his head, curious. 'Do you want to explain, Layla?'

'Maybe.'

Doc leans forward. 'Try—for me.'

Closing her eyes again, she draws a deep breath—the slow, deliberate kind capable of clearing a path to the darkest corners of her memory. Pressing pause at the point of her eighteenth birthday, she sees Wendy passed out drunk, and the Scott-family secret scattered around the base of the backyard incinerator. Scorch marks have left sentences cryptic, but what would become clear when Layla confronted her mother later in the day is how something as intangible as a shared secret can shift the power from parent to child.

Ever since, fury has burned inside Layla, and with hatred fuelling the flames, a bigger explosion, fiercer, was inevitable.

'Mum and I provoke each other,' she tells the doc. 'We've turned into a couple of bone-pointing she-devils. We curse and cast unkind comments; have done since Dad …'

She stops, switching her recollection to silent mode. The adorable Doc Dashing does not need to hear everything, including details about how easily Wendy caves into her eldest daughter because she fears Layla will carry out her threat and make the written confession public knowledge. The woman claims she has the most to lose. On that score, Layla disagrees.

'My parents robbed me of so much: my trust in people, my precious sister.' *My identity.* 'When Wendy accused me of being "evil like William" I made myself the epitome of evil—physically, at least.'

She replaced every item of clothing in her wardrobe with dark colours, dyed her nondescript brown hair blue black, and pierced her body. Whenever Wendy complained, Layla would laugh.

'I wasn't always a blue girl, Doc,' she says, raising the cannula-free hand to show off the navy-blue nail polish. 'And I don't like how I look or what I've become. Don't like much about myself at all.'

'Then why such a drastic appearance?' the young therapist asks.

'Goth facades work. They keep people at a distance, with some so uncomfortable I'm as good as invisible to them. Others treat me like I'm stupid or a waste of space. I don't care.'

Far from dumb, Layla had regularly ranked among the top ten percent of students in her year—until the secret stole her concentration, and addictions stole her youth. The first drug she experienced was not a drug, but control. Layla's constant threat to expose the truth soon turned her mother into her minion. When power no longer made Layla feel good, she switched to pills, and when expelled from school for breaking every rule in the book, she pushed every boundary to test her her mother and make her pay. That was until Wendy regained control by using, and emotionally wounding, the little sister Layla had vowed to protect.

'Tell me this,' Doc asks, repositioning a box of tissues from the hospital tray table to her lap. 'What makes you saddest when you think of your family?'

Layla scoffs and claws the hospital sheet, the edge speckled blue with wet mascara stains. 'You think these tears are over my family? Not likely, Doc. My stomach's hurting and I need the pain to go away. *I need to go away* before I do something to harm my mother, like she hurt my sister. Mum reckons Dad destroyed our lives, but Wendy takes the cake.' Layla yanks several tissues from the box to blow her nose, to breathe, to think.

'Your mother physically hurts your sister? Does she hit her?'

'And break a nail?' Layla scoffs and shakes her head. 'Mum's more into emotional blackmail, but because she can't control me, my little sister would cop the brunt. Like the morning Mum dragged Chelsea into the car and dumped her at the school swimming carnival. Water terrifies my sister, and Mum knows why. A bath—even a shallow one—could trigger a tantrum. I screamed and begged Mum to let Chelsea be, but she shoved her into the car anyway.

'Because I went to a friend's place to bunk for a week, I wasn't at home when Wendy returned that same day, packed a bag, and left a note saying she needed time alone. She was shacking up with a man who lives two suburbs away, but the woman didn't bother to collect my scared little sister from the swimming carnival. Aunty Rita did, taking Chelsea in, but the damage was done. Convinced her morning tantrum drove Mum over the edge, and Chelsea had broken our family for a second time, she blamed herself.'

'You moved into Rita's with Chelsea?'

'I wanted to but, no. With Chelsea aiming for uni—teaching is her dream job—she needed to focus. In case you haven't yet figured me out, Doc, I'm a dangerous distraction.'

'Why dangerous, Layla?'

She shrugs her response, averting her gaze to the high ceiling with its stark fluorescent strip lighting.

'Our father used to say, "The fish that keeps its mouth shut is the fish that gets to swim another day". By keeping the secret, I'm saving myself and protecting my sister. I'm way too loud, too opinionated, and too unpredictable to be around her.'

With Layla unable to trust herself and not slip up, the safest move was to cut all ties with Chelsea.

Then Layla cut herself.

If only cutting Wendy out of her life was as easily done. Instead, a despicable act, a secret, and a necessary pact bound the pair.

'Layla, will you tell me your secret?'

'Maybe,' she says from the hospital bed: rescued and now in recovery. 'One day, and just you.' *Never Chelsea!*

'Layla?' Trent's voice made her look at the laptop monitor. 'Where did you go just now?'

'You don't want to know, Doc.'

'Without exception, I want to know what's going on in that head of yours.'

'Ha! And that, right there, is why I date guys who want me for anything *but* what's in my head.'

'I see. Eternally the tough girl, eh? You don't have to be emotionally hard to overcome the hard things in life, Layla. It's okay to lean on some-one's love for strength. But understand, it's *your* love of self—not their love of you—that makes you courageous. You are so much more than you think you are. When are you going to believe neither your parents, nor their actions, define the amazing woman looking into that webcam?'

'When are *you* going to stop asking questions, Doc?'

The man chuckles. 'Once you realise you have all the answers. You've always known who you are inside and what you want. I've simply been here waiting for you to figure that out.'

'You're right.' She was no longer the terrified teenage girl, or the highly strung secret-keeper from her twenties, and this was exactly why she'd telephoned Trent. The man could still calm looney Layla, the loose cannon. 'And I have.'

Thanks to Doc Dashing, she was stronger and brave, but did that make her ready? Was it right to tell Chelsea at all, then leave her to deal with the truth alone? Someone would need to support her emotionally—someone Chelsea loved and trusted. *That won't be you once the truth comes out.* Her little sister's life was falling apart over a bloody house and her bloody-minded obsession with a man who had promised to care for his family but instead broke them one-by-one.

'I guess there can be no more questions from you, Doc, because I have no more to confess. You've heard every disgraceful, depraved, desperate Scott-family secret and I'm free, at last.'

But not without having paid the ultimate emotional price. *As if you haven't paid enough.*

'Tell me, Layla, how are you feeling right now?'

'Alive, thanks to you, relieved, still angry.' Her voice gave out, her fury turning to sarcasm, then shame. 'But as I have no more secrets, Doc, I guess we can finally stop meeting like this.'

'You're wrong, Layla,' Trent said. 'Now I know the truth, we can begin. I'd like to talk some more. My first appointment isn't until 9.30 this morning. Let me shower, dress and grab a coffee. I'll phone you back.'

'And pay your out-of-hours rate?' Although she laughed, it didn't sound genuine. 'I'll be fine.'

'I have every confidence. You are the strongest woman,' Trent said. 'You've survived on your own terms and, yes, you might have fallen a few times, but you got up and you grew stronger.'

'People like you picked me up.'

'Maybe so, but *you* control your life now; no one else. You'll do the right thing with the truth. That first day, you stared through the thickest blue mascara, but I saw through the mask. I saw desperation. I saw you. Thank you for letting me share your journey. Because of you, I'm a better shrink.'

'Did you just say the word "journey"?' Layla quipped. 'That is so last decade, Doc. Time for me to go. I must see my niece and my brother-in-law before flying back east tomorrow and then driving north.'

'North?' Doc queried. 'Where are you going?'

'Nowhere,' she said. 'And I plan on hunting down Nowhere Man, sitting in his precious Nowhere Land, to tell him what he's been missing.'

'Do I need to worry?' Trent asked.

'Certainly not about me,' Layla remarked. 'William Scott should worry. He might not be dead, but he's going to wish he was.'

1 7

CHELSEA

Thinking back on that very ordinary day long ago, nothing had told Chelsea she would never again see her dad wearing his signature wrap-around sunnies, the straw fishing hat he pushed down until his ears stuck out, and the zinc cream smeared across his nose and cheekbones.

'The stripes of a water warrior,' he'd say, while painting Chelsea's face.

'More like water weakling,' she mumbled into the caravan's mirror, squeezing a dollop of sunblock onto the pad of her index finger before spreading the zinc-based lotion over her nose and cheeks, war-paint style. *Time to be brave, to suck up some courage, and to try out the so-called self-imposed phobia therapy.* 'Let's see how far you get this time!'

'Nice look,' Tad called as Chelsea locked *Sea Esta's* door and looped the key lanyard around her neck.

'I'm channelling my childhood,' she called back to the man lounging in his camp chair, dog by his side.

'And I thought you were preparing for tonight's luau.'

'There's a luau?' She crossed the narrow roadway towards Tad. 'As in grass skirts and hula dancing?'

'Nice moves,' Tad said about her quick demonstration, 'but we stick to the feasting bit without too much tradition and no dancing. Simply B.Y.O. your drink, plate, dessert bowl, and cutlery. Ten dollars per head covers food and goes towards the communal kitty.'

'You have a communal kitty?'

'Sure do! Proceeds from the market day every second weekend also go into it. Elmie and Connie came up with the idea of combining artistic offerings with produce from those with land parcels large enough to grow vegetables, fruit, and herbs. These days, people come from across the district.'

Squatting to pat the dog sitting quietly by his master's chair, Chelsea said, 'I look forward to meeting Connie.'

Tadpole's expression clouded over. 'Ah, you won't. She died.'

'Oh, my goodness, no! When?'

'Close on thirty years.'

'Thirty?' Chelsea echoed. 'But Elmie said … We were expecting jam.'

'Yeah, well, Elmie's sister story is long—if you're interested. In the meantime, you have a strand of hair stuck in your sunblock.' As Tad reached out and ran a finger over Chelsea's cheek, she held her breath, waiting until he finished tucking the strand behind her ear. 'Looks like you're set for the beach.'

'Oh, ah, yes. It's been a while, but I figured slip, slop, slap was in order. But the beach can wait. I am interested in hearing about Elmie and her sister—unless I'm disturbing your work,' she added.

'My office hours are strictly Sandbar time. Pull up a pew.' Tad offered a folded chair, but Chelsea took the opportunity for a little puppy therapy, sitting cross-legged on the ground with the dog.

While she scratched Lucky's ear, Tad explained how Australia's White Assimilation Policy had assumed children with mixed parentage and lighter skin colour were more suited to a white society.

'Ripping kids from their parents and homes was a national bloody disgrace, but the Wandarri community of the day protected its own, as usual, with the girls evading detection by authorities for longer than others.'

'How did they?' Chelsea asked.

'Not sure if you know this already, but Bunker Headland has a network of war-time observation points, gun emplacements, and old ammunition stores linked by underground passages.'

Oh, Chelsea knew, all right. Mentioning the labyrinth of tunnels could have triggered a panic attack, if not for Tadpole's distracting story about two sisters torn apart.

'If you're interested, I'll dig out the dossier Prudence compiled to argue Wandarri's claim for a preservation order on the entire headland, in particular the south-facing bunker where both girls hid from authorities. I keep all my mum's memorabilia in the office.' He thumbed towards the caravan at his back. 'The current day committee remains determined to safeguard the bunker. You've gotta see the mural to understand. It's quite the artistic fusion, with both strong Indigenous influences and references to the Italian way of life. So one of a kind that I remember jokingly comparing the bunker mural to Michelangelo's Sistine Chapel. Next thing, cagey old Prudence grabs hold of the idea, calling it Sandbar's Sistine and insisting Elmie's and Angelo's works share similar themes: temptation, creation, expulsion, and devastation.'

'And does it?'

'Well, it depicts a special love story between a young Indigenous local and the Italian POW she'd helped hide from the authorities. Elmie's interpretation is very detailed if you know how to look, even identifying the part in the visual storyboard where her mum conceived—right there in the southern bunker—one week before their relationship was discovered and the soldier arrested and interned.'

'And you've seen this mural?'

'A long time ago.' Tad turned towards the headland that loomed above everything else to the north of the campground. 'This is the only view for me these days. But look closely and you'll see a dark hole three-quarters of the way up. That's the gunner's post—one of them—where soldiers kept watch, and where the girls hid. See it?'

'I-I think so.'

'Spotting it is not meant to be easy,' Tad said. 'There's a second lookout on the northern face of the cliff, but no one dares attempt that rabbit warren. Not until deemed safe by the defence services. I wish old Prudence was here to put a rocket up those Government bureaucrats. To date, all they've done is seal every tunnel access point and erect barbed wire fencing to annoy the locals who once traversed the headland to reach the northern beach. That said, while the rest of us have lived vicariously for decades through Prudence's dossier and Elmie's fabric designs, there was no keeping Elmie out. You've seen her kaftans? Her mother's painted walls are the inspiration.'

'I've seen one.' Chelsea recalled the mesmeric material. 'So, Elmie has a way in?'

'She's never admitted as much, and until engineers complete the long-awaited geotech reports there's no official accessing the headland, therefore no getting to Heartbreak Beach and the adjacent wetlands and forest. Unless, as I said, you're Elmie, or a daredevil—or Squid.'

'A squid?'

'Squid is a nickname for Talia's old man. Slippery old bloke and good with his hands,' Tad laughed. 'Reckons rules are made to be broken. I have a feeling he found a way through the old tunnels a long time ago, but he keeps stuff close to his chest, including where the fish are biting. He'll disappear for hours and come home with a catch big enough to share.'

'And he hasn't told you how he gets through?'

'Like I said, not much use me knowing.' Tad tapped on his stump. 'I'm also a lousy secret keeper.'

'And they took Connie away because of her skin colour?' Chelsea asked, keen to get back to the sisters' story.

'The government yanked both girls from poor Mary. Elmie had white skin, so a well-to-do family adopted her. They dumped Connie with children of the same colour at a child labour farm where she worked in market gardens. Elmie eventually found her way back here where she roamed the headland, revisiting the bunker and calling over the ocean to her sister.'

'Please,' Chelsea implored, 'tell me they found each other.'

Tad nodded. 'A few years before Connie's stomach cancer diagnosis. Poor old Elms. To this day she struggles to deal with all she's lost.'

'I understand accepting loss is difficult, but surely encouraging her to move on is more ...' Chelsea stopped talking aloud to tell herself, *Pot and kettle!*

'Like I said earlier, Chelsea, we live and let live around here. People find their way in their own time. And despite me going on and on, bemoaning the past to strangers, the Wandarri community is hardly a bunch of sad tragics. Most of us find our tribe—metaphorically speaking. Take me and Talia,' Tad said. 'She listens when I need to vent, and in return, I bake for her.'

Chelsea smiled. 'You bake?'

'Oi! Enough with the surprise face. I'm whipping up dessert for the monthly luau, which Talia and I coordinate. I promised trifle.'

'*You* make trifle?'

'Well, it's Squid's Spectacular Trifle recipe. He is the true trifle master in these parts—has been for decades—but Talia says he's in a flap over a phone call and a meeting in Ocean Sands tomorrow with an old friend. Must be someone special. Usually requires a seismic shift in the earth's tectonic plates to budge him from his piece of paradise on the hill. So, with Squid preoccupied, I'll be trifle king for a night. Come see for yourself. Not that you'll have much choice. We use the fire pit outside that camp kitchen.' He pointed across the road from *Sea-Esta* at the basic corrugated tin shelter covering a wood pile and huge dish-shaped fire pit.

'Easy decision then,' she said. 'Count me in.'

'I'm glad. You don't want to be one of those campers who gets here and does little else but sit inside their caravan watching TV.'

'I might—if your van had a TV,' she said, grinning.

'That's what I don't get.' Tad shrugged. 'Why bother coming if not to soak up all Mother Nature offers? Personally, I enjoy sunset walks. That's when the beach is at its best. There's something magical about the sea when the sun is setting.'

'But the sun sets in the west,' Chelsea said matter-of-factly. 'We're on the east coast, Tadpole. Surely sun*rise* over the ocean, and wondering what the day ahead holds, is better.'

'Prettier, perhaps,' Tad conceded, 'but a sunset stroll allows me to reflect on all the things I've achieved in the day. Speaking of which, work awaits. Oh, and a word of warning about Space Invader tonight,' he said. 'That's what we call Ivan, who sets up the roasting spit. You'll figure out why.'

With a final dog pat, Chelsea stood. 'And what does one wear to a luau?'

'With your hip action, you'd rock a grass skirt, but I'd go with long pants and long sleeves. We breed a discerning mosquito at Sandbar. One that comes out at sunset and likes attractive women with sun-kissed hair and sexy eyes.'

She laughed when she probably shouldn't have. But what the heck? The man seemed harmless enough and amusingly unperturbed by his occasional *faux pas*. Tadpole was a much-needed distraction, his enthusiasm for life and sunsets encouraging, and his unapologetic preservation of family possessions a pleasant change for Chelsea.

18

———

DALE

The sight of his daughter weaving around tables on the pub's alfresco dining deck surprised Dale straight in the chair.

'Way to go, Dad!' Gabby flashed her mother's smile. 'Never imagined I'd see you here on a Friday—or any day. Good on you for getting out and about.'

'I could say the same to you. What brings you here, little mama?'

'A well-deserved night of freedom with the girls while Mick plays dad with the twins. He all but locked me out of the house and said "go", which is why I'm early, although I think I can see Trudy One ordering a drink.'

'Trudy One?' Dale queried, squinting towards the bar and into the setting sun.

'Yeah! I've talked about the two women at work—Trudy One and Trudy Two. One day, they'll be my first official marriage celebrant gig.'

'Official?' Dale asked.

'As in lawful union. Trudy One, who works in Canberra, reckons same-sex marriages will get passed. It might be a couple of years, but by getting in first I can build my brand *and* a point of difference. I'll be the go-to for gay marriages.'

'That's my clever girl. All very sound decisions, I'd say.'

'Thanks to you, Dad.'

Dale was curious. 'Why me?'

'Well, I didn't get my decision-making skills from Mum.'

'Aw, Gabby, sweetheart, I wish you and your mum were—'

109

'Yeah, yeah, I hear you. Nice fedora,' she said, changing the subject. 'Another excellent choice of mine.' Gabby transferred the hat to her own head and struck a pose. 'What's the occasion, Dad? Meeting a friend?'

'A colleague is leaving.'

'Really?' Gabby made a point of glancing at the table for two he'd chosen for no particular reason except he wasn't really in a social mood. 'I see. Well, meet away!' She kissed him again and plonked the hat back on his head, laughing. 'Bumping into my dad in a Fremantle pub. That is the craziest and the coolest thing ever. I love it.' Then, as if sensing Dale's melancholy, she said, 'I'm sorry about you and Mum, but so glad you came to Perth. I'm super excited about Sunday. The twins love their Poppy. We can FaceTime Mum.'

'Maybe not. Mum's phone is playing up.'

'Oh? Okay, well, speaking of Sunday. Bringing a *colleague* is fine with me. Ooh, I see Trudy One waving. Must be our table. Better go, Dad. See you Sunday. Don't be late—and don't stay alone.'

'Wait!' He didn't want to make a fuss. The pub on a Friday was not the time or the place for what Gabby would call a 'D&M', but he worried about his daughter's relationship with her mother. Gabby was a loving wife and a great parent. She was a good daughter, too, but there'd been clashes—hurtful ones, as well as those mother and daughter moments of frustration. 'About your mum, Gabs ...'

Her grin dropped away. 'Sounds ominous.'

'She loves you,' Dale said. 'She wants to visit, but she's concerned about upsetting you more. Your Mum worries. Her relationship with her own mother was—*is*—problematic.' His daughter's Friday-night-and-I'm-free glimmer dulled as she dragged the spare seat beside him and plonked down hard, his moody and defiant little girl once more. As she leaned back, arms folded, mouth puckered, he said, 'She misses you, Gab. She wants the twins to know their grandmother.'

'I want the same, Dad,' she admitted. 'I miss her more than I thought I would, especially since the twins. I-I just never felt like a priority to Mum. She never cared about what I did.'

The words shocked Dale straight. 'Why would you think so?'

'Because, Dad, I never got that vibe at home. Any time I asked Mum what she thought or what I should do—about anything—she deferred to you. "Go ask your father", she'd tell me. Remember when I couldn't decide between a Dolly Varden birthday cake and a pavlova for my tenth birthday? Mum made one of each.'

Dale couldn't help but be amused. 'And this was a bad thing, sweetheart?'

'Yes! If you recall, I ate too much and puked up cake all over my new dress, and my best friend. The kids at school never let me forget. They called me *Dolly Varden Vomit Head*, and the puking-up incident followed me right through to my end-of-high-school formal when they crowned me *Dateless Dolly Varden Vomit Head*.'

Though said in jest, there was genuine hurt in her eyes. Dale moved to cuddle his daughter, but she shrugged away.

'Sweetheart, I had no idea.'

'I never said anything, but it was around that same time I decided to never grow up to be her—so agreeable and keen to please everyone. Only the strong make it today, Dad; not the Matildas of the world. Matilda Baker?' she said, responding to his quizzical expression. 'From school. Lived down the street.' Firing off the additional information achieved nothing. 'I'm sure I mentioned her, Dad. We kind of bonded because kids poked fun at her a lot, too. They were downright mean to Mati, but acceptance was so important that she'd say sorry for any reason, just to go along with the crowd.'

'I'm not following you, Gabs,' Dale said. 'What's this got to do with your mum?'

'Like Matilda, Mum never made waves. Even when Aunty Layla and Nanna were being mean to her, *she* would apologise to *them*.'

Dale waved away his daughter's concerns. 'Their family suffered a terrible tragedy.'

'Yes, and I believe Tyler and Travis—and not me—were the best thing for Mum.'

'How so, sweetheart?'

Another shrug. A sad one. 'Twins provided Mum with a legitimate reason to buy two of everything. No need to choose between the red and the blue, or the boat versus the race car cake. I get life hasn't been easy for Mum and she has *issues*, which is why, when people told me how much alike we were, I did everything to counter it.' Gabby teared up. 'Then, when I found out I was having twins, I feared becoming her—or worse, her mother. I wanted to be like Aunty Layla. She's so in control and doesn't care about anything.'

'Hey, hey, sweetheart. I so wish you'd mentioned this stuff before.' Dale tugged paper napkins from the holder on the table and pushed them into his daughter's hands. 'Mum's loved you forever.'

'She loves her dead father more. You understand that much. You've talked to Mum how many times about selling up? Every time she falls to pieces over Granddad's memory. I love you Dad, but I'm sorry.'

'Sorry for what?' Dale's thumb caught another tear on his daughter's cheek. 'Hey, come on.'

'You're so important to me, loving me, guiding me, but …'

'But what? What's this about?'

'I-I'm sorry, Mick is my family now. I love you, Dad, and as much as I want Mum around—I miss her, even though she makes me crazy—I can't turn into her, and I won't make *you* the most important man in my life, like she's done with her father. Does that make sense?'

'More than you know.' Dale shifted in his seat, turning to take Gabby's hands in his. 'I wish we'd had this conversation earlier. Family is important, and so is finding the one person who'll make you want to smile every day.' Dale tried sounding upbeat. 'That time you accused Mum of judging Mick? She admits to choosing the wrong words, and while I'm not defending her, I get where she was coming from. Her intentions were good. Growing through tough times as kids made both Mum and me more determined that our children would avoid heartache. Call her, Gab. Share your life with her. I promise you'll be glad. Now, *you* promise not to keep this stuff to yourself in the future.'

She nodded, and the pair sat staring at the last of the sun. 'Speaking of family … Aunty Layla and I met for coffee.'

'Oh?' While not his favourite person, if faced with a choice between Chelsea's sister or her irresponsible mother, Dale would pick Layla—if only because the pair stood in solidarity, sharing a frustration over Chelsea's father fixation. 'How is Layla?'

'Weird,' Gabby replied. 'Not weird, like when she visited the house. I mean, weird as in all she wanted to talk about was Mum—and you. I gave her your address and your new work number. She asked. Hope that's okay? And I hope your *colleague is* fun company tonight. You deserve happy, Dad. Hey!' She wiggled closer. 'Before the sun goes, let's do a selfie with you wearing your fedora.'

'Your Mum made sure I packed the hat. I love it *and* her,' he added, 'but marriages hit potholes.'

'And brick walls! You've wanted to get out of that house for as long as I can remember, Dad, so you'll understand why I had to leave. Smile for the camera!' Gabby positioned the mobile phone and squished up. *Snap.* 'If not Mick's job, I would've found another reason to move away.' Turning the camera on herself, Gabby inspected her makeup and fluffed her hair. 'All relationships have use-by dates. Even Mick and I work hard to stay the course. You and Mum might've been good once, and of course you'd still have feelings, but when it's time to move on for *you* ...' Another shrug. 'I'm simply suggesting you keep your options open. A woman who gets you and shares your passions could walk through those doors over there. So, at least be open to the possibility, Dad. It's a Friday night and you're too good a man to be on your own.'

'I'm in Perth for work, Gabs. It's giving Mum some space and time to miss me. I still love your mother.'

'And I love her, Dad, but when something's not good for you ... Anyway!' His daughter switched to Friday-fun-night mode, fussing with her hair, and blotting both moist cheeks with the tips of her fingers. 'Bet I look like crap.'

'You wear your resilience better than anyone, Gabby.'

A cheer erupting from the nearby table cut her hug short. 'Ooh, time I got over to the party.'

Another quick peck and a wave and his daughter dissolved into the alfresco bar crowd.

With the music volume cranking up, Dale felt uncomfortable sitting within cooee of his daughter's night of freedom. Also, Gabby's admission had disturbed him. He checked his watch, a gift from his wife to celebrate Dale moving from his finance administration job into field work as a children's guardian. While surprising his mates, Chelsea had supported the career move. She understood Dale in a way nobody else did, even suggesting, if ever there was a calling for him, it was taking kids from broken homes and matching them with the right foster family.

Dale Holt, the kid who came from nothing, knew every child deserved a chance to reach their potential and a safe and happy home life. Despite his wayward youth—or perhaps because of it—Dale identified opportunities. He'd come a long way, achieved so much. Why then, he mused, did he often feel like a runner-up to William Scott? And how had he fumbled so superbly with his own family?

The adjoining alfresco area was getting louder, and amid the cheers was his daughter's laughter; so much like her mother's. Whatever their individual faults, together Dale and Chelsea had produced amazing children. Gabby was confident, settled, and happy, while the twins were carving their own paths. Dale had nurtured all three, spoilt them, prepared them the best he could, and let them fly. Now *he* was flying the coop, confused and unsure of his future for the first time since meeting Chelsea.

The sound of an acoustic guitar, followed by the jarring screech of speaker feedback, drew Dale's attention to the band setting up in a corner of the outdoor deck. To one side stood Gabby and a girlfriend, the pair's body language suggesting a D&M in progress—to use his daughter's turn of phrase. Deep and meaningful conversations were not something men did much or well. The blokes Dale mixed with back east would happily and regularly share a beer, a joke, and a locker room, but never their emotions. Men rarely admitted to feeling lonely and unwanted. Most seemed resigned to their lot in life: toe the line, go with the flow, what will be will be. Not Dale. He had lost too many life chapters to the foster care system.

Time to turn the pages, write new ones, live life.

To date, however, Dale's socialising had been mostly cups of tea with potential foster parents. Some couples he screened were young—childless, for various reasons. Others, like Anna and Russell in their sixties, showed no signs of wanting to stop fostering. The world needed more people like Anna and Russell—a couple with no concept of empty nest syndrome and no desire to experience it. Such caring people, they couldn't be more different from Dale's corporate cohort, most of them parents who considered it socially acceptable to rejoice when no longer required to provide for the children. According to them, men did *not* suffer from empty nest syndrome. Women were the primary nurturers, tending the nest and struggling emotionally once the chicks could fend for themselves.

But as Dale discovered, dads also struggled with feelings of redundancy in their children's lives. Even before his children became adults, Dale had felt sidelined as a dad. When Gabby was around twelve, Chelsea had suggested it was no longer appropriate for him to enter his daughter's bedroom, or the bathroom, without knocking. While she'd delivered the blow softly, and he wasn't being asked to stop being a dad, Dale had experienced an instant disconnect. A pre-pubescent daughter meant things in the Holt household would be done differently, with Dale forced to adapt.

'And you did okay,' Dale reminded himself, noticing how his daughter stood out from the crowd.

Gabby was a capable young woman because he'd let her thrive in the same way his mate and mentor, Bill Field, had loosened the tether while still being there for him. God, he loved that man. Bill had shown young Dale the type of children's guardian he wanted to be when he grew up and became one.

Dale recalled their last catch-up. Bill had shown no signs of the cancer trying to impact his case load. Instead, he was at his desk doing what he did best—finding kids their forever families. Behind him was the familiar wall poster and quote. Featuring an archer—bow taught, arrow at the ready—the words read:

> *Parents are the bows from which children, as living arrows, are sent forth. The stronger the bow, the further and straighter the arrow flies.*

There was no questioning Dale's and Chelsea's parenting. They'd kept all three kids on the straight and narrow. But with their fledglings flying into new phases, Chelsea and Dale had turned into two people sharing the same void; at least they were before Dale walked away. Chelsea had likened his move to a mid-life crisis. Was she right? Dale swigged the last of the lukewarm beer. Was Perth about his discontent with her, or a pathetic and slightly creepy attempt to emulate his children's freedom? Maybe carrying the weight of decision-making throughout their marriage had brought him across the country and deposited him in a one-bedroom studio that had no hope of ever feeling like a home.

Gabby was spot on about one thing. Chelsea had deferred all decision-making to him, but it was wrong to assume it was indifference on her mother's part.

What is it about the women in my life? They certainly knew him better than he knew himself. If Dale was an expert in anything, it was identifying the early signs of childhood trauma and its effects later in life. He'd spotted the signs in Chelsea's behaviour in class, and in the attention-getting stunts that had landed her in detention.

Why was Dale only now realising he'd allowed his own traumatic childhood experiences to drive *his* need to find a place to belong, ultimately affecting his relationship? It was easy to blame a rough start to life. Do-gooders had all agreed *Baby Dale*—the infant delivered six weeks premature by cesarian from his deceased mother's womb—would need guarding and guidance. But post hospital, there'd been no protection afforded him until Bill came along on Dale's fifteenth birthday. As a boy, all Dale had wished for was to give love, receive love, and be valued. While each new foster placement had come with the promise of a family and a forever home, rather than a place to belong with people who wanted him, Dale remained a visitor, an interloper, a presence but with no place at the table and no picture on the wall. Worse still, he'd been an inconvenience to most; his only value to the so-called 'kind carers' was securing their regular government handouts.

Then Chelsea stepped inside the classroom and changed his world. Like him, she had needed to give and to receive love. Dale was incredibly lucky to find someone to protect, to make all the decisions for, and to make a home and a family with.

'So, what the hell are you doing here?' he muttered.

If this *was* a mid-life crisis, no career change, snazzy car, or high sea adventure would satisfy Dale. Much simpler, he wanted his wife to step with him into their next chapter because he didn't want to write it without her. He now worried that leaving her alone to miss him might backfire, as evidenced by her solo camping trip. Chelsea seemed not to need him like she used to do. *What's changed?* Or had they, as a couple, not changed enough and the moving-house mandate did little else but slice into that frayed connection?

As Dale tried counting each occasion he'd phoned Chelsea because he missed the sound of his wife's laugh, he heard his daughter's and saw her friends donning sparkly tiaras and huddling together selfie-style. He checked the time on his own phone. Should he call Chelsea and ask her outright? *Do you need me? Do you love me for me—and not because I fill a void left behind by your father?*

Thumb hovering over the call button, wondering if he should take his midlife crisis out for a test drive, he caught sight of two women walking through the doors to the deck. Sheila's eyes almost popped out of her head and the pair peeled apart in a kind of well-coordinated maneuverer. In jeans and a tight V-necked top, hair draped over her shoulders rather than pinched back in the usual ponytail, Sheila Matthews looked different. Younger. *Too young!*

'Hello there, Dale!' Lips puckered, she closed in on the cheek Gabby had kissed not ten minutes ago. 'We've booked a table for twelve inside and I'll be needing a man's insight to settle an argument Tessa and I are having.'

'I, ah, sorry, Sheila.' Dale shifted uneasily, knocking his fedora so it sat skew-whiff on his head. 'I'm going home.'

'Oh, well, can't blame a girl for trying.' She reached up to straighten his hat. 'Do I understand by "home" you mean to Scarborough Beach tonight? Or does your heart lie in Sydney?'

She knew the score. Dale had made a point of playing with his wedding band when in meetings, or repositioning Chelsea's photo every time Sheila perched her butt on his desk to *chat*.

'Lucky Sydney! I assume you know many people will be sad to see you go. You are admired, Dale Holt,' she added. 'I'll go now and catch up to the others. See you at the office on Monday.'

19

DALE

In the car and headed to Scarborough Beach, Dale detoured to the local bottle shop to buy a six-pack of beer. Approaching the drive-thru entrance, he slowed. Then, changing his mind, he sped straight ahead. Though he'd love another drink, he'd witnessed his sister-in-law's booze and drug dependency in action too many times early in his marriage. These days, Dale found other ways to feel good. It used to be spending time with his wife, sharing a meal or quiet time together once the kids were in bed. Often, a board game came out of the cupboard. As a Scrabble opponent, his wife could be quite intimidating. In a game of chance, she could be as lucky as anyone else. In Monopoly, however, his gorgeous wife was useless, with her indecision over which property to buy or sell once endearing. Had Dale inadvertently enabled the behaviour he now found so vexing?

As he steered the car through the Scarborough streets, Dale recalled his daughter's reaction to the work-supplied Toyota Land Cruiser.

'Ooh! You've always wanted a touring car. We can fit out the back seat with twin baby seats and go driving once a month. I'll ride shotgun with you while Mick leads the way on his bike. It'll be fantastic.'

Dale *had* dreamed of crossing The Nullarbor and driving isolated beaches of Australia. And while Mick was a top bloke—the love for his family humbling—Dale's preferred company was his wife's. Chelsea, however, was four-thousand kilometres away, pop-riveted to a house, and petrified of the ocean.

Parking his car in the apartment's designated space, Dale ambled towards the ground-floor pizza joint enjoying good trade, as usual. Preferring takeout, he headed to the counter until spotting a face in the crowd. The woman stood.

What the hell is she doing here?

'Hello, Dale. Figured I'd spot you if I waited long enough. I'm happy you did. We need to talk.'

20

CHELSEA

From *Sea-Esta's* cosy dining nook, Chelsea watched a man tease out red-hot coals with a metal poker. His outfit, comprising cowboy hat, jeans with boots, and a striped shirt rolled to his elbows, reminded her that while this caravan park sat on the edge of the Pacific Ocean, a little west was the Great Dividing Range. The mountainous, mostly green belt separating the coast from the country was the gateway to prime New South Wales pastoral land, where quaint B&Bs, offering luxury Wendy Scott would love, punctuated the landscape. Not that Wendy was lacking luxury with husband number-three having a proclivity for P&O cruises. Did the woman still nitpick over finding the odd fish bone? And did Layla, who as a teenager had deplored peeling stinky prawns, still refuse food that had breathed air before being served up on a plate?

'Fish don't breathe air through their mouth, silly,' Chelsea had told her big sister one time. 'They get oxygen from the water. Right Dad?'

'Sure do, and the fish that keeps its mouth shut doesn't get caught,' Dad added. 'Lesson learned, my girls.'

While William Scott loved giving life lessons, Chelsea had learned plenty on her own. She'd read books and asked teachers, but some information found *her*—coming in shouted whispers from her parents' bedroom while Layla sat alone in the lounge room, *Countdown* blaring through the TV speakers.

'Bloody hell, Wendy! I'm not sure what you expect of me. A lesser man would walk away. But I promised to honour and obey, and I've never shirked my responsibilities. I love those girls.'

'And if you love me, William, you'll stop being an embarrassment, get rid of the pathetic ponytail, and chuck out the ridiculous beach pants you wear absolutely everywhere. As for that outfit, you are not wearing the stupid magic jar choker to a wedding. Get rid of it, or at least cover the thing with a tie. You're no longer a sixteen-year-old surfer boy.'

'I wear a tie five days a week, Wendy. Besides, there are no hard and fast rules these days. Look what Martha Tighe wore last year to her son's wedding. You said everyone was talking about the inappropriateness of the cream-coloured monstrosity.'

'Yes,' Mum replied, 'and no doubt we'll all be talking about a similarly shameful choice for daughter-in-law-number-two's wedding.'

'Exactly,' Dad retorted, 'which is why no one will pay me any attention. And about my hair ...'

'Stop that!' Mum snapped. A slap and a giggle followed.

'You know the effect on that Samson guy from the Bible when Delilah lopped off his locks.' As Dad's big belly laugh softened, Chelsea pressed her ear harder to the wall. 'You don't want me losing my *va-va-va-voom* like Samson, do you?' Another giggle, then silence until Dad's baritone singing voice reverberated off the walls: '*Oh! My, my, my Delilah!*'

At that moment, Chelsea decided she would marry someone smart and funny, just like her dad.

'Come on over,' Tad called from the fire pit as Chelsea exited the van and slipped into her thongs.

Tote bag loaded with the required B.Y.O. items, she hung the key lanyard around her neck and tried inhaling some enthusiasm before heading across to join the gathering.

'Everyone, this is Chelsea,' Tadpole announced, pocketing the ten-dollar note she proffered. 'Welcome to Wandarri's legendary luau. Can I interest you in a traditional welcome beer?'

'Beer is a luau tradition?' Chelsea queried. 'Do you also offer a traditional lei?'

There was a beat of silence as Chelsea realised her mistake, then someone behind sniggered.

'Now there's an idea,' Tad said with a wink. 'Happy luau, everyone.'

A fizzy chorus of cheers, laughter, and carbonation erupted as the crowd twisted beer bottle caps simultaneously, tossing them into the fire.

'Elms!' Tad waved the latest arrival over. '*Giinagay!*' he said, quickly explaining the word belongs to the local *Gumbaynggirr* people; the original custodians of the land on which they celebrated.

Bra-less under the pink singlet, and her legs lost in loose-fitting harem pants, Elmie sported a crown of pink Frangipani flowers pushed low on her forehead.

'*Aloha!*' she greeted Chelsea.

'Our Elmie likes a good lei, don't you, Elms?' Tad chuckled. 'Let me squish over so you can sit that skinny butt.'

'No, thank you, cheeky boy. You're forgetting Connie and I help Talia.'

'Tals is running late,' he said, adding in a low voice for Chelsea's benefit, 'An emergency trip to the doctor with Kai after a mishap at home earlier today required a tetanus shot. He sure keeps his doctor busy, but most adventurous boys do.'

'Not only boys,' Chelsea said. 'I was quite the tomboy and loved the outdoors. My sister not so much. We were different.'

'Different how?' Tad asked.

'Well, for one, she liked boys.'

Tad's obvious disappointment drove his usual grin down. 'And you don't?'

'What I *meant* about Layla is she's older and boys soon superseded everything, including annoying little sisters.'

'Ah, puberty blues and priorities. I remember those carefree beach days,' he said. 'If you still enjoy outdoor adventures, about an hour's drive away into the mountains behind Wandarri is a nice walking track, and I happen to be dropping materials to Ivan tomorrow. He has a welder, and we need a bigger fire pit. Happy to have you along for the ride. You can drop by the caravan around ten. I'll be in there finishing paperwork. Or, if for some reason I'm not, use the two-way on the table in the annex to track me down. Way more range and more reliable than the mobile network. We can make a day of it if you like and have a pub lunch.'

'What about Talia and Kai?' she asked.

'Talia? Well, she's busy with the shop, but ...' He cocked his head to one side. 'I can check with her about Kai. She appreciates some respite. On a good day, Squid might hold the fort, but ... Oh, speak of the devil.'

Wearing a different peasant-style skirt, sky-blue and teamed with a flowing yellow shirt tied in a knot at her waist, Talia waved and headed Chelsea's way. Her other hand had hold of the energetic Kai.

'Looks like the tetanus shot is forgotten. Is Mr It-Wasn't-Me still brooding?' Tad asked.

'He's apologised a million times,' Talia said. 'Took his eyes off Kai at the wrong time. He has seemed distracted of late, but you and I both know how he is when the fish are biting.' Giving in to Kai's constant tugging, Talia let the boy go, yelling at him to slow down, and telling Tad, 'Keep watch while I do my catering bit.'

'Can I help?' Chelsea asked.

'Yes, keep Tadpole away from the food until we're ready.' She sent a wink his way and sashayed off.

Tad was telling Chelsea about the tourist drive through the hinterland when Ivan announced they should grab a plate and get in before the bugs. Moving in an orderly clockwise fashion, diners snapped metal tongs at the mound of freshly sliced meat, squirted sauce bottles, and scooped spoonfuls of coleslaw and salad. After loading her plate, adding peeled prawns on the side, Chelsea perched on one end of a long log away from the fire. After twenty-four hours of the make-do rations she'd brought from home, eating soon superseded speaking, while Talia and Tadpole, sharing the same log, never seemed to run out of conversation and things to laugh about.

What a difference! She and Dale seemed to have forgotten how to discuss anything other than the house and Chelsea's opposition to moving.

With her stomach full, and having twice escaped the man they called Space Invader, Chelsea was content being on the periphery of the party. She might have said goodnight an hour ago, except the campfire flames sparked memories of her dad one winter weekend while burning garden waste in the backyard incinerator. When embers had exploded into the night sky, raining down like burning confetti, Chelsea recalled holding the hose and being told by Dad to wet the cinders where they landed. But the flecks of fire never did land.

'The sparks all disappear in the air,' she'd told him.

'You're wrong,' he'd replied. 'Red-hot sparks turn black to trick us into thinking they're gone. Then we walk away and—*whoosh!*—those dead embers take on a new life. Not seeing something doesn't mean it's not there. Lesson learned, Chelsea-girl.'

A small explosion in the luau's fire ignited a medley of swear words from those gathered nearby, with cinders dancing skyward in a whorl before disappearing into the blackness. Even Tadpole jumped in fright, while Talia buried herself against him, her giggly scream lost in the man's bulky chest.

Chelsea stood. She had to get away fast from the fire, from the idea of disappearing embers, and from happy families.

'Thanks again for inviting me.'

'Going already?' Talia sounded genuinely disappointed. 'Sorry if Tadpole and I have been ignoring you. We're just—'

'Oh, no, don't apologise,' Chelsea gushed. 'I think maybe the fire's glare and smoke is too much. Nothing a cuppa won't fix. Nice to see you again, Talia. Kai is a lovely boy. Goodnight.'

21

LAYLA

'What's going on?' her brother-in-law asked. 'What are doing here? First, a visit to Gabby. Now me.'

'I'm used to quick catch ups with my niece. But when she told me you were in town, I wanted to speak in person before heading east tomorrow and seeing Chelsea.'

'Chelsea's not at home. Your sister is camping—at Sandbar.'

'Yes, and that's partly why you and I need to talk.'

Her brother-in-law shoved the travel bag across the seat opposite before sliding into the booth. 'About what?'

'The truth,' she replied. 'And I'll need you to get your backside into gear and get home to your wife because, when I'm done telling her, Chelsea will require support from someone she trusts and loves. That person is unlikely to be me ever again. So, Dale, I'm hoping you'll be there.'

'You've gotta give me more, Layla. More time and more detail. Getting away from work won't be easy with so many custody cases pending, but with a compelling argument, my boss might be agreeable to a short break.'

'No! You can't tell him anything. You can't tell anyone what I'm about to tell you.'

'My line of work demands confidentiality, so whatever this is about, rest assured—'

'You're not hearing me, Dale. *This* is life-changing, and believe it or not, your life—your marriage—is my motivation. But I owe it to Chelsea to tell her first.'

'Okay, Layla, now you're freaking me out. You've gotta tell me what this is about, or,' he said, taking the phone from his pocket, 'I'm dialling my wife and asking her.'

'Fine,' Aware there was no turning back, she reached over and gently forced his hand with the phone back to the table. 'Make it takeout for two, and I'll tell you what I'm going to tell Chelsea.'

22

CHELSEA

Having washed away the malodour of the night's fire, and with a teabag brewing, Chelsea picked up the little conch shell from the beside shelf and stroked the glossy surface before pressing the opening against her ear. Hearing the sound a shell makes, she wondered how it was possible for something so small to capture and store the sea's sounds for decades, while she struggled to recall the details of one day. Stranger still was how the white noise of the shell's inner sea calmed rather than stirred her ocean phobia.

Maybe the shell was whispering: *You've got this, the monster is not real. Time to get your butt to the beach, pronto!*

'Definitely tomorrow,' she said aloud, as if speaking locked in the commitment. 'And early.' Before beachcombers set about scouring the shoreline. Fewer people on the beach would mean fewer spectators, should she experience a meltdown like that time at Bondi.

Taking her tea outside to sit in the dark, only the light from inside the van shining behind her, Chelsea plonked into one of two folding camp chairs, her thoughts rewinding to the day she and Dale thought cramming three impatient youngsters in the sedan's squishy backseat and driving two hours to Bondi Beach—on a Sunday—was a good idea.

Six laps of the parking area later, Dale had somehow squeezed the station wagon into the smallest of spaces before unloading the kids and every conceivable floatation device. Their excitement palpable, the trio had followed their father like obedient ducklings across the bitumen, unaware Chelsea remained rooted by the car, her panic paralysing, major meltdown imminent. A fuss ensued as people pointed, and her pleading and distressed children danced on hot tar. Then, after an ambulance ride and three hours waiting in Emergency, it was back to the western suburbs with bickering children in the backseat and the setting sun branding their eyeballs.

'Sorry!' Talia said when Chelsea startled. 'I didn't want to interrupt, but you left before dessert and, well, Tadpole insisted you try his trifle.' She presented the paper bowl laden with sponge and cream and fruit. 'Being here with only your memories for company can't be easy. Do you want some?'

'Yes to trifle and company.' Chelsea smiled. '*If* I'm not keeping you from the party.'

'You're not.' Talia settled into the second camp chair beside Chelsea. 'We've reached that time of night when the crowd splits up into like-minded groups. Escaping the clean-up makes a pleasant change.'

'Ah, men gathering around the fire and women doing dishes.'

Talia laughed. 'Not quite. Misogyny—or any discrimination—demands a public flogging in these parts. Prudence Poulle wrote it into the first Official Wandarri Handbook. I'm joking, of course. We have rules—any official community needs guidelines—and while far from the perfect bunch, we manage most everything on a handshake.'

'What exactly is an official community?' Chelsea asked.

'In Prudence Poulle's day, the term used was *Intentional Community*, which to some out there translated into a pot-smoking commune intent on claiming Government handouts. Far from it, we remain good, self-sustaining citizens who contribute to society like anyone else, but with an emphasis on communing with nature.'

'I've never heard of one.'

'Communities don't advertise,' Talia said. 'There are similar places throughout New South Wales and around the country, all intent on reducing their carbon footprint and preserving precious habitats. The only time Wandarri brought attention to themselves was when fighting to retain the beach north of Bunker Headland as pristine coastal landscape. It's an example of how the area was before our political leaders allowed coastline over-development.

'Wandarri-ites were environmentally responsible long before most people had heard the term "sustainable living". The old vans you see skirting the campground's southern end are hangovers from an era when family groups time-shared. Some still do. The Wandarri Eco-Community —for the original parcel holders—is a gated section and further along the gravel access road.'

'Parcels?' Chelsea asked.

'Community land. Gifts from nature and from those who inhabited the country before us. These days, Wandarri parcels come with a hefty price tag and the older section still has original dwellings—shacks, mostly. The newer developments incorporate solar energy, which powers the caravan park and water treatment plant. How some folks live off the grid must be seen. Conservation Castles!' Talia chuckled. 'Ask Tadpole for a tour. It's a quiet time, until next week when school is out, and not all members reside here permanently.'

'Why not?'

'The realities of life mostly,' Talia explained. 'Family responsibilities, no reliable internet for remote learning and work, while those who inherited parcels from family members are simply reluctant. They either don't think they want this life or aren't ready to leave the rat race behind. Some singles have shacked up together and sold their spare parcel. One couple, both FIFO workers, rarely cross paths with each other. Wouldn't suit me, but everyone's idea of marriage is different. "To each their own" remains Wandarri's philosophy, even though the place has changed a lot.

'The village is ninety percent self-sufficient. There is a dam for our agriculture, rainwater tanks for drinking, plus we recycle responsibly in our purpose-built sorting shed. We have all sorts of professional people and intellectuals, but no class system. We're also very family oriented when it comes to passing on knowledge and ownership. Everyone contributes equally, except the elderly or infirm.' Talia's voice softened. 'Sadly, the one thing we haven't been able to do is maintain facilities to allow our elders to spend their final season in their homes. As a founding member, my old dad would prefer to live his days here, but medical needs make it tricky. We're desperate to rectify this, but such projects take time. Our newsletter keeps members informed of evolving agreements, topics of debate, and all hatches, matches and dispatches, while the luau—and Elmie—take care of gossip. Be warned! The woman doesn't miss a trick. I dread the day we need to make alternate living arrangements for her.

'Meanwhile,' Talia perked up. 'I love being on the hill. Kai is free to make as much noise as he likes, and the beach is closer than it looks—for those in the know. Perfect for a keen surfer and fisherman, and I have those,' Talia said. 'The best beaches in the world are at our doorstep. Nowhere better to raise a family. Nowhere!'

'Nowhere?' Chelsea echoed through a sigh. 'Yes, our family loved this place.'

'You didn't mention a husband when we chatted yesterday, Chelsea, but I noticed the tan mark on your ring finger. You and hubby never holidayed here with your own kids?'

'No.' Chelsea fingered the pale spot devoid of the gold bands. She'd tucked both rings safely into the coin section of her wallet, fearing the soft metal would lose its shape as she hammered pegs. 'When did you marry, Talia?'

'We didn't—not legally. Our beach ceremony was without a whiff of tradition. My father, bless him, walked me across the sand, then left us to speak our vows in private. He believed I was making a mistake,' she explained. 'Had Mum been alive, she would have made him see things differently; she would've been wonderful with Kai, too.'

Chelsea huffed. 'My mother's idea of being a grandmother is to send exorbitant amounts of cash in a card each birthday.'

Talia's hand was small and warm where she rested it on Chelsea's forearm. 'How sad to miss out on what's most important. Having a grandchild to spoil has been fabulous for Dad. Before the dementia, he enjoyed watching Kai become one with Wandarri.'

'You and Kai and Tadpole need to treasure every moment, Talia.'

The woman's questioning expression swiftly turned to amusement.

'Tadpole? Not likely—and he's not Kai's father, either. Speaking of my son … He's been running around the house all afternoon chanting, "Chelsea! Chelsea! Chelsea!". Funny how he's connected with you. Ordinarily, Kai is like his dad—a man who tolerates social interaction to a point, reckoning he gets enough at the shop. Every luau, he stays long enough to wash down a meal with a beer and to find out where the fish will be biting in the morning. Fish or no fish, the beach is his happy place.'

Mine too—once, Chelsea could have said, but she'd clap-trapped enough about her life to this woman and feared more embarrassing gaffs.

'Thanks for checking on me, Talia. And thank Tadpole for the invitation—and the trifle. It's the best.'

'About Tad,' Talia said, standing. 'While quite the catch, I wish any woman luck trying to land him. Not that he's a player,' she added. 'Although he was in his youth; inevitable with a mum who swanned around like the Queen of Wandarri. Girls who came for holidays all vied for his attention. When they said goodbye, however, they left Tad brokenhearted. Uh-oh, there I go over-sharing again. The man needs to tell his own stories. Speaking of Tadpole … He and Kai will be up to no good with the leftovers. See-ya 'round.'

As Talia wandered back towards the fire, Chelsea couldn't help thinking there was a message in the late-night *tête-à-tête* regarding Tadpole. But was the woman warning off a stranger, or protecting the long-time friend who'd suffered too many broken hearts? It didn't matter. Chelsea wasn't looking for love. She'd already found her soul-mate, even if he was trying out a new life on the other side of the country.

Washing down her trifle with warm tea, Chelsea snuggled deeper into the comfortable camp chair and took in a moon ten times more brilliant than the one she'd stared at through bleary eyes the night Dale told her what she already knew.

'We no longer want the same things, Chels.'

'Our priorities are different,' he told her. 'Maybe we were too young, or we married too soon. It's natural we might grow apart.'

Sitting forward in separate armchairs in the lounge room, the pair fell silent, mirroring each other: heads bowed, forearms resting on thighs, hands fisted and locked between knees.

'I still love you, Dale.'

'And leaving for Perth doesn't mean I've stopped loving you, Chels, or that I won't miss you. The thing is, I want to be *in* love with the person I'm married to. I'm not sure we're there anymore.'

'I don't understand,' she said, sounding as hurt as she felt. 'Is this some sort of mid-life crisis? Are you missing that light-headed, tummy tingling, teenage-crush sensation?'

'Aren't you?' His words slapped Chelsea speechless. 'Damn it, that came out wrong. Look, I'm happy to grow old, and yes, I miss the tummy-tingling bits—you can't crucify a person for that—but more than anything, I'm terrified we rushed into marrying, and the kids are the glue.' His head drooped lower still. 'Now they're grown, we need to figure out what makes *us* happy and if we're meant to be together.'

'I see, and the way to do that is by leaving?'

'It's been you and me since high school, Chels. I'm not sure who I am on my own. Maybe Perth is about testing the waters to see if I can live without you.'

Chelsea stiffened. 'And I'm assuming there will be plenty of fish to test over in those Perth waters?'

'Don't read more into this time away, hon. I honestly don't know anything, other than I'm incredibly unhappy my life has ground to a halt.'

Incredibly unhappy! Chelsea guzzled the tea dregs. For weeks, his words had plagued her, right up until the night before Dale was due to fly to Perth. Both had slept badly, with their routine morning cuddle slipping clumsily into what Chelsea could only call sad sex. Two hours later, she'd watched her husband walk out of their house.

Two weeks after that, she packed away her little pity party, convinced Vicki she would not turn to booze—or turn into Wendy—and returned to her long-standing classroom teacher support position, which she enjoyed for the rules and routines required when mentoring kids with cognitive disabilities.

Where were the rules for dysfunctional marriages? Was there one set for her and a different set for Dale, who got to dangle his line in those W.A. waters and wait for nibbles? Was Chelsea also supposed to wait? Not that it had occurred to her to do anything else. He'd said not to read too much into his relocation, and insisted most couples "had their moments", while some needed to "modify their lives" and "work through issues".

Friends had used all the above and more in the past to describe their marriage woes. But the night Chelsea broke down in the middle of her book club discussion—a novel about infidelity—Vicki had dragged her away for coffee, plied her with positive thoughts, and suggested she enjoy her freedom by hitting the club/pub scene to listen to a band. Twice Chelsea went along with Vicki before discovering there was little enjoyment seeing mature women dressing and acting like teenagers on a dance floor. Or worse, drinking in dingy dungeons, singing "I Will Survive", and lamenting their losses while posting soppy sayings on social media and waiting for true love to send them a friend request.

'I honestly can't be bothered,' she'd told Vicki over the phone one Friday afternoon. Standing at the end of her bed, her mother-of-three clothes strewn in uncoordinated combinations, she'd added, 'I own only two bras—one white and one skin-tone—and neither have fancy straps meant for public display with off-the-shoulder tops. Thanks, but the answer's no to tonight, and every night.'

Chelsea had her true love—no skimpy sequinned tops or tight skirts required. What those few nights out pretending to be single had done was let Chelsea see living without Dale was not an option. Now she needed to tell him, but with her phone on charge in *Sea-Esta* as Tadpole had suggested—"to help dry the innards out"—she didn't know the time; only that it was three hours earlier in Western Australia and a Friday night, which put Dale in prime water-testing time, or at home feeling miserable and missing his wife.

'Goodnight, Chelsea,' Tadpole called as he passed by *Sea-Esta.* 'Don't forget our date tomorrow. Weather should be good for the drive up and back.'

'Actually, Tadpole.' She stood, ready to head inside. A wind-shift was making the pounding ocean sound too close. 'I'll take a raincheck on that drive.'

'In that case, I'll tell Ivan he's got me for the day. He wants a hand with the welding. Goodnight. Sleep tight.'

After igniting a gas jet to boil the kettle for more tea, Chelsea settled at the dinette and reached for the phone, praying for a connection. It had to work. Dale had to hear every word loud and clear. As the screen illuminated, her attention shifted from the three bars of reception to the thirty-three Facebook notifications. *Thirty-three?* Launching the app, the first post in her newsfeed was Gabby's selfie-style picture with Dale in his fedora. The remaining photos of bleary-eyed young women—some sporting Bride of Frankenstein getups—were typical of a drunken hen's night. So why was Dale amongst the pictures?

Scrolling back over the images of pretty women with exaggerated poses, pouty lips, and red eyes, Chelsea zoomed to see beyond her daughter's close-up. A man was seated at a table for two, and in the company of a woman. The hat was familiar, not so the female. *Dale?* Was her husband dating, sharing a meal in a Fremantle pub while wearing the fedora she'd packed for him?

How dare he! Had she not declined Vicki's Bali suggestion, she could be doing her own bump and grind in a Kuta nightclub, and with a bevy of new bras to show off. Instead, she was at Sandbar Campground on a Friday night, fending off the Space Invader and avoiding the flirtations of a married man who, as it turned out, was *not* married, *is* rather lovely, and wants to spend the day with her tomorrow.

It's one day! Where was the harm in that?

23

CHELSEA, DAY 3 OF 7

There's no mistaking the roar of a wave swelling in height and strength. Then there's a moment of silence before the monster breaks and spews sea foam into the air. Chelsea holds on as the caravan lifts, rising higher and higher until it teeters on the wave's crest. Suddenly, the dumper breaks, and down, down, down goes *Sea-Esta*, tumbling over and over, filling fast. Chelsea must escape the water. But how when in place of the caravan's panes of hard plastic are porthole-type windows with rubber plugs wedged tight?

She screams. 'Help me! I'm drowning!'

'The plug, Chelsea!' Tadpole yells. 'Pull the plug, or your family will drown with you.'

'My family?' She turns to find Dale, Gabby, the twins, Layla, Wendy and … 'Dad? Oh, Dad, help me pick the right plug. We're drowning in this place.'

Her father laughs. 'You can't drown in a caravan, Chelsea-girl. Let your fear set you free. Become one with the sea. Be a mermaid.'

'But I'm not a mermaid. I have no tail. Layla! Layla, help me. Cut your hair, Layla. I need my tail. Help me!'

'No way!' Layla says. 'What good is sacrificing my hair for a tail when you're scared of the ocean?'

'Please, Layla, I'll try hard not to be. Layla?'

But her sister is gone, Dale is walking away with the children, and everyone else has deserted her.

Chelsea is alone, and she's drowning.

Screaming and gasping for air, the sheets tangled tight around her legs, a knocking on the window above her head startled Chelsea upright.

'You okay in there?'

'Hang on,' she said, jumping up and straightening her T-shirt and shorts before opening the door to find a one-legged Thaddeus teetering on two crutches and wearing nothing but striped pyjama shorts. He must have noticed Chelsea eyeballing his bare chest because when her eyes met his, Tad grinned.

'Sorry, didn't have time to change. Your calls for help woke me. Good or bad?' he asked. 'Your dream, I mean.'

'Um, bad—and weird. Thanks for checking on me,' she said, grateful the man-sized cardigan she'd packed purposely was within her grasp; Tad was not leaving. Slipping her arms into the roomy sleeves, she wrapped the garment tight and folded both arms across her braless boobs. 'I think I fell asleep listening to the ocean and, unlike most people, pounding waves don't lull me to sleep. I should've factored that into my camping plans.' The man's curious expression demanded she clarify, but not while half-awake, half-dressed, and mortified about admitting to nightmares at her age. 'Sounds crazy, Tad, but I can't explain.'

'You probably can,' he countered. 'We can clear up most things when we have a good listener. I happen to be *very* good, but only when coffee's involved. Your screams did wake me. Something about pulling a plug?'

'Best come in.' Chelsea stepped back from the door. 'I'll make us both a drink and tell you the part you played in my dream.'

'You're dreaming about me? Nice!' he said. Discarding the walking sticks outside, he part hopped, part pulled himself into the van before swinging his body onto the dinette seat. 'Fire up the kettle, then fire away.'

'How's that for weird?' Chelsea finished, having disclosed all she was prepared to, no matter how easy Tad had made the telling. 'You *are* a good listener.'

'Then you won't mind a question,' he said, doing that signature scratch-head-in-confusion thing. 'Why come to Sandbar Beach if you have a fear of the ocean?'

Chelsea stopped hand-batting the empty mug back and forth on the table but didn't look up. 'You might say it's a form of self-imposed exposure therapy. Confronting the source of an anxiety over and over can re-program the brain.'

'Hmm!' Tad sat back, bemused. 'And how's that therapy working out for you so far?'

'Not well, given I'm yet to step foot beyond the campground. I planned on a walk to the dunes today—early, while the ocean is calm. The nightmare was probably me getting worked up.'

'Can't comment on the dream analysis,' Tad said, 'but I can't find fault in your decision to hit the beach early. Nice way to clear the head, and a bit of Zen state of mind will shake off that nightmare.' He slid out of the dinette to stand. The man's agility was amazing. 'I'll let you get to it. Lucky and I are heading off for the day.' At the door, he let out a short, ear-piercing whistle before negotiating the single step to grab his walking aids and pause to whisper praise to his dog. 'Good boy! I hope you enjoy the beach, Chelsea.'

'I'll try,' she muttered as both man and his best friend limped away.

Too churned up to eat breakfast, she dressed in black gym pants and a T-shirt, hoping short sleeves was cover enough. Unlike mid-summer at home, until the sun warmed, coastal breezes chilled the air. With her dad's old cardigan—for comfort rather than warmth—she stepped into the early morning air, sat on the small step, and stalled by tying and re-tying her shoelaces. Then she searched the car and caravan for a puffer, finding one in her handbag, as usual.

Finally, Chelsea took a deep breath and headed purposefully towards the beach track while mentally poking around that special part of her memory for a suitable William Scott affirmation to provide courage.

AFFIRMATIONS WITH DAD, 1978

'What's a *affamayshon?*' I ask, standing on the shoreline.

'Well,' Dad starts, 'affirmations involve words or phrases that you repeat—either aloud or to yourself—to help make negative thoughts vanish.'

'You mean like when a magician says "abracadabra" and things disappear?'

Dad huffs a laugh. 'Affirmations are special, but they're not magic, and by themselves, they can't change anything. To work, an affirmation needs you, and what's inside—in here, and here, and here …' With each *here*, his finger-poke to my ribs forces a squeal. 'Alone, affirmations won't achieve much at all.'

I hike up my shoulders. 'Then why do I need one?'

'Because they make us focus.'

'What's a focus, Dad?'

'I'll explain this way.' He squats, taps my nose, and pulls me close. I'm leaning against his knee when the receding water sucks my feet down, burying them deeper in the soggy sand. 'Remember when you left your magnifying glass too long in the sun and it put a burn mark in your sister's journal? The one Layla got last birthday?'

'I didn't mean to,' I mumble through pouted lips. 'And I wasn't reading. Blame the bug.' I'd been in the backyard, following the ladybird's expedition over my sister's abandoned beach towel, when the tiny red-winged insect crawled across the pages of the book and stopped. 'It climbed up all by itself, Dad.'

'Yes, then Mum called you for cordial, and the magnifying glass stayed on your sister's book. Right?' He waits for my nod. 'You see, Chelsea, the object alone—your magnifying glass—contained no special magic and no heat until it concentrated all the sunlight on one spot. That *focus* made the glass powerful enough to change into something else.'

'I still don't get it,' I say. 'Change into what? It's a dumb toy.'

'I agree. Your magnifying glass has no special properties *until* we let it rein in the sun's energy. On its own, an affirmation is similarly powerless —mere words strung together. The power,' he says, 'comes from the conviction we bring to our affirmation. The stuff inside us—our energy when we chant—creates change. So, think of an affirmation as a magnifying glass for your conscience.'

I don't know what my *conshunsh* is either, or where to find it, but if Dad says I have one, then I must. He never lies.

'Can you teach me *a affamayshon*, Dad?'

'Okay, but you'll need to concentrate.' Shifting my body so he can stand, he says, 'Close your eyes and imagine mermaids.'

I snigger. 'That's too easy.'

'Shh,' he insists. 'Put all your energy into those mermaid images.

Picture them. They're happy and frolicking. Mermaids are not afraid, Chelsea. Be a mermaid, my darling girl. Repeat after me: Let your fear set you free; become one with the sea.'

24

CHELSEA

W as the bush track taking longer to traverse because Chelsea was older, or because she wasn't racing Layla to the dunes? Rather than two young girls leaving a father in their wake, Chelsea took metered steps, mindful of the breeding holes dug into the sandy terrain by the gregarious and industrious rainbow-coloured bee-eater birds. While powerless to stop sand sneaking into her shoes, Chelsea could avoid the sharp foliage of the Pandanus, and the protruding branches of Coastal Banksia and shady She-oak trees. All the while she chanted in her head: *Let your fear set you free; become one with the sea.*

Periodically picking up and pocketing bits of plastic, along with other sad signs of a selfish society, had been a useful distraction until, at the base of the dunes, a full-on panic attack triggered the familiar tightness in her airways, and numbness in both legs forced her to drop into a squat. At the same time, two young boys dragging brightly coloured boogie boards burst out of the bushes. Their father offered Chelsea an apologetic shrug as he hurried towards the designated beach access point designed to funnel foot traffic and reduce dune degradation. When the mother appeared and hesitated, concern clear in her expression, Chelsea forced herself to stand and unfurl her fist to show a discarded bottle cap. She smiled reassuringly at the woman, dropped the litter in her pocket, and followed the family up the dunes.

Using the rope handrail, she trod one wooden plank after the other until reaching a weathered viewing platform, its greying balustrade and bench seating polka-dotted with bird poo. Chelsea didn't care. Sitting was entirely necessary as all the breath in her lungs whooshed out in a short exclamation of both relief and surprise. Surprise because she'd made it this far on her own, and because the seascape—muted by thick sea mist—was more surreal than scary and totally unexpected.

The beach bore evidence of a war overnight; the clash of an ocean too quick to retreat, its casualties already decaying in the summer sun. While telling herself the discarded seaweed harboured no threat—that nothing was hiding under the ugly clumps—postponing her beach therapy for another day made sense. Even though Chelsea was the closest she'd been to facing her fear, tomorrow's conditions would likely be more favourable. At the very least, an overnight high tide might reclaim its dead, sweeping the battlefield clean.

Oh, for goodness' sake, Chelsea, just make a damn decision and do it.

Hugging her dad's chocolate-brown cardigan as tight as possible, and with her father's affirmation in her ear, she began the sandy descent down from the lookout.

Let your fear set you free; become one with the sea.

She dared not leave the hard, dry sand. Not even after spotting a victim of the retreating tide—an abandoned jellyfish with its bulbous, boneless, brainless body mostly made of water left behind to dry up. As a child, Chelsea would've rescued the creature, no matter what her dad said about it being a waste of time.

'Jellyfish are planktons,' he'd once told both daughters busily rolling the mass using their thongs as hand tongs. 'There is no saving them now, even if you make the water.'

'How do you know?' Layla asked.

'For a start, jellyfish don't have a heart. And most plankton can't breathe away from the ocean. They take in oxygen from seawater through their skin, and like any living thing, when kept from the one thing they need to survive, they shrivel up and die. Some ocean species will deliberately surrender themselves to the elements once they've served their purpose. People are no different if kept from the one thing we need to survive. The secret, my girls, is knowing when to give up.'

Tugging the cardigan tight, Chelsea looked out to sea. 'Did you give up, Dad?'

As the miasma of decaying sea life, wet weed, and salty spray settled around her, so did a profound melancholy at the sight of a lone fisherman on the shoreline. Though a long way up the beach, something about him —the way he stood at a deep green gully, perfect for bream—prompted a memory of her father and another warning: *Never sneak up behind a fisherman.*

Finding strange comfort in imagining the man on the beach *was* her dad, Chelsea made her way along the hard sand, wondering why she could recall such useless life lessons in detail, while memories of the man responsible for teaching her were fading.

Neither short nor tall, this angler's stoop was of a much older man. Or did it only look that way with his back to her, his peak cap pulled low enough to meet the upturned collar on his all-weather jacket? Closing in, content to watch—to maintain the illusion for a little longer—more fatherly advice came to Chelsea.

'Chatty folk are never welcome, Miss Fix,' Dad had told her. 'Especially the ones who ask too many questions, like "getting any bites?". If the fish *are* biting, no fisherman in his right mind will answer in the affirmative.'

'So, fishermen fib?' Chelsea had asked.

'It's not fibbing. Life comes with choices, and with rules that we choose to observe or ignore.'

'You mean like school rules about not speaking during a test?'

He'd nodded. 'And rules like honouring and obeying, and not tricking a man into marriage after another bloke's mistake.' He beamed at her scrunched face. 'There's also a rule that says fishermen never divulge secret fishing spots, or their bait of choice.'

'Why not?' she'd asked.

'You wouldn't tell your friends where to find the best rock pools and seashells, right?'

'No way.'

And no way could Chelsea walk by this fisherman today without a hello.

'How's it going?' she yelled into the strengthening onshore wind. 'Catching any?'

The fisherman twisted his body as far as the restrictive all-weather jacket allowed before promptly turning back to the sea.

'Sorry,' she said, stepping over a heap of brown weed. 'My dad did teach me to never be a chatty Cathy around fishermen, but seeing you here reminds me of him. He knew everything about fishing and, if you don't mind me saying, this tide is not ideal. With this wind all over the place he'd tell you only crazy men and crabs enjoy such conditions.'

Without a word, the man reeled in his line, picked up his gear, and hurried back up the beach.

As Chelsea watched him and his bright-green tackle box melt into the mist, a terrible thought hit her. *Was he Talia's demented old dad, and you've called him crazy for fishing in these conditions?*

'I'm sorry!' She shouted in the hope the wind carried her apology, because no way would she follow.

As it was, Chelsea was too close to the headland that had once dominated her bad dreams. In her young mind, the mass of rock and shrubbery had been a gargantuan tower, intimidating her, and dwarfing everything within cooee. The reality three decades on might be more a weather-beaten bluff, only about eight storeys high, but the defiant mass still dominated the skyline, stoically fending off the barrage of waves that constantly clawed at its foundations.

Suddenly wanting to hate the cliff for its resilience, especially given the fragile foundations of her own life, a confusing mix of emotions—more fury than fear—coursed through Chelsea. Turning back to the ocean, she pulled her legs to her chest and stretched the cardigan around both knees. Today, the sea's surface was calm, as if the waves couldn't be bothered. *Perhaps the relentless pounding and constant in and out exhausted them too.* The notion prompted Chelsea to think about the ebb and flow of people she has loved.

For the first twelve years, William Scott had been a constant and inspiring influence. With his guidance, had he not been taken away, what might Chelsea's life be like today, and might the Scott family be living happily ever after? As for her mother—in name only—Chelsea wanted to care, but Wendy never made it easy; nor did Layla. Thank goodness devoted, dependable Dale came along when he did, filling the void left by an indifferent mother and sister.

The youthful version of love with Dale had been the all-consuming kind, with their shared passion for parenting making them utterly and equally obsessive—in a good way. Without a doubt, Dale's constant can-do attitude had helped Chelsea through those early days of motherhood, and they'd been so happy until the house became a source of irritation for the pair. Like the ebb and flow of the tides, every time one of them pushed, the other drew away.

Maybe if you'd been more careful and waited to start a family!

'Hey, Dad,' she said softly, staring up at clouds scudding across the sky. 'Do you remember me asking you about baby fish? I asked if fish got married before having babies and you said ...'

'Some do, Chelsea-girl. Others get themselves well and truly hooked and yanked out of their watery world with no hope of surviving in a place they weren't made for.'

'Then fish are dumb, Dad. Why else would they not swim far, far away from the shore and hide in the ocean where they can't be hooked?'

'The lucky ones do swim away, Chelsea. Only the silly ones stick around, snagged good and proper by a fishwife.'

'You once called Mum a fishwife.'

'From the mouths of babes,' he laughed. 'You don't miss much, do you, Miss Fix? I'll have to remember that. And, yes, your mum hooked me.'

'And she didn't throw you back.'

'Nope, she sure didn't.'

'And you promised to honour and obey?'

'Yes, much to my detriment.'

Whatever detriment meant, Chelsea didn't know back then. 'And you and Mum made little fishies, right?'

'We did. A very sweet Miss Fix fish.'

'And a little Layla fish?' she'd prompted.

Rather than a verbal reply that day, Chelsea recalled her dad's expression had morphed into one of those far, far away ones when he'd gazed at the horizon for ages, saying nothing.

'Oh, Dad!' she whispered while staring at the same horizon three decades later, and unperturbed by the wet soaking through her gym pants, or the salty tears seeping between pouting lips.

Growing in number to surround her, a flock of seagulls gathered, taking respite on the ground, their bodies turned into the wind.

'Wasting your time with me. Feeding birds is taboo,' she said when one broke formation to ruffle its feathers and caw. 'Dad taught me wildlife must forage, and that includes you over there with the one leg. And you,' she told the brown-feathered baby with pleading eyes. 'Humans have programmed you to expect a handout, but there's an entire ocean of food out there. Go! Forage! Be a bird.'

Though her shouts failed to shoo the small strategist now triggering her mothering instincts, the shrill ring of her phone moved the flock in a flurry of feathers and squawking.

'Hallelujah!' she said, answering quickly.

'You can say that again.' It was Vicki. 'I've been worried sick. You never called back. Timmy! Stop biting your brother.'

'Sorry, my phone's been working as intermittently as the mobile reception.'

Chelsea was getting to her feet and brushing sand from her bottom when Vicki asked, 'What about TV reception?'

'Why? What's happened?'

'Cyclone Minnie! Flash flooding, gale-force winds, and massive tides. Timmy, leave him alone! When I couldn't raise you on the phone, hon, I figured the storm had washed you away, or Hairy Legs had murdered you while you slept.'

Relief swept through Chelsea. 'Oh, the storm. Yes, I slept very little that night, Vik, but you can quit the dramatics. And yes, I should've messaged. Thanks for caring, but I'm fine.' As a flash of reflected sunlight caught in her eye, Chelsea spotted the source partly buried near a clump of seaweed. Shaking the glass jar free of sand, into the cardigan pocket it went along with the plastic waste she'd collected earlier. 'And interestingly, Vik, Hairy Legs turned out rather lovely. Sure was one wild night.'

'Ah, so, Hairy Legs is why you're lacking sleep? You go, girl!'

'That's not what I meant. And it's not what this trip is about.'

'Why not?' Vik said. 'You reckon Dale's attending choir practice in the west all this time?'

Chelsea contemplated telling her friend about the photo on Gabby's Facebook post until Vicki spoke again.

'Why can't a woman have a holiday fling? Society accepts a man suffering through a mid-life crisis will dangle his line.'

'I'm not here for a fling, Vik.' Chelsea stomped on a tatty brochure, wind-whipped briefly into full flight and tumbling over the sand right towards her. 'I was miserable earlier, but I have wonderful memories of Sandbar. Today, I made the beach. I'm here now and on a mission to rid the sea of plastics one piece at a time, along with anything else that should not be here.' Taking the jar from her pocket, turning it over in her hand, a thought evolved. 'Don't worry about me. I'm better than expected, and I'll be home soon with a little magic potion, especially for you.'

Vicki groaned. 'If that's another name for hippy-harvested hemp or magic mushroom, I don't want to know.'

2 5

CHELSEA

Still smiling after Vicki's parting line, Chelsea heard her name. It was Tadpole yelling from down the beach. Despite the sandy terrain, he moved quickly and confidently on his prosthetic. Faithful Lucky trailed behind.

'I didn't notice you out there,' she said as he caught up. Chelsea's focus had been on anything *but* the water. 'And where were you hiding, fella?' She squatted to pat the dog, whose brown eyes were as good as any tonic, soothing the piercing sadness left behind by Fred's passing.

'This old boy is too clever to sit in the weather. He prefers the shade under the viewing platform. As you can see, his job is keeping my land leg safe and dry while I'm surfing.' Tad's nod indicated the prosthetic leg strapped to the dog's bright orange vest. 'A big, ol' wus, but one I can't do without.'

'Your ... land leg?' Chelsea queried.

'As opposed to the water prosthetic.' Tad rapped his knuckles just below his knee. 'Twenty years ago, these babies were mostly metal and wood; not designed for water. With no option for amputees like me who needed flexibility for surfing, I crafted my own. Took several prototypes, and more wipeouts, but we did it. Squid was the ideas man. He suggested the lightweight carbon fibre and the flipper-style foot, so we persevered and *voilà*!'

'Where there's a *will*, there's a way, my dad would say. His name was Will—William,' Chelsea explained. 'To him, nothing seemed impossible.

He'd tell me to reach for the horizon, because if I didn't, I'd never get there. Then he'd say, "You can go anywhere and do anything, Chelsea-girl".' Waiting until the echo of her father's voice faded, Chelsea said, 'He told me, one day when I'm ready to want more, I'll understand about reaching for the horizon.'

'Your dad sounds special.'

'Thanks.' She beamed. When was the last time anyone spoke highly of her father? For years, she'd fought against the tide of her family's indifference. Even Dale grew to despise Chelsea's constant husband / father comparisons. 'Speaking of dads,' she said, preparing to fess up. 'I might've bumped into Talia's dad fishing and called him crazy. Did you see him?'

'Talia's father? Fishing? Not likely. He's up in Ocean Sands, his beach days well and truly over years ago. Whoever you spoke to, it wasn't him. Could've been Squid getting in an early session. Tals reckons he's been oddly stressed, and he fishes when he's worried. Do you mind if we sit, Chelsea? I need to get out of this thing.' Without delay, Tad dropped to one knee, then twisted his body and kind of flipped onto his bottom.

Chelsea sat, too, the urge to query the man eclipsed by a desire to hug him for saying kind things about her dad. A need to learn more about Thaddeus Poulle, and a ripple of attraction caressed Chelsea. How strangely seductive to be so emotionally comfortable and so close—physically—to a man who wasn't her husband; a guy in the process of peeling his wetsuit down to his waist, no less.

Tad's relationship with the surf, understanding how the sea and the sand were part of his makeup, was not dissimilar to William Scott's. Oh, the comparisons she could make. Tad likely shared more similarities with him than Dale. What other explanation was there for the connection she felt. At that moment, Chelsea was the youthful version of herself when life with Dale had been flat out fantastic. Sitting on the beach with a man effectively living the life her dad would have loved had Chelsea blissfully aware of both his physicality and the potpourri of those of fun, family holidays: warm air redolent of coconut board wax, Hawaiian Tropic, and sun-cooked salt-laden hair.

That's it! That's the connection. Tadpole smelt like home.

Oblivious to her musings, the free-thinking, easy-talking larrikin with the mischievous smirk continued chatting about his travels, his passions, and life as a boy in Sandbar. Chelsea could relate to the love and respect he had for the woman who'd raised him—teaching him in the same way Chelsea's dad had guided her. But Tad's recovery story brought perspective to Chelsea's problems. Tadpole, it seemed, had suffered more than most, and lost more than most, yet he oozed positivity about getting up and getting on with life, albeit one shaky step at a time.

'My greatest achievement still today is getting into and out of a wetsuit.'

'You're pretty amazing.'

'Nah! I'm a bloke who's had his share of stumbles but keeps moving, which you can't do if you're holding on to all the wrong things. Even when it hurts like hell at the start, letting go of bad habits and cutting those anchor lines tying you to what used to be is the key to finding your *happy*.'

That Chelsea might find an element of *happy* sitting on a beach beside a man who was not her husband, but whose nearness brought a teensy touch of that tummy-tingling sensation she'd accused Dale of wanting, was both inconceivable and unnerving. Was Chelsea only now appreciating she was at the point in her life—a moment of awakening—that her dad had said she'd understand when she was older? Was little Chelsea Scott ready to want more and to let go in search of the horizon?

Chelsea Holt! What are you doing?

Preparing to leave, and to cover her uneasiness with a wisecrack about him using her as a windbreak, Tad's hand on her knee pinned Chelsea to the spot. *When did he move so close?* Their whole side—shoulders, arms, and thighs—touched.

'You look miles away,' Tad was saying. 'Where were you?'

'Um, the horizon?' The nonsensical reply fit her ridiculous reaction to this man. 'I should go.'

'To the horizon?' His face lit up, his laugh easy. 'That's a long way.'

Feeling her cheeks redden, and not from too much sun, Chelsea shifted to stretch both legs out in front, arms behind to hold her back straight. 'I've already come a long way, Tad. I'm sitting on sand and within cooee of the water. A massive achievement.'

'Beach today. Tomorrow the ocean?'

'No way,' Chelsea replied. 'Some things I'll never do.'

'Twenty years ago, medicos told *me* I'd never walk the beach again, much less ride a wave. Mentally, I was prepared to try. Physically, I needed a prosthetic that wouldn't drown me on my first wipeout—and there'd be plenty of those. Regaining balance after an amputation takes perseverance and good upper body strength, especially here in the core.'

'You have that,' Chelsea said, watching his hand trace the six-pack of abs. His grin said he'd noticed. 'I, um … About your water leg design. Dad was a bit of an inventor. A real ideas man with not enough weekends and nights to see them all come to fruition. Mum also hated mess, so the messy ideas stayed in his head. She'd complain he never tidied up after himself or had the commitment to see things through to the end. But I believe, given time—no long commute, no wife and kids taking up his weekends—he might've done more.'

'Genius is one percent inspiration and ninety-nine percent perspiration, but all credit goes to my mate, Squid. If he'd patented this design way back, he'd likely be worth a squillion.'

'You and your nicknames!' Chelsea laughed. 'If Tadpole is not intriguing enough, why would anyone choose Squid for a name?'

'Well, while a bloke called Tadpole can hardly question another man's moniker, I recall a boozy Secret Men's Business gathering when Squid slobbered on my shoulder, clamouring about being the chameleon of the sea. "The supreme marine master of disguises," the bloke had crowed. "Able to disappear before your very eyes. *Abracadabra*". And he did disappear that night; right outside to throw up, I suspect. By night's end, we'd all given ourselves stupid sea names. Let me think. As well as Squid, Dave and his son, Barry, chose Marlin and Nemo. Crazy guys! I chose Flipper. The kids at school christened me that in first grade when they saw my feet.' Tad waggled his slightly webbed toes. 'Not only was I born with these flippers, but experts say dolphins are supremely intelligent, adorable, and amazing swimmers. I'd have to agree,' he said with a wink. 'What would your ocean element be, Chelsea?'

'The seahorse, of course: serene, enigmatic, and as adorable as *any* dolphin. Also capable of changing its appearance to fit in with the environment—and I tend to blend in ...'

'Not sure I'd agree with the blending in bit,' Tad said, 'and you failed to mention seahorses are stubborn buggers.'

'Says who?' Chelsea demanded.

'Says anyone who knows how fiercely those gorgeous tails can grip seagrass to anchor them in turbulent waters. No budging a seahorse if there's something they're desperate to hold on to.'

Like a house! Chelsea almost laughed aloud. 'Sounds about right.'

Tad's grin shifted to cautious. 'I'm very glad I ran into you this morning, Chelsea. To be honest, I was worried after last night.'

'Worried? That's lovely of you, but do you worry about all your female renters?'

Tad scratched his head comically. 'Huh?'

'According to Elmie, I'm like "all the lovely ladies who stay in Taddy's van".'

'Ahh, those ladies! *Sea-Esta* regulars for the last few years. Jane and Vanessa with their two fluffy fur kids. They'd be here now if Jane—not her real name—wasn't filming in London. They come here to be not-so-famous in a place where flying under the radar is super easy. Lack of connectivity helps. There *was* a whisper a while back about erecting a mobile phone tower in the wetlands to the north until Squid made a fuss. Well, Talia made the fuss on his behalf. She's the diplomat in the family. Squid's like tapware. The bloke runs hot and cold.'

'Speaking of cold, Tadpole, your lips are turning blue. You're freezing.'

'Like scales are to fish, goosebumps are a surfer's armour. I'll be warm soon.'

'Not likely.' The sun was still low in the eastern sky, the wind stiffening. 'Sorry, that sounded very half glass empty of me. I'm not usually such poor company,' she added, feeling the need to explain. 'Ordinarily, I'd be at home at this time of year and being maudlin by myself because my sister and mother have never understood my need to remember Dad's anniversary.'

'We often share the same wounds but mend in different ways. The fact remains, whatever we lose—be it a leg or a life,' Tad tapped his stump, 'if it mattered to us, we grieve the loss. Just a bloody shame the rock crushed my pretty foot, because this one made me the butt of every joke at school, with the girls agreeing webbed feet were a deal-breaker and a turnoff.'

'Are you kidding?' Chelsea chortled. 'I wished for flippers—*and* a tail. Quite the opposite to my all-time favourite storybook while growing up: *The Little Mermaid*.'

'I wasn't much of a reader. My picture books were Prudence's National Geographic magazines. Later in life I enjoyed travel books, while these days, armchair trips are my preference—and by armchair, I mean by the fire in the camp kitchen with travel tips told by actual travellers. Did I mention I'm a great listener?' He grinned. 'I'm *also* a Disney expert. Haven't seen the Little Mermaid, but I'm an expert in *Frozen*. I do a mean rendition of *Let It Go. Let it goooo! Let it goooo—*'

'Stop! Please, don't,' Chelsea said a little too quickly.

'Deal-breaker?' Tad chuckled.

'Yes, but not for the reason you're thinking.' She explained how the *Frozen* storyline was about estranged sisters who lose their way and need to heal. 'And while I have nothing against Disney's Ariel as a mermaid, I prefer the original Hans Christian Andersen's classic—a story more complex, if slightly bizarre, about a mermaid wanting legs.'

'Now that's a plotline I can relate to. Do tell.' Tad seemed genuinely keen to hear, his body almost mirroring Chelsea's; her legs drawn to her chest, chin resting on knees, eyes squinting somewhere towards a single cloud thick enough to conceal what would otherwise be a brilliant ball of warming yellow sun still hovering close to the horizon.

'There's also a sister thread in the story. They care enough to sacrifice their beautiful hair to save one love-struck little sister. But in the end, the little mermaid must stab the prince and let blood drip onto her feet. Only then can she return to the ocean.'

Tad jerks upright. 'Are you kidding? The chick kills the prince?'

'No! She saves the prince by choosing to return to the ocean where her body dissolves, becoming sea foam.'

'Seriously?' said a bug-eyed Tad. '*Sheesh!* Give me a Disney ending any day. Preferably one about a hot-looking chick who saves the day by kissing the tadpole and turning him into the handsome dude he never was. How about it?'

Chelsea jerked back, avoiding Tad's puckered lips, and shoving his shoulder so hard she knocked him off balance. 'Oh, I'm so sorry!'

'Serves me right,' he said, accepting the helping hand she extended. 'I'm guessing that's a definite deal-breaker. Got a bit carried away with the story.'

'Yes, besides,' Chelsea said, quick to recover, 'the hot-looking chick kisses a frog, not a tadpole, and the only prince I ever wanted to save was my father. But, Thaddeus Poulle, you so remind me of Dad. I can't quite put it into words.'

'Allow me,' Tad said. 'Princely, witty, and devilishly handsome?'

'Ha! More like larrikin and mad about the beach—like I was until my phobia set in. But look at me now, sitting here, safe and calm. It's miraculous. You're good therapy.'

'The waves are my go-to place,' Tad said after a few minutes. 'Nothing was going to keep me out of the water.'

'I used to be the same, but hearing people constantly say Dad went doing something he loved was enough to make a twelve-year-old afraid to love the ocean.'

'Not a toe in the water since?'

'Nope! As a child, I blamed the king tide for taking him. Later, I blamed myself, so the idea of enjoying the things we'd done together felt wrong without him. The beach, and all it represented, soon became too powerful a reminder.'

'Naturally, you were afraid,' Tad said. 'Every swimmer and surfer in the world remain at the mercy of the ocean, with a change of weather or a moment of complacency changing the odds in a split second. Often, it's simply bad luck—or *good* luck in the case of Mick Fanning's recent shark-punching encounter. Real lucky!' At the sound of his name, the dog's head shot up, eyes alert to the next command. Tad patted him and the dog relaxed again. 'But you can bet on Fanning not quitting the boards forever. As tragic as my accident was, I sure as hell never considered giving away what I loved. Better that I let go of the self-blame, which is *the* most toxic and life-threatening of ailments.'

'How do you mean?' Chelsea asked.

'Losing a leg sucked big time, but I could relearn to walk,' he explained. 'Self-blame, on the other hand, cripples us before we can even begin to move forward. A giant bloody boulder crushed my leg. Nothing about that moment in time was my fault. It was a clear-cut case of the wrong place at the worst possible time.'

Chelsea hugged her dad's cardigan around her knees. 'Nobody said *I* was to blame. Not to my face. The coroner ruled "Death By Misadventure"—likely due to a medical event. A heart attack was possible, but the finding never made sense to me. Dad had the biggest heart of anyone I knew, and my recollections are of a tall, strong man in his mid-thirties. Even though we lived out west—no beach—he kept fit, rode a bike every weekend, and stayed active with projects at home. As far as I knew, there was nothing he couldn't do—except save himself that day. Why?' she asked, tears forming. 'He grew up on the beach, became a nipper, a life-saver, a local surfing star. He loved fishing, and was doing what he'd done hundreds of times, and on a day like any other.' *Except for the top-secret fishing spot*, she silently reminded herself.

'Maybe, Chelsea, it was a case of extraordinary events on an otherwise ordinary day,' Tadpole offered. 'No one was to blame for what happened that February 1938. No one even considered the possibility.'

Chelsea knew of the Black Saturday bushfires in Victoria a few years ago, but not a Black Sunday. Curious, she asked, 'What about Bondi?'

'It was a perfect summer beach day,' Tad explained. 'Approximately 35,000 people were looking for some respite from the heat. My Granddad was partway through his first lifeguard shift as a recruit when the sea suddenly changed. He told me it was peculiar surf, with a tremendous undertow. When the tide dropped, an unusually large sandbar formed, which encouraged beachgoers to venture a long way offshore while still only waist deep. According to Gramps, shortly after 3 pm, an eerie stillness fell over the beach. The ocean calmed, oddly silent, then three waves surged in rapid succession, hitting high up on the beach. The combined power of all three receding waves created a strong backwash, wiping away the sandbank and dumping hundreds of men, women, and children playing there into deep water. They were knocked off their feet and dragged out to sea.'

'And your grandfather witnessed this?'

Tadpole nodded. 'Whether a fluke or fate, Bondi Beach was mid surf carnival, which put seventy good swimmers in the vicinity. Beltmen mobilised on a mission to rescue those furthest out, but dozens of desperate men grabbed at the lines, the weight of them dragging the beltmen under. That's when Gramps and his mate started hauling the beltmen back in, while a powerful rip-like current dragged others out to sea.

'There'd never been such a catastrophic beach emergency. One minute the sea is crowded with drowning people. The next, Gramps said the beach resembled a battleground. Bodies everywhere needed resuscitating, but so few people knew CPR.'

'People died?' she asked.

Tad nodded. 'Five lives lost. Five—from hundreds—and all men. Strong swimmers, too. Strength is often no match for the force of a powerful sea, or the unpredictable nature of waves.'

The pair sat in silent remembrance, Chelsea repeatedly drawing the infinity symbol in the sand by her foot. 'Dad made sure Layla and I understood the sea's power.'

'Your sister's name is Layla?'

'Yeah, she's four years older. We were close once. She used to care.'

'Used to?' Tad queried. 'Not the type to sacrifice her beautiful hair?'

Chelsea huffed a laugh. 'My sister grew distant after we lost Dad, while Mum seemed to lose interest in everything, including me. I understood. I blamed myself; stood to reason they'd blame me, too. At night, I would beg the evil witches to return Dad, but the only thing the sea sent back was his spray jacket, found washed onto a beach to the south.'

Tad nodded. 'Even with today's technology, tides and currents make the ocean a massive, moving search ground. But you know what, Chels?' When he reached down and slipped his hand under hers, she curled her fingers and held on tight. 'While the sea will usually give up its secrets, often it will keep the extra-special things, like dads.'

'You're so lovely, Tad. Thank you. It's difficult being back here. I can hardly look at the rocky point and not picture him there.'

'*Our* rocky point to the north?' He looked towards the headland, then to Chelsea, his mouth agape. 'Why choose here for your self-imposed therapy? Talk about rubbing salt into a wound.'

'I hoped to bring about some sort of closure. I've let the tragedy define me. It still rules my life.'

'And you chose to come alone?'

'Chose? Not exactly.' Chelsea freed her hand to point out the suntan line on her wedding finger.

'Ah, gotchya!' Tad said, nodding. 'I should've guessed you were married when I first clamped eyes on you. Probably should've checked before trying the kissing thing. Must've been all our talk of frog princes and happy endings.'

Chelsea chuckled. 'I take it you're not married, Tad?'

'Thrice was enough for this fella.'

'Three times?' Chelsea sounded more surprised than she'd intended.

'What can I say? I make poor decisions. Officially, it's only one marriage. One was the live-in-sin kind, to which Mother said I'd "rue the day". As usual, Prudence was right. Unfortunately, I was naive enough to think a woman would love me without a piece of paper. Turned out, by not making our union legal, I made it too easy for her to walk. Number three was interesting,' Tad continued. 'There's no piece of paper strong enough to hold back love meant to be. Helena left me for my best mate. She and Snr Constable Carly O'Shea—both of NSW Police Dog Squad— plan on marrying as soon as it's legal. Lucky, here, will be the ring bearer.'

'Oh!'

'Oh is right, but not as colourful as my initial response to the announcement. Of course I gave them my blessing, but mutual friends found social occasions with the three of us uncomfortable. So, I got right away.'

'You said three relationships?' she prompted.

'Ah, yes, Kim!' he said, his mien changing, the larrikin no more. 'Kim died after a cave collapsed around her.' A beat of silence followed. 'One minute we're on the beach and getting all hot and heavy, so I'm urging her into the cave, away from prying eyes. We fell into each other, giggling like kids, and heard an almighty cracking noise overhead. Next, we're both under rubble. I was pinned by the leg, but close enough to hold her hand as she slowly passed on. I've never stopped wishing it was me who'd died that day, and that Kim got to raise our girl.'

'You had a child?'

'Have!' He nodded. 'At the time, I knew little about babies, except how to make one. Barely conscious after surgery, doctors told me they'd successfully performed an emergency cesarian. Little Elise clearly got her never-say-die attitude from her old dad.' The joker's mask cracked, and tears flooded Tad's cheeks. 'While I eventually forgave myself, Kim's parents did not, and with four good legs between them, the authorities determined an infant was better off in the care of her grandparents. I couldn't dispute the decision; I could barely look after myself after the amputation.'

'Where is Elise now?' Chelsea asked.

'Married and with a daughter—Fleur. The grandparents live in a big house a few towns north, which was partly why I settled back here. When Elise comes up from Sydney, which is often, she makes sure I get quality time with little Fleur. I only dropped Fleur at Ocean Sands the day before the luau. Kinda breaks my heart each time. Those girls are my everything, and they keep me on my toes—toes neither Elise nor Fleur inherited from me. God *can* be kind.' Tad's shoulders seemed to relax. 'And that, Chelsea, is why I've steered clear of relationships. Without you for company today, Lucky and I would be sitting here alone. So, come on, your turn,' he said.

'My turn what?'

'Tell me why you're camping alone. You're married. Where is the lucky bloke?'

'For twenty-eight years, Dale was right beside me, raising our family. For the last few months? Perth,' she quipped. 'We met in high school and clicked. Both of us had lost parents in tragic circumstances: Dale was an orphan when the foster system was a mess, and my mum walked away a few years after we lost Dad. With Dale and I both desperate to belong, it was natural we'd connect.'

'Your mother walked away?' Tad asked.

Chelsea nodded. 'The day she dragged me kicking and screaming to the school swimming carnival. I remember making a grab for everything: the front door, the letterbox, the light pole on the street, the car door. All the way to the pool, I screamed and yelled stuff.

'What sort of stuff?' he asked.

'I guess the sort that makes a mother not love a daughter, because she dragged me out of the car and said: "I can't live like this". She left me at the pool, and with my sister totally unreliable, Aunty Rita came and found me in the change rooms where I'd spent the entire day fending off my sports teacher who thought getting me in the water was the best therapy.

'Aunty Rita—not my real aunty—then took Layla and I back to Sydney. While I loved Rita, I hated her house with its ocean views. But beggars can't be choosers, right? Layla was old enough to come and go as she pleased, but I was enrolled in a new school, where I met Dale. We fell in love, we fell pregnant, and I was determined to be a better mother than Wendy.'

'And I'm sure you are,' Tad said.

'Not if you were to ask my daughter, Gabby. Apparently, I don't treat her like a grownup, while my sons grew up far too fast. I swear those boys were only out of my womb for a matter of weeks before they were dating girls. As for my husband, life has become all about "moving forward".' Chelsea's fingers curled into air quotes. 'He's seeing out his mid-life crisis in Perth. So, I guess that means we're separated.' There was something liberating about saying the words aloud to a stranger. But should she have said sort-of-separated? Or did that only make her sound pathetic and more indecisive than she already was?

'And on that note,' Chelsea announced. 'As lovely as chatting is, you officially *look* frozen, the sun is being contrary, much like my sister these days, and I need to finish my magic jar.'

'Your what jar?'

Chelsea presented the glass container before scooping up sand to create a layer over the base. Then, screwing the lid tight, she said, 'I'm collecting morning magic.'

'Magic, eh? And here's me thinking it's a pickle jar left behind by some moron with the munchies.'

'Dad would argue it all depends on how you look at it. Capturing the morning's magic in a jar was one of his idiosyncrasies. My father had a few.'

'Jars or idiosyncrasies?'

'Ha! Both, much to Mum's chagrin. Decorated jars popped up all over the place at home, either filled with sea glass or broken shells, or whatever the tide left behind. One day, after making the mistake of opening the jar and spilling the layers of coloured sand and shell over his desk at home, he'd sat me down and said, "Some things you mess with can never go back to the way they were. When the magic is gone, Miss Fix, you need to start over and build a new jar".

'So, the next morning, while still dark, Dad woke me, carried me in my pyjamas to the car—and we arrived at the beach in time to capture the first rays of sun. That's the magic bit, and I've clung to the memory of that morning—just him, me, the sea, and capturing morning magic in jars.' Closing her eyes, Chelsea stemmed the surge of new tears for an old memory. 'At that moment, I had Dad all to myself and … Argh, sorry!' She dabbed her cheeks with the cardigan sleeve that had dried too many tears over the years. 'By the afternoon, he'd tasked me to write gift tags, which he tied to jars with twine. The words were, *If I can't be with the sea, let the sea be with me.* Then we rode our bikes to Penrith train station and left the jars, like random gifts for morning commuters to find.'

'For your sake, Chelsea,' Tad said. 'I hope this Sandbar stay does what you need it to do. Being here works for me, but our experiences are not at all similar.'

'Maybe not the aftermath,' she said, 'but you and I both carry guilt. I questioned my actions that day. Still do. And while there's little *Eat, Pray, Love* with my Sandbar pilgrimage, I remain hopeful of a magical cure-all, as easy as making one of these jars.'

'Wanting to keep the sea close makes him sound like my kind of guy.'

Chelsea nodded. 'The more time I spend with you, the more similarities I see. I'm certain if he was still with us, he'd be at the beach every second and recording himself with a Go-Pro, too.' She nodded at the compact unit mounted on Tad's board.

'I post to my *YouTube* channel, motivate amputee kids to give surfing a crack,' he explained. 'I share accessibility tips and hold the annual Sandbar Surf Accessibility School right here.'

'There you go!' Chelsea slapped her thigh. 'Exactly the sort of project Dad would've got stuck into. He was the best teacher, and he loved nature. He wasn't made for city life.' When a bird landed briefly on the sand in front of them before flying off again, Chelsea recalled something Talia had said about her deceased mother. 'I do hope Dad is a bird or a fish and not tied to one place.'

'I'm thinking your dad is up there right now with good ol' Prudence.' Tad wrapped an arm around her shoulders, squeezing her close. 'While he's wondering what he can do to make you smile, Mum is giving me a big nudge.' He cupped his ear towards heaven. 'What's that you say, Mum? Oh, right-o. Mum reckons I should shut the hell up, make you a coffee, and find some happy biscuits. Reckon I should do what I'm told for once?'

'I thought you were going to help Ivan today,' Chelsea said.

'Let me think.' He tapped a finger to his chin. 'Welding with Space Invader—a man with no sense of personal space—or coffee with you. Come on, Lucky. Time to help me up, mate.'

26

CHELSEA

First ducking under the Tibetan prayer flags and motioning for Chelsea to do the same, Tad opened the caravan door, directing her inside.

'Head on in. Make yourself comfy. I need a second out here to make myself respectable. Oh, and sorry about Fleur's toys.'

By the time Chelsea had collected and repacked the coloured pencils, boxed a game of Snakes and Ladders, and put Barbie with her campervan accessories at the far end of one dinette seat, Tad was hopping up into his caravan. Dressed in navy work shorts, his Hawaiian shirt open, he set about making coffee by adding coffee grounds to a stovetop espresso pot, setting two mugs, and popping the lid off a biscuit tin.

'Happy Honey Jumbles, Happy Hundreds and Thousands, or Happy Honeycomb Crunch?'

Chelsea grinned. 'Is choosing one of each considered a decision?'

'No, but you're allowed. They're Fleur's favourites. Here's a picture of my little Honey Jumble girl.' He slid the phone with its photo app open towards Chelsea. 'Scroll away,' he added before returning to his coffee duties.

'Adorable,' she said of the pictures showing a pretty, dark-haired girl. 'I guessed she would be.'

'Yeah, takes after her Pop. How often do you get to see yours?' he asked, delivering both black coffees to the table with a carton of milk from the fridge.

'I've flown to Perth a few times. Short visits with Gabby are all we're managing for the moment, but we're working on it. Whoops! Swiped too far. Sorry.' She nudged the phone back, but not before appraising the wild-looking woman in the black and white photo as both attractive and avant-garde.

'Ah, Prudence in her prime.' Tad towelled his hands dry before moving through more screenshots, stopping at a second picture. 'I was trawling through old photo albums and files to find information on Bunker Headland for the geotech engineer, when I realised how much history was sitting in boxes. Now I'm creating a digital memory album of Wandarri when under Prudence's rule so Fleur can know her great granny. For the engineers, I'll copy the original letters and journals in which Prudence detailed, among other things, the Warrior's battle with Council over the coastal erosion. In particular, the headland and cave formations. Too late for me, but …' He opened a cupboard above the dinette. 'This is the file, I think.'

The big, bulging scrapbook landed with a thud on the table. Flipping the cover, he scattered the loose newspaper clippings aside. One headline read: *WANDARRI WARRIORS WIN SAMSON AND GOLIATH BATTLE.*

'May I?' Chelsea asked, her hand poised over images depicting the lazy evolution of the Sandbar Campground and coastline: landscapes, crowded beaches, black and white images showing hunky surfer boys standing tall alongside taller boards stabbed into the sand. Decades of pictures and news articles, all featuring the establishment and growth of Wandarri Intentional Community, changed to news stories about other happenings, including safety concerns for beachgoers, prohibiting access to the rock shelf from Sandbar Beach, and access to Bunker Headland. As Chelsea's page turning quickened, she half-expected to see her father's face among the headlines: *DAUGHTER MAKES WRONG DECISION - FISHERMAN LOST.*

'And this ring binder …' Tad sat beside Chelsea to thumb through the scores of plastic sleeves, 'is the dossier regarding the headland. Photos of Elmie's bunker mural will be in here somewh—'

'Wait!' Chelsea's hand slapped the table. 'That picture!' She flicked back two sleeves. 'What is this, Tadpole?'

'Armament and gun emplacement remnants from World War II,' he replied, nonplussed. 'Bunker Headland was important to our nation's defence. Ironically, it was the tunnels dug between bunkers that old-timers reckon caused the 1970 landslip. Prudence's goal was to kick the government of the day into shoring up and safeguarding the headland

and adjoining rock platform. A spate of rockfalls since, including the northern cave formations, has kept the reserve's walking trails and the adjoining coastal scrub area to the north off limits.

'Only recently did the government earmark twenty-three million to make safe and reopen Bunker Headland and, pending the geotech reports, they've promised a historical walking trail to show the important role the area played in defending the coastline. Eventually, the public will have access, all the way down to Heartbreak Beach.'

'Heartbreak Beach?'

Tad nodded and tuned the page to point at another article. 'An unfortunate name for the section of coastline touted to be "the most pristine coastal wetland in the state". To have something so picturesque and tranquil co-existing alongside remnants of a war makes the place more special. Don't you think?'

Disagreement sat on the tip of Chelsea's tongue. But she was only half listening, her gaze glued to the giant structure in the photo she held tight.

'At least no development and no formal access road has meant no freeloader campers,' Tad continued. 'A local cultural burn some time back found evidence of an itinerant squatter deep in the scrub. The campsite was decades old, and the shack demolished, after which Talia's dad began monitoring the area—they have a bird's-eye view from the shop. Squid took over the task ten years ago, doing bi-annual patrols on behalf of Wandarri's Land Care Committee.

'What does this round object look like to you?' she asked, pointing to the picture still in her hand.

'You mean apart from what it actually is—a big ol' rusty wartime gun emplacement?'

'Yes, yes,' she said impatiently.

'Okay, well,' Tad pondered. 'It's big, round, and with a chunky length of chain fixed at the centre.' He sat back, hands cupping his mug. 'I'd say it looks like a giant plug in the ground, just asking to be pulled.'

'Exactly! Like in my recurring nightmare when I'm drowning and everyone's yelling at me: "Pull the plug!". Why would I have such a dream?'

'A therapist told me nightmares are a coping mechanism,' Tad said. 'By changing the narrative and removing the sinister elements, we lessen the hurt, and we recover—in a way.'

'Well, I never got over what happened, even though Mum and Layla insisted I "forget and move on".'

'How did your sister cope?' Tad asked.

'Oh, Layla discovered more *novel* ways to numb the pain. My sister self-harmed, which I only found out when Mum slipped up while talking on the phone to Rita. Here I was thinking Layla and I were different when, in fact, we'd both coped in much the same way.'

Tad's stare zeroed in on Chelsea, concern deepening the lines on his forehead. 'You also intentionally hurt yourself?'

'No, I didn't mean physically.' Chelsea smiled, but in a nervy way given the spoken confession was a first. What she was about to admit to this sweet stranger not even Dale knew. Acknowledging the truth herself had taken almost half a lifetime. 'Every reminder of how I failed Dad, every reminder of the man—the mementos and photographs, the family gatherings, the house he'd loved—was a mental cut in my mind. By holding onto so much of him, I guess you could say I've been kind of self-harming; wanting to bleed, to feel pain, to feel punished.'

When Tad found Chelsea's hands fisted on her lap, the warmth, the comfort in strong fingers clasping tight was yet another reminder of the way her dad's hands and hugs had reassured and encouraged his girls. Leaning closer, the man thumbed away a tear Chelsea was unaware she'd cried. Then he pressed the flat of his palm where her heart banged against her ribs.

'And you're holding tight to so much in here. And ...' He reached up, tapping the side of her skull twice. 'In here. Try letting go, Chelsea. *"Let it goooo! Let it goooo!"'* he sang tunelessly. 'But if you won't sing, then talk. I'm a good listener, remember?'

She was encouraged by the genuineness of his offer. 'Trouble is, I'm no longer certain it's possible to verbalise what happened that day with any accuracy.'

Three decades ago, she'd sat and talked with a policewoman. Today, she recalled nothing of the conversation, only the officer's smell and the sing-song way she'd asked questions, like Noni on Play School.

'Remembering the day was too painful and remembering him was unappreciated by my family. As for my nightmares, they bear no resemblance to reality. The short version is,' Chelsea said, 'one different decision that day and, like sliding doors, Dad might've been here today.'

'He'd hate that you're harbouring guilt, Chelsea. Take a deep breath, think,' Tad suggested. 'You remember the policewoman by her scent and voice. Right?' When Chelsea nodded, he added, 'Then close your eyes and go back to earlier in the day: What do you smell, see, hear?'

Despite Chelsea's disquiet, the replay—part adventure, part horror— began flickering on the insides of closed eyelids like a reel on a dodgy home movie projector. Then—*BAM!* With cinematic accuracy, Chelsea was back on that bush track, tired and thirsty and complaining.

'Dad kept telling me: "We're close, Chelsea-girl". We weren't, though. Not really. I so wished we'd gone to the beach to fish, like normal. Instead, I'm traipsing behind, head down, disinterested and pouting. With little sunlight, the dense bushland and overgrown tracks are a continuous messy carpet of leaves, pine needles, and sand that catches in my thong straps and rubs my skin raw. Suddenly ...' Chelsea flinched at the brightness. 'We're stepping out of the screen of trees and into a sunny clearing. It's incredible!'

'What do you see?' Tad asked in a whisper, his finger repeatedly stroking the back of Chelsea's hand in a hypnotic pattern. 'It's a good memory, Chels. You're smiling.'

'Oh, yes! It's very good. I'm on the top of the world up here on the headland, like being on a tall stage and facing an amphitheatre of sun-speckled ocean. There's a choir of sea gulls squawking over the susurration of windswept Sheoaks, and the wind ... Wow! It almost whips my hair out of the elastic band. So billowing and constant, the birds overhead aren't even flapping their wings. They're hovering in close formation, reminding me of white bunting let loose at one end. It's magical, like Dad promised, and I've forgotten the long trek and my hurting feet. I'm so high up, in awe of the horizon, and doing what I love more than anything else in the world; just me and my dad on an adventure. Until ...'

'What happens next?' Tad prompted.

'I'm sad.' Chelsea's shoulders slumped. 'I'm so wishing I'd listened to Mum and worn more than my swimming costume under the flimsy fabric of my spray jacket. It took so long to reach the headland, and the rock platform is so far down—the escarpment steep. No way can we reach the secret spot, so I tell Dad, "I don't want to stay here". And Tadpole,' Chelsea said, looking at him, 'I ... I don't think I want to go there now. Not in person and not in my mind.'

Tad slipped an arm across her shoulders. 'You're okay. I'm right here.'

Perhaps it was safer telling a total stranger. Not only would she never see the man again—because she'd made up her mind to go home tomorrow—he wouldn't criticise or judge her.

And so, feeling safe snuggled against Tad, her head on his shoulder, Chelsea dipped into that rock pool of memories to detail all she remembered about that day.

Neither Tadpole nor Chelsea spoke for a long while after she brought her story to a close. She did cry, though. Chelsea cried the tears of a shattered, guilt-ridden twelve-year-old.

'You can't blame yourself,' Tad said, sitting up to massage away what was most likely a cramp in his shoulder from holding her up so long.

'I can. I made stupid mistakes. It's why I've kept pushing the details away.'

'Bad mistakes aren't the same as bad decisions; not when you're young and scared.'

'Had I not turned my back on the water, I would've seen the wave. I could've warned him, and he might not have slipped on my shell collection. Then I left him alone on the rocks, injured. Then I got lost in the dark, so I waited at the big plug, but Layla never did arrive with the usual warning from Mum. A man found me wandering close to camp the next morning. A stranger.'

'You did the right thing getting to safety. Imagine if you hadn't? Your children and grandkids exist because you were brave.'

'Dad was brave,' she responded, 'and he was supposed to be safe. The tide wasn't meant to be high. The tide lied.'

2 7

LAYLA

Is this brave or stupid?

'You're about to find out,' Layla muttered while peering over the cafe's railing to scan the open-air carpark below.

He looked like every other holidaymaker in the baggy pants, sandals, and a loose-fitting shirt, but she knew the person. He wore no hat, had almost no hair, and his shoulders hunched, but there was no doubt in her mind. The man getting out of the rusty Pajero was him.

With no expectations, and no idea how the meeting would play out, Layla knew only that if hell had no fury like a woman scorned, the revenge of a rejected daughter had to be ten times more dangerous.

Today's reunion might be long overdue, but she was under no illusions about the dilemma she was dropping in the man's lap. The only illusion in play was the one William Scott had pulled off thirty-four years ago, with his deceit starting a domino effect that would see the family he left behind slowly and agonisingly self-destruct.

Layla had deliberately picked a public place to meet—The Lucky Lotus, a small but busy resort an hour's drive from Sandbar Beach. Doubling as a pickup and drop-off point for whale watching tours, all the comings and goings and excited exchanges meant father and daughter could sit at a table in plain sight and among complete strangers.

Sitting at the table, hands pressing down on jittery legs, Layla's gaze danced back and forth between the door and her bag with the tiny container of helpers. Today required something to let her stay composed, stay the course, and stay long enough to say her piece and no more. Popping a third non-alcoholic, grape-flavoured magnesium relaxant jube, Layla decided against standing or waving.

No way! Let the bastard search the expansive eatery and bar for her, like she'd searched the endless ocean for him that day, thirty-four years ago.

28

LAYLA, 34 YEARS AGO, 1981

With each goblet of wine, Wendy's complaints intensify. By her fourth, she's drunk with fury.

'I'm so over waiting. Go to the beach, find your father and sister, and tell them to get back here—fish or no fish.'

Layla groans at the order, even though the task is not a new one.

'If he thinks I'm eating at some God-forsaken hour again ...' Mum announces to the entire caravan park.

Unsure what 'God-forsaken hour' means—and not game enough to ask—Layla is trying to master the art of fire-making. Dad makes it look so easy, and a prepared fire will mean faster food on her plate. Layla is starving.

'Do I have to go, Mum?'

Of course you do! At least once every camping trip, Layla is required to deliver an ultimatum to her fishing-obsessed father. Thankfully, finding him is never difficult. Sandbar Beach has two deep gullies: one at the southern end near the bluff, and the other—best for bream—to the north.

By the time she's dawdled along the bush track, grumbling and mumbling to herself, any earlier beachgoers were already back to their caravan or tent preparing food before dark. Only one lady wearing tie-dyed pants, a flowing cheesecloth top and a headband, remains on the sand, her mesmerising salutation to the setting sun momentarily distracting Layla and delaying her trek to the far end of the beach. The green gully a little short of the estuary is her dad's pot of gold. But when he's not at the gully, Layla wonders if they've crossed the estuary, forgetting about the high tide.

She squints at the rocky platform now in full shadow. Seeing two distant figures in semi-dark conditions is unlikely, and shouting over the roar of an incoming tide is a waste of energy Layla doesn't have because Dad's tardiness is also depriving *her* of food until 'some God-forsaken hour'.

Back at camp, her mum is wild with wine and anger. Setting her glass aside long enough to slap a cheese toastie in a pan, she serves the sandwich burnt side down on a plastic plate. An hour later, having slammed her body onto the double bed, Mum's snores echo around the tiny interior.

When sunrise brings the numbing realisation that Layla's sister and father never returned to the campsite, a contrite, hungover, and hysterical Wendy drives to the public telephone box outside the bait shop on the hill. She dials triple zero to raise the alarm.

On the beach, locals dot the dunes, scouring the shoreline and scrutinising every white cap, every low-flying bird, every sun flare on the water's surface; the occasional call of 'There they are!', 'What's that?', or 'I see them!' nothing more than vivid imaginations. Never far away from Wendy and Layla is a young—very young—policewoman, her purpose to console, to reassure, and to answer questions.

The possibility of joining the police service briefly distracts sixteen-year-old Layla. She could do the job. She loves protecting people; constantly looking out for her little sister is proof enough. A distant shout snaps her head around. Someone way down the beach is waving wildly. Being young and barefooted, Layla easily sprints along the sand ahead of the policeman wearing cumbersome boots and a gun belt. When she reaches the yelling man first, her lungs ready to burst, it's her heart that kind of detonates inside her chest. A bashed-up bucket buffets back and forth on the shoreline—a green bucket covered with mermaid stickers.

The devastating discovery sends a disbelieving Layla back to the caravan with her mother, and grateful to be cosseted from the premature pitying of strangers. As the afternoon sun bakes the metal roof and

Wendy melts into a sobbing heap on the bed, the nice policewoman's words prepare them for the worst.

'No!' Unable to breathe, Layla breaks free of the caravan, rushing outside and falling to her knees.

She's looking skyward and pleading with whoever is up there to let Chelsea come home safe when the policewoman catches up, crouching down. With a protective arm wrapping tight, Layla makes a final silent appeal. She's promising to protect her sister forever when the policewoman's radio screeches to life with news. Two locals have found a distressed Chelsea and are currently making their way through several-hundred metres of dense scrub.

'Good news about your daughter, Mrs Scott,' she quickly tells Mum. 'Seems she tried to make her way back to camp but became disoriented in the dark. She's spent the night alone in the bush.'

Mum's allowed to see Chelsea straight away, while Layla's forced to wait until her sister is questioned by police, and to hear the same whimpered reply to each question.

'I should've stayed.'

When Wendy's immediate response was to shake more detailed answers out of Chelsea, Layla's promise to protect kicked in and she shoved her mother, screaming at her to stop.

Her sister recovered from her physical injuries, and eventually recalled more about the incident—as much as a traumatised twelve-year-old could —but the details often came in nightmares, later manifesting in a phobia of the ocean. Layla, on the other hand, never forgot the moment a stranger emerged from the beach track with her little sister, knees scraped, feet bloodied, eyes wet and wide.

2 9

LAYLA

Fast-forwarding thirty-four years…

What Layla couldn't foresee was how her promise to protect Chelsea would ultimately drive them apart. And all because William Scott had made himself disappear that night. But, those memories, combined with decades of destructive anger, now negated any nervousness about seeing the man she held responsible for ruining all their lives.

Trent once said Layla's strength, and not her weakness, was what allowed her to keep the secret all these years. Then he'd quoted some ancient Chinaman—*Tzu something-or-other*—whose various quotes adorned his walls. One saying had made its way in ink onto the soft flesh of Layla's forearm.

Being deeply loved gives you strength.
Loving deeply gives you courage.

But her lack of both traits had stopped Layla tracking this man down, even after figuring out what her mother had always known and never shared, and despite the clues being right in front of Layla. Unsure which re-reading of the pieced-back-together letter had let the penny drop, the answer—suddenly and absurdly apparent— was right there.

I'm keeping the parcel.

From years those words haunted Layla. How special could one parcel be? She imagined an important package spectacularly wrapped in pretty paper, the mysterious contents clearly more precious and prized than any person. Why else would he leave his family but take *it*?

One day while arguing with Wendy, the irony behind the treasured mystery parcel hit Layla. The same man who'd objected to his wife's material possession obsession had walked away from his family valuing one thing—a parcel of land in a place called Wandarri. Crazier still, Wandarri, Layla learned, was the official name for the old Sandbar Beach community of fishing tragics and squatters. Was it William Scott's audacity, or a deliberate strategy, to hide in the place where he'd allegedly died?

Layla eventually stopped wondering. Every so often, though, she let him into her head, but the idea of tracking him down usually ended in one of her infamous booze or razor blade benders. That was until recently when she reached out to a friend of a friend of a friend whose grandfather used to be mayor of a local council on the New South Wales north coast. While a long shot, the conversation had alerted her to online articles about The Wandarri Warriors and their fight against development. The resultant Wandarri Eco-Community—a tight-lipped bunch of hippies living together—sounded fascinating, and their defiance over the decades appealed to Layla's delinquent side. Another tipoff led her to a retirement village. The ex-commune old-timer with a terrible case of verbal diarrhoea, and gifted with incredible recall and a fondness for *Skype*, recalled two rock-fishing accidents from the late eighties / early nineties.

Maybe she could have extracted answers from her mother years ago—Layla *had* wielded the power in their twisted relationship—but why bother learning about the day or the man she never wanted to remember? Once considered a good father and teacher, his only legacy was pain, with his last lesson the hardest of all …

How was it possible to love someone so much that you hated them for leaving you.

Never did Layla imagine sitting at a table opposite the man, but there he was, walking towards her, his expression unreadable. Soon, she would get the answer she'd wanted—deserved—and straight from the horse's mouth.

Why *did* William Scott choose such a cruel way to walk out of their lives?

As he advanced through the chaotic courtyard with its maze of tables and chairs, Layla channelled the never-felt-before fury into actions. With a strangely steady hand, she poured water from a bottle into two glasses, repositioned the condiment tray and table decoration to one side, then deliberately positioned her handbag. Only then, as she pressed back into the chair to steel herself, arms folded to disguise the exaggerated rise and fall of her chest, did the man's double take suggest she'd caught his eye.

Blood boiling, and with cortisol spiking to corrode her earlier courage, Layla's body instinctively shifted into fight-or-flight mode, albeit briefly. In her mind, there was absolutely no ambiguity, and no fleeing. She was ready to fight for a life lost—hers and her sister's.

'Look at you!' He sat in the opposite chair. 'This is so—'

'Stop right there.' Layla interrupted. 'Let's skip the big reunion bit. We're way beyond that crap.'

His face twitched into a smirk. 'So, after all this time, it's going to be like that, eh? Fair enough, I suppose. I am curious, though, Layla. First, I see Chelsea in Sandbar. Now you're here. Please, tell me your mother is not about to lob as well.'

'Wow! Smiling and jesting.' Layla scoffed. 'This is amusing to you? Destroying your family and your daughter's life is something to joke about?'

The pair eyed each other like a couple of stray cats in a narrow alley until his gaze flickered to the bar at the back of the open-air eatery.

'Do you suppose they'll sell me a beer this early? Want one?'

'I doubt it and no,' she retorted. 'Thanks to you and Mum, I developed a drinking problem in my teens. Like I said, our meeting today need only be brief. And about Chelsea,' she added, staring hard. 'Stay away from my sister. The last thing I want is her stumbling upon the truth, especially if I'm not around to support her.'

'I saw her, but don't worry. I'll be staying low from now on until she leaves.'

'I see, and then you'll get back to living your happy-ever-after existence, safe in the knowledge you will have traumatised us all sufficiently enough to never come back ever again? Oh, how wrong you are.'

Layla's conviction intensified. She was the sly cat taunting an oblivious bird. She was also about to throw those cage doors wide open and let the cat amongst the pigeons. Another facial twitch exposed his unease, alerting Layla to the power shift. She'd seen the same in Wendy when forced to submit and fess up to the insurance money scam.

'Tell me, *Dad*, when you saw Chelsea, what did you see exactly? Hmm? Was it her pain? Her confusion? The toll of self-destruction that started the day you disappeared?' Layla clenched her jaw, fists too. 'Sitting here now, do you see my pain? Do you realise what this is doing to me?'

'You need to calm, Layla.'

'No!' Yanking her hand off the table thwarted his attempted physical contact. 'You gave up the right to control me. What you did, especially to your precious Miss Fix, was despicable. You broke our family; you broke my sister; now you're breaking her marriage. You've been nothing but a cancer eating away at Chelsea's happiness. She's a gentle, accepting soul, and a wonderful mother to amazing children. *Your* only legacy is deceit, and it's destroying everything she loves. Worst of all, *Dad*, we were sisters until your greed, your indifference, and your dishonesty ruined us. Oh, don't look so freaking shocked.' Layla smacked the table hard enough to rattle the condiment containers. 'Do you never think about anybody but yourself?'

'I do, Layla,' he said, the words soft and steady. 'I see your pain. I'm sorry for putting that in your life. You were never meant to find out. As for Chelsea … I'd needed her that day, but she was young; the young forget,' he said. 'They recover.'

'No, they don't.' Layla snapped. 'Chelsea's kept you on such a pedestal. No one can compete, which means she's set to lose the one person who *is* good for her—her husband. I may not be a Miss Fix, but I refuse to let you ruin our lives more than you have. Silence is no longer the way to protect Chelsea. It never was, and that was *my* mistake, which I'm rectifying.' When the deep furrows of William Scott's brow showed confusion and something indistinguishable, she said, 'Let me spell it out for you. I lied on the phone. Sorry! This meeting is not about reconnecting. You're here because I'm done keeping your secret.'

'Layla?' His voice ground out a warning. 'What are you planning?'

'Honestly? I didn't know until just now. My intention, when I found out Chelsea was at Sandbar Beach, was to find my sister and save her stumbling into your life of lies. But I'm done covering for you. In fact, *Dad*, I plan on knocking you off that pedestal once and for all by exposing you for the lying, false-hearted creep you are.'

William stiffened, shifting nervously until perched on the seat edge—a bird uncertain if it should fly away or stay. 'Don't do this, Layla.'

'Destroy your carefree existence, you mean? Why not? You tore us apart, you selfish bastard.' Every head at a table of Japanese tourists turned. Clearly, some words, or certain tones, spanned language barriers. Layla didn't care. 'You assumed Chelsea was young enough to forget, but the daughter who idolised you still carries guilt. Can you not fathom the damage you've done? Did you think money would help us all move forward? I tried, believe me. I tried every method I could to forget you, but once the brain takes the sights and sounds of a moment, a memory is made. Happy or heart-breaking, it's forever etched in our minds.'

'Then why hurt your sister with the truth now?' he asked.

Layla had to laugh, if only to slice the smug expression off his face. 'You have this all wrong, *Dad*. Because of you, I've been hurting the sister I love for decades. Yes, when I found out the truth, I wanted to tell the world what you'd done, until Mum said the police would lock her up and take Chelsea away. So, I walked away. I left my family out of love, *Dad*. Why did you leave?' Layla's mask fell away, tears welling. She fought them back. 'In your letter to Mum, you claimed to love us. What sort of love?'

'A father's love,' he retorted, 'and I loved you girls equally and undeniably. Never your mother, although I tried. We were friends and nothing more. We hung out at the same spot on the beach, she was friendly and pretty, but older than me and with different ideas about the future. I had plans for my life,' he added without a whiff of emotion. 'Until that one night on the beach after her twenty-fourth birthday. There was a bunch of us and all drunk.

'It was one time, Layla. "One stupid decision", as I told my parents. First time with a girl and I make her pregnant. Should've got myself a lottery ticket. Instead, I got a wife and a baby. Not until two years into our marriage—mid-argument—did Wendy fess up.' He leaned forward, resting his elbows on the table, fingers steepled and flexing. 'Your real father and I were at the same beach party. We were good mates and surfing buddies. He lived next door to your mother's house, yet I never knew they were an item. No wonder he declined to be my groomsman— no reason given. Next thing, without warning, the family up and moves. The penny should've dropped then. Kevin Hodge went on to live my dream life.'

Up to that point, Layla had been holding it together, feeling strong, calling the shots, until hearing his name sucked the might right out of her.

'Kevin Hodge is my father's name?'

With such obvious indifference in William's nod, the man might have been answering 'yes' to a cup of tea.

'We were nippers with dreams of following the pro surfing circuit.' William's thoughts seemed to drift. 'Kev went on living with his parents for years, travelling anytime he wanted. No responsibilities, no mortgage. If there was an upside to my moving out west with your mother, it was not seeing his surfing successes headlined in the Manly Beach Daily.'

When William stopped to gulp water from a glass, Layla asked, 'You're saying Kevin knew about me?'

'Wendy told him, hence the sudden move out of town. But here's the real kicker. Unbeknownst to everyone—including her parents—he'd offered marriage and suggested Wendy move into his parents' place so she'd have support while he chased his surfing dream. She declined his proposal. Your mother wasn't interested in being a stay-at-home surfing widow and living with her in-laws. Apparently, I was the more reliable option.'

Unsure how, Layla found her voice—softer, unguarded. 'And when you found out the truth? You stayed with Mum?'

He shrugged. 'No choice. Your birth complicated our relationship. You see, Layla, I loved you.'

As the cacophonous courtyard chatter turned into white noise, those three words—I loved you—fell around Layla like snowflakes: serene and beautiful, but complex and sadly short-lived. Spoken by a man she'd spent most of her life hating, his words became barbs of ice: one poked, one prodded, the third pierced her heart. But oblivious to Layla's pain, his storytelling continued.

'Then, of course, there was your mother. A woman who slaps a man with one hand while seducing him with the other.'

'What are you talking about?'

'Convinced a baby of my own would fix her and I, and our marriage, she went off the pill to fall pregnant.'

'Of course,' Layla gushed. 'Miss Fix! I get it now.'

'I desperately wanted Wendy to be right and to make us work,' he said. 'And just like the moment I held you in my arms, I fell in love with Chelsea. But it didn't change enough. I was drowning in suburbia and working hard to support a difficult and demanding wife. At first, I looked for ways to escape *with* her, like taking a round-the-country camping trip. But, when it was clear I'd be trapped in that house and in a life I hated until I died, I decided dying was my way out.'

'You couldn't divorce and live someplace else, like any honourable man would do?'

William stiffened, his old-person stoop all but gone. 'I am an honourable man *and* hardworking. While providing for our family and being loyal to the same insurance company for years, my salary simply didn't stretch to supporting more than one household or mortgage. Wendy left me no choice. But I looked after you girls financially,' he added. 'Money would provide you both with choices. Choices I never had. Whatever else you think, Layla, I never regretted loving you and I will *always* be your father.'

The words sounded right; they sounded real. Had Layla closed her eyes and imagined another scenario, she could have …

'No!' A resurgence of the old grief hit hard. It was the same anguish she would fold up, pack away, and try suffocating in a suitcase crammed with crushless travel clothes and comfortable walking shoes. But no matter the destination, Layla could never escape the bitterness and the baggage her parents' lie had brought into her life.

'Yes, Layla,' he insisted. 'My words are the truth. I tried with your mother, but I was no good as a husband, and no good as a family man, even though I loved you girls. I risked my life *because* I loved you. Sure, I could have stayed, but existing isn't enough. Cautious people live to their nineties miserable. Other people make the most of every minute. I needed to live, and the only way out was to—'

'Die! Not to mention risk something terrible happening to your youngest daughter?'

'In my heart I knew my adventure girl would cope. She was smart and brave.'

'Well, your adventure girl spent the night alone and lost on that headland.'

'She wasn't alone,' he said. 'I followed her and kept watch. Only when I had to, when I knew help was coming, did I disappear.'

'… leaving her to help you pull off insurance fraud,' Layla finished. 'A very upstanding and loyal father and employee, *Dad*.'

'If you knew how those companies operated back then, you'd understand what they paid out to us was a drop in the ocean. What I did, they deserved.'

'Deserved?' Layla queried. 'You stole from them.'

He nodded. 'You can look at it any way you like, but please see it from my perspective. Every day, another example would come across my desk. The company short shrifted customers without a second thought, denying claims and finding loopholes to reduce payouts. In those days, people didn't question, and there was no Google and mass hysteria. Grieving families didn't share their lives online. They didn't suspect or question paperwork and payout figures—if they even knew what to ask. Businesses back then relied on ignorance. Without proof of death for probate purposes, families of missing persons waited seven years. Even then, claims were often left to some overworked, underpaid processing clerk.

'If the circumstances of my fishing accident hadn't provided the Coroner with enough evidence to make an early Inference of Death, your mother would've waited years before seeing any money. I knew, if you were to get on with your lives, there could be no doubt as to my death, and no delay. That's why I did what I did, the way I did it. And I took out my form of insurance by making sure to spill the beans on my boss's shonky accounting practices after I was gone. An anonymous word in the right ear did the trick,' he added. 'Management would've been so desperate to "do the right thing" and do it fast. My claim would sail through.'

'And I suppose you consider whistleblowing a form of redemption.'

'Not at all, Layla. I made a choice. Either take charge of my future or live in the hope a bad home life turned into a good one. And that is no way to live. But I left you and your sister well-off. You had real estate, trust accounts your mother couldn't touch, and you had each other. That was the plan, at least.' The way his voice snagged, combined with the hand tremor as he lifted the glass of water to his lips, made no impact on Layla.

Crocodile tears! Though tempted to suggest he shouldn't try conning a con artist, she instead asked, 'How long had you been planning this escape?'

'Planning?' He scoffed. 'There *was* no plan until, as luck would have it, I saw the name Liam Scott in an archived file and realised one man's death could be my rebirth. I'd long ago lost the *will* to live my mundane existence, so I removed the *Will* from my name and mentally removed myself from my life bit by bit. How to disappear came to me when I picked up a new tide chart. I realised a predicted king tide would coincide with our annual holiday.' He stopped to sip more water. 'William Scott would die at Sandbar twelve months later. It was a calculated risk that could have gone terribly wrong for me but, like I said, I'd been drowning in that house and in my marriage for years. Turned out, the moon and the tide saved me.'

'Oh, my god!' Layla's stomach spasmed so violently she had to hug her belly to hold back the urge to throw up. Already shaking mad, her body started rocking, the pressure in her head making her eyeballs pulsate as she stared William Scott down. 'People actually spent days searching the ocean. I searched. Where were you?'

'Nowhere,' he said with a toss of his shoulders and a smirk. 'They sent in search helicopters and mapped the ocean's currents, but I was never in the water. Even if they'd thought to look up, my hiding place blended in with the environment. Camouflage works for soldiers, and it works for sea creatures like the humble cephalopod. I only had to stay put, stay very still, and wait for the danger to pass.'

'Where did you go afterwards?'

'Anywhere and everywhere, until drawn back to Sandbar. For a few years, I lived in the middle of the bush, until a nosey park ranger stumbled upon my shack. After he razed it to the ground, I walked into Sandbar as Liam Scott, claimed my land parcel—no questions asked—found a jack-of-all job, and fell in love with the locals—and they loved and accepted me. Like I said, no questions asked, no demands.'

'Why risk confessing to Mum?'

'The letter …?' he mumbled, his remorse clear in the stone-cold tone. 'That was a mistake.'

Layla barked a laugh so hard, heads turned. 'Me sitting here today is proof enough of that fact.'

'Yes, you are here, Layla. So what now?' he asked, clearly not sharing in her amusement. 'I used to say you were like a beach umbrella. No guessing when you might take off.'

'Well, William / Will / Liam / Whoever,' she retorted. 'There's no holding me back and you can't stop me.'

His stare contemplated hers in a kind of whoever-blinks-first-loses way. 'Can I at least ask you for a head start? There are people in my life to consider, things to be settled and—'

'Arrangements to be made?' Layla finished with a scoff. For a second, she almost felt sorry for the man. Was making him suffer, like he'd made them suffer, not revenge enough? 'Relax, William. I won't be dobbing you into the police and putting myself under scrutiny—unless I'm forced. We've both made mistakes,' Layla admitted. 'The difference is, I'm going to correct mine. I suggest you consider doing the same by fessing up to your lovely wife sooner rather than later, because Chelsea will learn the truth, and I can't be sure what she'll do. One thing is for certain. While she'll need a shoulder to cry on, it won't be yours—or mine.'

For a second time, worry dragged his shoulders down, 'Layla, please—'

'Stop speaking!' She flashed a warning palm at him, her irritation skyrocketing. 'You don't get a say. You destroyed my dream of having a baby sister; to see her grow into a woman, to have her confide in me and share experiences, and grow up to emulate me. Little did I know, as half-sisters, she would never be like me at all. Hell, I don't know myself anymore. Only that, despite everything, my love for Chelsea is why I've stayed away. As of today, that stops.' Layla paused to breathe, to slow her racing heart. 'I'm going to find her at Sandbar because I want to be close by when you break her heart all over again. Protecting each other is what loving sisters do.'

'You clearly haven't thought this through, Layla. If you love her, why hurt her?'

'Oh, no, William, you're not hearing me. I'm the sister she thinks doesn't give a damn, while you are her hero, and your memory over-shadows everything and everyone. No man can compete with the great William Scott. Not even her amazing husband, Dale. So, no, *I'm* not telling Chelsea. You are. Only then will the hero-worshipping stop, and with luck she'll save her marriage. So, *Dad*, listen carefully because this is how it's going to play out.'

Layla finally had his attention.

When done speaking, she stood. Seven hours behind the wheel of a car, combined with a hideous case of jet lag, allowed her to stay stony-faced. Or was the controlled exterior because she'd never pictured this unlike-liest of moments, and she no longer harboured expectations of the man who'd influenced her formative years?

'I think we've covered everything.'

'For Christ's sake, Layla, what is it you expect of me?'

'Nothing. I haven't needed you since I was a teenager. A man who's been more mentor than you once said if I expect nothing from people, they won't disappoint me. So, William, I expect nothing. But you should expect I'll follow through on my threat to expose your secret life.'

A ringing bell and a burst of activity distracted the pair. Chairs scraped and a cacophony of excited voices rang through the cafe as tourists, eager to escape the humid courtyard, headed for air-conditioned buses.

'Please,' he said, mopping sweat from his brow with the back of a hand, his earlier arrogance reduced to an uncertain stare. 'At least think about what this will do.'

'Oh, believe me, since finding your letter, I've done nothing *but* think about what *you've* done. Some birthday present! But,' Layla reached a hand into the bag she had purposefully positioned on the table prior to his arrival, 'I guess some things must've rubbed off on me when growing up with you, *Dad*, because I, too, had an insurance policy in place for today.' Extracting the mobile phone from the side pocket, she made a point of stopping the voice memo function. 'I reckon we've covered everything. Thanks for making time to meet. Wish I could say it's been a pleasure.' Standing—strong and sure—Layla tossed her bag strap over one shoulder. 'And remember, this is not a choice, William. You screwed with our lives. Now it's my turn to determine *your* fate. Should you fail to show as arranged, I may change my mind about involving the police.'

'Layla, I—'

'No! We're all done here. Expect a call within twenty-four hours. I'll tell you when and where you'll meet with Chelsea and me—once I've prepared her as best I can. Or perhaps we might drop by the shop. *Squid's Bait & Tackle*, right? Talia sounds so nice over the telephone. Twenty-four hours, okay?' Layla made to leave, tucking the mobile deep into her bag. 'A bit of advice, though. Use this time to think about what you've done, knowing twenty-four hours is *nothing* compared to all the years I've been forced to think about it.'

Miraculously, Layla's legs got her away from the table, out of the cafe, and back to her resort room, where she threw up in the toilet, then threw open the bar fridge door. She stood back and stared hard at the tiny, bright-coloured bottles lined up like soldiers on the shelf. Then, in the mirror above, she caught sight of her battle-weary reflection.

'What do you think you're doing?' she asked, unsure if the question related to the booze, or to what she was about to put herself and Chelsea through.

Probably both.

LAYLA, DAY 4 OF 7

Her decision to stay overnight at the resort had been a good one, and she'd slept more soundly than expected, waking to a Lao Tzu text from Trent:

> "Mastering others is strength. Mastering yourself is true power."

Layla's grip on the steering wheel matched her fierce mental determination. Soon enough she was whizzing past littoral rainforest while listening to the distracting dirge of local breakfast radio and hoping the snaking stretch of road ended before she threw up her guts—again. A welcome straight section of highway saw her car, and her thoughts, drift dangerously. But as she neared her destination, the undulating ribbon of narrow roadway switched from gravel to bitumen as often as Layla changed her mind.

When activating the wipers to clear her windscreen of the dead bug and dust inundation, she noticed a minuscule crack. What danger might such damage pose if ignored? Layla should know the answer. The Scott family's secret had been like a stone chip in her life—a constant threat that would one day splinter and break.

Suddenly, a Sandbar Campground sign confirmed her destination was close. Too close. Layla had to slow down—both the car and her racing heart. In fact, she needed to take a breather, refocus her thoughts, and pick the remnants of smashed butterfly from the windscreen in front of the driver's seat. Steering the car into the same small clearing as a motorhome, she raised a hello hand to the family of three seated in folding camp chairs. The beaming child, likely around four—five if small for her age, like Layla had been—waved back. Driving past the well-loved Winnebago to park up, she was adjusting the rearview mirror to mop mascara stains from under her eyes when she noticed the little girl wore all pink.

When around the same age, Layla's world had turned very rosy. The bedroom got a fresh coat of pink, Wendy and William stopped arguing, and Cabbage Patch Caroline took up permanent residence at the back of the wardrobe. Despite the always-peeing, always-pooing, and always-screaming real-life baby not as easily put aside, Layla was determined to be the best big sister ever. And when old enough, she would be the best wife, then the best mother.

'I'll have it all,' she had told her father.

He'd hugged her and replied, 'Find the right person, make the right choices, and the world will be your oyster, Layla-girl.'

Even after Dad explained the old-fashioned saying, Layla had wanted to question why an adult would make a slimy shellfish the symbol of 'having it all'.

Unfortunately, she never did live the dream. Worse still, to this day, eating an oyster reminded Layla of her first tongue kiss.

Fifteen at the time, and on holidays—their second-last at Sandbar, as it turned out—Layla had become bored with board games and the confines of a stuffy caravan. Taking a walk, she'd followed the sounds of kids laughing and came across the local teen hang-out spot among the dunes. Not far from an old boat shed, a dozen kids sat cross-legged around a collection of Coolabah wine casks and passed around a cigarette.

Two fast drinks later, Layla was necking with a blond-haired boy until sand tried finding its way into all the worst places—his hands, too. But it was the guy's enthusiastic kisses, like slimy molluscs sliding over her lips, and the boat shed's splintered wooden floor that ended the petting session. Unforgettable for all the wrong reasons, Layla wished she'd stayed a naive young girl with the world as her oyster.

Instead, she would soon learn that her parents were liars, the truth leaves scars, and protecting her sister would require a lifetime commitment.

By eighteen, she was the custodian of an unthinkable lie and burdened with the worst birthday present in the world because she'd bowed out of a weekend sleepover on Ginny's family's brand-new boat—and for the most puerile reason. Her period.

Having wished and prayed she'd get them like all her friends, they'd come on as Ginny's parents were packing stores into the car. Rather than admit she was unprepared and pathetically uneducated—because her self-absorbed mother had never bothered with 'the talk'—Layla's humiliation that day had set her fate.

31

LAYLA, 1983

'You must come,' Virginia pleads. 'How can you get so sick so quick?'

'Um, I, ah … *Oooh!*' Layla grunts and grabs her stomach as the very real cramp stabs her belly low down and deep. 'Tummy bug, I guess.' She doesn't admit to the wad of toilet paper inside her knickers making her want to scratch. 'I'll have to go home. Sorry.'

'It's your birthday,' Ginny whines. 'Mum bought champagne. And you haven't seen my new bathers.'

'What if it's contagious? Mum's been crook,' Layla adds, lessening the lie with a pinch of truth.

Her mother hasn't 'been well' since 'the accident'—two phrases the adults use when referring to the family's tragedy. Aunty Rita still visits regularly to sort out the refrigerator—a task otherwise known as chucking out the booze to make room for fresh vegetables, which Layla cooks each night before hitting the study books. If she *is* to 'have it all' like Dad says she can, she'll need top marks in every end-of-year exam.

Mrs Peters stops packing food into a big icebox. 'I'm sorry you're unwell, Layla, dear.' She looks at her watch.

Aware the reason for the sleepover is to make an early start, ensuring the boat's smooth passage through the heads and into open waters, Layla shrugs sheepishly. She hates lying to her best friend, but the truth will change nothing. Why be on a boat if you can't swim in the water? Do boats even have toilets? Feigning illness might seem like overkill, but it's embarrassing enough to only be getting her period now.

Layla once asked her mother why she was so much later coming on than other girls at school. Wendy had been dropping panty liners and feminine spray products into the grocery trolly at the time.

'Stress delays menstruation, and we've had our share.' Then she muttered something about the whole menstruation business being a curse, and Layla should enjoy not having *it* while *it* lasts.

'Virginia, dear,' Mrs Peters says, 'if Layla's not well, it's better that she heads home. Our drive to the mooring is long and winding.'

That's grown-up talk for *no one wants someone with a contagious lurgy on a long car trip—or on a boat—no matter how big something called a Halverson Cruiser might be.*

The dawn's early rays are only just sun-striping the neighbouring acreages when Mr Peters slows the car on approach to the Beach Shack.

'Just drop me here, Mr Peters. I'll walk the rest,' Layla says, planning to sneak into the house and into the shower without waking Mum and getting the third degree. 'Have a great time,' she adds tearfully before waving her best friend away.

Taking the sloppy joe she'd purposely sat on during the car ride—in case—and tying the sleeves around her waist—in case—Layla takes the side path to the backyard. She's hoping to find period products in the pool house—the old outhouse/laundry Mum insisted Dad renovate the year they got the Clark Rubber pool. Finding no pads, and uncertain about tampons, Layla makes do with multiple pairs of knickers she's reclaimed from the washing pile.

With her emotions ranging from excruciating embarrassment to extreme ecstasy that *it* had finally happened to her, Layla is rinsing out her shorts in the tub and glancing out the window—across the weed-infested wasteland their backyard has become since losing the keen gardener in the family—when she spots smoke wafting in spirals from the rusty drum incinerator.

'Dad?' The word ends on an optimistic high note.

But he isn't at the incinerator, beer in hand and busily burning pruned tree branches; nor is her mother asleep in her bedroom at the front of the house, as expected. Wendy Scott is draped over the sun lounge, simultaneously snoring and gurgling through her open mouth. This isn't the first time Layla has found her mother passed out. Grief, combined with the accumulation of chemist bottles in the bathroom cabinet, mostly keeps

Mum in a comfortably comatose state: in front of the television, in bed, and even in a bath turned cold.

Some months ago, when it seemed Aunty Rita's tough-love approach might bring Layla's mother out of the dark place she regularly retreats to, a letter arrived. While Mum never shared the envelope's contents, whatever was in the little orange pill bottles in the bathroom perked her right up when combined with a cask of wine.

Scattered around the sun lounge this morning are family photo albums displaying picture-less captions and unoccupied corner mounts.

'Mum?' Layla tries tapping her awake but gets only a garbled utterance. 'Mum?' When her mother's mouth sags open, Layla tears up, shaking harder 'Please, wake up, Mum.'

A part-snort, part-gurgle turns into a cough and a moan before Mum rolls onto one side. 'Call Rita. She'll come get you girls. Leave me alone.'

If asked, and despite battling illness herself, Aunty Rita would collect both girls and take them back to her beach house, which was literally on the beach. Unlike Chelsea who loves Rita but never looks out windows overlooking the beach, Layla loves searching for cruise ships and planes, wishing she and Chelsea could travel far, far away.

While at Aunty Rita's, the girls got so much love, Layla resented coming back home to a mother too wrapped in her own misery to deal with her daughters' grief. But Layla has never begrudged caring for Chelsea, often using treats to coax her sister out of her bedcover cave.

Like Aunty Rita, Mr and Mrs Peters are such good huggers. Ginny reckons it's because, as police officers, they see every day how precious life and family are.

'Yeah, sure!' Layla grumbles while swilling and downing the dregs of warm wine from her mother's discarded goblet.

So much for sipping her first champagne while boating around the beautiful blue waters of the Hawkesbury River. The only thing floating at that moment is the incinerator's scorched flotsam on the pond-scum green waters of a neglected above-ground pool. As a gust of wind scatters more ash from the incinerator, a tumbleweed of charred paper and photographs barrel across the backyard, some impaling themselves on the chain wire boundary fence. Before long, they'll be on the neighbouring property. Mr Baker won't be happy.

After collecting all she can, Layla returns to the patio and dumps the lot in a plastic box—the stackable, lidded variety that ordinarily stored her father's fastidiously filed family tax records and bills. About to try waking Mum again, Layla notices one particular sheet of paper sticking out from the bunch. Different from the rest, this single note has her father's distinctive left-handed scrawl.

Although singed at the edges, the words are decipherable—the content devastating.

Sitting on the shower floor, back pressed against the wall, her knees crushed against her chest, Layla stares blankly at her innocence swirling in red around the drain hole and washing away. Gone! *Time to grow up, Layla.*

Only when the water runs cold does she get out, dry herself off and start rummaging under the bathroom sink, studying the excess period products but making do with a pair of disposable paper knickers—the type with a built-in mini pad. They feel odd, but not as strange as the face staring back from the mirror.

'Who am I?' she asks. 'Who is he?'

'Layla? Layla!' Mum calls while jiggling the door handle. 'Unlock this door immediately.'

Secreting extra mini pads under the wrapped towel she's tucked across her barely there breasts, Layla shouts back, 'Go away.'

More knocking follows, as desperate as Mum's voice. 'Virginia's mother called to check on you.'

When? Layla wonders. Since locking herself in the bathroom, she'd heard nothing other than running water and the words *he isn't dead* and *who is he?* beating a persistent drum in her head.

'Let me into the bathroom this minute, or—'

Layla flings open the door. 'Or what, Mum? Or you'll tell Dad?'

Pushing past her startled mother to make a dash for the bedroom—relieved to find her sister's bed unslept in—she slams the door and turns the lock.

'Open up immediately, Layla.'

'Why? Who is there to care if I rot in this room?'

'Please, sweetheart, you're confused.' Her mother tries a softer approach. 'Let me in and I'll explain.'

With her latest birthday present—the Japanese-inspired happi coat that were all the rage—hugging her body, she slides the door's privacy lock and steps to the side, no longer concerned about the full ashtray on the dressing table. But her mother says nothing, walking instead to the window and easing the venetian blinds apart as if expecting to see someone in the street.

'Watchya looking for, Mum? Dad coming home?'

With fury evident in every furrow of her mother's forty-one-year-old face, she snaps. 'This will *never* be his home, and he will *never* be back.'

Layla steels herself, swallowing any remaining sarcasm along with the urge to cry. There are too many questions. 'So, where is he?'

'Nowhere,' Mum says. 'He doesn't exist. He's no longer alive. Not to us, not to the insurance company, not to the world. Forget him.'

'You're a drunk,' is all Layla can think to say. 'I'm not talking to you. I want Dad.'

'Too bad because he's gone. That's how he wants it. And there's no coming back from the dead.'

'I'll show Aunty Rita what he wrote. She'll know what to do.'

Something like a switch in Mum flicks, changing her face from smug to suspicious. 'Where is the letter?'

'Safe!' Layla replies. 'You should never burn off with a belly full of booze. Are there more letters? Do they say where he is?'

A dramatic chest grab is Mum's play for sympathy as she surrenders herself to the small stool at Layla's dressing table. 'There's only the one letter. Best we don't know more about where he's gone,' she adds, almost philosophically.

Tears prick at Layla's tear ducts. 'Best for who? Not me. I want the truth. Tell me, or else—'

'Oh, grow up, Layla,' Mum says, opening the wooden jewellery box on the dresser and lifting the top tray to extract Layla's ciggie stash. Taking one for herself, she tosses the crushed packet of *Stuyvesants* onto the bed. 'Join me?'

Layla's jaw drops. 'What are you doing?'

'You're not a child,' she replies, dragging deep. 'You are a grownup who must accept the facts. Your father started a new life.'

'W-without us?'

'The letter suggests so.'

'But ...' Layla settles on the edge of her bed, tears mingling with snot before raining over her chin. 'How long have you known? You're not even upset.'

Another drag on the cigarette. Another sigh. 'A little over a year. And of course I'm upset—for you. The fact your father needs more than we can give does not surprise me in the least. I'm more surprised he stayed with us for as long as he did. I believe he wanted to leave sooner, but he had commitments.'

'What commitments?'

'You and Chelsea,' she says, voice stoic. 'I tried to protect you, and I'm sad you had to find out this way, but you'll understand in time. He loves you girls.'

With pinched eyes and agonising accuracy, Layla launches daggers at her mother. 'Even though I'm not his daughter?'

Mum's expression chills. 'What counts, sweetheart, is he loved you as if you were.'

'You tricked him, didn't you?' Layla waits while her mother sucks another lungful of smoke. 'I hate you. I *hate* you. I'm going to tell Rita. Or I'll tell Ginny's parents what a terrible mother you are and how you drove Dad away.'

Rising slowly from the stool, pausing to grind the cigarette into the ashtray, her mother walks to the bed and puts her face inches from Layla's, both hands on her shoulders and squeezing so hard Layla's forced up and onto her tippy toes.

'Well, Miss Tattletale, look around. See all the pretty bed pillows, the latest clothes, jewellery, makeup, music cassettes? Go on. Look!' she hissed. 'I've given you so much. I've cared for you and your sister—cared we didn't look like the neighbourhood hillbillies—but I'm tired of you girls wanting more, and of mean people talking about us. And I'm tired of this house.'

When Mum turns back to the dresser, Layla assumes she's about to pinch another cigarette from her stash. Instead, a random handful of jewellery turns into flying shrapnel.

'Look at all this. Curlers to curl, straighteners to straighten, clips and scrunchies and ribbons—all so you can keep up with Ginny. Money does not come out of thin air, Layla. Your father's insurance payout was a generous one, and there'll be more for you both in trust funds; more than you'll know what to do with at twenty-one. But that's your father! Happy to deprive me in favour of you girls, as if he doesn't trust I'll share.

'Well, your mother is done sharing herself ragged. It's time I took back. These are mine!' A pair of silver hoops hits Layla in the face before falling to the floor. 'Go ahead and tell the truth, you ungrateful girl. See how long you stay friends, as I doubt Ginny's wonderful parents are the type to consort with criminals. Oh, and forget about our birthday shopping excursion next week, and the portable stereo I was planning to buy. In fact, forget about birthdays, full stop. And while I'm certain Mrs Peters will make a better mother than me—' Mum gasps as if breathing for the first time. Then she cries—for real this time; Layla has seen enough crocodile tears over the years to spot the difference. 'If you tell Ginny's parents, or anyone else, *anything* other than your father died in a terrible and tragic rock fishing accident, we will all suffer. You and Chelsea can certainly say goodbye to the pretty things—and to each other.'

'Why? We've done nothing wrong.'

Mum snatches up more bits from Layla's dresser. 'Thanks to your father defrauding his employer, these are the proceeds of a crime.'

'But I knew nothing about anything. You claimed his insurance.'

'The letter arrived well after lodgement of our insurance claim, and I was as shocked as you. And it was Rita who dealt with the paperwork, mostly because … Well, you know how devastated I was.'

'Devastated?' Layla snorts. 'Is that another word for drunk?'

Mum stiffens, clears her throat. 'Your father left the policy document, along with instructions detailing what I needed to do in the event of his death or injury, *and* to not delay doing so—a deliberate move on his part, no doubt.'

'But why?' Layla cries.

'You're asking me why he left, or why he felt the need to rip an already aching heart out of my chest and make me despise him?' Mum shakes her head. 'I only know this conversation is over. I'll admit no more; not with your threat to tell the world. Some cocky corporation lawyer at your father's firm will have me locked up for fraud. They'll certainly take our house, all our money, and you and your sister will have nothing. They may even go after Rita and her house.'

'But it's a lie.'

'Yes, a big, fat, ugly lie. And, yes, I kept quiet and kept the money for you and Chelsea—for *our* financial security and *your* futures. And why not? None of us asked for this burden, but as of now, because you came home when you were supposed to be boating, you're as involved.' Mum tugs another cigarette from the packet but doesn't light it. 'If you want to tell Ginny's parents, or anyone else, that's your choice. Don't forget, when they ask why your father walked away from you, tell them the truth about that, too.'

'What truth?' Layla asks.

'That you, me, and Chelsea weren't enough. I'm sorry I didn't do a proper job of burning the letter. We might've avoided this scene, but …' She shrugs. 'Here we are. Happy birthday! Time to grow up.'

'I'm already grown up,' Layla insists, eyes now heavy with unshed tears refusing to fall. 'I want to know what you know—everything.'

Mum smirks. 'Very well, my grown-up girl, but understand this. You can't be selective, and you won't like everything I tell you. That's not the way it works. There'll be questions I can't answer because I don't under-stand myself, but by sharing what I do know, Layla, I hope you'll consider your sister's future and the devastating impact of telling your version of the truth. Because I will dispute it. I'll tell them you're a troubled child.'

'And I'll show them I'm not. I'll tell them how I look after my sister when you're too drunk.'

Her mother's face reddens. 'Excellent strategy! They'll claim I'm unfit and take me away, leaving poor Chelsea to foster care.'

Layla flinches. 'They wouldn't.'

Mum nods. 'At least Chelsea is young enough for another family to want her. Girls your age are, well, you said it yourself. You're all grown up and needing good exam results to support yourself. Alternatively, we destroy the letter—and properly this time.' Her mother extends a hand and wiggles *gimme-here* fingers. 'Where is it?'

When Layla doesn't budge, her mother moves to the dresser, rifling through personal bits, including her undies drawer where she'd hidden the extra mini pads.

'Stop, Mum! Here! You want the damn letter destroyed?' Layla takes the folded note from her robe pocket, rips the sheet, and lets the tiny pieces snow over the wicker bin with its dirty cotton buds and snotty tissues. Then, cradling the basket close to her chest, she announces, 'I'll do the burning this time.'

Mum's voice tracks Layla down the hallway and out the back door. 'And get that head of yours in order before your sister gets home from her sleepover. Remember, Layla, this is your father's doing because we weren't good enough.'

3 2

LAYLA

'No wonder you ended up suicidal and on Trent Dashwood's sofa,' Layla muttered while scratching the last bit of black-and-white butterfly from the windscreen.

Whenever she'd sulked or pushed the boundaries like a brat in the past, Trent would pull her into line by imposing rules, and encourage her to accept and value herself, saying: 'Layla Scott, you are enough, and you are worth loving'.

The hot doc had been exactly what she'd needed, and once she'd accepted his help, their regular one-on-one sessions shifted to scheduled group therapy check-ins, finally transitioning to 'as needed'. By that stage, Layla was completely and utterly dependent and in love. In her mind, Trent was the father she never knew and the lover she never dared to want, because her heart wouldn't tolerate more rejection when he discovered Layla was not enough. And so her attraction remained another secret to keep; although she'd suspected Trent had known, because he stopped being her shrink, putting her instead under the watchful eye of a sober coach to help her stay substance free and find her a job.

But without the mind-numbing booze and barbiturates, Layla struggled to contain her emotions around her sister. And so she has kept her distance, kept her secret, and kept something Trent once told her at the forefront of her mind.

'Being sensitive is not weakness, Layla,' he'd said. 'And repressing your feelings does not make you strong. It's the opposite. We're all born brave, but we learn fear from a young age. Then we grow and learn what courage is. The truest version of courage comes from our willingness to experience every emotion, even at the risk of a broken heart. You only need do one thing every day,' he'd said while tapping a finger against her skull. 'One small thing to trigger fear—in here. Then, go ahead and do it anyway. You'll be surprised to discover what you've been missing.'

While she'd nodded and promised Trent she'd try, Layla was fully aware the thing she missed most—and would go on missing—was her sister.

Might confessing after all this time be the beginning of a beautiful connection? Or might their relationship end up resembling the remains Layla was still picking off her windscreen?

33

TADPOLE

Tad closed in on the car idling at the private entrance to Wandarri Eco-Community, and studied the woman standing trance-like nearby. 'G'day! Can I help you?'

'Not if I'm close to Wandarri and Sandbar Beach. Am I?'

Squinting at the embroidery on her peak cap—*World Eco Tours*—Tad said, 'Yes and no.'

'Yes *and* no? What kind of absurd answer is that?'

'Simple, really. Yes—if you own a parcel, and no—if, as your hat suggests, you're a stickybeak planning to share what you find with the world. Wandarri-ites value their privacy, and the bona fide visitor should know which bower they're looking for.'

'Bower?'

'Hmm, figured as much. Sorry, but it's residents and their invited guests only beyond this point.' He directed her attention to the sign stating as much. 'Sandbar Campground entrance is further along. And you'll find ample sightseeing opportunities, depending on what you enjoy. What floats your boat?'

The woman cracked a kind of smile—possibly to make up for sounding disproportionately upset by his questioning. 'Floats my what?'

'It's a saying. This part of the country has something for every traveller, so I'm wondering. What do you want to see? What do you love? What gets you up in the morning? What drives you?'

'Oh, I see, well, too easy,' she replied, the smile growing more genuine and maybe a little smug. 'I want to *see* my sister; I *love* my own bed; the alarm on my clock radio *gets me up in the morning*, and Charlie from the bus company *drives me* into my office in the city. He's the sweetest Pakistani man who smells of curry and entertains his passengers by singing Bollywood songs. Any more questions?'

Tad huffed a laugh. Yes, he had more, like why this woman joked through sad eyes, and why her face was stirring such familiar feelings. Despite the stiff veneer, Tad liked her. He liked sass. He also liked women in their raw state, preferring his food the same: no artificial colouring, additives, or preservatives. Tad was too long in the tooth to ignore his heart health—physical and emotional.

'I am looking for someone,' the woman said, more an afterthought. 'Perhaps you know her?'

'Perhaps tell me who *you* are, and we'll go from there. I'm the caretaker at Sandbar Campgrounds.'

'Oh, great. Hi, my name's Layla, and I need—'

'Layla?' he queried. 'That's weird—in a good way. It's not a name you hear a lot, but I might've met a Layla. Long time ago now. A bunch of kids and me on Sandbar Beach, a warm summer night, a little too much Moselle. But it was the Stone's Green Ginger Wine chaser that did me in.' He had her attention now. 'Yeah, she was definitely a Layla.'

'Good heavens! You're that Tadpole?' Every speck of stiff facade fell away.

'The one and only, but only to my mates and good-looking chicks who wander uninvited into beach parties.' He removed the peak cap and ran a hand over his balding head. 'Had more hair on top back then. Yours was long, right? I recall eating it at one point.' His grin widened when she laughed. 'A bloke never forgets his first crush.'

'It was dark! You hardly saw me.'

'I felt you,' he said, his face warming as he glanced back towards Kai in the car's passenger seat. 'Ah, sorry, I mean, I felt a connection. It was nice.'

Glancing towards Kai, she lowered her voice. 'You *felt* a lot, as I recall.'

'And then you squealed,' Tad said, 'which got me quite the reputation afterwards.'

'Really? You mean you neglected to mention to your mates that my vocals were less of the orgasmic variety and more due to a massive splinter in my butt?'

'Letting people come to their own conclusion isn't illegal, is it?' he quipped.

'That depends,' she said, the spark in her eyes dulling. 'Thanks for the memories, Tadpole, but I need to find my sister.'

'That would be Chelsea.' Tad hoped his unease didn't show.

He hadn't spoken to Chelsea today. Last night they'd both drunk too much, and he'd held her until she fell asleep. Then Tad crashed out on Fleur's stretcher in the annex and when he woke, his visitor still dead to the world, he'd left her there to sleep it off.

'Do you know where my sister's camping?'

'Sure do! Head towards those gates up there and park the car. My little mate and I will take you. Chelsea moved into a van and there's only one car per site,' he explained. 'Them's the rules.'

CHELSEA

Fact: waking in a hot, claustrophobic caravan with a hangover was not fun, and the cold shower did little to invigorate Chelsea. Adding to her disquiet was waking in a stranger's bed—with said stranger nowhere in sight—and with a cotton wool mouth, the beating of one-thousand drummers behind her temple, and with eyeballs burning from too many tears.

Last night, while pouring her heart out, Tad had poured red wines, his hugs and reassurances offering her empathy and understanding. How was it a stranger could comprehend the way sadness had reshaped her life so dramatically? Dale tried, but his life experiences were different. His parents' death, while tragic, hadn't been an accident, and he hadn't been involved or responsible for their demise. Rather, his drunken father had got behind the wheel to drag race, egged on by a wife—eight months pregnant—who was keen to beat her ex-boyfriend. An orphan shunted from place to place, Dale hadn't experienced love or genuine paternal affection in the way Chelsea had with her father. For Dale, the closest thing to losing a parent had been farewelling former case worker, Bill Field, who'd succumbed to a protracted illness.

Tadpole, on the other hand, had loved and then lost in tragic and traumatic circumstances. He also knew the pain and torment that came with self-blame. So, on that score—not that she was scoring—it was natural Tad would relate to Chelsea's inner battles better than Dale ever could.

Unfortunately, Tad not only knew how to pour wine, but he also made the tastiest Pasta Napolitana. Added to that, he was a gentle gentleman who'd cared enough to let Chelsea commandeer his very comfortable bed.

Though keen to thank Tadpole, she hadn't spotted him all day, which, given the way she felt, was probably a good thing. She'd barely been off her own bed, except for a beach walk. *Yes, another one!* Greasy food might've helped her recovery, but with no hot chips within cooee, lunch had comprised bread and butter with a side order of imagination to turn it into a hot and salty chip buttie.

Unable to sleep much during the day, she'd scanned the various tourist brochures by the bed, including a Wandarri Eco-Community information booklet featuring a set of guiding principles that read a lot like rules for visitors, with several topics covering food scraps and composting, sight-seeing options in Ocean Sands, and recipes to stir more food cravings in her. After a cuppa and a sweet snack, Chelsea read the Fisheries Depart-ment booklet containing both useful and useless facts about fish breeds and their quirky behaviours.

Now, standing over *Sea-Esta's* small sink, Chelsea stared indifferently at the half-drunk and cold cup of tea, at the bread crusts—a landing field for flies—and at the coconut crumbs from her protein balls currently marching across the sink, courtesy of a line of black ants. Some ants she washed down the sink. Others she wiped away with a wet tissue and an apology.

Having changed into a fresh pair of shorts and a tank top, Chelsea was taking the rubbish bag to the bin when Kai's *Swish! Swish Swish!* noises reached her. She'd barely slipped her feet into the rubber thongs when the boy and Tadpole came into view. Walking alongside was a woman wearing a stylish hat and sunglasses. Chelsea's immediate thought was: *Oh oh! The mysterious and famous Jane! No longer filming in London, Jane, Vanessa, and their two fluffy dogs are here and keen to claim their booking.*

The woman's stride showed purpose—unless all women with wafer-thin bodies and long legs stride rather than stroll—and her smile, though small, looked familiar. In fact, as she neared, the woman looked a lot like …

'What the hell …?' Chelsea felt the rise of irritation, then unease. 'Layla?'

Neither made a move to embrace, even though the sunglasses

coming off to reveal puffy eyes and dark circles tempted Chelsea. Something was very wrong. What else would bring her sister to Sandbar? Had Layla tried calling or messaging Chelsea's water-logged phone? Had a lack of replies forced Layla to drive here and deliver the bad news in person?

'Thaddeus! It seems you've found my sister.' She deliberately refrained from using his nickname. 'Layla, this is—'

'We've met,' she responded.

'And that's my cue,' Tad said. 'I'll leave you to catch up. See you around, Chels. You too, Layla.' He nodded, nudged Kai, and whistled his way towards *Thisldo* where Lucky waited beside a camp chair, tail wagging.

'Interesting guy,' Layla said, her eyes following as he and Kai walked away. 'If you don't mind, I'd like to step inside the van and out of this heat.' Without waiting for a response, Layla led the way.

Plonking herself and her handbag at the dinette table, Chelsea perched anxiously on the bed, her gaze glued to the woman—part sister, part stranger. About to open her mouth to speak and demand an explanation, Layla barked an order at Chelsea.

'Explain to me what the hell you're doing in this place.'

Whoosh! All concern vamoosed itself right out the caravan door. Layla wasn't unwell or the bearer of bad news. She was as self-absorbed and demanding as the last time they'd butted heads. Over what, Chelsea couldn't recall, but she could guess.

'You tell *me* what's going on, Layla?' She might've demanded to know why her personal life mattered after decades of not giving a damn. She refrained and reached for her last bottle of wine, raising it in a part olive branch, part hair of the dog manner.

'A little early for me,' her sister replied. 'Wouldn't mind a hot drink.'

'Since when?'

'I'm recovering … from a long-haul flight,' Layla said. 'Tea without the nip of annoyance and inquisition would be nice. First, though, I need to pee. Then we need to talk. Do I require a key for the toilet?'

Chelsea shook her head. 'No, but before you go. How did you know I was here?'

'Gabby told me. We usually catch up when I stop over in Perth.' Layla must have read Chelsea's face because she added, 'I figured you knew. It's no secret.'

With a mind too busy wondering what her daughter had said to make Layla come to Sandbar—her sister's *last bloody place on earth*—all Chelsea managed to say was, 'You turning up out of the blue has thrown me.'

'And you coming here on your own has worried me,' her sister retorted. 'What's going on with Dale?'

'Are you hungry? I have microwave dinners.' Chelsea turned her back to ferret through the one food cupboard she'd stocked.

'Yes, I'm starving, but you're changing the subject. When I get back from the loo, you and I are going to talk.'

35

CHELSEA

Chelsea tried several conversation starters—any subject other than her marriage—but years of sporadic communication between sisters made for slim pickings, much like the reconstituted chicken pieces in the pasta meal she'd divided over two bowls. If Chelsea was going to drink more booze—and this random and yet-to-be-explained reunion required alcohol—she needed food.

'Heard from Mum recently? Is Sandbar her next port of call?'

Layla shook her head. 'Genoa, in Italy's north-west region.'

'I know where Genoa is, Layla. I may not be as well-travelled as the two of you, but I'm not a total ignoramus.'

Layla prodded a bit of pasta with her fork. 'I got them a good deal on a Mediterranean cruise,' she said. 'The ship hooks up with a European river cruise.'

While her sister rambled distractedly about stopovers and shore tours, impatience attached itself to Chelsea's growing list of emotions.

'The guy hasn't run out of money then?'

Layla sat back and huffed a laugh. 'Who knew there was a fortune in recycling garbage?'

'An improvement on Tammy Watson's dad, I suppose,' Chelsea muttered. She drained her wine, grateful for the numbing effect of alcohol, and again offered the bottle to her sister.

'Not yet, thanks,' Layla said, quick to cover her still-clean glass. 'How could anyone forget Mr Watson's whacky invention?'

'You mean the automatic sanitary disposal device he designed?'

'And remember Tammy turned up for the Easter bonnet parade at school with an Aussie cork hat made from—'

'Tampons!' the pair shrieked in unison.

'As if a coat of paint made them *not* look like tampons,' Layla spluttered. 'Oh my goodness, the principal's face!'

As the night wore on, and their quiet moments grew longer, Chelsea wondered if Layla was thinking the same as her.

'I've missed this,' she said, happily soaking up the big-sister thing. 'I wish you'd tell why you're here; assuming it's not only to charge your laptop.' The pair poked their tongues at each other—kids again. 'Sure you're not unwell, Layla? You look tired.'

'I look old,' she joked, 'and jet lag's a bitch at my age. What used to be twelve hours of lethargy now wipes me out for days.'

'Why don't you ground yourself? Get a desk job.'

'Believe me, I've contemplated taking a break and a move away from the city, but I don't know what might happen if I was to stop in one place, or what that place might look like.'

Swallowing her last mouthful of the tasteless pasta, Chelsea rested her fork on her plate before pressing for an answer.

'Why drive all the way here with jet lag? Of course, I'm happy to see you. More shocked, but that's because, well, you are the last person I expected.' Chelsea drained her glass, grateful for the liquid courage having done its job.

'Since we're being open,' Layla piped up. 'For someone who's happy to see me, you look determined to get wasted. Time to talk.'

Lifting and dropping shoulders heavy with too much wine, Chelsea sighed. 'And start where? I'm sure you're not the least bit interested to know I had a Dad moment.' Chelsea had expected an eye roll, or one of her sister's *who-cares* expressions. Instead, concern deepened the lines on Layla's forehead. 'Kai, the boy with Thaddeus, gave me this.' Reaching into the fruit bowl, Chelsea presented a cuttlebone. 'And you'll never guess. He calls them mermaid surfboards, like Dad and I used to do. I loved lots of things about the beach,' she said, starting to tear up. 'And I used to love my home and my husband, and Dale loved me back. Now he's having his mid-life crisis on the other side of the country.'

'And that makes this guy you call Thaddeus what, exactly? Hmm?'

'Just stop, Layla. I don't owe you any explanations, other than I'm renting this van from him. *And* he's a total gentleman; so easy to talk to. He knows about Gabby and Dale in W.A. He was on Facebook.'

'Who was on Facebook?' Layla asked, shifting Chelsea's wine glass to the far end of the table. 'Tadpole was?'

'No, no!' The growl brewing inside Chelsea since her sister's arrival became a bark she couldn't hold back. '*Dale* was on Facebook. The man is moving forward and in the company of a woman—one half his age, I'd say.' Chelsea snatched the phone from the fruit bowl, navigated her way to Gabby's Facebook page, and shoved the screen in her sister's direction. 'I reckon what's good for the goose can be acceptable for the gander—and Tadpole is lovely.'

'No way, Chels. This post isn't what it looks like. The picture is harmless and easily explained. Ask Dale?'

'How would you know anything?' Chelsea retorted. 'And no, I have not asked him. I've had other family matters on my mind. The most recent is sitting opposite me in *my* holiday accommodation.' A jolt of annoyance straightened Chelsea's spine. 'Look, Layla, let's clear up a few things. One: why are you here? Two: no need to worry about me; I'm fine. Three: I'm not cheating on Dale, and I have no intention of cheating on the man I've loved my entire adult life. I am not moving on, and *I* don't jump into bed with every Tom, Dick, and Harry.'

'I never said you did.'

'But I saw your expression, Layla. You and I are different. You're more like Mum. I was always more Dad.'

'You won't get an argument from me about that,' Layla grumbled. 'You and I are very different, Chelsea, but you didn't get all William's genes. You are not a deplorable human being. Dad is a bastard.'

Shocked straight for a second time in as many minutes, Chelsea glared. 'I see you've matured. We clearly cope differently, Layla, and you turning up and name calling is not helpful. But to be totally honest right now, I think I've drunk too much for this conversation. I need sleep. I'll meet you tomorrow. Where are you staying?'

'This folds down into a bed, doesn't it?' Layla said coolly while running her hands underneath the tabletop. 'This van looks much the same as Vinnie; it had a latch *thingamy* to convert the dinette into a double.'

A dozen responses lapped at the edge of Chelsea's brain, but too much wine washed the lot away, launching her out of the seat in a hurry.

'I think I need to pee, or puke, or something.'

'Come on, sis,' Layla said. 'I'll help you.'

The hit of night air had been Chelsea's undoing, knocking her out the second she'd succumbed to the comfy mattress. Not until the pins of unfiltered morning sun pricked her eyelids had she realised she was on the bed. She opened one eye, then the other. Her sister, fully dressed and on her side, faced Chelsea. They lay so close, Chelsea had to pull back and squint to focus.

Layla with the long legs and tiny waist had been, in Wendy's words, "the attractive one" and "real model material" until, late in Layla's teens and into her twenties, their mother had bemoaned her pretty daughter's blue phase. Everything—hair, nails, and makeup—took on shades of blue, mostly dark, while Layla's wardrobe turned black, and body piercings and tattoos turned the model-material sister into a real-life Barbwire Barbie.

Up close, without the facial embellishments, and under the morning sun's spotlight, the myriad minuscule skin piercings remained noticeable holes in Layla's nostrils, brow line, and along her ear cartilage.

'Hey, Barbie!' Chelsea nudged. 'Time to wake up and get your own Barbie Dream Camper.'

CHELSEA, DAY 5 OF 7

Within an hour of waking, both sisters had showered and eaten toast and Vegemite for breakfast. Now they sat across from each other, sipping instant black coffee from matching James Dean mugs. Wearing jeans and a shirt, her hair a style-less bob, Layla not only looked her age, but she appeared strangely subdued. Rather than drinking her coffee, she swilled and stared, while her other hand toyed with the mobile phone, tapping it awake every few seconds as if time was an issue.

Having managed an entire hour in each other's company this morning, and without a single cross word, Chelsea wondered. Might this return to Wandarri go one step further and fix her relationships with the living as well?

'Thanks, sis,' Layla said out of the blue.

Assuming the heartfelt gratitude was unrelated to the coffee refill Chelsea was partway through pouring, she asked, 'For what?'

'Nothing. Everything. Just saying it aloud. A while back, I embraced gratefulness as my daily addiction. I focus on the little things and I'm not sure I've said "thanks" to you enough.'

Careful to keep any surprise out of her expression, Chelsea said, 'You also haven't said why you drove eight hours to see me when we've spoken fewer than eight times in as many years.'

'That can't be true. Eight?'

'Pretty close,' Chelsea returned. 'We text. Guess I can be grateful for that.'

After a beat of silence, her sister looked up from her phone, all calmness gone. 'This is a mistake.'

'What is? Coming here?'

Another beat, and with another check of the time on her phone, an increasingly anxious Layla said, 'Yes—and no. Yes, if we don't pack up and just get the hell away today. Now! And no if it means connecting like we did last night. I want that so much. I want us in each other's lives. We *are* sisters. We'll always *be* sisters, no matter what.'

This conversation was way too heavy for a hangover, but for such an outburst from Layla, they'd obviously bonded, and more than Chelsea could recall.

'And you, Layla, were a terrific sister and a better mother to me. You walked me to school, made sure I had lunch money and hankies, helped with my homework ...'

Layla winced. 'Not too helpful in the homework department. But Chels, I can learn to be a better sister—if I'm not too late.'

'Late? Of course not.' Chelsea reached out, recognising this moment of sisterly solidarity as the perfect opportunity to plonk the elephant smack bang at the centre of the dinette. 'Layla, how often do you think about Dad?'

Groaning her discontent, sullen Layla was back and snatching her hand away to pick up her phone—again. 'For heaven's sake, what's it matter how often? Can we stick to talking about us, please?'

'But given you're here ... I figured it was Dad's annivers—'

'Well, you figured wrong. I'm here for you.'

'Then why drive out here now when in a few days we could've caught up at the house? Isn't this your "last-place-on-bloody-earth"?'

'Yes, but I've missed you. I miss us.'

Had Chelsea's jaw dropped or was the heavy feeling in her mouth years of unspoken words scrambling to form sensible sentences?

'And you're right, Chelsea, I'm not comfortable being here in this place, or in this van—and I need more than Vegemite toast.' Layla jolted to life. 'I have a better idea.'

'Better than what?' Chelsea queried.

'Better than staying here. Let's go together—now. There's a terrific resort about an hour's drive. Pool, cabana, a great cafe—'

'Cabana boys? Vicki would love that!' Chelsea laughed. Layla did not. Her sister was suddenly serious, her fidgeting with the phone erring on fanatical.

'Vicki? Oh, I remember her. Invite your friend to join us.' Layla was up and opening the small wardrobe, extracting tops and jeans Chelsea had stacked on the shelves. 'Where's your bag?'

'Stop, stop! What are you doing?' Suspicion snapped Chelsea straight. 'What's going on?'

'I'm packing,' Layla said. 'We'll get three adjoining rooms and have a slumber party. You can drink all the wine you want and throw up—preferably in a toilet within stumbling distance.'

Chelsea stood, ready to rescue every clothing item from her sister. 'Will you please leave my things alone and sit down?' With a gentle shove, Layla slipped back onto the dinette seat where she resumed the incessant phone fiddling.

Chelsea switched seats, squeezing next to her sister. 'Shift over.'

'See?' Layla quipped. 'This caravan is too small for both of us.'

'I wasn't expecting company,' Chelsea responded. 'But you're right about this van being like Vinnie the Viscount. Remember when I chucked a tantrum over broad beans and refused to come out from under the table?'

'I do. Mum gave you a whole bowl and a fork and told you to eat the lot.'

'Yes, I sat underneath, where you are now, secretly scratching the letters Y-U-K on the underside of the table. I showed you, remember? It was right about where your hand is now and ... Layla? Layla, what's wrong? Here! Water,' Chelsea said, forcing her sister's clawed fingers from the table edge. 'Drink the water.'

'I can't, Chelsea! I can't be in here. Please, can we go?'

'Layla, I'm here for a reason. It's that time of the year.'

'Yeah, and you would make sure Mum and I never forgot.'

'So what?' Chelsea didn't care if she sounded like a brat. 'I promised to remember, always.'

Layla wrapped an arm around Chelsea. 'I'm sorry and so grateful for this opportunity to be with you. Come here.'

The pair cuddled for several minutes, Chelsea's head resting on Layla's shoulder. *What a rollercoaster of a reunion!* About to ask her sister why now and why here, she looked up and saw tears of real regret in Layla's eyes.

'I've made mistakes, Chelsea. My most recent was yesterday.'

Chelsea shifted to face her sister. 'What did you do, Layla?'

'I met with a man. He's the reason I came to see you.'

Layla was looking for relationship advice—from Chelsea? *How ironic!*

'He must be a special guy to bring you all this way.'

'Not at all. I shouldn't have bothered.'

'Meeting him was your mistake?'

'One of them,' Layla replied.

'And that's behind you wanting to leave so quickly now?' Chelsea was guessing, but the sudden mood change, and the fear in her sister's eyes, was worrying. 'It's because he's here? And he poses a threat?'

'Not if we go—and go now.' Layla flipped the lid on the Apple laptop, the screen filling with a sparkling pool and palm trees. 'I still have the resort's website open. We can pack and be having a bang-up banquet by lunchtime. My shout.'

An unexpected rap on the caravan and an 'Only me!' made both women start. Layla looked positively petrified.

'It's just Elmie,' Chelsea announced, flinging the door open.

'Hello, dear. Heard you had company. A sister, no less.' Quicker than a blink, the old woman climbed aboard, handing Chelsea the foil-wrapped plate.

And there it was, Chelsea mused, the difference between a house and a caravan. Despite having walls with windows and doors that locked, when parked in a campground, a caravan had an openness that invited people in.

'And aren't you lovely!' Though brief, the woman's effusive embrace had Layla looking like the proverbial stunned mullet. 'Connie suggested you might like maple syrup with your pikelets.'

'Food is exactly what we need. See, Layla? No need to rush anywhere. We can share a bang-up pikelet banquet right here.'

'Good-o,' Elmie said. 'I'll leave you gals to enjoy. Bless the food before us and bless the family beside us and the love between us. Cheerio!'

Layla huffed, shutting the door firmly and putting her back to it. 'We'd certainly have more privacy at a resort.'

'Privacy is not what I need,' Chelsea said, wondering where that gratefulness addiction had gone. 'Please, can we eat while the pikelets are warm?'

Layla's answer was in her groan as another knock sounded. 'What now?'

Tadpole stood at the fly screen, looking apologetic. 'Sorry to interrupt. I can come back. Dropping off a brochure is all.'

'Don't go on my account,' Layla said, nipping out the door. 'I need space.'

'Sorry about my sister, Tad, and the mess. Come in.' Chelsea shoved the table's contents to one corner before sitting. 'Layla is the untidy one in our family. She used to step out of her clothes and leave them as if her body had spontaneously combusted. And she'd leave her journals open as well. Big mistake!' Chelsea's prattle was an attempt to cover up her sister's rudeness; nothing she wasn't used to doing. 'Layla also left her school-books taking up space on the dining table. Case in point.' As Chelsea pushed the laptop to one side, the device trilled, and a text message flashed onto the screen.

Bold and capitalised, **MUM** was the first word Chelsea made out. The reflection of Tad's Hawaiian shirt obscured most of the text.

When Tad left, she'd take a closer look. But the words did look very much like:

> Think about what telling your sister the truth
> will do.

3 7

TADPOLE

Tad had stayed with Chelsea long enough to drop the brochure and scoff a pikelet. He knew better than to get involved when there was clearly family trouble afoot. But he liked Chelsea—and her sister, who was currently sitting in her car, door open, mobile phone in hand.

'G'day again, Layla.' He leaned an elbow on the open driver's window. 'I wanted to say … About you and me and your sister …'

'Don't worry,' Layla said with a flick of one hand. 'I'm not announcing our history.'

Tad whooped. 'Not sure a couple of sexed-up kids and a grope a long time ago qualifies as a history. Don't keep anything from Chelsea on my account.'

'And in my experience, Tadpole, some things are better left unsaid.'

'Well, if you don't mind *me* saying,' Tad ventured. 'Things between you two seem, ahh …'

'Strained?' She shrugged. 'We're not the closest family.'

'She was close to your father.'

Layla's expression said *watch out*. 'If Chelsea's spoken of our family, Tadpole, she will have told you he was her hero, Mum was mostly absent —in one way or another—and I'm the sister who doesn't give a damn. That's my description, not Chelsea's.'

'And yet here you are,' he said plainly. 'Giving a damn.'

'Because I do love my sister. And I can tell you, this is the very worst place for her right now, which is why I'd like to take her home—today—for her own good.'

Tad's intrigue spiked. 'What does "for her own good" mean? We've spent a bit of time together, talking, and I like her. I know, I know,' he added. 'She has a husband who she loves. No harm in enjoying a lady's company. We've talked, Layla, nothing more.'

'Well, whatever she's told you, Tadpole, I miss my sister. I'm not a big part of her life, but not a day passes that I don't have regrets and wish things could be different.'

'Don't tell me this,' he said. 'Tell her.'

Layla softened. 'Keeping my thoughts and my distance is the only reason we're still on talking terms. Me in close confines makes her mad. You didn't notice?'

'I think your sister's sad about your relationship, not mad at you. I also think it's strange that the two people she loves—you and her husband—think distance is helpful.' Tad knew Layla's raised eyebrows were a warning flag, but the Prince of Faux Pas was well beyond worrying about upsetting people with the truth. 'If life has taught me anything, it's saying what needs sayin' while you have the chance.'

Irritation flashed over the woman's face as she alighted from the car, slamming the door. Where was the flaunty woman who'd oozed sass and attitude? This morning she seemed restless, self-conscious, and fixated on the V-neckline of a sky-blue top that wrapped around her body to tie at the back.

'I'm not sure why I'm sharing with you,' she said. 'One quick bonk in a dilapidated boathouse hardly means you and I have some kind of—'

'Hey, steady on! It wasn't that quick. It wasn't even a real bonk.' Tad's nudge seemed to knock some of the tightness from her shoulders. 'All joking aside, and to be clear, my intentions are completely honourable. Your sister is trying hard, but she needs something only you can give her.'

'Oh really? What?'

Tad chuckled. 'It's as obvious as Superman's undies how much she wants you in her life. I might be a bad almost-bonk, but I'm observant.'

'Oh, that would make a catchy Tinder profile.'

Sharing a grin with her, Tad said, 'I remember your laugh. You should do it more often. Great therapy.'

'I'll take your word for it.' Layla smiled—for real this time. 'Bet you're glad we were only a one-nighter, hey Tadpole?'

'Oh, I dunno,' he replied. 'Life with you would've been interesting. Might've needed a whole lot of *Dettol* and *Band-Aids* though.'

38

CHELSEA

Left alone in *Sea Esta* to mull over the text message, Chelsea's rollercoaster of emotions had completed several *loop-de-loops* before coming off the rails and smashing to smithereens. Twenty minutes later and tempered by mistrust, she fixed her stare on Layla as she stepped up into the caravan.

'Alone, at last.' Her sister shut the screen door. 'Are you ready to accept this place is full of busybodies who want to know the ins and outs of a duck's … What's with the serious face, Chelsea?' Dropping into the dinette seat, Layla plonked her phone on the table. 'Did you eat all the pikelets?'

'I hate to sound like one of your busybodies, Layla, but a message from Mum popped up on your laptop seconds after you stormed away, and like your journal that time, I read it. Let me share it.' Jerking the lid open, the screen lit up, while the colour from her sister's face drained. 'It reads, *Think about what telling your sister the truth will do.* Care to explain?'

Like a curious but cautious cat swats an object to check if it's something to fear, Layla's paw smacked the computer lid shut. But not before a faint notification tone sounded. This time on her mobile.

'Go ahead, sis, check. Might be more dark family secrets I'm not supposed to hear about.'

'No, no,' she said, head shaking. 'This isn't what you think, Chelsea.'

'Really? What is it?'

'A mistake. Another one,' her sister replied. 'The mobile reception out here is supposed to suck. You said as much last night.'

'It's erratic,' Chelsea quipped. 'Much like our family relationships; a connection that's intermittent at best and usually at the most inconvenient time, like now.'

'When did you become so angry?' Layla asked.

Chelsea hardly recognised her own laugh. 'When did *you* begin to care?'

'Why, why come here after all these years, Chelsea?'

'Because I'm lonely and confused. But you'd know all this if you'd bothered being my sister. You'd know how empty my house and life are with the kids gone. And now Dale.' Chelsea snatched her hand out of reach. She couldn't look at her sister.

'Would it help that I saw Dale in Perth on the same night as that Facebook post? He went home early and alone, Chels. I was at his apartment when he arrived. We talked.'

Chelsea's jaw almost locked open. 'You what?'

'He wouldn't cheat on you. He loves you. He understands.' Layla ferreted in her handbag, eventually coming up with a complimentary travel-sized packet of ten Aloe Vera-softened tissues. 'Dry your eyes and we'll pack up and leave all the bad memories behind. I'll explain everything, only not here.'

'No!' Chelsea snapped. 'This place is not the problem. I came to be on my own and I plan to stay on my own. I *want* to remember. But you are right about one thing. This caravan is way too small for us both. You need to go.'

'Where?'

'Home?' Chelsea suggested. 'Or to your five-star resort with a pool and cocktails. I don't care. I don't want to deal with you or Mum right now. I need a walk, and when I come back, I want to be alone. I'm getting used to it.'

39

CHELSEA

Surprised by the level of activity on the beach to the north of the viewing platform, Chelsea turned towards the less crowded southern end and headed towards the smaller bluff.

Drawing closer, she noticed an elderly man standing beside five abandoned surfboards. Wearing white compression stockings with sandals and shorts, he wielded a walking cane in the air, his voice blowing in the wind.

'Can I help?'

'Boys!' he chuckled as Chelsea sidled up to him. 'S'pose I was one, once. Cheeky buggers must have my genes. Been keepin' the grandies down here and out of everyone's hair. Now I can't get their attention. Slippery rocks are no place for an old man. Bound to go arse up, as they say.'

With a rock shelf also no place for Chelsea, she was about to wish him luck and walk away when the shriek of a troubled child reached them. Another scream, shriller than the first, left her little choice.

'Stay here. I'll go.'

After assessing the safest route, furthest from the water, she moved cautiously, skirting water pools, evading crevices, and sidestepping obstacles until spotting the squatting boys. All five appeared in good spirits and chanting.

'Get it! Get it! Get it!' The biggest boy, his hair the colour of rust, brandished a driftwood spear.

'Stop!' Chelsea chastised, startling all five.

'But the crab nipped my brother. We was trying to get it back into the sea.'

Chelsea doubted the story. 'This little guy will be fine without your *help*. Crabs aren't like fish; they don't need water to breathe. So, I suggest you suck on that finger of yours and learn a lesson.' Craning her neck to look over a boulder, she raised a thumbs-up to the man on the beach before turning back to the boys. 'We don't disturb tidal pools. They're too important.'

'Important how?' the smallest asked.

'Well …' Though keen to leave, she couldn't help reprising a William Scott lesson or two. 'Tidal pools are tiny ecosystems with hundreds of living things, like crabs, relying on them for food or for safety, or for breeding.' The concept of copulating crustaceans amused her audience. 'Removing the things they need to live is no different from someone raiding your house and emptying your fridge. If you saw it happening, you might even nip at the intruder stealing your food.'

'My mum fills our fridge when it's empty,' a boy said.

'Yes, and every life form in these pools depends on the tide doing the same as your mum. Filling up supplies.'

As if on cue, a wave crashed too close, sending a creeping swathe of seawater around Chelsea's ankles. Dropping to her haunches, suddenly as green as the sea cabbage clinging to the rocks, she braced and prayed she didn't vomit in the tidal pool.

Try explaining that to five curious onlookers!

'Are you crying, lady?' a boy asked. 'Did you get nipped?'

'No,' Chelsea said. 'Nothing in the ocean *wants* to hurt you.'

'Except sharks,' another boy touted. 'I'd kill a shark.'

'Let's move to where it's safe and I'll tell you a secret about sharks. Then we'll head back to the beach. Okay?' The boys needed no other incentive to follow. 'Ready?' All five salt-crusted heads nodded. 'Around your age, I learned sharks only ever move forward.'

'Why is moving forward so important?' a boy asked.

Out of the mouths of babes! Chelsea might have laughed if the words hadn't hit home so hard. No doubt Dale could provide that answer for them all.

'Hey, check this out,' said the one blond boy in the group who'd wandered to an adjacent pool. 'Whadaya reckon this is?'

Chelsea recognised the odd-looking fish with spots from the fisheries pamphlet in the caravan.

'An Epaulette shark,' she said. 'Tiny, as sharks go, and not at all inter-ested in you as food. He's stranded himself here to enjoy his own personal smorgasbord.'

'Ew, gross,' a boy said, peering into the rock pool. 'I'd want more to eat than what's in here.'

'And sometimes this fellow will, too, so he'll *walk* over rocks to find a fresh food source. Then he'll bide his time to conserve energy and oxygen because he's smart enough to know the tide will come in and away he'll go. Speaking of the tides …' Chelsea swallowed her panic as more lacy foam refreshed rock pools and inundated crevices near the base of the bluff.

'Let's go. Your grandad wants you back.' And she couldn't get away fast enough.

'It was Grandad who told us to stay out of the water and out of the way while they search,' the redhead said as they headed for the safety of the sand.

'While who searches? For what?'

'The old guy who lives at the shop,' another said. 'He was rock fishing near the other headland and never got home.'

Talia's father? Missing?

While the soft sand high up the beach slowed her run, nothing could stop Chelsea. Poor Talia will be frantic, and little Kai so confused. Should she go to them, perhaps provide some comfort? If anyone understood, Chelsea did. But no, the woman had an entire community for support. This was no time for nosy strangers.

Passing the crowded viewing platform, she overheard two men talk-ing. One she recognised from the luau.

'Is it true?' Chelsea called to him, moving nearer.

Space Invader nodded. 'Unbelievably, yes. Talia raised the alarm after returning from her overnight stay in Ocean Sands.'

'If you ask me,' said the second man, 'I'm not sure this fuss isn't simply a case of her old man stayin' until the fish go off the bite. Remember the time he came back early hours with a haul big enough to share with the entire community? Secretive bugger never shared the fishing spot.'

Chelsea had elbowed her way to where the mates stood. 'By "old man" you're referring to her dad, right?'

'No love,' Space Invader replied. 'Six months ago, Talia settled her dad into care in Ocean Sands. That's why she stays overnight from time to time. No, no, we're talkin' about Squid missing. Folk around here call him her "old man" coz of the age difference. Tadpole was the first to use the moniker. A mate stirring a mate, but with a touch of good-natured revenge, given Tad and Talia go way back. Thick as thieves, the pair was as kids until Talia grew up. Then Squid arrived on the scene and they fell for each other hook, line and sinker.'

Space Invader's mate chuckled. 'Won't stop her getting up Squid when he returns with a tale as big as the fish he's toting. Can't blame her.'

'I hope so,' Chelsea said.

'Yeah, we've got blokes checking all known fishing spots, hoping it's as simple as a fall and he's hurt a leg and can't walk himself out. Oi! Steady on!' Space Invader grabbed Chelsea's arm, supporting her, and guiding her through the packed platform. 'Gangway, folks, we need a seat.'

'I'm fine, really,' Chelsea said as the crowd parted like soldier crabs. 'I want to help look for him.'

'We all do, love, and we can help by waitin' and watchin' while those with the know-how do their thing.'

40

LAYLA

The December sun seeping through her eyelids woke Layla. But the crunching of gravel under tyres and a creeping police car lifted her out of the camp chair.

'You in there, Chelsea?' she called, surprised by the time showing on her phone. The combination of warm sun, a comfortable seat, and too many days without restful sleep had been her undoing. The police vehicle was now stopped alongside a group of people, all pointing as if directing a lost driver, although the beach was an odd destination. 'Chelsea?' she said louder, and with more urgency.

The only times Layla recalled seeing cops in full kit hitting the beach had been—

'Oh no! No, no, no!' An abandoned green bucket with mermaid stickers burst out of that memory box. 'Chelsea? Chel-sea!'

Not stopping to lock the caravan door, Layla raced barefoot across the campground and onto the bush track. Weaving around stragglers, she knocked shoulders with dawdlers, cussing without concern, and clambered up the dunes, stumbling onto all-fours several times. A sense of dread stopped Layla at the top as if she'd walked headlong into an invisible pane of glass. Then she saw her.

'Chelsea!' Glimpsing her sister let Layla breathe for the first time. 'What's going on? I saw a police car and ... What's with all the people? And why are you crying?'

'Oh, Layla! It's just like Dad.'

'W-what do you mean—Dad?'

'Another fisherman is missing. Talia reported it this morning.'

Layla's gag reflex forced a cough. 'T-Talia?'

'She owns the bait shop with Squid,' her sister explained needlessly. 'You met their boy with Tadpole. Poor Kai. It's like Dad all over again. Can you believe it?'

Layla choked out a 'No' before her legs gave way and she dropped to the sand in a heap, head spinning.

'Layla! Layla, open your eyes. You're frightening me.'

A circle of concerned faces hung over her, the mass of bent-over bodies blocking the sun. The most worried expression belonged to her sister.

'Don't fuss. I'll be okay.' She sat as if to demonstrate and to drink from a proffered plastic bottle.

'You passed out. You *are* ill,' Chelsea insisted. 'And it's serious. That's why you've come.'

'I fainted from dehydration,' Layla snapped, annoyed at the growing attention. 'I fell asleep in the sun. Can we go back to the caravan, please? I need to talk to you about Dad.'

All concern vanished from her sister's expression. '*Now* you want to talk about him! Where were you and Mum all those years when I needed to talk, to cry, to grieve? Forget it, Layla.' Chelsea snatched her elbow from her sister's grasp. 'I need to be here, watching and hoping. It's what people do. It's *all* I can do, other than be there for little Kai.'

As much as she wanted to drag Chelsea away, tell her this stunt was likely a diversion, and right now the man of the moment was hightailing it or making plans to do so, Layla squeezed her sister's hand tight.

'Believe me, Chels, waiting and wishing are not unfamiliar to me. I stood on this very beach looking for you, and when I thought I'd lost you, I made a promise.'

'What did you promise?'

The confession seemed to soften the sharpness in her sister's stare. 'I'll tell you, but I fear I'll pass out again if I don't get out of this sun. If not the caravan, can we at least move away from people? Up there.' Layla pointed to a dip between two dunes, the snarl of Banksia branches providing a patchwork of shade.

Begrudgingly, Chelsea led the way, plonking onto the sand to sit cross-legged and to sulk, like little sisters do.

Layla settled beside her. 'Don't get worked up over this missing fisherman.'

'I'm not "worked up". I'm shattered for Talia. While not exactly friends, we chatted and I sensed a genuine connection. Not only to her, but with Kai.'

Layla cast her mind back to the sweet-sounding woman who'd taken the telephone from her son, then jotted a message about a catchup her husband couldn't afford to miss.

Poor, naive woman! Should Layla find Talia and warn her not to waste her time mourning an unworthy man?

In his letter to Wendy, William Scott had claimed his deceit was no less wrong or hurtful than being tricked into marriage and rooted in the suburbs, in a house he never wanted to live in. Worst of all, Layla mused while stealing a glance at Chelsea crying silent tears, the man had left his grieving twelve-year-old daughter behind to root herself in the same house. William Scott did not deserve Chelsea's tears back then—and not now.

'I feel your stare, Layla, and it's freaking me out. Whatever you have to say about Dad, go ahead. But I won't tolerate you sticking up for Mum. She hasn't bothered to be a proper mother to me since I was twelve. She blamed me. I'm aware of that.'

'You're wrong, Chelsea.' Drawing both knees to her chest, like an armour for her heart, Layla racked her brain to find the words with the least amount of hurt in them. 'Like us, sis, when it happened, Mum was sad. And then—'

'And then she wasn't,' Chelsea countered. 'The pair of you barely tolerated my need to keep Dad's memory alive, so I don't care to think about Mum at this point. I've come here for some *me* time and to reconnect with someone who *did* love me. Dad might've jokingly called this place Nowhere, but it's somewhere to me. I feel him here, and I don't want any anti-dad attitudes. Your negativity is not okay, and frankly, Layla, given the situation playing out before us, it's unacceptable and deplorable.'

Maybe Layla should leave Sandbar while some semblance of sisterly connection remained—even if that connection was a shared hatred of their mother. What would she achieve by revealing their father's deception, other than replacing one giant ache in her sister's heart with another? Unfortunately, Layla had set the ball in motion, and her ultimatum had left William Scott with the next move.

And what a move he took!

Clearly, the man could not be trusted. It was up to Layla, even though hurting Chelsea will be *the* hardest thing; ten times harder than pressing the tip of that blade into the soft flesh of her own wrists. She rubbed a thumb over the blue heart tattoo. Twice, she'd tried to disappear off the face of the earth. Twice, strangers had saved her.

Layla let the sand drain from her hand like her fist was an hourglass. Hopefully, time would heal their wounds. But at that moment, with both sisters mirroring each other—shoulders hunched, chins resting on bent knees, eyes fixed on a gloomy seascape—Chelsea seemed as fragile as the torn sheet of notepaper back at the caravan. The brittle barely holding together with sticky tape turned brown with age.

'I'm scared,' Chelsea said, nudging a dried cuttlebone on the sand. 'Why have you come? What aren't you telling me?'

As her sister turned the white, chalky object over and over, Layla knew where Chelsea's thoughts lay because she'd been there that day, too, and equally captivated by the man and his mesmerising stories of the sea.

Collecting cuttlebone with Dad, 1977

'What a beauty!' Dad points at the line of high-tide detritus. 'Nab that one, Chelsea.'

'And these?' I ask excitedly.

'Yes, those as well, Layla. Big is better.'

'What are you going to do with the shells, Dad?'

'They're not shells, remember? They're the discarded bones from the cuttlefish.'

'Bones? Whoa! Better not get one stuck in our throats.'

Dad laughs when Chelsea grabs her neck and writhes on the sand before playing dead. 'You'd look pretty funny chowing down on a cuttlefish bone. Up you get, Miss Fix.' He tugs her upright. 'Besides, they're not fish. They're molluscs, like squid and octopus.'

I shudder at the thought of icky sticky tentacles getting stuck in my throat. 'I don't like them.'

'*Ewww!* Me either,' Chelsea pipes up.

'But you like magic, right? Think of cuttlefish and squid as the magicians of the deep.'

'What magic do they do?' I ask.

'They disappear, as quick as this,' he says with a finger-snap, 'and no matter how hard you look you won't see them.'

41

LAYLA

Finding the right words to tell her sister was Layla's next struggle. If she managed, should she string out the sordid details, or think like a Band-Aid? The quicker it's done, the less painful the procedure. Then a phone beeped with a notification. Chelsea's phone. Her sister immediately dropped the cuttlebone, dusted sand from her fingers, and shared the screen with Layla.

'Tyler's Instagram. A new profile picture,' she announced. 'My gorgeous, goofy boy.'

'Travis' popped into my feed yesterday,' Layla said, checking her own phone. 'Those boys sure love a selfie.'

Chelsea arched her eyebrows. 'You follow *my* boys on social media?'

'And Gabby,' Layla announced without a second thought. 'It's how I stay a part of your lives. I've missed having family. Sorry if sharing yours is wrong.'

Her sister's eye roll spoke reams. 'It isn't wrong, Layla. The invitation was there any time. You simply stopped coming over to the house.'

Layla snorted. 'Nothing simple about it.'

She had to tell her sister now, but how? She could deliver the news like a flu shot. A quick jab would be painful, but what hurt the most was the truth that slowly seeped under the skin. Should Layla tell Chelsea a diluted version, or subject her to every despicable detail, and straight from the horse's mouth? Every word was captured on the phone in Layla's hand.

'You won't want to hear this, Chelsea. You may even hate me, but … Scoot!' Layla shooed a persistent seagull. 'I hate Dad for what he did to us.'

'Hate? Layla, for goodness' sake! Dad did nothing to us. He died doing what he loved. He slipped on shells I wasn't supposed to collect and rather than stay and help, I left him alone to fend off a king tide.'

'Chelsea, you were not meant to stay, and definitely not to blame. You were a scrawny twelve-year-old girl. He was a seasoned rock fisherman, fit and knowledgeable. If he'd wanted to save himself, he could've. Trapped and injured people desperate to live find the willpower and strength to free themselves. William was fit and prepared, but he had a plan in which you unknowingly played a part. A plan all about timing and the tide. His success relied on you getting lost and not finding your way off that headland in the dark. You did exactly what he wanted you to do.'

'You're crazy, Layla.'

Yeah, you're right, Layla mused. *I'm crazy. Ignore me. Forget what I said. Live your happy life in oblivion because I love you too much to cause you pain. But, Chelsea …*

'Just listen to me, please. I'm telling you this because I love you.' Layla pressed the flat of her hand on her sister's back, rubbing between her shoulder blades, wanting to soothe. 'You were twelve and terrified. Neither of those things makes you responsible. And I didn't lose contact because I blamed you or hated you. I stopped coming to the house because I struggled to watch you worship that man.'

Chelsea shrugged Layla's hand away. 'That man was our father.'

'Hmm, yes.' Layla prepared to introduce the final excruciating drop of truth from the syringe. 'I've wanted to tell you this so often, but every time I made up my mind, Mum would pop up and remind me of all I stood to lose. The woman has an exasperating sixth sense, like she's constantly in my head and knows when I'm weakening. That's when she calls and—'

'And sends text message reminders about things I'm not supposed to know?'

None of the people milling around the dunes or wandering back and forth on the beach noticed the two women speaking too loudly. Most observers gathered closer to the shore, eyes turned seaward, heads shaking with lost hope.

'Look, Layla, I'm more than overwhelmed by current events, and more than baffled about why you'd choose this moment to talk. I'm still confused about what you're doing here. Catching up? Reconnecting? Or,' Chelsea said, the pain starting to show in her eyes and in the accusatory tone, 'are you here to throw yours and Mum's jet-setting life in my face, and rub in the fact you have a better relationship with my daughter than I do?'

'Sure, yeah, that's my purpose. The shitty sister, as always.' Layla prepared to stand. 'Guess I'll see you in another three decades. Enjoy your return to Sandbar.'

'Wait! I'm sorry.' Chelsea's hand and her pronounced pout pinned Layla to the spot. 'You're not a terrible sister. Please, please, just tell me what this is about. Then we can talk about seeking a professional to help you work through the dark thoughts about Dad.'

Layla smiled, somehow. 'Oh, believe me, I've tried to forget what he did to our family—and mostly in all the wrong ways. By the time I could think clearly enough, and I was ready to reconnect, you had Dale, and the babies were … Well, you were all so happy. You'd finally let go of your grief.'

'My grief, yes, but not my memories of Dad.'

Layla nodded. 'Which is why I'm here—to help you let him go. You claim to have made mistakes and bad choices, but none were as bad as my mistake. I was wrong for letting you believe he died.'

'Believe? Are you having some sort of drug-induced episode?'

'No, I'm off that stuff. Years of therapy,' Layla said, plunging the most painful part of truth into her sister. 'He planned to go missing. He wanted to disappear.'

4 2

CHELSEA

Her sister's revelation was such that it grabbed Chelsea by the throat and the heart. Her response—unspoken but clinging to the edge of a laugh—finally spilled out, the part scoff, part hoot spooking the same stalking seagull on the sand in front of the pair. Envious of the bird's ability to take off at a whim—to escape—Chelsea was about to leave when she saw three decades of tears rolling down her sister's cheeks.

'Bloody hell! What's got into you, Layla?' She sagged back to the sand and wrapped an arm around her sister's juddering shoulders. 'This makes no sense. What aren't you supposed to tell me? Why are you here? And why, why, why would Dad *want* to disappear? I was there that day. I saw his leg and the blood.'

'He was faking,' Layla said with a steely voice. 'He left because he didn't love his life with us enough to stay. On the rocks, you saw only what he wanted you to, like the blood you described to the police. You told them he'd stayed because the tailor was running, right?' Layla waited for Chelsea's nod: small, scared, uncertain. 'And remember how adamant Dad was about bleeding tailor without delay and keeping the catch fresh in salt water?' Another nod. 'You weren't there to witness his fall.'

Although not a question, Chelsea answered with a small head shake, her body sagging with the burden of guilt. 'I was collecting fresh cunjevoi.'

'But why catch more fish? Dad's diktat was to never take home more than you need, and he had ample for dinner. Besides, hooking tailor requires bait fish. Chels, sweetie, that day wasn't even about fish. He sent you to collect the bait so he could execute the plan because timing was crucial. Then he wanted you frightened and confused and convinced his injuries were bad. The blood-filled rock pool was perfect. But like I said, if a trapped farmer can lift a tonne of quad bike to get out from underneath, do you not think a seasoned rock fisherman—a fit one—wouldn't endure the pain of a banged-up knee to escape an encroaching king tide *before* it swept him into the sea?'

Though desperate to find a fitting defence—like maybe he did try—the dam wall behind Chelsea's eyes burst, leaving silence between the sisters to hang as thick as the afternoon sea mist, Chelsea's memory foggier still.

'How can you be sure he didn't try, Layla?'

'Because I can. And I'm sorry to blurt all this out. I've had years to come to terms with the truth and I still shake my head over a man planning his death—his disappearance—down to the tiniest detail. A plan that may or may not have worked—and involved traumatising you in the process. He didn't overlook the king tide in his *Tides Table* booklet. He knew the tides chart by heart because William Scott didn't plan to die, Chels. He wanted to get lost, and he counted on you detailing his lie to the police. Who would question your version of the events? Please,' Layla pleaded. 'I swear this is true. The tide was his accomplice, and you were his alibi.'

Cupping her head with both hands, Chelsea squeezed her eyes tight, either to help orient her thinking or dull her sister's utterances.

'I understand self-blame, Chels, and how never forgetting is a form of punishment. But selective memory—not seeing what we don't *want* to see —is a survival tactic. You're a survivor.'

Chelsea wanted to laugh, or shout shut up, or walk away from her deranged sister. She might've done all three, had disbelief and despair not drained every speck of energy.

'Why take such a risk, Layla? Why wouldn't he walk away like any other unhappy family man?'

'Money,' Layla said. 'A life insurance policy that relied on lazy assessors, assumptions, and a police report containing the evidence of a traumatised and very believable twelve-year-old witness. The Coroner's Court had no reason to delay granting probate in advance of findings; that's what speeds up policy payouts,' Layla explained in a matter-of-fact voice. 'He worked the system he knew well to become another tragic rock fishing fatality; one of many to occur every year along this coastline. The police had needed little convincing. Having seen many fishermen suffer the same fate, they quickly closed the case, declaring William Scott officially dead. Only he wasn't.'

'But I … How …? Where did he go?'

'Nowhere.'

Chelsea's head jerked up to scrutinise her sister's face. 'No, no, not Nowhere. Don't tell me that.' Craving the comfort that came from her happiest memories, Chelsea picked up the discarded cuttlebone, clutching it tight like a magical totem.

Layla reached out a hand, but Chelsea resisted her attempt to connect. 'Please believe it breaks my heart to tell you. He resurfaced here as Liam Scott and made a new family. He married Talia.'

As much as she wanted to scream at Layla, a 'No' lodged in Chelsea's throat. She could barely breathe or think, let alone speak.

'I understand you'll be hating me right about now,' Layla said. 'I've hated myself for keeping the secret, but I've wept over you idolising the man who destroyed our relationship. He ruined my life, Chelsea. And while the truth is a horribly cruel thing to blurt out, I can no longer sit back and watch him ruin yours.'

'Enough, Layla! Whatever this is, I don't want to listen to your lies. I don't want you near me at all.'

Layla grabbed Chelsea's forearm, pinning her to the spot. 'I'm not lying, Chels, and I will go, but not until you have emotional support close by.'

'Me?' Chelsea's squawk made heads turn in the sisters' direction. Undaunted, she stared at the cuttlebone clenched in her hand, and like a bird sharpens its beak, Chelsea honed her next words for maximum hurt. 'I am *not* the one needing emotional support, Layla, but I suggest you get some. You are delusional. Now go! Leave me!' She jerked her arm away and jumped to her feet. 'We're done.'

'Okay, okay, I'll go,' Layla conceded, standing. 'But not until you've played this recording. Listen carefully and you might think differently about me afterwards. Take it.' She thrust the phone forward. 'What we talked about is all here.'

Chelsea's face flinched. 'You've recorded us?'

'No, I recorded Dad and me. Figured you'd want proof. Take the phone. Listen over and over if you need to.' At that, Layla picked up Chelsea's limp arm, slapped the device on her palm, and poked at the screen's play button. 'The start is garbled while I'm waiting for him to sit. But please, listen to the end.'

Unmoving, Chelsea stared at the device, then up at her sister, now walking away. 'How do I know this is Dad?' she called.

Layla turned her back to the ocean, her exhalation long and loud. 'You'll know. And when you're done,' she said, 'I'm here for you. Always will be.'

Preparing to hurl the damn mobile device at her sister's retreating figure, both frustration and fear curling Chelsea fingers tight, a faint but familiar voice reached her ears. She raised the phone.

'I saw her, but don't worry. I'll be staying low from now on until she leaves.'

Even with the speaker volume up high, some words were difficult to make out. Not her sister's.

'I've been hurting the sister I love for decades.' Then: *'I left my family out of love, Dad. Why did you leave?'*

A loud bang, like a fist thumping a table, jolted Chelsea, but the recording played on. *'You are her hero, and your memory overshadows everything and everyone. No man can compete with the great William Scott. Not even her amazing husband, while I remain the sister she thinks doesn't give a shit.'* Another thud echoed. *'So, no, I'm not telling Chelsea. You are. Only then will the hero-worshipping stop, and with luck she'll save her marriage.'*

As the recording fell silent, and the shame and contrition that had coiled itself inside Chelsea all these years wiggled its way out, she dragged her face from damp, tear-soaked knees to scan the beach.

Picking her sister out from the shoreline crowd was easy enough. Knowing what to say was the hard part.

Layla couldn't know of Chelsea's approach. And yet somehow she did, reaching a hand behind, ready to reconnect—to be sisters again. As their fingers entwined, Layla turned to face Chelsea, no words needed. Then, finally and for the first time in years, the Scott sisters hugged and cried together, their tears this time for what they'd found.

Each other.

Layla pulled out of the embrace first, stroking a hand over Chelsea's hair before peeling wayward strands stuck by salty spray and tears. 'I'm so sorry.'

'No, Layla, this isn't your fault. I-I just don't get why he'd choose Sandbar. This place was ...' Chelsea swallowed. 'It was *our* magic place.'

'My guess is he figured we'd never return without him. For over three decades, he was right. Then Gabby said you were here, and I had no choice. I had to find you before you bumped into him.'

Chelsea's rapid blinking squeezed fresh tears to the surface. 'Oh, my! I-I think I might've bumped into him.' She whispered, almost to herself as each moment rose to the surface of her mind: the man staring from across the fire pit at the luau, the fisherman on the beach, the person behind the shop curtains as Chelsea had sipped lemonade. Had he recognised his youngest daughter and stayed hidden to listen? Or had Talia told him about the pathetic woman who still burst into tears over her dead father?

As Chelsea's knees buckled, Layla stopped her from falling, both hands gripped tight and shaking as if waking Chelsea from a bad dream. 'Hey, come on. Be strong. You're hurting right now.'

'You, too, and for all those years. Yet there I was, constantly shoving his memory down your throat. No wonder you were never sad at birthday and Christmas events.'

'Mum taught me early to lie, not cry. She did a good job.'

Chelsea jerked away so abruptly, she almost stumbled. 'Mum? She was a part of this ruse?'

'Not initially,' Layla replied. 'She didn't know, and she didn't plan. Her grief was real until his letter arrived. That's when Mum changed. Remember the time she threw everything in the bin? On one occasion, Wendy did a lousy job of destroying evidence in the old incinerator. I found the letter he'd written to her, basically explaining why, and to reassure her we'd be financially secure if she followed his instructions. I read the note and I ripped it up. Told her I'd chucked it. Fortunately, I stuck the thing back together. It explains a lot.'

'Where is it?' Chelsea asked.

'In my bag, in the caravan.'

'And you're telling me Mum's known all this time?'

'Look, you can choose to hate Mum—and me. I hate what he did to you—to us both. I hated myself and the world so much I turned to anything and everything to ease the pain. My hatred nearly killed me. Hating is not the answer.'

Chelsea wiped a tear from her sister's cheek. 'And I thought Mum couldn't stand to look at me; that's why she left me at the pool and offloaded us on Rita.'

'No, no, she walked away from us both, but not before off-loading her anger on me, bemoaning her wasted life. She said things I've never forgotten. Words like *"I might not be the storybook mother, but at least I stayed to pick up and put away: housekeeper, cook, laundry maid. That's been my sole purpose since I fell pregnant at twenty-two. Twenty-two!"* Then she added, *"Did anyone ask how I saw my future, or what I wanted from my life?"* She even said she'd squandered her youthful beauty on a man who grew more ridiculous and embarrassing every year, and that she wasn't raising two children; she had three. *"I was stuck in this pathetic excuse for a house and watching you girls, with your beauty and boyfriends and bright futures, remind me every day what I've lost and will never get back. Never!"*. I know that speech verbatim, Chels. Hard words to forget.'

'Wow, sis, didn't we hit the jackpot?' Chelsea's huff was more resignation than rage. 'A mother who resents us and a father who didn't want us?'

'If it helps, I believe he did love us. That's why he went to such extremes to leave us money. But the man needed his freedom more. Maybe if Wendy had not been so stubborn—putting the kybosh on the things William wanted and enjoyed—their marriage might've been different. If she hadn't insisted they buy "in the boonies" rather than rent closer to the beach scene he loved, our lives might be different. Even though the man detested the house, according to *The Rule of Wendy*, "families made memories in their own home and not in a stranger's rental".'

'He hated our house? You can't be serious. No, no, not The Beach Shack.' Chelsea hung her head and cried shambolic tears, her cheeks now burning with anger, confusion, and contrition. Dale had said the same about homes and memories.

'I hate hurting you, Chels, but you needed to know, especially considering what's happening in your life right now. William Scott was a miserable man who tolerated the daily commute and all the material things Wendy claimed made a home.'

'Yes, that same home he once told me he was drowning in. I remember now. We were on the headland that day. He started to cry and said he'd been treading water for years, and he was tired.'

Chelsea closed her eyes to stem the rise of resentment, but she couldn't control the sharpness in her voice, like an invisible slap to her sister's face.

'For goodness' sake, Layla! I'm almost fifty. You couldn't tell me before?'

'I was protecting you from the anger and bitterness that sets in and eats you alive from the inside. You and Dale were happy, or so I thought.' Layla reached out a hand to dab Chelsea's cheek. 'The truth would have destroyed you, and to what end? William had caused enough hurt.'

'But you didn't give me the option to learn the truth. You and Mum decided for me. And stop calling him William. He's our dad.'

'Listen to the recording again,' Layla said. 'Better still, read the letter. You'll find the original in the side pocket of my handbag back at the van. On my phone is a photographed version with a filter applied to sharpen the text. Zooming in will help decipher the words lost to the folds. Take it.' Layla dropped the mobile device into Chelsea's cardigan pocket.

'He can't have loved us,' Chelsea muttered through held back sobs.

'Guess that depends on your definition of love,' Layla said. 'He could've done a Skase: packed a bag, cleaned out the bank account, fled in the middle of the night.'

'Done a what?'

'Remember when they found that millionaire living a lavish lifestyle in Majorca? One day, before I knew his actual whereabouts, I asked Mum if Dad was living on a tropical island and protected from intruders by hi-tech security systems. She laughed and said she didn't care. Then, on my first overseas trip, I looked for him in every face, always holding onto the tiniest kernel of hope. But what a waste of emotional energy. He hadn't fled the country to hide out in some exotic port. The clue had been his letter all those years. The man was living less than a day's drive away from the home he hated.'

'But how could he be certain Mum wouldn't get mad enough to dob him in?'

Layla huffed. 'And give up all that money? No way! She was damned if she told the truth and damned if she didn't.'

The tide was on the turn, a wave's white foam closing in on the high-tide line of marine waste.

What do you know? Chelsea asked the ocean. *Tell me.*

While no answer came, the next wave seemed to keep its distance before slinking away, as if aware it had done something very wrong.

Chelsea needed to get away from the beach and from Sandbar. In five minutes, she could be back at the caravan. Fifteen minutes more, having thrown every belonging in the car, she could be on the road and headed back to her boring life in an empty, pathetic excuse for a house. Once there, it would be just her and the walls and sideboards adorned with memories she'd dusted dutifully for years. She'd unpack, put on a load of laundry, and after tidying the house no family member cared to live in but her, she could sit and wait for the family dog they no longer had to want dinner, or for her boys to need her, or for her husband to decide he wanted to come back.

'Chelsea? Chels, sweetie, when you've read the letter and listened to the recording again, there's one more thing I need to tell you.'

'No, no more,' she pleaded, mentally exhausted. 'I need time.' Chelsea turned so sharply the sand gave way. Though thankful Layla's quick reaction again stopped her from falling, she shook free of the handhold. 'Let me be, please, Layla. I have to be angry with you for a while. Just a while.'

The direction Chelsea ran didn't matter. As long as it was far away from people, from the sea, and from the lying tide.

In the quiet of a mostly deserted campground, she was nearing the serenity of *Sea-Esta* when the shrill ring of a phone made Chelsea curse and reach into a pocket. Realising her mistake, she cursed again.

'Damn it!'

'Well, *you're* not Layla,' the voice said.

'No, I'm Chelsea. I've answered her phone by mistake.'

'Oh, you're the sister!'

'I beg your pardon?'

'Sorry, that sounds rude. Layla probably hasn't mentioned me. Is she there?'

'I left her on the beach,' Chelsea said, struggling to unlock the caravan before realising it was not locked, her ire rising. 'Let me take a message, okay?'

'I'm Trent,' the man announced, as if she should care to know. 'How are things progressing? She's doing okay?' The questioning tone sounded more caring than curious—but cautious—and for a moment the voice was a calming salve to Chelsea's pain.

'Maybe, Trent, you can phone back, and I won't answer.' She slammed the door shut behind her and busily scanned the compact space for her sister's belongings. 'The call will go to messages. Okay?'

'Ah, on second thoughts,' the man said, 'don't mention I rang. She'll accuse me of holding too tight. She's probably right.'

The guy sounded far too sweet for Layla.

'I worry, and I was sitting here wondering how things were working out for her. She loves you very much. I hope we meet socially one day, Chelsea, even though I feel like I know you already.'

You can't possibly know me, Chelsea might have replied, had her impatience not skyrocketed with the discovery of the crumbling paper in the side pocket of her sister's bag.

I no longer know myself.

'Chels, wake up,' Tadpole called from across the way, his voice breathy, his rush exaggerating his limp. 'Where's Layla?'

'I'm not sleeping.' Chelsea rose from the camp chair she'd fallen into after reading a letter that prompted more questions than it answered. Tadpole's eager enquiry, and the dark circles under red eyes, raised more. 'I left Layla on the beach. Why, what's wrong?' She slipped the folded letter safely in her cardigan pocket, then reached for his hand, clasping it tight. 'You have news?'

Tad nodded. 'Some, finally. With Elmie protecting Talia like a bulldog, and with the coppers tight-lipped, I've been relying on Wandarri's grapevine. Only now are we hearing the truth …'

Tempted to tell Tadpole she'd had her share for today, tears filled his bloodshot eyes. 'What's wrong, Tad?'

'Squid's not the only one missing. He isn't the only one to not make it home. Talia is inconsolable and I'm bloody useless to her. I don't believe it.'

'Believe what? What are you trying to say?'

'Going solo is unsafe, but Squid prefers fishing alone. Always has,' Tad blathered. 'He says chatter chases away the fish. So why take him? I've asked myself a million times. Talia visited her dad overnight, but when needed, I ordinarily looked after him.'

'Who? I'm confused.' Thunder cracked open the clouds, and rain bucketed down. 'Tad, come inside the van, you're trembling. What's wrong? Who did he take fishing?'

'His son,' Tad said in a rare, beaten-down voice. 'Squid took Kai. They're both missing.'

Without a word, Chelsea took off, sprinting shoeless towards the bush track and the beach beyond. Tad called a warning, but she didn't stop. Little Chelsea Scott ran and ran.

43

CHELSEA

As the concerned and the curious deserted their posts for the dry comfort of a cabin or caravan, Chelsea understood. Only those who knew the pain of keeping watch, prepared to sacrifice their safety if it meant spotting and saving a precious life, would dare endure a beach in a deluge. To prove the point, more thunder cracked, and the diehards who'd gathered in mournful groups, and those who'd paced the shoreline solo, now raced each other back to camp. Even Layla was gone. One man stayed, camera poised, ready to capture any sign of life to become an Instagram star.

Chelsea considered telling him he was wasting his time, but could she be certain of anything while still recovering from her sister's truth bomb, and with one explosive question ticking away in her head?

Is William Scott fooling them all for a second time?

Along the sand to her left, a young board rider moved into Chelsea's peripheral vision and paused, possibly contemplating the squally conditions. Zipping up his wetsuit, he rubbernecked the strange woman in the now-see-through white T-shirt and rain-soaked shorts. Another thunder crack, followed by raucous cheering up the beach, saw the teen abandon his board where it stood in the sand. He raced back up to where mates congregated under the now-empty viewing platform, the glow of their cigarettes in the shadows like flitting fireflies.

Catching a glimpse of the unmissable hair—the colour of rust— Chelsea recalled the boys who'd stared through innocent eyes while she'd explained how a trapped epaulette shark waits for a wave to make good their escape.

Is William Scott waiting—again—to escape detection—again?

He used to tell his daughters, "The really clever sea creatures wait and watch and listen to the wave's whispers. The sea is slick, and it can trick, but if you never take the ocean for granted, Chelsea-girl, you'll have nothing to fear".

Is William Scott slick? Is this disappearance another trick? Is it even possible in 2015?

Disappearing had been doable in a little-known and isolated local fishing spot and campground circa 1980. How would a person pull off the same stunt with so many people in proximity, so many zoom lenses poised, so many constant calls for help posted to Facebook?

'Where are you?' she called towards the rocky platform, her gaze intent on finding signs of life hiding in the headland's shadows.

All the while, watery tentacles sneaked over the shale surface, like a child's fingers sneaking over the tablecloth to claim the last treat after Christmas lunch. How often had her mum slapped Chelsea's cheeky hands away from the mixing bowl and cream beaters saying, 'no more'? Had Wendy done the same to her husband, denying him what he'd craved? Had she forced him to leave them, to create a new life with a new wife? Were Layla and Chelsea daring him to disappear again, this time with his son?

'No, no,' she yelled into the susurration of squally winds and rain, 'not a special boy like Kai. You wouldn't!'

The whispered reply came back, confirming what Chelsea already knew.

It's possible. It's possible. It's possible.

44

CHELSEA

There was one way to find out, but the dangers posed by crossing an outgoing estuary meant she couldn't reach the rocky platform via the beach. Should she lose her footing, she'd be washed into the deep green gully and carried out to sea in the adjoining rip. That's after the rocks and razor-liked barnacles gouged her skin. Should she survive the fierce and fast-moving current, Tad had said both the northern side of the rock shelf remained inaccessible from the Sandbar Beach side. But hadn't Tad also inferred old Elmie knew of a way in?

How difficult could it be?

Another option was to race back to camp, find Tad or the police, ramble incoherently about her dead father being alive and, if they didn't cart her away there and then, the police might take goodness knows how long to find Elmie—possibly interrupting pikelets 'with her sister'—and force a confession regarding illegal trespass of a historical defence force location. Maybe then, they'll have coerced the whacky old woman to tell them how she accesses Bunker Headland so they can have it sealed back up.

Oh, Chelsea, YOU are the crazy one!

But was she crazy enough to do what no one else is doing? Where were the boats? Where was the rescue chopper dispatched from Lismore, even though the monochrome landscape—the sky heavy with cloud and the sea gun-metal grey—made impossible search conditions. Even the imposing Bunker Headland was surrendering to the dense sea mist.

Would air crews see anything in this weather? Maybe the authorities had already decided, based on the circumstances, the exercise was more likely recovery than rescue? But what if, thirty-four years ago, people had looked sooner and harder and concentrated their efforts on land rather than sea?

What if you did that now, Chelsea? The fastest way to the truth was undoubtedly via the northern stretch of sand Wandarri locals called Heartbreak Beach. From there she could access the caves and the rocky platform. Something was better than nothing.

With no time for indecision, and with the teen's abandoned board sticking proud of the sand now firmly in her sights, she chanted to herself, *Let your fear set you free. Become one with the sea.*

Suddenly sprinting towards the abandoned board, she took a death-like grip and dragged it to the waterline. Soon waist deep, the first wave—sharp with cold—stabbed her belly. Despite a bigger-than-normal surf, and the undertow that pulled and pushed hampering her progress, Chelsea ignored the desperate teen's pleading. *You're moving forward, Chelsea, even if it kills you.*

'Hey, lady!' The teen's cussing, mostly muted by the sound of wind and waves, was the last thing Chelsea heard as she planted the board, threw herself on the deck, and paddled for her life, headed for the green gully's rip to take her out fast. She was not going back to shore, and no longer was little Chelsea Scott afraid. *Nothing is lurking beneath the surface. Nothing can hurt you. Nothing.*

'Only more of the truth, eh Dad?'

But Chelsea was already three decades beyond the worst hurt in the world. The angriest of oceans couldn't stop her now. Not once she was beyond the shore, beyond the fear, and beyond the breakers.

To anyone looking on, Chelsea might appear insignificant in the vastness of the ocean, but her purpose was far from small.

'Time to give up your secrets,' she told the undulating and strangely stagnant surface on which the board now bobbed. 'No more lies.'

Word about the bonkers board nabber must've reached camp because the shoreline was again crowded. One person frantically waved a red umbrella. *Layla!* Her sister was frightened, and for good reason. *Had* Chelsea stopped to consider the ramifications of her dash into the ocean, she would likely not be freezing and afraid and straddling a stolen surfboard more than a kilometre offshore. But this was no longer about Chelsea or her phobia. This was about a small boy, supposedly missing with his father.

'Or am I right and you're up there, hiding in plain sight?' Chelsea screamed at the distant headland. 'Were you up there somewhere evading capture thirty-four years ago, Dad? Are you seeing me now, like when you watched and listened from behind the shop curtain? Tell me. Show yourself. I want the truth. Now!'

Chelsea used to tell her sister, and later Dale, how she would summon her dad for chats late at night when in her bedcover cave. She could conjure him up anytime, awake or asleep, and he would wrap her in his warmth, in his wise words, and in his advice. But, like sea mist whenever she moved or reached out, there was never anything there, and nothing reassuring to hold. The man had lived in her imagination and in her dreams—the good ones—just as he'd lived, still lives, in every room of the house.

Because you've let him, Chelsea.

He was beside her now in his flowery board shorts, bobbing on his vintage board, and wearing the choker necklace Mum reckoned made him look like a hippie.

'Things don't just vanish, Dad,' she said into the wind. Her mother would spout the same line whenever someone in the house grizzled about not being able to find something in their bedroom. 'Or can people disappear—if desperate enough. Is that right, Dad? Did you make yourself disappear?'

The reply came to her as rolling thunder, accompanied by a rapid firing of forked lightning determined to unpick the horizon's tight seam of ocean and sky. But unlike the crowd on the beach earlier, Chelsea no longer looked to the sea for answers, nor to the headland.

Chelsea had the answer. She only needed to pick through that detritus of memories inside herself for one moment in time, years ago. The answer was in her father's wise words:

'Never play Hide and Seek with a cuttlefish. Lesson learned, Chelsea.'

LESSONS WITH DAD, 1977

'It's what cephalopods do,' Dad says, as if I should already know. 'Like the octopus and squid, the cuttlefish make themselves disappear to evade predators.'

'What's a predator, Dad?'

'Someone or something that wants to hurt you,' he answers. 'When sensing danger, the cephalopod evades capture by changing colour to blend into the landscape, much like a bug takes the shape of a thorn and an insect can look like a stick. There's a lesson in there, Chelsea-girl.'

'What lesson, Dad?'

He pokes my ribs and forces a giggle. 'Never play Hide and Seek with a cephalopod, of course.'

'I'm too grown-up for Hide and Seek. Besides, Layla always wins.'

'Ah, but the secret to winning is to be a cuttlefish, an octopus, or a squid. Layla will never find you.'

'How do you mean?'

'Simple!' he explains. 'Next time you play, stay super still and in plain sight.'

I scrunch my face. 'Huh?'

'Blend in,' he says. 'Your sister will be so busy looking in all the usual places, she'll miss the obvious.'

'Promise, Dad? I really wanna win.'

He nods. 'I've told you before, if something is important enough, you can do anything and go anywhere, Chelsea-girl.'

When he loads my beach bag with more dried cuttlebone, I ask, 'What are you going to do with all these? We have so many already and Mum complains about the stink.'

'Never mind about Mum. I have a plan for these—when I finally make time for me.'

'When will that be, Dad?'

'When little squirts stop asking questions and Mum stops asking for everything else. That's when I'll go live on a beach and make beautiful things from all these cuttlefish bones.'

'And when will that be, Dad?'

'When I'm ready to want it more than anything else—more than life— I'll make it happen. Come on, Chelsea-girl. Time we headed back to camp.'

45

TADPOLE

'Here!' Tad shoved his land leg at Layla. 'Look after this and I'll look after your sister.'

'Please, please, bring Chelsea back to me, Tad. Tell her we all need her.'

Tad nodded and hopped to the waterline, aware this rescue, even in his book, was next level ludicrous. In a heaving swell on a stormy day, and with his one leg and a borrowed board—no time to fetch his own—he was somehow supposed to spot a surfer wearing blue shorts and a white top.

And there she was, sitting stiff as a board, on a stolen board, and with both legs dangling in the murky depths.

'What do you think you're doing?' he called on approach.

'I have to do this for me.'

'Well, whatever "this" is,' Tad said, sitting up, 'did you have to *try* on another bloke's board without permission? Time to get it back to its owner.'

'I'm not going in yet. I can't.'

'Look, I get that a missing rock fisherman is going to hit you hard, but it's best we leave the sea search to the chopper crew, and you, sitting out here, won't achieve anything.' He didn't add that surfers know such gnarly conditions are dangerous, especially with onshore winds turning the surf into an unrideable mush.

'What chopper? Where?' Chelsea looked up at the sky. 'Do they even care?'

'Our region has one unit. They were diverted to a highway head-on.'

'Because a missing rock fisherman is just another of those "Too late to rescue. Recovery only" situations you mentioned after the storm that first day?'

'Layla wants me to tell you she's sorry, she loves you, and to get back to the beach so she can hug you and never again let go.' While Tad knew the poignancy of the message had required he pause, the changing weather said otherwise. 'She shoved me into the water and begged me to hurry. So, Chelsea, now I'm begging you.'

He might be shouting into the wind—literally and figuratively—but what other choice did he have? The woman had to want to return, and under her own steam. He couldn't pick her up and carry her back.

'I understand,' he shouted over a wind gust. 'There's no better place to think or maybe scream than out here. I get it. I've needed to look at the world from a different angle many times to make sense of my life. Sitting out here beyond the breakers does that, and more.'

For Tad, the ocean was about connection. As a lifelong lover of surfing, he was no stranger to the rush of riding a wave. Having the energy of it flow through him was surreal and enlivening. This situation was the opposite. With Chelsea bobbing up and down on the borrowed board, her unblinking gaze glued to Bunker Headland, he was growing more nervous by the minute.

'Chels, come on,' he called, 'this current will soon have us north of the rocky point, and that's heading into Heartbreak Beach territory. Let's get a wave back to shore before it gets any darker. I'm feeling a little vulnerable with my one remaining and incredibly good-looking leg hanging off a board.'

Finally, Chelsea looked at Tad, her expression deadpan. 'You've got more chance of dying in a motor accident than you do from a shark attack.'

'Yeah, well, I'm not partial to either. Besides, your sister will kill me before anything else, unless I get you back to the beach.' Driving a hand into the water to partially turn his board towards the shore, he said, 'Come now. You'll be helping me impress Layla.' Finally, a flicker of a smile. But when Chelsea made no attempt to move, Tad paddled alongside and anchored himself to her board. 'Can I at least know why you're out here?'

For a moment, he thought she was ignoring him. Then ...

'You talk about seeing your world from a different angle. Right? Well, as a kid, I loved the beach. Thirty-four years ago, that stopped, and I let what happened change me. You might assume I'm only out here to look for a man lost to the sea. I'm also looking for that twelve-year-old girl.'

Sitting side by side on boards, the pair bobbed over the rolling waves and going nowhere fast, like horses on a watery carousel.

'So, Chelsea, what will you do when you find that little girl?'

'Grow up,' she said, turning to look at him, the harshness back in her voice and her eyes. 'I'll sell up, move forward with my life, and hold my husband. Then I'll … Oh, wait! What's that?' She pointed towards Bunker Headland. 'Close to the top. I see colour.'

As the woman stretched out on the deck, arms poised and ready to paddle, Tad managed to grab the board's trailing ankle strap. 'Whoa, there! Hold your horses and let me take a look before you go galloping off.'

He blinked to squeeze the salty water from his eyes and to make out the unidentifiable shape.

'Could be a kid's snagged kite,' he shouted back at Chelsea. 'But more likely it's safety bunting that's come loose. Over the years they've added loads to deter walkers.' More of a worry was what looked like a fresh landslide. As Tad no longer frequented the headland, and when surfing he rarely ventured north of Sandbar Beach, to see the escarpment from this angle unsettled him. 'Even if you could get onto the rocky platform, there's no safe way up.'

'There was a track three decades ago, Tad. Still is, I'd say.'

'But in what condition? Just look at the gaping bloody hole. That landslip is another reason why Bunker Headland remains off limits. Not even the rule breakers are stupid enough to try.'

'All evidence to the contrary,' Chelsea said. 'Please, let go of the board.'

'Even if you find a way up, Chelsea, I can't help you. With one leg, I'm totally useless.'

'No Tad,' she yelled, the worsening weather making conversation almost impossible. 'The day we met, I saw my father in you. But, Thaddeus Poulle, you are far from useless—and a good man. The only truthful thing to come out of my dad's mouth was telling me I can go anywhere and do anything if I want it desperately enough, which means, Tad, you won't stop me. I've wanted nothing as desperately as I want the truth. And if I'm right, it's up there. But it's mine to find. That's why, even if you could help, I'm going alone. And another thing,' she called, her body now horizontal to the board, arms ready to paddle. 'I'll happily list for Layla all the reasons you and your one leg are a million times more impressive than most men with two. And you're brave,' she added, 'because you, my friend, are heading back to shore to tell my sister what I must do.'

Short of physically restraining her, and likely coming off second best if he tried, Tad gave up. Like Prudence, this woman had a mind of her own. As the sky opened, firing skin-stinging shrapnel, and pitting the ocean's surface, the best he could do was find out where the chopper was, fill them in, and then break the news to her sister. He imagined Layla's response. It looked a lot like the storm in play—all dark, thunderous, and dangerous.

CHELSEA

Fear drove Chelsea around the point, making for the shore, and unsure which scenario scared her more—what she would find, or what she wouldn't.

For one exhilarating moment, as the waves drove her towards Heartbreak Beach, Chelsea was twelve again; flat on the deck and paddling—her eyes wide with excitement and determination, the board and her body one. Preparing to pop up tall and confident, despite the foaming closeout wave, she heard her dad urging her on.

'You're doing it, Chelsea-girl. Keep coming, keep coming.'

But Chelsea was no longer twelve, nor nimble and fearless, and without the vertical wall of wave a surfer needed to stand, the crest broke hard and all at once. Without a secured leg rope, the surfboard slipped out from under her, somersaulted dangerously several times, and speared the water surface, forcing Chelsea deep inside the turbulent wash to avoid being struck.

Pummelled, pushed, pulled and dragged down until thrown against the sea floor, her entire life passed before her eyes in what seemed like less than a nanosecond. Then nothing.

It was all over.

The monster she'd once feared had spat her out onto the sand and, unlike the borrowed board further down the beach, Chelsea *was* in one piece, flat on her back, and in considerable discomfort. With an uncontrollable shiver making the simple task of poking her finger inside waterlogged ears ridiculously difficult, she tilted her head back, eyes wide, and let the light rain wash away the stinging salt and sand. To relieve the tightness in her lungs, she administered two puffs from the pocketed reliever that had miraculously survived the ocean's rough and tumble.

Eventually standing on wobbly legs—no time to waste—she made for the headland. But with the rock shelf already awash with the white foam of an incoming tide, Chelsea steeled herself, half crawling and half climbing to reach the start of the track she knew was there—somewhere. When a noise overhead took her attention, she slipped, scraping her heel, her ankle bone, and her elbow. The pied oyster catcher bird had swooped in for a stickybeak, landing uncommonly close and again sharing its call, but a noise overhead drowned out the gentle *pleep-pleep*.

A person. A shout.

Unable to see beyond the bluff's dense foliage, and ignoring the agony of barnacles needling bare feet and the sting of sliced skin, Chelsea found the start of the overgrown walking track and solace in the sandy surface and the cool cushioning underfoot from coastal grasses and pigface plants. Starting out steep, the climb soon took on a zigzag pattern, which meant getting nowhere fast—or so it seemed. The higher she climbed, the stronger the wind, but not once did Chelsea look down to check her progress. The only way was up, and the breeze-battered shrubs shaped by persistent winds suggested she was getting close to the top. So bent over was one section of foliage she passed through, the branches had formed a kind of underpass, bringing relief from what was now lashing rain and wind. With denseness, however, came darkness to reduce her field of vision and turn tree roots into trip factors.

'Damn it!' Landing hard on her left hip, and with a burning sensation on the heels of both hands, Chelsea carefully crawled forward, hoping she'd find a sturdy tree limb to help right herself. Forward also meant reaching the light, the glow up ahead momentarily blinding her into a squint. When she focused her salt and sand-scratched eyes, she let out a gasp and stumbled backward, her feet sending a spray of loose earth into a gaping void. The walking track ahead of her was all but gone.

Then she saw *him*—a man—precariously perched amid the crumbling remains of the cliff face, and barely clinging to a collapsed concrete bunker. *And not just any man.*

'You're—' Unsure if her next word was going to be *alive* or *hurt*,

Chelsea said nothing. She was too intent on telling herself to wake up from what had to be another baffling and bad dream. *Except it's not.*

'Chelsea-girl, help.'

How? Scan the area for a branch or a sturdy vine strong enough and long enough to reach and pull him to safety? Two metres would do. *Then what? Take his weight and trust no more land falls away?* More rubble raining over her father and smashing on the rock platform below decided for her. Remarkably, the tangled remnants of concrete and steel supporting him stayed in place.

After the clatter of falling rocks came the caterwauling of an anxious crowd looking on from afar. The landslide had exposed a slice of Sandbar Beach to the south. People gathered there, mere specks on the sand but distinguishable: Talia and Elmie in their unmissable outfits, Tadpole with Lucky, and Layla. All watching, and all barred from helping by the high tide and a surging estuary.

'People know I'm here,' she told the man. Despite everything, even the bloody thigh wound, her words were calming. 'Help will come.'

'Good, because I'm clearly going nowhere, no matter how much I might want otherwise. This steel rod has my leg pinned.' He yanked hard on the length of colourful construction bunting—a makeshift tourniquet —his expression a portrait of both pain and repentance. 'I can't get to Kai, and I need to make sure he's okay.'

'I understand. You don't want him scared,' Chelsea said, the sharp end of her stare further impaling him to the crumbling cliff face. 'You don't want him left alone to survive the night on this headland with its dark forest of gnarly limbs bursting with ghoulish Banksia men.'

'Please, Chelsea-girl, find my son,' he said. 'Forget about me.'

Forget about you? Momentarily tempted to laugh, she steeled herself. 'Your son is the only reason I've come.'

'Then, please, find him. I pushed Kai to safety seconds before the earth gave way. If he's run off, it's because he's confused about what to do. The headland is not new to him, but I've taught him not to tell anyone about our secret spot.'

Secret spot? His words were as good as a punch to Chelsea's stomach.

'He's familiar with the place. We've played Hide and Seek up here. He's likely in the southern bunker. He goes there with Elmie. He loves her storytelling.'

'Elmie's bunker?'

'From here, head towards the tunnels and the wartime gun emplacement. Remember? You called it "a big plug".'

'Do I remember?' she mocked. 'It's coming back to me, Dad. All of it. Your cruel lies. Your fake tears that day.'

'I'm seriously sorry for what you went through,' he said, grimacing with more pain. 'If I could've done one thing differently, it would have been to leave you at camp with your mother and sister. But even if you'd let me, going without you was so out of the ordinary. People would've questioned why I went fishing alone on the very day I go missing.'

'So, Layla's right. I *was* your alibi.'

'Chelsea-girl, you were so much more to me. Such a curious girl and always questioning. There was no way for me to explain starting a new life together, so I couldn't take you away with me. Whereas Kai … He doesn't ask questions. Kai is … Well, he's Kai.'

'You were actually taking him? No!' she cried, determined to not sob aloud. 'This can't be real. Do you know how much I wished and dreamed and hoped you'd come home? I've held so tight to your memory, Dad.'

The earth underfoot shifted. Or was the tremor she felt Chelsea's world falling apart—her life, her beliefs, and her trust plummeting and smashing onto the rocky platform below—and with the man responsible right there, watching. Could he not see *her* about to crumble and fall? Did he not love his daughter as much as he cared about his son?

'I promise to answer all your questions once you and Kai are safe. A few metres more and you'll be at the top and on solid ground. Find my boy. He'll trust you to keep him safe; you've bonded already. And I know you're a wonderful mother, because now and then Wendy acquiesces to send family photos or news. Right now, though, you need to go.'

Yes! Yes she did.

With the sky her only guide up, she forged an alternative path, eventually finding flat ground. *At last!* But the climb wasn't over. Up and up she went, coming across a dozen stairs barricaded by fallen trees and fortified by sticky spider webs. Taking up arms, a cobweb-battling branch firmly in hand, she charged up the rotting steps, stopping at the entrance to a tunnel; one of several on the headland, as she recalled.

Over three decades ago, her father had urged Chelsea to trust him, but nothing looked familiar. The tunnel entrance was caged, but the wire bent back to make a small gap. *Enough for a child and for a tiny woman*, she thought. *A brave one!*

Chelsea edged close enough to call the boy's name in case he was hiding inside, but the echo too quickly faded. She tried again, louder— desperate.

But with no reply, and no other choice, she breathed herself skinny, turned her head sideways to avoid the protruding wires, and sung out, 'I'm coming, Kai, ready or not.'

Desperation drove Chelsea through the dark and dank confines, the stench of something rotten—something dead—turning her stomach. Making herself small, as if a child again, and in her bedcover cubby, she squinted in the darkness while, step by shaking step, she made her way along the increasingly familiar and frightening tunnel. There were, at irregular intervals overhead, cracks with guiding shards of dying daylight, which she counted, stopping suddenly at three. *This is wrong.* The tunnel had taken her and Dad *towards* the secret spot track and both bunkers. She was retracing her steps, and she was wrong. *Again.* Turning back, giddy and disorientated, she braced the walls with both hands to stop herself from slipping on the slime underfoot.

Out of the tunnel and gulping fresh air, the southerly wind was cooling on a face wet with tears she didn't realise she'd cried. With no time to waste, Chelsea turned south to hunt down the inconspicuous southern bunker. *Elmie's bunker.*

And there it was, like a burrow built into the side of the cliff.

Despite only a narrow opening for observing the ocean, there was enough light to appreciate the painted walls Tad had said told the story of a mother's love and sacrifice for family. And there, tucked in a corner and covered with kaftan fabric, was Kai.

'Hey there, little man,' she whispered while gently rousting the boy and rearranging her face to show fun rather than fear. 'You must be the Hide and Seek champion, but we must hurry away from here. Mum needs you home.'

'Dad! Dad! Dad!'

'Yes, Dad needs you to be safe.'

Taking a calming breath, she'd just gripped his hand, ready to lead him away, when the remains of war rattled around them. Starting as a low growl, the noise grew, the ground under her feet juddered and the smashing sound of falling rocks echoed in the hollow space. Pulling Kai tight, fearing Elmie's bunker was about to suffer the same fate and fall to the rocky platform, Chelsea bent over, buried her yelp in the boy's hair, and imagined Layla waiting on the beach, and no doubt feeling guilt over Chelsea's current predicament. But all blame lay with the man she was prepared to save—for Kai's sake.

'Look! Look! Look!' Kai said, pointing beyond the slit of concrete where soldiers had once kept watch.

The helicopter. *Finally!*

Grabbing the swathe of fabric from the floor, she asked, 'Have you ever flown in a whirlybird?' When the boy shook his head, she added, 'Me either. So let's hurry and that's exactly what we'll do. Take my hand.'

Fifteen shards of light later, and with the sound of a helicopter somewhere overhead urging Chelsea on, the pair emerged from the tunnel. They'd made it through the maze and back to the open space with its dilapidated tin huts on the periphery and the giant plug dead centre. But the helicopter had already turned tail, the crew's reconnaissance of Bunker Headland completed too quickly. *Can they not see a man needs help?*

'Hey! We're here!' she screamed, letting the wind catch the silken kaftan fabric as she ran into the clearing and climbed onto the big plug.

It worked. *Thank you, Elmie!*

'Kai, sweetie, let's get you ready.'

Having circled back, the aircraft hovered while a crew member lowered himself to the ground nearby.

'Look at me,' Chelsea said as she squatted before an increasingly confused Kai. Holding his shivering shoulders, she explained, 'The harness is the fun bit. It doesn't hurt. That nice man will use it to lift you safely into the whirlybird. Okay?'

'Dad! Dad! Dad!' Kai cried, his agitation growing as the crewman neared, rescue harness at the ready.

'Yes, Kai, sweetie, you'll see him soon. But going with the man now will show Dad it's not scary. I'll go now to tell him to look up at his very brave boy.'

'Sorry,' the crewman shouted over the deafening *thwop! thwop! thwop!* of blades. 'I'll be straight back for you.'

With arms akimbo, as if proving she was uninjured, Chelsea yelled back, 'Leave me. I'm not the one needing urgent help.'

He unclipped a second harness from his kit and thrust it towards Chelsea. 'We don't leave anyone behind unless we have to, and it's less traumatic for all of us—this little guy included—when Mum is on board. Let's go, little guy. Mum will wait right here.'

'You don't understand,' Chelsea insisted.

'I do understand,' he cut in. 'Delaying in these conditions will drain our fuel fast. Let's go.' He signalled his crew.

'But Kai isn't my son.' With the crewman already out of earshot, only she heard the words. 'He's my half-brother.'

Despite wishing she could've raced back and tell her father Kai was safe, Chelsea had waited.

Only when dangling midair, like a limp puppet, did the enormity of what she'd achieved and all she'd seen squeeze more tears from her eyes. She cried harder still once safely bundled into the chopper. Freed of the harness, headset in place, she cradled Kai, rocking him and reassuring him, all the while keeping his face pressed into her body as the pilot took in a wide arc, flying out to sea before turning back towards land.

'About his dad,' she ventured. 'Will another rescue chopper come with a medical team?'

If the crewman's carefully controlled expression didn't vividly portray his reply, the bleak, bare, and broken face of a distant Bunker Headland said it all.

CHELSEA DAY 6 OF 7

Other beachgoers might assume Chelsea was there for the same reason—to pray and hope. She wasn't, of course. Chelsea was not a part of the growing collective of Wandarr-ites intent on paddling out in honour of the man they lovingly referred to as Squid.

Overnight and working against an incoming tide, several teams, made up of local volunteers and police, had searched the rubble-strewn rocky platform by torchlight. But the ocean had won, beating back rescuers and sweeping the battlefield clean by morning. What the retreating tide hadn't washed from the rubble, a work crew had continued to comb through since daybreak. Cadaver dog and all, they were yet to find evidence or remains at the base of the cliff, with the term 'recovery effort' being reported in news bulletins and the sea once again blamed for taking a beloved family man.

At the base of a dune, knees bent and pulled close to her chin, Chelsea kept her back to the headland, preferring to observe the abundant board shorts, Bali shirts, bikinis, sarongs, and sunhats, the colourful array of clothing a contrast to the gloomy day. Feeling conspicuous in her plain three-quarter pants and a shirt, she watched the goings-on from a distance. Though connected in ways, Chelsea was not on the beach to commemorate or mourn. Had Layla got her way, Chelsea wouldn't be on the beach at all. The pair would have left that first day and found a resort pool to lounge around while the sisters reconnected. Chelsea would be none the wiser, and Kai might be with his dad.

As choices go, staying in Sandbar had been neither right nor wrong, but last night with Layla could have played out differently. So many high emotions followed by long silences and meaningful moments for two sisters trying to heal. Had the pair acted like adults and made up after their yelling match, Chelsea wouldn't have spent the evening alone in *Sea-Esta* wanting her sister back, crying over her husband's absence, growing angry at her father, and angrier with herself for sticking around for this afternoon's paddle out for Liam 'Squid' Scott. But Tadpole had asked her to stay, and she kind of owed him. Layla remained nowhere to be seen, her departure not unusual, nor unexpected. Since the age of eighteen, disappearing was something her sister routinely did, often for months on end.

At least Chelsea now understood why.

In contrast to the busy beach, the ocean appeared impassive. But Chelsea knew better. William Scott had taught his daughters 'the ocean is motion' and constantly moving and propelled around the globe in sweeping currents.

'There's no holding back a restless wave,' he'd said.

'And no turning it around, either,' Chelsea muttered.

With the sun sinking behind the dunes, and people gathering in groups on the sand, Chelsea recalled Tadpole saying an east coast sunset helped him reflect on his achievements. Chelsea's successes—the ones to be celebrated—were small, like learning to appreciate who she was, what she was capable of, and importantly, knowing what she needed to do next. The answer, so tiny, had sat on her various bedside tables for thirty-four years. As she passed the little conch from one palm to the other, Chelsea pondered the many marine lives this one small shell had protected before snatched from a tidal pool by a selfish girl who knew better.

The hermit crab lesson had been one of Chelsea's earliest. William Scott had understood the curious creature because, like the hermit crab, when he outgrew one house, he simply went on the hunt for a new one.

MUSICAL (MOLLUSC) CHAIRS WITH DAD, 1976

'Just this one, Dad. Please?' The shell is light in my hand. 'It's empty,' I add.

'Remember the rules,' he replies while lovingly uncurling my fisted fingers one by one. 'Besides, being empty is more reason to leave a shell behind for the squatters of the sea.'

'What's a squatter?'

'Squatters borrow places to live. Hermit crabs outgrow their houses, so they find an abandoned shell, attach themselves, and tote it around wherever they go.'

'Like we attach and tow Vinnie the caravan,' I say.

'Kind of, but for hermit crabs, there can be too few to go around because little girls take shells as keepsakes. When someone takes a shell away, like a chair in your Musical Chairs party game, a crab misses out. Remember how you got upset on your birthday?'

I nod and, although the conch in my hand is my favourite of all time and very pretty, I tilt my palm and send it back into the water with a plop. 'Can we stay and see if a hermit crab finds it?'

Dad shakes his head. 'Could be a big wait. Not even sure why they're called hermit crabs,' he says, 'except that they tuck themselves inside borrowed shells and rarely poke their heads out. Kind of like Mum when we're caravanning.' Dad chuckles. He has a great laugh. 'Even weirder,' he says, 'is hermit crabs aren't hermits at all. There can be hundreds living as a community in complete harmony, and happily swapping shells or finding new and bigger ones.'

'Is that like Mum wanting a bigger caravan so she can fit more junk in?'

Dad doesn't answer yes or no. Instead, he throws back his head, lets out a big burst of laughter, and walks away, leaving me pondering the rock pool, now home to my very favourite conch shell. My very, very beautiful and hard-to-leave-behind conch shell.

Chelsea might've read more into the recollection than was rational, but it was impossible to not compare the conch to The Beach Shack. She'd self-ishly kept both. How had she not understood Dale's discontent? He was living in a borrowed shell and drowning in William Scott memories. She'd been reckless with her husband's love, throwing away her relation-ship rather than throwing away boxes.

Time to right two wrongs. Standing, she brushed the sand from her bottom and strode purposely towards the southern end of the beach.

Squatting beside the rock pool and observing her reflection, Chelsea opened and upturned her hand. The plop of the little conch, the way it spiralled to the bottom of the pool, stirred the water's surface. Hopefully, the ripple effect of Chelsea's return to Sandbar will also eventually calm and, while impossible to forget completely, she'll learn to remember her father differently—the way he deserved.

'Ahoy there!' Tad called as Chelsea neared the viewing platform. 'Missing you already, and right when I could do with some delightfully distracting company.'

Although keen to pack her things and bid Sandbar Beach goodbye, she paused long enough to say, 'You're sweet. I'm going to miss you, Tad, but I'll be back—after I've sorted my life and two generations of stuff in and under the house. Thank goodness I have a sister willing to help.'

'Should my ears be burning?' Layla emerged from behind the dune, joining them, and surprising Chelsea.

'You stayed? I-I thought you'd left me here.'

'I'm never leaving you again.' The sisters hugged so tight, with Layla pulling away to ask Tad, 'Do you mind? I need a minute with Chelsea.'

'No problemo! I have things to do and people to see. The community is putting a thank you event on for the volunteers. Hopefully, the rain stays away. Maybe you'll be there?' Tad whistled Lucky to his side and called back as he walked away. 'If not, it's good to see you two patching things up.'

'I honestly thought you'd gone,' Chelsea said.

Layla slipped into the lookout seat and smiled up at her. 'No choice but to stay. I can never let you out of my sight again. You know all my secrets.'

'I sure hope that's all there is. It's a lot to reconcile. I dread Dale's reaction when he hears how much Dad hated The Beach Shack. An abandoned shell no one wanted but me was how he once described our home. I'm unsure how much damage I've done to my marriage, but I'm going to fix it.'

'Newsflash, Chels, you're not losing Dale—not over a house and not over a woman. Don't take my word for it. Call him.'

'I plan to, and thanks to you, I won't be starting the story from scratch when I see him.' After a minute staring at the horizon, Chelsea asked, 'Do you reckon it was Dad's plan to—?'

Layla's gaze zeroed in on Chelsea. 'Do *you* really want to let your head go there?'

'No! But what if—?'

'No more "what if". Second guessing is no way to live. I hate what he did to our family. What he did to us. But that's behind us. It's over. Done.'

Watching her sister finger trace a heart tattoo that did a lousy job of disguising the scar, Chelsea knew. No longer was the reason her attractive, older sister had progressed from alcohol and drugs to self-harm a mystery.

'There can be no more secrets, Layla.' When her sister nodded, Chelsea added. 'Let's shake on it.'

'Seriously? We're not children, Chels. We don't cross our hearts and hope to die. But I also wish we weren't grownups. How about we promise without the symbolism?'

'And if you weren't a grownup?' Chelsea asked. 'If we could go back to being kids, what would you want to do right now?'

'Too easy,' Layla replied. 'I'd run away. Wanna come? I'm serious.' Her sudden burst of enthusiasm suggested so. 'Let's go *somewhere*. Anywhere but bloody *Nowhere*. Let go of this place and let *him* go.'

A distant commotion of colour caught in the corner of Chelsea's eye as a woman emerged from between the dunes further north. *Talia! A woman mourning a husband. A mother wondering what next.* Chelsea contemplated what she could say to comfort Talia until a burst of wind-driven sand slapped sense into her. The same gust caught Talia's hippy skirt. As the fabric flapped wildly but fleetingly, the flurry of red, green, and yellow reminded Chelsea of the lorikeet that once crashed into her kitchen window. On that occasion, she'd stood back and waited, because a stunned bird will recover if left alone. Not intervening, though, had been difficult.

'I can guess what you're contemplating,' Layla said. 'Forget it.'

'You don't think Talia deserves the truth?'

'What truth? That her husband is a fraudster and a liar? Do we tell her who *we* are? Should we make her question his love for her and let her see he's lied to her every day of their lives together?'

'Hasn't he?' Chelsea asked. 'And not just Talia, but Kai and Tadpole.'

Layla shrugged. 'Sure. But you'd also be forcing the woman to keep a secret, and I know the effects of doing so; like when constantly compelled to pretend you're missing a person—one you both love and hate at the same time. I know Talia will go through life pretending she's okay. But she'll be lying to her son and everyone else. The lying will impact her, change her, challenge her to keep going.'

'What if Dad wasn't pretending to love his life here? What if me coming back ruined everything?'

'I'm not listening to this, Chelsea, but if you want to tell Talia, that's your decision. And now is your chance. Walk on over, give her the full story, and watch her question everything she thought was true and good about her life. Then wait for her to discover how keeping a shocking secret from family and friends soon severs those precious relationships. Pretty soon, she'll cut all ties. Then she'll self-destruct, and poor Kai will go through life wondering what he did to make his mother sad one minute and angry the next. She'll start drinking because alcohol eases her pain, but grow to fear the truth will one day slip out because booze loosens lips. For that reason alone, she'll shut down around Kai and everyone she loves.

'And when it all hurts too much and gets too hard, she'll look for a way out—several times. If she's lucky, someone will see she's worth saving. They'll let her rant and they'll care enough to pull her through, giving her some semblance of a life back. They'll show her she is worth loving, but it'll be too late,' Layla said. 'She no longer trusts the word *love*. When a man tells her "I love you and I want to be with you forever" she'll question herself and him. I know what I'm talking about, Chelsea. I am that person. Is that what you want for Talia?'

'No.'

'Look,' her sister continued, 'you hate Mum and you think she ran out on us and too easily moved onto a new husband. Like me, Mum did what she did to cope. You and I are lucky. Don't scoff. I'm serious, ' Layla scolded. 'We know the truth and, going forward, we'll have each other.'

Through tears, Chelsea's eyes locked on the horizon. 'I like your idea of running away. I once asked *him*—Dad—how long it would take to swim to the end of the ocean. He replied, "There is no end. It's all about perspective. What you see is only the horizon. The sea goes on and on." So, I asked him where it goes.'

'And what did he say?'

'He said, everywhere and *nowhere*.' Chelsea huffed and dusted off a cuttlebone. 'He also claimed to be a chameleon of the sea.'

48

CHELSEA

Earlier, while staring at that unreachable horizon, with blustery winds from the south doing their utmost to penetrate the borrowed jumper, Chelsea had watched a bunch of teenagers tasked with building a bonfire on the sand.

The same gusts now carried their rowdy exclamations and the smoke of a fire refusing to cooperate. Having watched their struggle, and many kindling trips behind the dunes, Chelsea walked over and surrendered William Scott's brown cardigan.

Aghast at the crazy lady's actions, Chelsea smiled at the group and muttered, 'Where there's smoke, there's fire. Lesson learned, kids.'

Now, alone on the viewing platform, and having found warmth and comfort from the contents of Layla's suitcase, Chelsea again sat on the periphery to watch the goings on, unsure about her fascination. Was it the fire—again—or the fact people were lamenting the loss of her father?

'You came.' Tad sat beside her, placing a comforting hand on her thigh.

'Sort of,' she replied.

'In need of an ear?'

'That all depends,' Chelsea said. 'Do you need to hear a story about a mother who used her children and dog as an excuse to hold on to a house? I'm that mother, in case you're wondering.'

'Go on.'

'I should've listened to my children *and* to my husband,' Chelsea began. 'They wanted out of that house years ago. They tried telling me.'

'You obviously have your reasons for staying.'

'*Had*, Tadpole, and no,' she said resignedly. 'Like those stubborn seahorses, I was clinging and refusing to let go. I had to make a safe home for my family, and prove I could be a good wife and a better mother because my mum sucked big time. But being back at Sandbar has made me realise I've selfishly held on to all the wrong things, including one empty conch shell.'

'Letting go can be scary, Chelsea.'

'Yeah, my daughter once told me I was afraid. And I am,' she confessed. 'I'm terrified about selling the house.'

'Even the stubborn old seahorse will eventually loosen its grip and let fate have its way,' Tad said. 'Do you know they're monogamous? The seahorse finds a mate to cling to in turbulent waters, and when the time's right, the pair let go together and ride the current. I reckon, if your guy is half as intelligent as a seahorse, he'll be hanging onto you real tight. As for the kids? I'm no expert, but it's said those who fly early are proof we've done a pretty decent parenting job. I can't take full credit for mine, but I was a kid once, and I made mistakes. In fact, maybe while you're confessing, I should tell you something. I, um, well, there's this incident in my past I want to share with you. It involves Layla.'

As Tad's long-winded confession sank in, along with the memory of her sister's splinter and the resultant infection, Chelsea guffawed. 'That's it?'

'*Not* the reaction I'd expected,' he said.

'What *did* you expect? You and Layla had a quick grope when you were teenagers. I recall the splinter episode involved a boy on the beach. I didn't laugh back then, of course. I was sad for my sister.'

'Speak of the devil.' Tad raised a welcoming hand at Layla making her way up from the shoreline. 'Reckon I might get myself another beer—for old Squid. Let's go, Lucky, mate.'

'Wait! Before you go.' She caught him by the elbow. '*I* have a secret, too, but—'

'It's okay. We're allowed secrets. If it *is* one to tell, you'll know the right time.'

'Hey!' Layla plonked down beside Chelsea. 'Amazing, isn't he?'

'Which one? The dog or the man?'

'You know exactly what I mean. And look at old Lucky. He's like a pup on the beach. I took a dip earlier, but I still feel old. Then again, you were the water baby. As kids, I always knew where to find you. Looks like I'll have to get used to it again. Seems you can't stay away.'

'I am learning to trust the water. I think I'll stay another day. Sitting alone on the beach helps.'

'You weren't exactly alone just now.'

'He's good company. Tad and his love of the sea have helped me more than he knows. For so long, I've stayed away from something I love, and all because of what Dad did.'

'Oh, I get that.' Layla wrapped an arm around Chelsea, pulling her close. 'I stayed away from you.'

Chelsea rubbed a thumb over the heart tattoo on her sister's wrist. 'That must've hurt.'

With the tiniest nod, Layla said, 'Wounds heal.'

'That reminds me. I meant to ask … Was your healing helped along by a honey-voiced man called Trent?'

Surprise, and maybe a pinch of concern, widened her sister's eyes. 'How do you know about Trent?'

'I don't *know* anything. Relax. I accidentally answered your phone and forgot to mention it. But he seemed keen that you didn't know he'd called; said you'd think he was checking up on you. He asked if you were okay. Are you?' Chelsea glanced back at her sister's wrist. 'Now?'

'Trent was the shrink who let me see how harbouring blame leads to certain self-destructive behaviours.'

'Then why didn't you care I was blaming myself for Dad?' Chelsea instantly wished she could retract the question.

'Look, Chels, I went off the rails for a long time, too full of myself. By the time I was thinking clearly, I figured the damage had been done and I hoped you would move forward with your life and beautiful family, but … If I *could* go back, I would.'

'I know, and speaking of moving on …' Chelsea said. 'Does Mrs *I'm mid-Mediterranean cruise don't bother me* know the skeleton is out?'

Layla shrugged. 'I'm not returning her messages. I'm done. I don't want to stay in touch.'

'Why not?'

'Because love didn't bond me to Mum. Lies did. And it turns out, she was worse than William. He at least married the woman he thought he'd knocked up because it was the honourable thing to do. Then you came along—Miss Fix, the golden-haired, magic marriage cure-all. But there was no fixing a marriage that wasn't salvageable, any more than you could save a man who didn't want to be saved.'

'The lies stop with us, and they stop today,' Chelsea said.

'Agreed. You are the most important person in my life, and I'm feeling like I might—*might*—get my sister back. Can I hope?'

'Layla, you've always had me. I love you.'

'Ditto.'

49

CHELSEA - DAY 7 OF 7

'Dale!' Chelsea jumped to her feet, brushing sand from her cut-off shorts, and blindly tidying her wind-blown hair. 'Why are you here?'

'Because you're here.' Her husband's words, his presence, and his embrace unravelled Chelsea in all the right ways. 'I've missed you, and after what Layla told me, I asked for a few days off.'

'Oh, I've *so* missed you. I can't believe you've come.'

Life made sense around Dale. Steadfast in calm times, he'd kept his family safe and together, even when life's raging currents tried pulling them apart. Now standing on the sand in his shorts, an open shirt and thongs, Chelsea saw the boy with sun-bleached hair who'd moved his school bag to the floor for her, then moved his life to a suburb far from his beloved surf beach.

Not until he'd left for Perth had Chelsea appreciated that it takes a family to make a shell a home. Had Dale's moving out not brought her back to Sandbar, she might not be in his arms and relishing the hug that unfailingly felt like home.

'Thank you for finding me, Dale.'

'I got a little lost myself, Chels, but I'm here now. The GPS got me as far as Wandarri bait shop, where I ran into a bloke who told me I should try the beach. I was about to question the validity of his tip—I figured he was talking about another Chelsea Holt—when he called out, "You're a lucky man". So, I got to thinking, wifey. What's a bloke supposed to make of such a statement from a stranger, hmm?'

'Absolutely nothing, Dale. Stop teasing. That was Tadpole.'

'I guessed as much. Your email pinged as soon as I got off the plane. In it, you mention he was in your dreams.'

'Yes, err, no! You're making that sound wrong. I didn't *dream* about Tadpole. I was talking with Tadpole about the giant plug from my dream and I … Look, sorry for rambling. I'm slowly getting my head around all this, which is why I wrote that long-winded email, rather than call you.'

What she'd written turned out a safe way to confess to her family's sins, with the writing process cathartic. Beginning as one unwieldy rant, composed while too angry to sleep, the early morning revision had both censored and softened the news, while also making more sense. But there were gaps to fill.

'I didn't mean for you to drop everything, Dale.'

'I was more than ready to come home, and seeing Layla in Perth … Well, Chels, you are the woman who makes my life right. Shh!' He placed a finger to her lips. 'I never intended walking away from all we've built; I'm not your father. My preference is to walk through what's left of our lives by your side, and I see this—being here—as meeting you halfway. From here, we'll decide the next direction together.' They hugged for a second time as Dale whispered in her ear, 'Oh, and Gabby wanted me to tell you she is more than willing to choose our direction. And, I quote: "The west"—as in Western Australia—"is awesome all year round".'

Chelsea pulled back, her tone a sober one. 'There's something important I need you to understand, Dale. In the past when I've struggled to choose, or in the future if I ask your opinion, please know it's not that I can't or won't decide. Maybe it's not been obvious, but I respect your views. I've cared about what you and the kids want.'

'What do *you* want?' her husband asked. 'Besides time to process the past week.'

'Like I wrote to you. I'm over nostalgic wallowing. I hope you still have that real estate agent's card?'

'Don't rush on my account, Chels. In fact,' he added, smiling. 'We could get some work done. Maybe spruce up the boys' old room. They'll be home soon.'

Chelsea squealed, clapping childlike hands. 'Both boys?'

'They wanted to surprise you, but I said you'd had enough to last a lifetime and to leave the telling to me. While I'm finishing my Perth secondment, they'll begin sorting the house and contents. What's the good of having two strapping lads if we don't use them for the heavy lifting? Oh, and I suggested they start with their closets.' Chelsea chuckled at the notion and, as usual, Dale laughed love. 'Layla will supervise them in your absence and hire a shipping container.'

'My absence?' Chelsea questioned. 'Where will I be?'

'Perth, I hope,' he replied. 'Gabby needs you.'

'Gabby has never needed me, Dale.'

'She needs her mother, Chelsea, trust me, and you can't work on a relationship long distance; my secondment has confirmed as much. Speaking of work, I'd love my colleagues to meet you.'

'And after your secondment ends?'

'We decide together. I have a few ideas to toss around. Will you come to Perth for a few weeks and help me pack up, Mrs Holt?'

'Hmm, well, while I look forward to seeing you in business mode, Mr Holt, I do prefer this understated board short, shirt and thong look you've got going on.' She'd hooked a finger in his waistband, letting the elastic snap back onto bony hips. 'I'm so glad I married you.'

Stripping down to the togs she'd packed, never for a second thinking they'd get wet, Dale asked, 'What are you doing?'

'What does it look like? Let's have a quick swim before heading back to camp. Tomorrow we can take off and find a beach cabin closer to home. How about it, Mr Holt?'

The surprise in Dale's expression could not have been more obvious if it were in neon. 'If it's possible, I may have just fallen in love with you more, Mrs Holt.'

Waiting until he'd shrugged out of his T-shirt, Chelsea stole a quick kiss and said, 'Race you into the water, slow poke!'

EPILOGUE

'Welcome back!' Tadpole's embrace felt good. 'Nice bit of *wheel estate* you got there. And g'day to you, Layla.'

'Hey, yourself!' she replied. 'The difference with our *wheel estate* is we plan on wearing out those tyres.'

'And who have we here, Lucky?' Two scruffy white dogs barked on cue. 'Sit! Good boy!'

'This is Hub and Cap,' Chelsea said. 'They're sisters. We rescued them.'

Tadpole grinned. 'Cute!'

'Yeah, brilliant idea!' Layla chuckled. 'Three months! A twenty-foot motorhome! And four-thousand kilometres from one side of the continent to the other.'

'The dogs were also a kind of self-imposed therapy,' Chelsea explained to Tad. 'We did stop at two.'

'Thank goodness,' Layla grumbled as Tadpole eyed the motorhome.

'Congratulations on your decision-making *and* on the choice of wheels. She's a beauty, but a big change from four solid walls.'

'And it's home for the foreseeable future now the house is gone. Sold to the highest bidder—a consortium with plans to develop a fancy Over 50's lifestyle village for people with big caravans and big dreams of doing the big lap of this amazing country.'

'What about your boys needing a home base?' Tad asked.

'Surprise, surprise! They're not boys. Travis and Tyler are making their own lives, like Gabby. My children and I love each other, and like me they can go anywhere and do anything, but it's wrong to rely on others for fulfilment, especially our kids. And there are no guarantees they'll be there in the way we want or need. We all get one life, one chance for happiness.' Chelsea paused to smile at her sister briefly, knowingly. 'Personally, I'm excited to be hitting the road. Being here and witnessing Wandarri's tight community-mindedness, I see a life in the suburbs as far more isolating than travelling the country. All the years I lived in the house, not once did anyone knock on my door and offer pikelets. Poor Elmie …'

'Yeah. I was with her when she passed,' Tad said. 'She seemed content and ready.'

'How do you know?'

'She smiled and told me Connie was pestering her for tea and pikelets. Speaking of happy,' Tad said, 'the devilishly handsome Prince Dale got his girl, and the girl got her fairytale ending—the happy Disney kind.'

'He always had me, Tadpole.'

'Yeah, well, you had the potential to be a pretty nice port in a storm. Then I realised the ship had already sailed, and the real purpose for popping into my life was to re-introduce me to your sister—and at a time when we're both ready for a new challenge. As a couple, we'll have our work cut out for us, but I'm game. Don't tell her I said that.'

'Sorry, but we don't keep secrets from each other,' Chelsea said, smiling. 'But seriously, Tad, spending time with you let me see how much I needed to be with Dale.'

The man's smile grew so big it almost split his face. 'Hmm, I'm going to take that as a compliment. You're meeting up with him in Perth?'

'Yes, by then he will have organised his long service leave replacement and handed over his case files. In his job, doing anything short notice is difficult, but he's trying. We're both going to try. Gabby, too. In the meantime, Layla and I will enjoy the sights while learning how to be sisters again. She'll fly back from Perth, leaving me to enjoy my grandbabies. Speaking of … How's little Fleur? Bet you miss Kai. I can't believe Talia simply walked away and left the shop for the Wandarri community.'

Tad shrugged. 'For years, she talked about taking her parents' ashes north so Kai could meet his grandmother's family. But when she wrote back to say her family needed her to stay, I was curious. Then again, Talia's devotion to family is undeniable. Loyalty is part of her DNA. Maybe I'll see her again. Maybe not. Where she is, I'm not sure. I may never know. You could circle those islands for years and never find the person you're looking for.'

A question hung on Chelsea's lips until Layla stepped up into the motorhome, launching herself piggy-back style at Tadpole.

'Come on, sis, let's you and me and the piddle and poo pooches get this show on the road. And I'll see *you*, Mr Thaddeus Poulle, when I get back.'

'Great! And while you're gone, I'll get busy on that project.'

'What project?' Chelsea queried.

Her sister laughed. 'De-splintering my new abode.'

'Not sure how your sister got on the top of the waiting list, Chelsea, but I'm glad she's got a Wandarri parcel. That particular shack has sat empty for years, and the Wandarri Warriors could do with a woman like Layla. Prudence would approve.'

Chelsea had said little upon hearing the news, and she remained concerned about her sister claiming the family parcel, quizzing her one day about it.

'What goes around, comes around,' Layla had announced after learning a vengeful and greedy Wendy had somehow extorted William's only remaining asset.

When confronted with Layla's ultimatum, however, their mother had handed the parcel over, choosing to keep the secret *and* her marriage. Layla was *that* determined and convinced Wandarri Eco-Community was the right move for her. Layla, the crusader, had fights to fight, and saving Elmie's bunker topped the list.

'Give Dale my regards, Chelsea,' Tad said. 'And remember, it's a big country, and you are two lovelies travelling alone.'

'With a couple of killer dogs on board,' Layla quipped. 'And a sister whose bite can be every bit as ferocious as her bark. Right?'

'You should talk! It helps that I no longer imagine monsters everywhere. Speaking of which,' Chelsea added, grabbing her sunhat. 'Ten minutes and we can set off.'

The sea laved the shore with small, agitated waves, as if it, too, was tired of the blame. Lace-like lines of white foam bubbled and lapped at Chelsea's feet, creeping higher to claim more footprints. If only recollections of her father were as easily wiped. But no matter how high the tide, some memories will never completely wash away. They will remain the tidal detritus to pick through and discard—or to treasure.

At least the ocean was back to being a friend, albeit the kind that required a certain cautiousness and restraint. Chelsea might one day learn to trust the tides again—and herself—knowing the more she fights life's ebb and flow, or the more she thrashes and clings to her loved-ones, the more she risks drowning and pulling others down.

Better to trust in the rhythm of life and ride the wave, she mused, while staring at the horizon and hearing William Scott's ultimate lesson.

'Remember, Chelsea-girl, just like you can't see where the earth ends and the ocean starts, you must convince yourself it's okay to not know some things.'

ACKNOWLEDGMENTS

Like the tide, this story has rolled in and out, the plot lapping at the edge of my mind to tease and tempt me for a few years now. And so, I have again dived into the deep and terrifying depths of self-publishing to bring you a story close to my heart. (But not the for reasons you might think.)

It was around 2015. Jeannette and I were camped in a caravan park (northern NSW) when a much-loved local failed to return home from rock fishing. Even those of us who didn't know the young man watched, waited, cried and hoped. The sea eventually gave him back. But out of respect I let this fictional story of a grieving community grow in my head.

The Tides That Lie is ENTIRELY fictional, and I thank you for choosing to read this, my 7th novel.

Huge hugs to those who supported (tolerated) me throughout the writing and publishing process. Special thanks to my wise readers (Jeannette McAnderson and Sharon Horton), to Lily Malone (author) for making me 'kill my darlings', and to Kris Lewis—the sister I am grateful for every day.

And to you, lovely readers, for buying my books (or asking your library to buy in) and sharing your love of fiction with others in your conversations, online reviews and on socials. Your enjoyment inspires me to keep telling my kind of small-town stories.

Jenn J xx
www.jennjmcleod.com

JENN'S FULL-LENGTH FICTION

HOUSE FOR ALL SEASONS

A Calingarry Crossing novel & 2013 #5 bestselling debut novel (AU).

Four women, four lives unravelled. The truth will bind them forever.

Bequeathed a century-old house, four estranged friends return to their hometown, Calingarry Crossing, where each must stay for a season at the Dandelion House to fulfil the wishes of their benefactor, Gypsy. But coming home to the country stirs shameful memories of the past for all four, including the tragic end-of-school muck-up-day accident twenty years earlier.

Sara—a breast cancer survivor afraid to fall in love;

Poppy—an ambitious journo still craving her father's approval;

Amber—spoilt and addicted to pills and cosmetic procedures;

Caitlin—a doctor frustrated by her flat-lining life.

At Dandelion House, the women will discover something about themselves as well as a secret tying all four to each other and to the house forever.

For more info: **books2read.com/House-For-All-Seasons**

SIMMERING SEASON

(The 2nd Calingarry Crossing novel)

A country hotel, an unexpected house guest, and a school reunion. Maggie's perfect storm is about to lift the lid off a lifetime of secrets.

Dan Ireland, a work-weary police crash investigator still hell-bent on punishing himself for his misspent youth, has ample reason for not going home to Calingarry Crossing for the school reunion, but one very good reason why he should—Maggie Lindeman.

Maggie is back in Calingarry Crossing trying to sell the family pub, while also dealing with a restless seventeen-year-old son, a father with dementia, a fame-obsessed musician husband back in the city, and a dwindling bank account.

The last thing she needs is a surprise house guest for the summer.

Fiona Bailey-Blair, daughter of an old friend and spoilt with everything but the truth, whips up a maelstrom of gossip when she blows into town in search of answers.

This storm season, as Maggie's past and present converge with the unexpected, she'll discover ... *there's no keeping a lid on some secrets.*

(First published by Simon & Schuster, *Simmering Season* is **the 2nd Calingarry Crossing novel**)

For more info: **books2read.com/Simmering-Season**

Also available in audio with bonus song track: Aurora/Ulverscroft

HOUSE OF WISHES

(The 3rd and final Calingarry Crossing novel)

Three wishes, three mothers, three generations:

Dandelion House is ready to reveal its secrets.

Dandelion House, 1974

Two teenage girls—strangers—make a pact to keep a secret.

Calingarry Crossing, 2014

For forty years, Beth and her mum have been everything to each other, but Beth is blindsided when her mother dies, and her last wish is to have her ashes spread in a small-town cemetery.

On the outskirts of **Calingarry Crossing,** when Beth comes across a place called Dandelion House Retreat, her first thought is how appealing the name sounds. With her stage career waning, and struggling to see a future without her mum, her marriage, and her child, she hopes it's a place where she can begin to heal.

After meeting Tom, a local cattleman, Beth is intrigued by his stories of the cursed, century-old river house and its reclusive owner, Gypsy. The more Beth learns, however, the more she questions her mother's wishes.

When meeting Beth leads Tom to uncover a disturbing connection to the old house, he must decide if the truth will help a grieving daughter or hurt her more.

Or should Dandelion House keep its last, long-held secret?

For more info: **books2read.com/House-of-wishes**

Also available in audio: Download or ask your library.

SEASON OF SHADOW AND LIGHT

Sometime this season … the secret keeper must tell, the betrayed must trust, the hurt must heal.

When it seems everything Paige trusts is beginning to betray her, she leaves her husband at home and sets off on a road trip with six-year-old Matilda and Nana Alice in tow.

Stranded amid rising floodwaters, on a detour taking them to the tiny town of Coolabah Tree Gully, Paige discovers the greatest betrayal of all happened there twenty years earlier.

Someone knows that truth can wash away the darkest shadows, but …

PRAISE FOR JENN'S NOVELS

Click through to more reviews on Goodreads
House for all Seasons (Calingarry Crossing Collection)

"The author has created a living, breathing small town, peopled with wonderful people - an amazing achievement."

— GREG BARRON, AUTHOR

"Captivating."

— WOMEN'S WEEKLY, MARCH 2013

Simmering Season (Calingarry Crossing Collection)

"A tangled wed of loyalties, guilt, and secrets. A great read."

— NEWCASTLE HERALD

Season of Shadow and Light

"McLeod delivers a story packed with pathos, Aussie wit and a great sense of place… an irresistible tale."

— ROWENA HOLLOWAY, AUTHOR

The Other Side of the Season

"Jenn's writing is evocative, gorgeously descriptive and transports you to the places she writes about."

— MICHELLE, BEAUTY & LACE BOOK CLUB

A Place to Remember

"I read 'The Thorn Birds' about forty years ago and still remember it. Similarly, I think the emotion and poignancy of this story will stay with me too."

— JANE HUNT (UK)

House of Wishes (Calingarry Crossing Collection - final)

"…a clever story. I was shocked as the truths emerged - absolutely did not see them coming. Absolute page turner. And TEARS! OMG!

Kathryn Ledson, Author

ABOUT THE AUTHOR
AND OTHER JENN J. MCLEOD TITLES

(Marie Miller image)

Five times published with Simon & Schuster AU & Head of Zeus UK, *House for all Seasons* was **#5 top-selling debut fiction novel**. Simmering Season is the second, with her sixth book, *House of Wishes*, the third and final stand-alone Calingarry Crossing novel.

As Australia's nomadic novelist, in a purple & white caravan called Myrtle the Turtle, Jenn is ticking things off her bucket list & finding rural landscapes to inspire more friendship & family relationship stories with a backdrop of country life.

JENN'S TITLES

House for all Seasons
Simmering Season
Season of Shadow and Light
The Other Side of the Season
A Place to Remember
House of Wishes
The Tides That Lie
All eBooks or visit www.jennjmcleod.com